I0699534

SAVING KRAKOW

K.R. KIEHL

ISBN 979-8-9898433-1-2

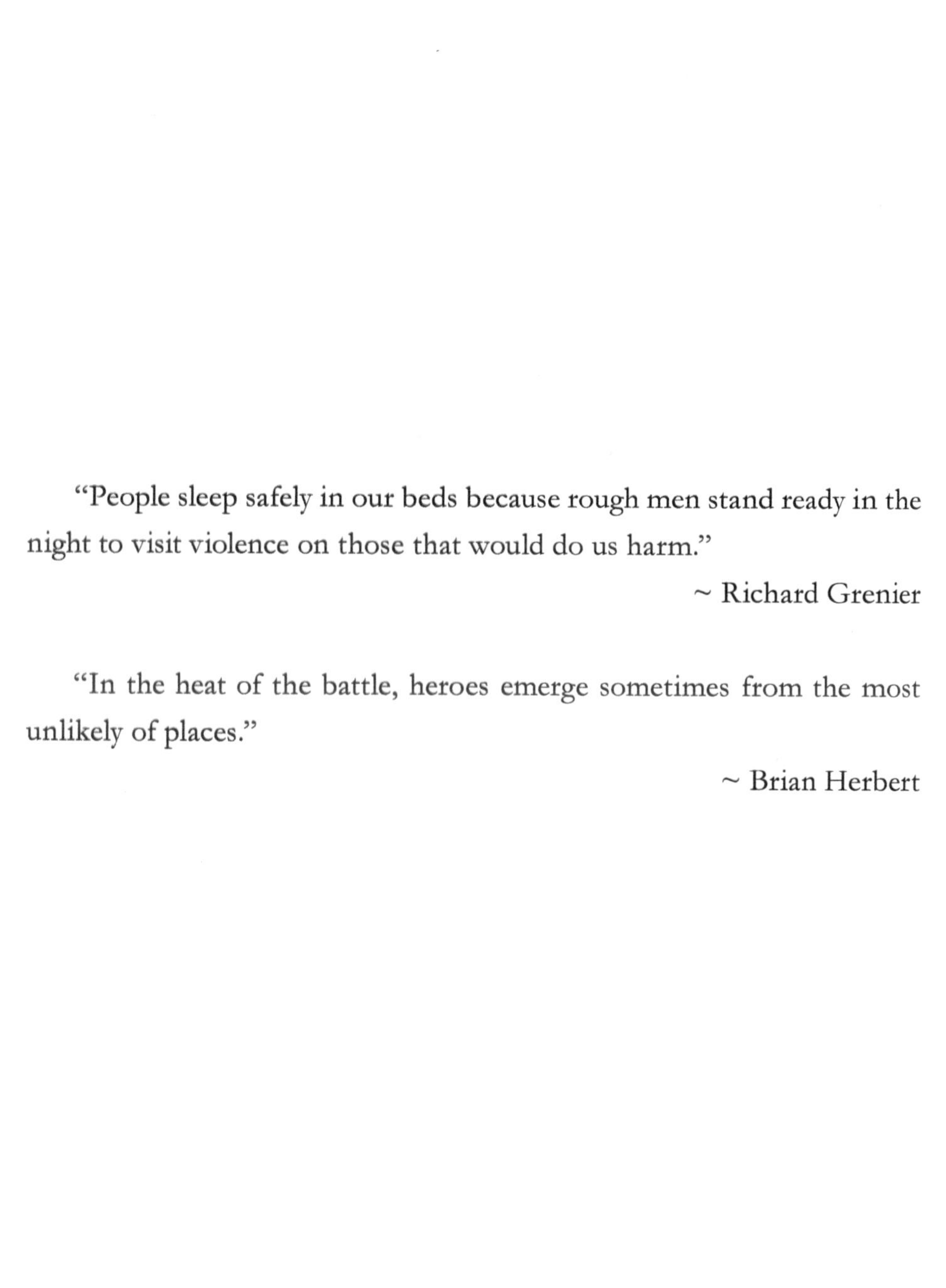

"People sleep safely in our beds because rough men stand ready in the night to visit violence on those that would do us harm."

~ Richard Grenier

"In the heat of the battle, heroes emerge sometimes from the most unlikely of places."

~ Brian Herbert

TABLE OF CONTENTS

PART ONE

Historical Note: Germany, Poland, Belarus, Ukraine, and the Soviet Union from 1920 to the 1939 Nazi Invasion

The planet post-World War I was not an orderly place, and no place was in more disarray than Poland, which found itself the focus of a power grab by the nascent Soviet Union that was consolidating its territory and influence after its own 1918 revolution. To create a buffer against Germany and Russia, Poland's Józef Piłsudski launched a Kiev offensive into Ukraine in 1920 with hopes of forming a federation. At this time, the League of Nations did not recognize the borders between Poland and the former Russian Empire. However, after a successful counter-offensive by the Red Army that almost reached Warsaw, Minsk was recaptured by the Soviet Union on July 11, 1920. As a result, a new Byelorussian Soviet Socialist Republic—what would become today's Belarus—was declared on July 31, 1920.

After the conclusion of the Polish-Soviet War, Poland and Soviet Russia divided Belarus between themselves with the Treaty of Riga. The People's Republic of Belarus spent two years preparing for a national uprising but abandoned their plans when the League of Nations recognized the Soviet Union's western borders on March 15th, 1923. In West Belarus, over 30 thousand families of Polish veterans were relocated to land previously owned by the Russian nobility. By the time of the 1930 elections, however, Belarusian representation in the Polish parliament significantly decreased. Starting in the early 1930s, the Polish government implemented policies aimed at assimilating all minority groups, including discouraging the use of the Belarusian language, thus causing financial struggles for Belarusian schools.

On September 1, 1939, Germany's forces invaded Poland, starting a raging conflict that would last six years and spark an international uproar. In response, France and Great Britain declared war on Germany just a few days later. Poland was completely overrun by German troops on September 17th. Towards the end of the month, Hitler and his allies finalized plans to divide up Poland with the Soviet Union claiming the eastern region of Galicia and all land east of the Bug River through the secret Molotov-Ribbentrop Pact. On September 17, 1939, the Soviet Union began its own invasion of Poland. The Byelorussian Soviet Socialist Republic gained control of Western Byelorussia, previously part of Poland, resulting in a brief period of growth for Belarusian culture and language. By October 1940, Belarusian was being used in over three-quarters of schools, even in regions with minimal Belarusian presence. In Western Belarus, countless individuals, including many Poles and Jews, were imprisoned, deported, and killed to enforce Sovietization.

When the Soviet Army began their invasion of Poland in mid-September, most of the Polish army, 100 thousand soldiers, retreated to nearby countries, though some areas did put up token resistance. Eventually,

Poland was split between Germany and the Soviet Union. The estimated number of Polish casualties was almost 200 thousand while Germany suffered an estimated 44 thousand.

By October of 1939, Germany had gained control over the majority of western Poland. In a unique agreement between Germany and the Soviet Union, the remaining regions of Poland were ruled by the Germans as the "General Government." Hans Frank, a lawyer and loyal follower of Adolph Hitler, was chosen as the sole civilian leader of this area with its main base in Krakow. The divided land was then organized into four separate districts: Lublin, Krakow, Radom, and Warsaw. Following the German-led Axis invasion of the Soviet Union in 1941, Poland fell under German occupation. The intertwined rule of these two forces resulted in devastating losses for Polish citizens, both in terms of human life and in resources.

In June of 1941, Germany launched its surprise invasion of the Soviet Union smashing the earlier pact. Hitler was confident that Operation Barbarossa would result in a swift victory. Despite initial successes, the grueling campaign dragged on and ended in defeat because of German strategic errors, a resilient Soviet force, and the ravages of the infamous Russian winter.

PROLOGUE

November 1923, small village south of Chertovichi, Belarus

The village near Chertovichi was nestled among rolling hills and towering pines, their branches reaching towards the grey sky of November. The small houses, made of wood and stone, were dark and weathered from years of harsh winters. The village was filled with the aroma of wood smoke and burning leaves, intermingled with the scent of freshly baked bread wafting from the open doors of the bakery. The whiff of horses and livestock also lingered, a sign of the village's deep ties with the land. The village was quiet, save for the occasional sound of a horse or cow in a nearby pasture. The leaves rustled in the crisp wind, creating a gentle whisper that winter was coming, filling the village with an eerie calmness.

Nadya Bravo, a woman in her late twenties, with dark hair pulled back into a messy bun and deep blue eyes filled with love and concern, looked down at her son. She wore a simple dress, faded from years of use, and her hands were rough from hard work as a seamstress. The room was filled with the comforting scent of lavender from the fresh linens on the bed, mixed with the faint hint of wood smoke from the fireplace down the hall.

As she tucked her son, Sergei, into bed, Nadya was met with a difficult question. "Was Father a good man?" the young boy asked.

"But of course, Sergei," his mother replied confidently. "Your father was the best of all men."

Confusion and sadness crossed Sergei's face as he continued to ask questions. Why had his father left them? Did he even love them? Nadya reassured him that his father loved them very much, but he had been taken away from them by others. Sergei couldn't understand why someone would be taken from their family. Sergei's mother explained that his father was a teacher with strong beliefs about their country, Belarus. He had taken up arms and fought for the identity of Belarus and religious freedom.

Inspired by his father's courage and dedication, Sergei expressed his desire to also become a teacher. But then he remembered his *dziadzka*, his Uncle Konstantin Bravo, who was a priest. He wanted to follow in their footsteps and be both a teacher and a priest.

Nadya gently reminded him that he would have to choose one path but could still be a good man, a wonderful teacher, and a devout Catholic. Sergei then asked when they would see Konstantin again and if he had also been taken by the government. A shadow fell over Nadya's face as she responded, "I don't know, my dear. Konstantin is not here, he's in Krakow. Remember? He's working for the church there," she reminded her son.

"Yes, I remember," replied Sergei with a smile. He reached into the box next to his bed and pulled out the rosary beads that his Uncle Konstantin brought him from Saint Mary's church in Krakow. The dark wood and amber embossed medallions gleamed in the light.

"Do you remember when we visited Krakow to see your Uncle Konstantin?"

Sergei beamed, "Yes, it was such a long train ride," he said as he thought back to his first trip to the medieval city several years before. His first glimpse of Krakow thrust him into the past, its medieval spires casting long shadows across the cobblestone streets. The weight of centuries pressed into his young bones as he walked beside his mother, her hand a reassuring tether in this ancient city that bore the scars of countless struggles.

The trio navigated through throngs of people toward Rynek Główny. Sergei's eyes widened at the sight of the grand square, a tapestry of life and commerce woven together within the embrace of time-worn buildings. Sergei's gaze lifted to the resolute spires of Saint Mary's Basilica. They pierced the sky with an austere elegance, their red-bricked majesty an un-yielding testament to the passage of centuries. Its imposing facade held firm against the onslaught of time, having witnessed the rise and fall of countless men who dared to claim dominion over the city.

The Sukiennice, or Cloth Hall, stood at the heart of it all, its presence a monument to the days when Krakow pulsed with the trade of empires. Merchants hawked their wares with a fervor born of necessity, each shout-ing and calling a reminder of the precarious balance between prosperity and poverty. The air was thick with the scent of leather and iron, the rus-tling of fabric and clink of metal goods mingling with the urgent cries of commerce. Horses adorned with red and white tassels stamped impatient-ly, their bridles glinting in the sunlight that filtered through the gathering clouds, their hooves clacking rhythmically on the stone.

Sergei's remembered eating his first and second *paczki* and then his fingers trembling slightly as he reached for the third, its glistening sugar glaze catching his eye like a siren's call. The aroma of the rose and mar-malade jelly pastry filled his nostrils, a fragrant promise of sweetness that resonated within him. Yet even as the soft dough yielded to his bite, the indulgence exacted its toll; a queasiness churned in his gut, a reminder of excess.

Nadya grabbed her son's hand, bringing him back to the present. "Do you understand the significance of Krakow, Sergei?" Her tone bore the weight of history. "In the 10th century, it was among the wealthiest towns in all of Europe, flourishing under the careful stewardship of commerce and trade. King Kazimierz," Nadya continued, her expression solemn as if she invoked the spirit of the ancient monarch himself, "ushered in the Golden Age. It was a renaissance that transformed Krakow into the envy of the world." Her eyes locked onto Sergei's, imparting the gravity of her next words. "During those hallowed years, the city became the epicenter of intelligentsia, art, and education. Scholars, artists, and thinkers converged here, drawing from the wellspring of enlightenment that King Kazimierz had cultivated."

Sergei nodded his head as he listened to his mother's lesson.

"Many say there is magic here," she continued, "that Krakow is more than stone and mortar—it breathes with an enchantment known well to the Galacians."

"Yes, Mama, Krakow is also special to me, and I cannot wait to return."

"Good, Sergei. Now use the beads Uncle Konstantin gave you and pray. Pray for your father, your mother, your *dziadzka*, Father Bravo. And don't forget to pray for Belarus," Nadya instructed.

Sergei held onto the holy beads and said a prayer for each important person in his life and for his country. His mother watched him with love and rubbed his head as he prayed. "Momma, can you tell me a story? I finished my prayers and brushed my teeth."

"Yes, my darling. Do you want to hear the dragon story?"

"Yes!" he said eagerly.

His mother already knew his answer; she read him the same story every night. Sergei retrieved a leather-bound book from under his blanket and handed it to her. Nadya Bravo carefully opened the book and began to read the parchment pages.

As she started, "The Legend of the Wawel Dragon" Sergei's eyes lit up with excitement as he snuggled deeper into his warm cocoon of blankets to listen to his mommy read.

"The Wawel Dragon was a fierce creature that lived in a cave beneath Wawel Hill and terrorized the inhabitants of King Krak's town in medieval Krakow. To appease the monster, they would offer it cattle and young maidens. The King hired many knights to slay the dragon, but none could succeed until Skuba, a clever shoemaker, came up with a plan."

"Mama, how did they trick the dragon?" asked Sergei with a smile on his face.

"Oh, my dear Sergei, you know this story even better than I do. You remember how he tricked him."

"Please continue, Mama," the little boy urged.

"The King commanded the shoemaker to defeat the dragon. So, Skuba stuffed a ram's hide with sulfur and pitch and placed it in front of the dragon's lair, hoping to deceive the evil beast."

"What happened next, Mama?"

"Stop right there, or I won't finish the story." warned Nadya playfully.

"Yes, Mama."

"The monster emerged from its lair and immediately devoured the fake ram. But the sulfur burned its throat and made it run to the Vistula River for relief. Despite drinking from the icy water, the dragon could not extinguish the burning sulfur, and gases began to build up inside it. Eventually, the gases caused the beast to explode, killing it instantly. The people of the town hailed Skuba as a hero for saving their city. The King agreed and offered his daughter's hand in marriage to the brave shoemaker. They were wed, and Skuba became a member of the King's court, a celebrated hero of the city, and happily married to a princess. The end."

Sergei smiled sleepily as his mother finished the story.

"Mama, what does it mean?"

"Well, to me, it shows that intelligence is more valuable than strength or riches. And doing good and making the right choices are most important."

"Mama?"

"Yes, my son?" she said with exasperation in her voice.

"I want to go to Krakow and slay a dragon!"

"You will, my dear. You will one day. Now go to sleep."

CHAPTER ONE

BEGINNINGS AND LOVE

September 1938, Chertovichi, Belarus

The first light of dawn barely touched the cobblestone streets of Chertovichi as Marta Alicja Piasecki stood before a small looking glass, fastening the buttons on her modest dress. She was a slender woman of nineteen, her features delicate yet strong. Her brown eyes were filled with determination, despite the dark circles beneath them from sleepless nights spent worrying. The garment was unadorned yet meticulously cared for, its fabric worn soft from countless washes. With hands practiced in frugality and precision, she tied the strings of her apron around her slender waist, securing it neatly against her dress. Today, no stray lock of her long, curly brown hair would dare fall into the dough she would soon be kneading, as her hair was tucked away in a tidy bun at the nape of her neck.

Her warm eyes, usually alight with youthful hope, instead showed worry, reflecting the seriousness of the times. The world outside was teetering on the brink of chaos, but within the walls of her father's bakery, there was bread to be made. There was life to be sustained. Marta stepped out into the cool morning air. She moved with purpose, her steps quick and determined, as if by sheer force she could ward off the encroaching shadows cast by the specter of war.

As she approached the bakery, the scent of freshly baked bread fought valiantly against the ominous mood that lingered over Chertovichi. It was an aroma steeped in warmth and familiarity, an antidote, however ordinary to the uncertainty of these dark days. Pushing open the heavy wooden door, she entered the sanctum of hearth and flour, where her father, Jakub Piasecki waited.

"Good morning, *Tata*," Marta greeted him, her voice melodic. Her smile was a beacon as she embraced him, his robust build a testament to years of labor among ovens and dough. Jakub returned her embrace with equal affection, his short, graying hair and warm smile serving as the anchor she clung to amidst the storm. "Marta, *moje dziecko*," he murmured, using the tender Polish term for 'my child.' In that moment, the bakery was not merely a place of business; it was a bulwark of normalcy, a humble fortress safeguarding a father and daughter from the brutality of the encroaching war.

"Let us begin," Marta said, releasing her father and stepping towards the heart of the bakery where the day's work awaited. Each loaf they would shape carried the weight of resistance—resistance against hunger, against despair, against the very forces that sought to strip them of their heritage and hope.

Today, like every day, they would bake bread. They would endure. They would prevail. Marta planned to take care of her baking duties, eat a small meal of bread and jam, and go to church this evening for a holy day of obligation.

Later that day, Sergei Bravo, now a young man of twenty, but still with dreams of slaying a dragon, strode into the modest dining room of his mother's small house where a steaming pot of borscht and freshly baked rye bread awaited him on the table. He entered the room with a confident stride, his broad shoulders and tall, muscular frame commanding attention. He had dark hair and piercing blue eyes with a sharp jawline and serious demeanor giving him a formidable presence.

As he entered the kitchen, his mother sat at the supper table. Her face showed a mix of worry and exhaustion from her day's labor, but it brightened upon seeing him. The smell of dill and beetroot wafted through the air, blending with an underlying tension that had infiltrated every home. The threat of war looming over their country was all too real. In the 1930s, Western Belarus had been under Poland's control, but now there was a possibility of being invaded once again by Germany under Hitler's aggressive foreign policies in Eastern Europe. Nadya constantly feared for her son's safety if he were to be called to defend their contested land.

"Tell me, Sergei," his mother urged, her voice tinged with both pride and apprehension, "how do your studies fare?"

Sergei ladled the ruby-red soup into his bowl, blinking against the steam before he met his mother's expectant gaze. "Well, Mother," he began, his eyes alight with fervor, "the more I learn, the more I am convinced that teaching is my true calling."

His mother nodded solemnly, passing the dark bread. "Education is a powerful weapon," she intoned. "In these times, it may prove mightier than the sword."

"Indeed," Sergei agreed. "I will equip our youth with knowledge, arm them with wisdom to rebuild what has been shattered." He spoke with an earnest intensity, his determination slicing through the oppressive atmosphere like a beacon of hope amidst the encroaching darkness. The meal progressed with animated discussions about lesson plans and literature, Sergei's aspirations unfurling with all the energy and joy of youth.

After supper, Sergei donned his coat and stepped out into the chilly evening air. The streets were somber; the usual buzz of the town had dulled to a murmur under the shadow of occupation. Still, as he made his way towards the church, he exchanged polite nods and greetings with the townspeople he encountered.

The townsfolk respected Sergei for his steadfast nature and his loyalty to the community. Even Old Mrs. Petrova, who watched the world pass by from her window, offered a frail wave which Sergei returned with a respectful bow of his head. Each interaction, no matter how brief, was a silent pact of mutual support, a shared acknowledgment that their spirits would not be easily quelled.

The heavy oak doors of the church closed with a sonorous thud behind Sergei, sealing him within the sanctum of worship. His footsteps fell in solemn cadence on the cold, stone floor, their echoes whispering like specters through the cavernous space. In the pews he found refuge. Marta Alicja Piasecki also sat in the pew in silent prayer. Sergei settled into the hard wooden bench with a reverence that belied his youth. His gaze lifted from the somber reality of the world outside to the celestial display above. The stained-glass windows, resplendent in their vibrant hues, depicted scenes of divine intervention and human salvation. Each panel told a story of a struggle overcome by faith. As his eyes traced the intricate lead lines framing each colorful shard, Sergei felt the weight of his own resolve pressing against his chest.

In front of him, Marta folded her knees onto the unforgiving stone floor, her silhouette bathed in a soft candlelight from the nearby stand of votive candles - each representing someone's prayer. A warm smile traced her lips, and her hands moved with a grace that belied the rigidity of her surroundings, fingers tenderly tracing the beads of her rosary in a rhythmic cadence of prayer. Each bead was a word, each pause a breath, as she wove her petitions into the fabric of the sacred space around her.

Sergei Bravo's gaze was drawn to her like a moth to a solitary votive candle in the dark expanse of night. He watched, observing Marta's soft presence, his heart thrumming a staccato beat within the cage of his chest. The serenity that radiated from her formed an aura, a silent testament to an inner fortitude that seemed untouched by outer strife.

Every stolen glance was a brushstroke on the canvas of his memory, the muted sounds of her supplications reaching his ears, not as words, but as a melody to soothe even the most tormented of souls. Sergei's throat tightened with the effort of suppressing emotions that, coming out of nowhere in an overwhelming wave, for he found himself captivated, ensnared by the tranquil beauty she embodied in this otherwise severe and cold world.

In those fleeting moments, Sergei allowed himself the indulgence of imagining a different life, one where the brutality of war was but a distant nightmare, dissolving with the sunset. But reality anchored him firmly, the weight of his duty and the somber knowledge that such dreams were as fragile as the silence that now enveloped them.

Marta's whispered amen signaled the close of her devotions, and as she lifted her gaze from the crucifix clasped in her hands, it collided with Sergei's, their eyes locking in a silent exchange. Shadows danced within the church's cavernous expanse, but between them flickered a spark—an ember of recognition of some deep, new emotion which, though they had often nodded to the other in passing, each only now recognized. Sergei found himself momentarily adrift in that gaze, the cerulean intensity of his own eyeing the soft glow in Marta's. Something ancient and familiar stirred within him.

The solemnity of the moment gave way as their fellow congregants gently nudged them back into reality, yet that shared look lingered. A murmur escaped Sergei, quiet enough not to disturb the sanctity of their surroundings yet audible to Marta's keen ears. "Do not think me foolish or falsely poetic," he began hesitantly, "but I wonder if you ever think of the woods." He hung his head. "They call me. Amidst the trees, there is a stillness, a respite from this world."

Her response was immediate, a gentle laugh, not at all dismissive but almost delighted. "Yes," Marta breathed. "I understand what you mean. I go there to seek quiet. The ancient oaks and pines seem to be talking, and I feel their peace wash over me so I can forget the day's cares."

They sat, two silhouettes etched against the dimming light filtering through stained glass, bound by a mutual longing for the serene refuge of the woodland.

After that mass, a brief introduction turned into a budding friendship. At first they would meet at church for mass and then say an abrupt good-bye while longing to meet again. The meetings expanded and evolved into short dates, at a café for conversation over coffee and cakes, then to walk in the woods.

On one such, as fall gave in to winter but before the snow, Sergei Bravo's boots crunched against the frostbitten earth as he made his way through the somber forest, his breath a ghostly mist in the chill morning air. Marta walked beside him, her arm linked with his, their steps in harmony. The towering pines stood sentinel around them, whispering secrets of ancient times long before the tread of soldiers and the drumbeat of impending war.

On this day, a familiar walk in the woods, Sergei shared his feelings about the future and his feelings for her. "I've thought much about the future," Sergei began, his voice barely above a whisper. "I wish to be a teacher, and I hope to kindle knowledge even in such dark times."

Marta's eyes met his, not with the somberness one might expect at such an admission, but with a spark of shared conviction. "And I..." she paused, her hands clasping together as if to gather her hopes within her grasp, "I dream of nurturing our community closer to heart. The bakery—my father's life work and now mine—it could be more than just a place for bread. It could be a sanctuary of warmth, where the scent of fresh loaves and the sweetness of pastries remind us of all the comfort of home, especially when it feels like the world is fracturing around us."

"Have you ever thought of what lies beyond these trees, beyond the strife?" Sergei asked, his voice barely rising above the murmur of the woodland.

"Often," Marta replied, her warm hazel gaze lingering on his face. "I dream of a place where the chiming of church bells drowns out the clamor of conflict. Where we can teach, and bake, and…." Her words trailed off, but her meaning hung between them—palpable and poignant.

"Where we can live without fear," Sergei finished for her, understanding the unsaid. They halted, standing within the cathedral-like enclave formed by interlocking branches above and all around them. Here, in this secluded space, they shared their aspirations to build a life. Their bond, rooted in the love of the land and their faith, grew stronger with each confession of hope amidst despair. Sergei, envisioning himself at the head of a classroom, imparted his yearning to nurture young minds. Marta, with a tender smile, spoke of the bakery she wished to inherit from her father, a sanctuary of warmth and sustenance.

As the sun pierced through the boughs, casting dappled light upon them, Sergei leaned closer to Marta, his resolve hardening. "No matter what comes, I swear to protect our dreams," he whispered, his voice firm and resolute.

"And I will stand with you," Marta affirmed, her fingertips tracing the line of his jaw.

With the stealth of shadows converging, they sought refuge in an enclave shielded by a thicket of brambles. There, concealed from the world's prying eyes, they surrendered to the urgency of their hearts. Sergei cupped Marta's face, his fingers weaving through her curly brown tresses. Their lips met in a stolen kiss, the taste of sweet defiance against the world outside their hidden sanctuary.

"Promise me something," Marta murmured, her voice barely rising above the rustle of leaves beneath them.

"Anything." Sergei responded, turning to face her. In the low light, her eyes flickered with a resolute spark that matched the intensity of his own.

"Promise me you'll remember this—us—in your darkest hours. When the world rages, remember our love. Let it be your shield."

Sergei pulled her close, his arms wrapping around her as if he could ward off the approaching storm with his embrace alone. "I will carry you in my heart through the hard times that are certain to come. You are my light, Marta. Nothing can extinguish what we have."

The somber melody of a church bell echoed distantly, marking the hour, and reminding them of their mundane duties. They shared a final, lingering kiss, a bittersweet fusion of passion and longing. Marta retreated to the safety of her father's bakery and Sergei to his studies, the thoughts of each on their hopes for a future together, in a place without the threat of war and violence hanging over them.

Weeks later, as winter settled in and dusk fell over the quaint streets of their Belarusian village, they sat nestled in the alcove of the church they both cherished, a place that once echoed with their laughter but was now heavy with silence.

"Have you seen the flyers?" Sergei's voice broke through the hush. "They are enlisting men... it's only a matter of time before I am called up."

Marta clutched her shawl tighter around her shoulders, the wool rough against her fingers. She nodded; her hazel eyes clouded with the same worry that creased her brow. "I've heard whispers at the bakery," she admitted, thinking of the mothers, loaves clutched to their chests, gathered in a corner worriedly discussing whose son had gotten the visit or the telegram telling them to report for duty.

"The front lines..." Sergei continued, his jaw set in a firm line that belied the tremor in his hands as he brushed a fallen leaf from his lap. "If I am to go, Marta, it is not just the fighting that terrifies me." He swallowed hard, the sound sharp in the stillness. "It's the thought of being torn away from you—of leaving you alone."

His determination flared up. "But know this," he said, his voice gaining strength from the depth of his resolve, "my every breath, my every step, will be to return to you. This chaos will not consume us. Not our dreams, not our love."

March 1939, Chertovichi, Belarus

Sergei Bravo's hands trembled slightly as he slit open the seal of the envelope, the stark red emblem on its face a harbinger of news that no young man wished to receive. The letters within seemed to blur before his eyes, each word a hammer strike against the foundation of his world. *"Order for Immediate Conscription"* it read, and beneath, Sergei's name inscribed as formally as a headstone. His breath hitched in his chest, disbelief coiling tight around his heart. This could not be real; it was just yesterday he had been discussing lesson plans and the future of education with his mentor.

"Bravo, Sergei is hereby conscripted into the armed forces with immediate effect," the letter continued, the formal language a stark contrast to the chaos it represented. Duty and loyalty warred within him. Sergei felt as if he were standing on the edge of an abyss, the gravity of his situation pulling him ever closer to the void.

Marta Alicja Piasecki's warm hazel eyes caught a glimmer of light as she stepped out of the shadowed interior of her father's bakery at the end of the day. Her usually radiant smile faltered when she saw Sergei's figure approach, his gait heavier than usual. The way his dark hair lay flat against his forehead spoke of the many times he must have raked his fingers through it in distress.

"Is everything alright?" she asked her stomach already knotted with foreboding.

He handed her the letter without a word, watching as her gaze quickly scanned the contents. Marta's complexion paled, her curls seeming to lose their buoyancy as the weight of the words pressed down upon her. A hand flew to her mouth, stifling a gasp, while the other crumpled the edges of the paper in a vice grip. Tears welled unbidden, spilling over to trace paths down her cheeks.

"This can't be," she murmured, her voice barely rising above a whisper. The world around them seemed to fall away, leaving only the two of them locked in this moment. Marta's chest constricted with a heaviness so profound it threatened to crush her from within. She clutched Sergei's arm, seeking solace in his strength, yet acutely aware of the fragility of their shared dreams.

"War is coming to our doorstep," Sergei said, his voice steady despite the turmoil that raged inside him. "Every part of me wishes to stay. But I can't ignore this call. To defend our home, our people—it's bigger than us."

Marta wiped the tears from her eyes, searching his face for reassurance they both knew he could not provide. "And what of the dreams we've nurtured, Sergei? Our plans to marry in the spring…. How can we just let them go?"

"This war may delay us," he replied, his piercing blue eyes reflecting hope, 'but it will not define us. We must hold fast to our love, for it will be a compass in the darkest of times."

"Promise me you'll return," she implored, her voice breaking on each word. "Promise me that you will write so that I can know your life. And I will write to you so you will know mine."

"I promise."

The time for departure came like a thief, stealing the last remnants of warmth from their embrace. Sergei shouldered his bag, its weight insignificant compared to the burden in his chest. He faced Marta, her once radiant countenance marred by grief and fear, her long curls lacking their usual luster.

Their final goodbye was a silent communion, a sweet soft kiss that spoke of both love and parting. Sergei embraced her tightly, then, he turned away, leaving behind the woman who held his heart.

He walked through the town, the cobblestone streets echoing with the footsteps of other men called to arms, an invisible thread linking each sorrowful departure. They moved as one, a somber procession shadowed by the specter of war—a stark contrast to the serenity of the church steeples that pierced the skyline.

As he joined his comrades, Sergei cast a lingering glance back at the life he was leaving. Amidst the dread and uncertainty, a steadfast determination took root. He would fight for the future, for Marta, for the peace they yearned to reclaim. The camaraderie of the soldiers around him bolstered his courage, a shared understanding that each step forward was a testament to their collective strength.

The train station loomed ahead, a gateway to the unknown. Sergei stepped aboard the car, and, as the train pulled away, chugging toward the heart of conflict, he whispered a prayer into the din, a solitary plea for protection and a swift reunion with his beloved. The wheels clacked out the relentless rhythm of departure, yet Sergei held steadfast to the images of Marta and the home they cherished.

CHAPTER TWO

INVASION OF POLAND

0430hrs, September 1st, 1939 - Hannover-Langenhagen Airfield, Germany

As *Oberleutnant* Johann Verloren strode toward his aircraft, the First Lieutenant could see *Feldwebel* Dieter Koch already on the tarmac, his sergeant conducting final inspections of the aircraft. First Lieutenant Verloren was the pilot of a Junker JU-87 bomber aircraft that the sergeant was inspecting. The JU-87, known on the battlefield as a Stuka, was a small fighter bomber aircraft capable of transporting 1200 pounds of bombs while still maneuvering quickly in the air. An air siren called a Jericho Trumpet was mounted under the gull wings of the aircraft, its piercing shriek the much-feared harbinger of the deadly chaos known as the Nazi *blitzkrieg*, the lightning war whose arrival was announced by air attacks on unsuspecting cities just before it dropped the bombs. While training, he learned to exploit the psychological aspects of the shriek of his aircraft by diving on targets and sounding the shrill horn even after releasing the payload. Verloren was proud of his aircraft, as it was one of the newer versions to come off the assembly line on the base. They camouflaged the aircraft dark green with glass observation windows covering the pilot's seat and the gunner's seat. The glass observation platform gave unobstructed views from the front, left, right, and rear for both crewmen.

Sergeant Koch, the JU-87's crew chief and radio operator, also served as the second-in-command and gunner for the German killing machine. Koch had enlisted in the Luftwaffe air support services soon after completing secondary school. He found some success as a strong noncommissioned officer maintaining the JU-87s during their debut in 1937 in the Spanish Civil War. He was a proud Cologne resident and missed his hometown, even though his service took him to exotic places. To keep him connected to his home, Koch had painted a small blue and white flag and the saying *Kolle Alaaf!* Cologne above all! on the tail of the aircraft, a tribute to his famous city. The sincere gesture had gotten him in hot water with the squadron commander with three days restriction to base last month. However, no one ordered him to clean it off the tail before this mission.

When the Sergeant saw his commander approaching, he smiled, came to attention, and saluted. Lieutenant Verloren asked, "What is it, Sergeant?" as he saluted back. "Why do you extend such military courtesy today on a flight line in the dark?" He had a smile on his face.

"Sir" the sergeant shouted, "this is going to be a big day for us. You have a big mission today, and I am your second-in-command to ensure you do not mess it up." He winked at his superior. "This is such an important day that King Göring has made an appearance. We need to assemble in the hangar in fifteen minutes."

King Göring was better known as Reich Marshall Hermann Göring, the Minister of German Aviation and confidante of Adolph Hitler. Göring was not only responsible for overseeing the air raid plans of the Polish invasion but also was the lead planner for the overall ground effort in Eastern Europe. Göring did not feel that Germany was ready for war but supported the Führer's urgings that the time was right. Just two days earlier, Hitler had named Göring the chairman of a newly created Council of Ministers for Defense of the Reich to serve as an advisory war council. The Reich Marshall had arrived earlier at the airfield in a convoy of black Mercedes-Benz Grosser 770s. He was now standing in the center of the hangar with his SS protective service detail behind him and the JU-87 aircrews in a horseshoe shape in front of him.

"Gentlemen," the Reich Marshall said in a low tone. "Today is a historic moment in the next chapter of our empire. This squadron was hand selected to lead the first wave of the invasion in Operation Wasser Kante. You must all do your jobs and succeed for the invasion to be a success," he paused dramatically, "and for the war to be won by the Third Reich. *Meine Herren*, make no mistake. This is a pivotal point in all our lives. Your squadron will prepare the battlefield. Then the ground forces will finish the destruction. *Meine Herren*, you have trained for this day for months and will be victorious." He paused and looked across the young faces, and then looked down.

The commanders, aircrews, and pilots all watched the Reich Marshall with a certain seriousness, waiting for his next words.

The Reich Marshall raised his head as if he finished a prayer, looked at the crowd again, and screamed, *"Gehen mit Gott!"*

The pilots and aircrews, many hoping God was indeed with them, rushed to their waiting JU-87s, boarded, and waited. The crew chief approached each and gave the go ahead, shouting *"Heil Hitler"* while he saluted the pilot. Lieutenant Verloren returned the salute. Blood and Honor! he shouted, *"Blut und Honor!"*

Sergeant Koch, now in the back of the JU-87, did a radio check with the tower and then used the internal radio. "Sir, the tower cleared us to get in formation by the runway."

"Jawohl, Herr Sergeant! Let's move towards our destiny." The Sergeant rolled his eyes but pressed his thumbs together as a symbol of good luck.

At 0430hrs, First Lieutenant Verloren's aircraft took off from the airbase and joined the formation on the mission to attack Warsaw. The JU-87 squadron linked up with the security team of several Messerschmitt BF 110 fighter planes before they crossed the German border into Poland toward their objectives.

As the flight formation approached the Vistula River, Koch radioed his Lieutenant that half of the formation was splitting off and navigating toward Gdansk for the first air attack of the invasion. His team's mission was to bomb high military value targets in Warsaw, preparing for the Wehrmacht ground attack. After the planes broke off, the remaining group stayed in a tight formation for the last leg of the journey to the outskirts of Warsaw.

At Plock, Verloren's aircraft started receiving radio messages. "Weiss leader of all teams. Staffel Captain clears us to move towards the objective and hit all targets of opportunity. *Zum Vaterland!* Acknowledge," Sergeant Koch spoke into the radio in a firm voice. "Weiss 5 acknowledges. *Zum Vaterland!*" Koch turned on the internal radio system to notify his commander of the order. "Herr Lieutenant, we have received clearance to identify targets of opportunity and bomb at will.

"Jawohl, Koch, *Danke*. It's so peaceful up here. Doesn't seem like a war has started...."

The shriek of multiple JU-87s activating their horns startled both Verloren and Koch moments later. They watched as several JU-87s dove at targets just south of Plock. About a quarter mile from the link-up, three JU-87s bombed a bridge, an ammo depot, and a radio communications site next to the Vistula River. The ground shook as the bombs exploded, sending debris and smoke into the air.

Immediately after the explosion, a squadron of Polish P-11 fighters appeared on the horizon. The Polish aircraft quickly engaged the German Messerschmitt force. To the Germans' surprise, the P-11s had an advantage and quickly shot down two Messerschmitts, torn metal and debris falling into the Vistula River.

The smell of exploded ordinance and burning buildings filled the air. As their aircraft approached Wyszogrod, Verloren spotted his primary target, a railroad bridge crossing the Vistula River.

"Brace yourself, Herr Koch. We are diving!" The JU-87 dove toward the bridge at an astonishing speed. "Bomb, Koch, Bomb!" screamed Verloren. Sergeant Koch pulled the bomb lever as they crossed over the bridge. The middle part of the bridge exploded and caught on fire, the rest of the bridge collapsing into the river. As the JU-87 rose from the river and continued south on the Vistula River, a P-11 quickly appeared alongside. Koch began to scream, "P-11, rear port!" The Polish plane was so close that Koch could see the enemy tail gunner fire at his plane. The bullets whizzed above the rising JU-87. Verloren yanked the control stick as hard as he could, causing the aircraft to shoot up into the air, the P-11 fighter passing quickly. The German fighter fell in behind the P-11 which was now zig zagging to avoid attack. Veloren locked on the P-11 and engaged with both guns. The tail of the P-11 burst into flames, and the plane fell violently into the river.

Coming closer to Warsaw, Verloren's JU-87 entered the Kampinoski Forest. Both he and Koch spotted a bridge ahead and immediately notified other bombers of a potential target. Ahead, Koch noticed an unusual form jutting out of the trees—the raised barrel of a Bofors anti-aircraft gun moving slightly from its fortified position and fixing on their aircraft. Koch screamed, and Herr Oberleutnant Verloren muttered, *"Schiesse!"* as a shell from the Bofors pierced the tail of his JU-87. The explosion violently separated the tail of his aircraft from the front pilot's cockpit. The Lieutenant could hear Koch scream as the flaming tail fell into the forest.

Watching the burning plane with some astonishment from his Polish Guard anti-aircraft post in the forest was *Starzy Szeregowy* Sergei Bravo, Private First Class Bravo. Just a few minutes earlier, he had been bemoaning the bitter morning cold of their position on the edge of the Kampinoski Forest while wondering if the war was ever going to come to Poland, reflections rudely interrupted by the abrupt screeching of the Stukas' horns announcing an impending attack.

My training instructors were right, thought Bravo, the *Jericho Horns sound like the scream of a demonic beast, like the scream of the Wawel Castle dragon.* He was on night watch; the rest of his teammates were in various stages of slumber inside the artillery bunker on the front edge of Kampinoski Forrest. He was currently sitting in the gunner's seat of the Bofors gun. Many armies in Europe used the gun, which was originally produced in Sweden but then manufactured in Poland to Polish Army specifications. His French instructors in artillery school had showed him how to load the gun which, fully crewed, could shoot 156 rounds per minute.

Bravo, dressed like the rest of the conscripts on his crew, wore a tan jacket and trousers with cuffs wrapped by cloth puttees that met the tops of his black high ankle boots. The equipment they issued him in basic training was next to him and included a blanket, backpack, and mess kit. His brown leather belt held ammunition pouches. Leaning against his backpack was his bread bag and entrenching tool. His olive-green steel helmet was not on his head, as ordered by his training instructors, but sitting on the floor of the gun pit. He had only arrived at the anti-aircraft post a few months earlier, having completed his basic military training and anti-aircraft gunner school then serving as a clerk in a training unit before this deployment to protect a bridge north of the forest along the Vistula. After being drafted in 1939, this was his first operational assignment, and about as different from his previous life as he could have imagined. After graduating from secondary school, he'd studied to be a primary school teacher, a placid life rudely interrupted by his conscription, tearing him from his life in Chertovichi, in western Belarus, a part of the 2nd Polish Republic since 1918. He dreamed of life, of life with Marta particularly, after the army and returning home to be a teacher, maybe headmaster, but certainly a husband and hopefully a father.

After several months of boredom, the morning's events signaled a brutal change in pace. Just as Bravo had been contemplating a hot mug of coffee, his teammate and target spotter had shouted: "Stuka! Stuka! Stuka!" Half a squadron of German aircraft darkened the dawn sky. Bravo sighted the Bofors gun and watched as several Messerschmitt aircraft zoomed by his position, leaving them unnoticed and unscathed. Bravo aimed at several JU-87s and locked on one, coming directly toward his defensive position. As the JU-87s approached, Bravo's spotter yelled "Fire! Fire!" Bravo pulled the Bofors firing handle several times, sending explosive rounds towards the attacking machine, hitting the Stuka's tail, and splitting the aircraft in two, the pieces pinwheeling into the Vistula River.

Bravo's teammates were now standing around him and cheering. Bravo barked, "All of you. Get into position. There will be more." On cue, several more German Luftwaffe aircraft swarmed over the area like bees after their hive has been kicked. Two of the Messerschmitts began to fire on Bravo's position. "Get down, get down!" he ordered. Bravo remained in the gunner's seat and took aim at the offending Nazi planes. Boom! Boom!

The attacks continued throughout the day but slowed as it became dark. Although just a crew member, at twenty-one his age made him a natural leader, as he was significantly older than the rest of the crew and had significant life experience. The gun crew paused for a moment to eat and to change the worn-out gun barrel. A cleaning was also necessary to ensure the weapon was ready for future engagements. Private First Class Bosko from Lublin was eating a piece of black bread when he saw two men walking toward their position. He alerted the rest of the crew to pick up their rifles.

As the two men approached, the crew identified them as superior officers and quickly came to attention. Lieutenant Colonel Josef Lider, the anti-aircraft defense commander, barked, "At ease." The old sergeant major, a veteran of World War I and former farmer from western Poland remarked jokingly, "Sir, look at these bums lying around like they are having a smoke in downtown Warsaw. Who would guess that they had the most kills today and saved the asses of Fighter Brigade?"

The battery commander looked at the crew of former farmers and salt mine workers and did not see a single career soldier among them. "Gentlemen," he said, "you all performed beyond expectations today and saved the Polish people to fight another day. Who is in charge of this group?" He asked.

"No one, sir. We all sort of work as a team." Bosko said in a whisper. "Well," he continued, "Bravo is sort of our big brother and always knows what to do." The other team members nodded their heads. Bravo, university student from Belarus, looked down at the ground as the rest of the men looked at him.

The old sergeant major barked, "Bravo, come forward!"

Bravo was leaning against the defensive position wall and came to attention. He purposefully marched toward Lieutenant Colonel Lider, stopped immediately in front of him, and came to the position of attention. The battery commander saluted back and turned him towards the rest of the gunner team. Reaching into his pocket, the commander produced the black insignia of sergeant and showed it to the rest of the crew. The old-World War 1 noncommissioned officer stood on the other side of Bravo while both he and the battery commander pinned the stripes to Sergei Bravo's collar.

The sergeant major came to attention and barked, "Gentlemen, we present to you Sergeant Bravo!" The other team members beamed with pride. Bravo's face flushed.

After the commander left, Bravo sat on top of an ammo can and smoked a cigarette. He could not believe the day's events. His brain raced. He had seen more death and destruction today than he had seen in his entire lifetime, too much, and now he longed for the peace of his village. Being with Marta and his family in Belorussia seemed better now than any adventure. But the Polish Army had drafted him, tearing him away from his life as a schoolteacher. In the few months that had passed since his conscription, he had done everything asked of him, and done it well. "I will do my duty," Bravo thought. "But I'm not sure this is the life for me."

As Bravo sat, the shriek of the diving Stukas began again, and activity buzzed around the forest. "Sergeant! Sergeant," Bosko shouted. "The planes are coming back!"

The newly minted sergeant rose to his feet and ordered, "Man your positions. Bosko, you take the gunner's seat. Private Nowak will help as the assistant gunner. The rest of you take cover."

"Yes, Sergeant!" the crew member yelled and complied.

Sergeant Bravo shouted, "Poland is not lost!" as a new squadron of attacking Messerschmitts and JU-87s swarmed over their position on their way toward the center of Warsaw. Bravo continued to fight, taking down another Messerschmitt later the next day. His gun position would shoot down eight Nazi aircraft during the first few days of the invasion.

CHAPTER THREE

CROSSING THE THRESHOLD

March 1940, Chertovichi, Belarus

The door to Piasecki's Bakery creaked with a timeworn familiarity as Sergei Bravo stepped over the threshold. The aroma of freshly baked bread, a warm and yeasty perfume that had always been interwoven with his memories of Marta, enveloped him like a comforting embrace. The golden loaves in their wicker baskets seemed to stand as silent witnesses to countless mornings when he had watched Marta deftly weave through the shelves, her laughter mingling with the chime of the bell above the door.

He had served admirably with the Polish Army's Freedom Brigade. But the German force was too much for the Polish volunteers and conscripts. Most were killed, and many who did escape were captured and imprisoned. After several weeks of fighting, the Germans occupied Warsaw. Those still alive fled back home to other parts of the East. As Sergei and his crew members traveled back across the battle lines toward the Belarussian border, near the city of Lvov, a Russian patrol intercepted them. Sergei and his Polish comrades were loaded into a train car that was headed to a Soviet prison camp in the east. However, when the train stopped for supplies, Sergei and a few other soldiers broke through the floor and slid off the train undetected. In the confusion, Sergei had escaped a fate that would most certainly have been a long incarceration. And so, he had made his way back to Chertovichi, hiding in barns and ditches during the day and travelling all night. After several days, Sergei arrived home, still wearing his full-dress uniform adorned with sergeant stripes. He was ready for a new chapter in his life. A return to his studies. But first he would find Marta.

Sergei's heart thudded against his ribs. His anticipation was laced with a nervous energy that made his hands tremble imperceptibly. He brushed a fleck of flour from the counter, the cool, powdery texture grounding him as he scanned the bakery for a glimpse of her.

Will she recognize me? The thought was a sharp blade of anxiety cutting through the warmth of the bakery. The months apart had etched lines of worry into his young face, a testament to the harsh realities of war.

Suddenly, the curtain behind the counter fluttered, and there she was—Marta Alicja Piasecki, her long, curly brown hair cascading over her shoulders like the gentle flow of the Vistula River. Her warm hazel eyes locked onto Sergei's, and for a charged moment, all was still. Then, with a piercing cry, Marta rushed toward him, her apron billowing around her, such was her haste.

"Ser-Sergei!" Her voice cracked with emotion, a poignant cry amidst the noise of the busy bakery.

Their bodies collided, two souls seeking refuge in the eye of a tempest. Sergei's arms enfolded Marta in a strong embrace, his hands pressing her firmly against him as if to meld their spirits into one indomitable force. Marta's arms wound tightly around his neck, her fingers clutching at the fabric of his coat with desperate fervor.

"Thank God," she breathed, her words a fervent prayer against the canvas of his jacket. "Thank God, you're here."

In that embrace, the world outside faded away. Here, in the sanctuary of the bakery, surrounded by the vestiges of normalcy, they stood resilient.

Despite the brutality that raged beyond the walls of Piasecki's Bakery, within this hallowed space, Sergei and Marta found solace in the strength of their connection—a bond made even stronger by experiences lived apart.

The reverberations of war seemed distant in the close quarters of the bakery as Sergei and Marta, still entwined in each other's arms, began to speak.

"Where will we go after all this?" Marta's voice was a soft whisper, her question laced with the urgency of their reality.

"I need to finish school," Sergei replied with conviction, his eyes alight with the fire of determination. "Beyond the reach of this conflict, there is a life waiting for us."

"Children?" Her question hung between them, imbued with both hope and the stark acknowledgment of the sacrifices they might have to endure.

"Many," he affirmed, the promise sparking a defiant light in his blue eyes. "They'll know peace, Marta. They'll walk through woods in a land we've reclaimed."

"Will you still teach?" Marta's fingers traced the line of his jaw, her touch grounding him even as his heart waged its own battle against despair.

"Always." Sergei's answer came swiftly and surely. "I will fill their minds with knowledge and their hearts with courage. Our children will be scholars, dreamers... leaders who remember the past but look forward to the future."

"Then let's promise...." Marta's words trailed off as she searched his face for the unwavering commitment she knew so well.

"Let's promise," Sergei echoed, "to make a home that will be a sanctuary from the world's chaos."

The vow settled over them like a mantle, a heavy responsibility yet one buoyed by the irrepressible spirit of two souls intertwined. In the quiet of the bakery, Sergei and Marta pledged themselves to the future—a future conceived in defiance of oppression, nurtured by love, and destined to transcend the ruins of a world at war.

"I wish for us to marry," she whispered, her eyes alight with a mixture of fear and love. Her hands, dusted with the flour of her father's bakery, reached out to clasp his own. "Despite all we've faced, Sergei," Marta continued, her voice steady, "I long for a life crafted by our own hands." Her curls tumbled over her shoulders, framing a face that had weathered uncertainty but still bloomed with love's defiant vitality. Sergei met her eyes, his heart full, a glimmer of happiness between them, imagining a quiet future with Marta in their small village.

March 1941, Secondary School No 2, Volozhin, Belarus (Minsk Region)

The school was a crumbling, grey building with chipped paint. The surrounding area was desolate, with abandoned homes and empty streets. But the classroom was bustling with students, each desk occupied by a student. Their faces varied in expressions, some eager and attentive, while others seemed bored or tired. The chalkboard was covered in notes and sketches, evidence of previous lessons. The books on their desks were dog-eared and well-loved from frequent use, the desks themselves battered and scarred. The classroom smelled faintly of chalk dust and old books. Underlying this was the hint of sweat and nervous energy from the students as they waited for the lesson to begin.

Students filled his classroom as Sergei Bravo was erasing his chalk board and preparing an outline on the board for his next lecture on Leo Tolstoy. The students pulled out their books and sat quietly until he had finished and turned around to face them. "*Dobraj ranicy,* class!" Sergei said. Good morning!

The class responded with the formal greeting required of students, "*Dobraj ranicy,* Sergei Bravovich!" Using the teacher's first name and family name was the tradition in Russia and Belarus.

Sergei began his class introduction in a soft tone. "Class, today we are going to discuss one of the great Russian novelists, Leo Tolstoy. He is the pride of Russia and the world for such works as *Anna Karenina* and *War and Peace*. He was also nominated frequently for the Nobel Peace prize before his death in 1910. He is one of my favorite novelists and the main reason I went to school to become a literature teacher. Today we will discuss his novel, *War and Peace*."

Aleh Petrov, a stocky twelve-year-old with blond hair, rocked from side to side in his chair. As Sergei turned toward the board to address his first point about Tolstoy, he heard Aleh's high pitched voice. "Sergei Bravovich?"

"Yes, Aleh, do you have a question?"

"Yes, Sergei Bravovich. My father says you were a war hero before you were a teacher. Is that true?"

Sergei's face flushed as he spoke, "Yes, Aleh, like many in our village, I served in the war, though hero is a bit much. We should focus on our lesson for today; you will enjoy it...."

"My father says you killed many Nazis and were an important soldier." Aleh challenged.

"Well, like others in our village, I fought against the Germans in protecting Warsaw, but we were unsuccessful, I'm afraid." Sergei's head dropped.

"My father says you were also a prisoner and escaped home to Belarus. Is that true?"

"We should really get back to our lesson, Aleh. The rest of the class wants to learn about Tolstoy and his contributions to literature."

"*Tak*, Sergei Bravovich," Okay, Aleh conceded, knowing that his teacher did not want to discuss his war service.

I'm no war hero, Sergei was thinking. Yes, he had many 'kills' during the first days of the invasion of Warsaw.

As Sergei began his lesson, there was a knock at the door. Sergei glanced up to see the school secretary standing at the door. He motioned for her to come into the classroom.

"Excuse me, Sergei Bravovich, but I have a note from the school director for you. She handed him the folded piece of paper, which he read quickly, a summons to Director Ivanov's office.

"I'm sorry, class, but I have been called to the school director's office for a meeting. Please begin reading Chapter One of *War and Peace* until I return."

Bravo hurried down the hallway to Director Ivanov's office. When he approached the office, he could see Ivanov sitting behind his desk and speaking to two men. The men were tall, similar in height, and wearing dark gray business suits with white shirts and patterned ties. As Sergei walked into the office, the older man turned and said, "Sergeant Bravo, please sit down." It was more of an order than a suggestion. The younger man stood up and motioned for Sergei to take his seat.

"Sergeant Bravo, I'm Vasili, and this is my comrade, Boris." Boris nodded his head at Sergei.

"I'm sorry, but I am no longer Sergeant Bravo, just Sergei Bravo, literature teacher for Secondary School No 2."

"Sergeant Bravo, we would like to talk about your service to your country." Vasili said.

Sergei turned his head away from the men and stared at a clock on the wall.

That's what they want. They are here to arrest me for running away from the capture.

"Are you not Sergeant Bravo? The Bofors crew commander with the Freedom Brigade? Responsible for three downed Nazi aircraft. Leading his team to shooting down nine Messerschmitts and Junkers?" Vasili asked.

Sergei Bravo turned toward the men and gazed at them, unsure of what they wanted.

"Sergeant Bravo, who fought valiantly with his comrades until all was lost? Sergeant Bravo who escaped capture from a Soviet unit and came back home to Belarus?" Vasili again inquired.

Bravo stood up from the chair as his body tensed. Bravo's voice raised, "Comrade," he said tensely, "I am a citizen of the Soviet Union and serve our country as a teacher here in Belarus. I am proud to be a citizen of this country. I am no hero and not a soldier anymore. I am just a teacher and no longer interested in combat service for my country. I have sacrificed."

"Comrade, we believe you have more to give to Mother Russia. You are Belarussian through and through, but still think you are a Pole sometimes. A hero doesn't just stop being a hero and run away. We believe a man like you wants to give more to his country."

"If you are interested, you will meet us tonight. The Hotel Europa in Minsk. Here is fifty rubles for your time and transportation. Be there by 1800hrs. If you do not show, we will know you are not interested. But we will come back. Or we notify the police that you are a fugitive from the army and the Russian military."

"Who are you?" Sergei asked.

"Come tonight, and you will find out. We are just comrades who want the best for the Soviet Union. *Do svidaniya*, Sergeant Bravo." With that goodbye, he was dismissed.

Later that afternoon, Sergei found himself aboard the train from Chertovichi to Minsk. After arriving, he took the carriage from the train station to the Hotel Europa. The hotel had a long history, first opening in the late 1800s with financial support from the wealthy Polyakov family of Minsk. It was also the first hotel at the time in Minsk, even Russia, that had an elevator. Over the years, the intelligentsia and bohemians visited the Hotel Europa, which also hosted famous Russians, like the artist Marc Chagall and the poet Vladamir Mayakovsky.

Sergei was in awe as he stepped down from the carriage and viewed the facades and the stunning workmanship of the exterior. He had never experienced such elegance in his life. The hotel itself faced Minsk's Cathedral Square, which intersected with Gubernatorskaya Street. As he walked in through the front door, Sergei was again struck dumb as he saw the cathedral-like interior with glass and overhangs that appeared to run into the sky. The hotel itself was progressive and designed in the art deco style of the time. Mixed with his awe was fear. *I should not have come here*, he thought as he climbed the hotel steps. *I do not know who these people are and what they want from me.*

Sergei had arrived earlier than the agreed upon time. He left his duties at the school and gone directly to the train for the hour trip to Minsk. He figured he would have a cup of coffee at the restaurant and then search through the common areas of the hotel to find Vasili and Boris. As Sergei walked into the hotel restaurant, Saulevich's, he saw both men sitting at the bar, drinking glasses of beer. The men immediately saw Sergei as he walked into the dining room. Boris was smiling as Sergei approached.

Vasili did not turn around but said in a faint voice, "We should get a table in a private area so we can talk." Boris snapped his figures to get the attention of the maître'd, who quickly approached from across the other side of the room. Soon, they were sitting at a table in a private room off the main dining room. To Sergei's surprise, servers began bringing food to the table, *zakyski*, small plates of food including a platter of sausages, pork belly, smoked meats, a variety of pickles, and sliced rye bread. The last server, who seemed to know both Vasili and Boris, brought a tray with a bottle of Minsk Kristall vodka and three small crystal glasses embossed with gold trim. Vasili was intently staring at Sergei as Boris filled and handed out glasses of vodka.

"Sergeant Bravo," Vasili began, "we believe you can help us in our war efforts."

"Please call me Sergei or Sergei Bravovich. I'm no longer a soldier. I tried to explain earlier to you. I'm just a teacher."

Boris leaned forward and broke his silence. "We know a lot about you, Sergeant Bravo. We spoke to your commander from Warsaw, we spoke to people in Chertovichi who know you. We spoke to your former crew from the Kampinoski forest. All of them say you are loyal. A leader. A genuine patriot and defender of your Russian homeland."

"I'm still not sure why anyone would want me. But I must ask. Who are you?"

Vasili smiled and leaned back in his chair as he took another sip of his vodka. "We are from The Big House."

"Big House?" Sergei asked.

Boris again spoke. "We are Cheka. We believe you can help us to defeat the Germans and others who threaten the Motherland."

Sergei sighed. So much for the quiet life of a literature professor. "What can I really do for the Cheka?" Sergei inquired.

"Yes, you are a *kacap,* a simple bumpkin from Belarus," Vasili remarked, emptying his glass. "A country that the Soviet Union and other eastern countries have conquered and controlled over the centuries. For a dirty Belarussian and a Polish simpleton, you have many talents. You speak German, Polish, and Russian. You have led troops in combat. And you are loyal to a fault. In our work, you must believe in what we are doing at all costs. You are also committed to teaching, a skill we need to recruit and train the next generation of patriots."

"I do not even know what a Cheka does."

"You will blend with the populace wherever we send you and be the eyes and ears of the Party. You will also perform specialized tasks when we need them done. We will train you in the skills needed to live the Cheka life—how to build bombs, how to use a clandestine radio, and, yes, how to kill and not just with a variety of weapons but also your hands. And then we will place you with an army unit. You will hear from us when we require your service. You will be trained and available when we need you even though months may pass without any contact."

"I'm not sure I'm right for this. I only wish for a quiet life."

"Well," Vasili said, sounding reluctant, "we offer no guarantees should you walk out that door."

"I promise to consider it, but I am really sure I am not your man. I am sorry," Sergei said as he stood up and walked toward the exit of the dining room.

"Sergei, should you have a change of heart, you could continue the fight for your country. Or we notify the authorities of the location of a deserter. The choice is yours." Vasili said with a smirk on his face. "We will be here tomorrow. Call and ask for Vasili."

On the train ride back from Minsk on the evening of their first meeting, Bravo pondered what it all meant. He understood that Cheka was a group of unconventional secret police who worked autonomously for the greater good of the country. Cheka, the word itself, was the slang term for the NKVD, formally the People's Commission for Internal Affairs. He had seen Cheka officers when he was in Warsaw during his first battles with Germany. They did what they wanted and often advised unit commanders on management of the unit and how and when to attack, all while keeping the goals of the Soviet Union as the highest priority. Cheka also meant bad business. Spying, political violence. But his bigger problem was Marta and his love for her. Could he leave her again? There was also the real threat of imprisonment. What to do? The Cheka or a Russian prison for desertion and escape? He would go directly to see Marta, and they would discuss what was best for their future.

Sergei arrived back in town on the last train back from Minsk. He was carrying an official letter in his hand that Boris gave him when he departed the hotel. Marta was sitting on the steps in front of his home. Her head was down, and it looked like she had been crying.

"Where were you!" Marta yelled as she stood up from the steps. This was the first time Sergei had seen his girlfriend upset or show any other emotion than happiness.

"I was in Minsk." he said flatly.

"Minsk? Why on God's earth would you be in Minsk? Why would you leave town without telling me? Or your mother?"

Sergei explained the details of the meeting with the NKVD officers. He handed the envelope to Marta. She read the letter, and her eyes swelled again with tears.

The seal at the top was unmistakable, a stark symbol of power—the emblem of the NKVD. Her heart slammed against her ribcage.

"Because of your skills and unwavering dedication to the cause," the letter began in an austere tone, "you are summoned for recruitment into the ranks of the People's Commissariat for Internal Affairs." Marta felt a cold chill surrounding her. She knew, beyond any shadow of a doubt, that life as she had known it was about to fracture into the before and after.

"You are leaving me again?" she said.

"Ah, Marta," he whispered, his head hanging and his voice a low rumble of unspoken fears. "They have chosen me. And they have threatened me if I do not go."

"Must you go?" she asked, though they both knew there was no room for choice in such matters.

"I must," Sergei affirmed, his resolve fortified by the same sense of obligation that now threatened to cleave them apart. "For our country, our people... for us. I also do not have much of a choice." He laughed bitterly.

"They are threatening to send me to prison for desertion if I don't rejoin the Soviet army ranks."

In the front steps of Sergei's home, they held each other close, the steady cadence of two hearts synchronizing in the face of looming separation.

"Stay strong." Sergei murmured into her hair, breathing in the scent of lilac and linen. "And faithful—not just to me, but to the hope that this war will end, and that I will return to you." Sergei's mother looked on as tears streamed down her wrinkled cheeks.

"Always." Marta replied.

Both entered his apartment and Sergei packed an old travel bag. Their final goodbye was silent. Sergei leaned forward and kissed Marta on the forehead. He stepped back from Marta, put the bag on his shoulder, and walked in the direction of the train station.

CHAPTER FOUR

THE BUTCHER OF KRAKOW

April 1941, Wawel Castle, Krakow, Poland

Hans Frank, known behind his back as the Renaissance Prince of Krakow and the Butcher of Poland, sat in a high-backed chair in the Wawel Castle. He wore a tailor-made grey worsted-wool suit, a heavily starched, white-collared shirt, and a blue and white Italian silk tie. He had his hair brushed back, which emphasized his prominent forehead. He had full and pouting lips, and thick eyelids that appeared too large for his button-sized eyes. Frank observed the group while he drank a cup of coffee from a china cup with the blue and yellow seal of the Jagiellonian dynasty, one of the many antiques taken by the German occupiers when they first arrived in 1939.

The large hall of the Wawel Castle overflowed with opulent displays of art, artifacts, and looted treasures from all over Europe. In one corner hung the famous Lady *with an Ermine*, a masterpiece by Leonardo da Vinci, its delicate brushstrokes and vibrant colors drawing the eye. Ornate tapestries and grand portraits lined the walls, while Persian rugs adorned the floor. Sunlight poured in through the large windows, casting a warm and gilded glow over the room. At the center of it all stood a grand conference table, adorned with intricate carvings and two gleaming silver candelabra. The office hall was vast and opulent, with high ceilings and ornate decorations adorning the walls. The hall was lit by grand chandeliers, making the ornately decorated walls and high ceilings glow.

"I continue to emphasize the will of the Führer, that Poland was the first colonial region of Germany." Frank paused and caught the eyes of each staff member sitting at the table. "Germany's interests must prevail here in Poland."

Seated before Hans Frank, Governor-General of occupied Poland, were his primary staff and lieutenants, those who administered this vast area of Poland not directly ruled by Germany. To Frank's right at the head of the ornate table, sat Arthur Seyys-Inquart, the Deputy Governor-General Administrator, then Colonel Scherner, the SS *Truppenungsplatz*, the head of police and security for Krakow. Across from Scherner was the commander of the internal security police (KdS), Lieutenant Colonel Max Grosskopf, SS-Brigadeführer, Dr. Otto Von Wachter, the Krakow District Governor, sat at the end of the table facing Hans Frank. Several other aides and assistants filled out the rest of the table and were on hand to take notes and address further questions asked by the Governor-General. The men were summoned monthly to Wawel Castle to brief the Governor-General on all progress of strategy, security, and management of the Polish population.

"*Guten morgen*, Governor-General and *meine Herren*," Von Wachter began. "The campaign to expel the remaining *Juden* from the city of Krakow to holding facilities and camps on the outskirts of the city has begun."

"*Sehr gut*!" Governor-General Frank said loudly, slapping the table with his hand. "But what about those *Juden* needed for essential services to the General Government?"

"We will issue an order soon to move essential *Juden*, about 12 thousand, to the newly created Jewish Residence Zone. Like our operations in 1939, as we continue to identify members of the Polish elite, intelligentsia, and academics, we will send those without useful skills to Sonderkation Krakau and the rest to Auschwitz. We should complete this operation in another thirty days."

The Governor-General turned to Colonel Scherner asking, "And Herr Colonel, how about our general defense and control of threats?"

"*Jawohl*, Governor-General," Scherner said "Our police battalions continue to identify threats, those who support the resistance and former Polish officers sympathetic to the Russians. Our combat units continue to actively patrol."

"*Danke*," the Governor-General nodded his head, and turned to Lieutenant Colonel Grosskopf to receive his report. Lieutenant Colonel averted his eyes, looking down at his notes and spoke. He was dressed in the green wool dress uniform of the *Sicherheitsdienst*, or SD, Hitler's secret police.

"*Guten morgen*, General-Governor," Grosskopf said. "There has been a high level of threat activity of late."

Frank nodded, "*Sehr gut*, Herr Lieutenant Colonel. What are we doing to prevent the attacks and identify the perpetrators?"

"The SD has increased intelligence collection activities, including interrogations of suspected underground members, debriefings of key Ghetto staff, and active use of our source network throughout the administration zone. SD soldiers continue targeted raids several times each night and have uncovered caches of weapons and valuable intelligence about the partisan movements and the plans of the Polish underground, the Armia Krajowa, which appears resolved to drive us from Krakow and is planning additional attacks against German government forces."

Frank frowned, staring intensely at Lieutenant Colonel Grosskopf. "But what are our plans to quell these disruptions?"

"*Mein Herr*, we have had much success in enclosing the *Juden* people in the Krakow ghetto, which now holds between 15 and 20 thousand Jews. They are secured by barbed wire fences and stone walls with heavy patrols by the SD and associated police units. They cannot escape."

Frank rubbed the back of his neck and was drumming his fingers on the long antique table. "And progress on the plans for the ultimate solution?"

Lieutenant Colonel Grosskopf leaned forward in his chair and adjusted his tie. The other senior officers in the room all appeared to shift in their chairs at this awkward question.

"*Mein Herr,* Under Operation Reinhart, we plan to move the residents of the ghetto to the forced labor camps in Belzec, Sobibor, and Treblinka."

"*Sehr gut,*" Frank said as he nodded. "What about the activities of Hauptsturmführer Wirth?" This was more sensitive territory, as this SD captain, known among the officers and soldiers as "Christian the Cruel," tended towards a more direct, ruthless—and openly violent—approach to "controlling" those judged anti-German, meaning any Jew at all, it seemed.

Grosskopf looked up and noticed that all the faces at the table were looking at him. "*Mein Herr,* yes, Captain Wirth is making progress. After conducting his first experiments at Grafeneck Castle, we appointed him as the administrative director at the Bradenburg Center. He has since perfected the use of carbon monoxide gas with large scale automotive systems. Wirth is confident that this will be the most efficient method for large-scale euthanasia."

Hans Frank looked down at the table at his officers and crossed his arms. "We must do away with them. They're like rats in cages in the Ghetto. Best to exterminate them as Herr Hitler directs us." Hans Frank declared, looking down at the table at his officers and crossing his arms.

CHAPTER FIVE

BACK TO SCHOOL

June 1941, NKVD School, Moscow, Soviet Union

Lieutenant Sergei Bravo stood at the gate of the schoolhouse. He peered at a red brick building with a large protective wall on one side. The NKVD School was a formidable building, made of dark gray stone and towering over the surrounding cityscape. Red flags with hammer and sickle emblems fluttered proudly from its rooftop. The school was on Bolshoi Kiselny Street and was within 300 yards of the famous "All-Russian Insurance Company," otherwise known as Lubyanka, the dark ornate mustard-colored building that now served as the headquarters for the NKVD, the People's Commissariat of Internal Affairs. Bravo had taken the train from Minsk after a few days of transition leave at home with his family. A series of train stops and then he arrived at the Kursk station, completing his journey with a hectic metro ride to the NKVD training center. It had never occurred to Bravo that service to his country would entail so much training at so many schools.

What had followed after he submitted to Vasili and Boris's "request" to support the Motherland and their government had been a whirlwind. Vasili, he learned, was Colonel Vasili Zarubin, a rising leader in the NKVD, and Major Boris Rodas was a counterintelligence specialist and infamous NKVD interrogator. He was still fearful that they might imprison him for deserting after the invasion of Warsaw and his detention by roaming Soviet troops as he made his way back home. Of greater concern was the unknown. What would they expect of him, and would he meet those expectations?

After his recruitment into the NKVD, Bravo had been commissioned into the Army, then sent off for subsequent basic officer and calvary training at Moscow's Budyonny Red Army Cavalry Academy. Sergei thought fondly of his experience at the cavalry school. The Academy stood tall and imposing, with its red brick walls and intricate carvings adorning its doors and windows. The courtyard was always bustling with activity, with soldiers marching in perfect unison and horses being led to and from the stables.

And now here he was, a few short months later, reporting for duty, he reflected, hearing the gate guard's words, "Welcome to the Brick House, comrade!" The soldier had said this with pride and a smart salute. "The commandant will meet you in the Great Room."

"*Spasibo*, Comrade Mladshiy Serzhant," Bravo replied in thanks. He made his way into the schoolhouse and eventually found his way into the Great Hall, also known as the Cheka Memorial Room. On the far wall of the room was a memorial to fallen NKVD and Cheka agents. Bravo approached the wall and looked at it curiously. He examined the large NKVD shield, red and silver with a dagger and a hammer and sickle overtop. Underneath the shield was the inscription: "Without mercy, without sparing, we will kill our enemies in scores of hundreds. Let them be thousands, let them drown themselves in their own blood. For the blood of Lenin and Uritsky." As Bravo finished reading, he heard footsteps behind him and turned.

"Lieutenant, you made it. Welcome home." Commissioner of State Security Service Yuri Petrov, the Commandant of the NKVD School, addressed him. Beside the Commissioner and dressed in uniform was Colonel Vasili Zarubin, the older NKVD agent Bravo had met in Minsk.

Bravo came to the position of attention and greeted both gentlemen. "Comrade Petrov. Comrade Zarubin. Good evening."

"Lieutenant Bravo," Commissioner Petrov said, "we came to wish you luck on your future tasks. We plan to train and push you to your limits. But we are here to reassure you that you made the correct decision to join our fight."

Zarubin added, "You will doubt yourself, but understand we do not doubt you. This will be the hardest thing you have ever done in your life and the most rewarding." After the brief greeting, they dismissed him, summoning an orderly who showed Bravo to his barracks, issued him newly pressed uniforms, had him examined by doctors, and finally led him to his first orientation class later that evening.

The next morning Bravo sat with others of similar looks and backgrounds in the gray classroom in anticipation of the first lecture by the course coordinator. Many of the students, he would learn, were from sister-countries associated with the Soviet Union before the war but which later had become Soviet republics. In a break during in-processing he met two others from Belarus, two from Vilnius, Lithuania, and five from Tbilisi, Georgia. Half the class was from the mainland, hailing from Moscow, Leningrad, and Samara. A senior state security captain entered the room, and the room of budding NKVD agents examined his actions. The captain wore a tan uniform like that of the cadets and senior leadership. However, his uniform was adorned with campaign medals and recognition of service from the earliest days of the NKVD in 1917 and service in the Russian Civil War. His face was ruddy and serious looking, as if it had a story to tell.

"Comrades," he began, "I am Vlod, your course director for the duration of your studies. You will listen, learn, and begin your transformation into agents of the NKVD today. We are going to push you every day. This work is not for everyone, so we want to eliminate as early as possible those who do not meet the standard and are unsuitable to represent the Motherland. In our last two classes, we had two students commit suicide under the pressure of this course. It is rigorous, yes, but you were all selected because we believe you have the correct traits to succeed."

Vlod paused for a moment and made eye contact with each of the students. Some looked away, and some couldn't keep their eyes off him. "Will you be the one who commits suicide? Will you be the one who is eliminated from the course because you do not have the skill, desire, or ambition to meet the standards? Do not be confused. We may look like a university, but most universities don't kill you—or teach you how to kill. We have physical training every morning, even when the famous Moscow snow comes. Based on your skills and background, some of you will specialize in learning other critical languages, others will become sabotage and guerilla warfare experts, and still others, masters of interrogation. All of you will master espionage tradecraft and hone your ability to assess and recruit people to provide information about threats to our homeland. Now, let's get to work." Vlod opened his lesson plan and began the mandatory discussion on the importance of Marxism and the success of the Soviet Union.

The next morning, an NKVD cadre abruptly woke the new cadets at 0400 hours and quickly ordered them to assemble in their physical fitness uniforms in the courtyard. There was a half inch of snow on the ground, and the temperature on the headquarters wall read 35° Fahrenheit. After a quick head count, Vlod marched the group around the courtyard then immediately brought the formation to a run. The formation left the campus at a quick pace, heading toward Lubyanka Square. As Bravo gasped for breath, he tried to distract himself by recalling the details of the building, its history. The NKVD cadre officer had explained on the first day that Lubyanka Square was neo-baroque style with a façade of yellow brick designed by Alexander Ivanov in 1897. Bravo was amazed that the hammer and sickle on the front of the building appeared to glow in the darkness. He could also see the domes of Saint Basil Cathedral on the horizon, its nine towers reminding him of flames coming from a bonfire.

Lieutenant Levan Berdize, a stocky, blond-haired cadet from Georgia, was running next to Bravo in formation, his loud breath coming out of his mouth like small puffs of smoke. "What is this insane Cheka trying to do to us!" Berdize gasped. "Is he going to run us across the Moskva? It's frozen!"

"He may be crazy, but he is a tough bastard." Bravo whispered.

"I think he's trying to kill us before we kill ourselves," Berdize said, choking on the cold air.

"He knows about killing and death. He led Chekas in the Spanish war. He is a true patriot."

"I think he's crazy!"

After the arduous run, Vlod ordered the students to clean up and report to the dining hall for a quick breakfast. After the serving of dark, dense rye bread, eggs, and hot tea, the trainees were ordered to the gymnasium for Samba and other hand-to-hand combat training. In this first phase, trainees were physically conditioned, taught advanced self-defense tactics all while being indoctrinated in the ideologies of the Soviet Union, a routine that would endure for the next month. They spent several days per week at nearby firearm ranges learning to master the Nagant revolver and Tokarev semi-automatic pistol, the preferred weapons of the NKVD agents who worked in close quarters.

A month later, Sergei found himself, along with his classmates who had made the cut, moving to new quarters on a campus southwest of Moscow, the so-called Special Purpose School in Yasenevo. Previous budding Chekists had given it the name "The Forest" because it was set in a rural area covered in ash trees. While the Brick House had laid the foundation, Bravo was now learning the real work of an agent. His classes trained him in using spy gadgets such as micro-listening devices and cameras and the use of harmless looking items like lighters and transistor radios which, using cleverly hidden compartments, could transfer intelligence and film covertly. He also began paramilitary training with classes on explosive handling, kidnapping, and assassination techniques like how to eliminate targets using poisons that couldn't be detected in the bloodstream. After about two weeks of training and orientation, he began operating as an NKVD "agent" in the mock town inside The Forest training area. The town resembled a typical small Eastern European city with stores, cafés, and other buildings.

The NKVD agent trainees would conduct missions to spot and assess targets to gain operational intelligence. This information was then used to develop training intelligence to plan a raid to "destroy" a government facility by the NKVD student teams. After several months of training at the Forest Facility, the NKVD trainees went back to the Brick House for final instruction, review of NKVD policies, and foreign language refresher classes.

About a week before graduation, Bravo was summoned to the Commissioner's office to discuss his performance in the course and his first assignment.

He quickly entered the office and sat in a brown leather executive chair directly in front of the Commissioner's desk, not quite knowing what to expect. The officer was drinking tea and reviewing a dossier marked "S. Bravo."

"Comrade," the old Cheka began as he leaned forward over the desk. "You have received high ratings from all of your teachers for your superior performance here."

"Yes, sir." Bravo said as he rose to attention.

"Please sit down, Comrade Bravo, you are a good soldier and an excellent officer. However, we need agents who are thinkers and able to work covertly and act less like a soldier."

"Yes, Comrade Commissioner, I understand."

"Bravo, you know the Germans are moving rapidly to invade Moscow. They have already engaged in three decisive actions on the Eastern Front. The allies call this attack Operation Barbarossa. Comrade Stalin is creating a new special operations force that will focus on attacking the rear area of the Nazi lines. We need strong clever men who can gather intelligence, look for spies within our ranks, and provide Moscow with information to identify and neutralize key Nazi commanders, police officers, collaborators, and traitors in the area. We would also ask you to assist the Red Army regular forces close to our beloved city. Bravo, do you think you can commit to this very important and dangerous assignment?"

Bravo heard talk of the new unit. His classmates were eager to join and be on the front line. A few of the friendly instructors had already provided a background on the new commander and given Bravo a sign that he would be a strong candidate for a special assignment protecting Moscow.

Lieutenant Bravo again stood quickly to attention and said, "Yes, comrade!" and almost shouted the motto of his new the unit: "Any place, any task!"

CHAPTER SIX

WHERE DO YOU BELONG?

Order No. 001435 by the People's Commissar of Defense USSR
2 October 1941
People's Commissariat for Internal Affairs, Headquarters Moscow

(1) Personnel of the NKVD Special Group are merged and reassigned to the 2nd Separate Motorized Brigade of Special Purpose of the NKVD of the USSR. The new newly created unit is directly subordinate to the People's Commissar of Internal Affairs Lavrentiy Beria.

(2) Colonel M.F. Orlov assumes the role of Commander, 2nd Separate Motorized Brigade of Special Purposes of the NKVD (OMSBON) effective 1 October 1941.

(3) As of 1 October 1941, Colonel I.M. Tretyakov assumes the role of Deputy Commander in the 2nd Separate Motorized Brigade of Special Purposes of the NKVD (OMSBON).

(4) Effective 1 October 1941, Captain A.A. Maksimov is assigned as the Major of State Security, 2nd Separate Motorized Brigade of Special Purposes of the NKVD (OMSBON).

L. P. Beria

Peoples Commissar of Internal Affairs

***

November 7, 1941, Red Square, Moscow, Russia

Lieutenant Bravo was cold. *Damn cold.* He had been standing in formation in front of his detachment since 0500. His senior officer had notified him at 2300 hours the previous evening that he should assemble his men and be on the parade field early the next morning. There was a meeting on November 6th at the Mayakoskya metro station to celebrate the 24th anniversary of the great socialist revolution. At this event, Chairman Stalin ordered leaders of the All-Union Communist Party to hold a military parade the very next day.

This is ridiculous, Bravo thought. *Some German units are about twenty miles from the city, and the Luftwaffe could strike and kill all the leadership of the Red Army.*

Even at 0500 the parade field was bustling with activity. The garrison senior noncommissioned officers were staging units facing the rostrum of the Lenin mausoleum. Other units were being staged outside of the gates to march into Red Square on command when the band played. This was the first time Bravo had been inside Red Square; he had run around it but had never been permitted to venture inside.

From his position near the center of this important place, he was amazed by what he saw. The soaring brick red walls sloping high on one side, which protected the Kremlin, impressed him. Thin round towers rose at the corners of the walls, each topped with big ruby red stars. Under the rostrum was the squat, blocky brown-red building that held the mummified body of Lenin. Prominent on the square, Bravo could also see St. Basil's, the church built by Ivan the Terrible, a vast collection of chapels and towers. All of Red Square had a mystical feel since it had been snowing since yesterday, the white powder covering the cobblestones and accumulating as the temperature had not risen above about 20° degrees for several days. Bravo ached with exhaustion. When he had first received the news that his next assignment would be with OMSBON, he felt excited about living the glamorous life of a *Cheka*. He looked forward to traveling the country and enjoying luxurious meals in the finest hotels in Russia, just like the officers who had recruited him. He also knew that the NKVD engaged in bad business, espionage, and political violence, sabotage, even murder. He was not sure if this really was the life he wanted. There were plans for Bravo, but his assignment now was to establish minefields on high-speed avenues of approach to the city. He and his detachment had spent days placing the mines, recording the routes, and supporting internal security operations as the German army raced toward the capitol.

Bravo, dressed in his best full-dress uniform and standing in front of his platoon, grew excited as the parade was about to start. At 0750, he watched as Chairman Stalin and other prominent officials of the government lined up on the snow-covered rostrum.

Bravo saw a white horse coming from the Spasskaya Tower Gate and trotting toward the stage. Sitting atop the magnificent creature was Marshall Budyonny, who sat well, bringing the horse to a stop in front of General Artemyev, the chief of the Moscow Garrison command. The general saluted Marshall Budyonny provided a brief report, and then accompanied the Marshall in a review of the troops. The Marshall dismounted after the troop review and joined the dignitaries on top of the Lenin rostrum. All Bravo could think was how cold his hands must have been, holding the reins.

"Here comes Stalin," Bravo said to the troops behind him.

Bravo watched as a short, mustachioed man with black hair and a large nose, his dress uniform heavy with medals, made his way to the podium. A technician adjusted the microphone for Stalin before he spoke.

"Comrades," he began, "we salute the men of the Red Army and Navy, commanders and political commissioners, working men and working women, collective farmers- men and women, workers in the intellectual professions, brothers and sisters in the rear of our enemy who have temporarily fallen under the yoke of the German brigands, and also those valiant men and women guerrillas who are destroying the rear of the German invaders!"

Shouts of approval came from the troops and those observing the ceremony in the stands.

Bravo listened as his supreme leader congratulated the crowd on the 24th anniversary of the October Soviet revolution. Bravo sighed in relief as Stalin recognized that the country was again under attack by the German brigands but insisted that the Soviet Union was now heroically repulsing the enemy along the entire front. This assurance from the supreme leader sparked louder cheers of support from the parade field and the stands filled with men and women observing this historical speech.

Snow began to fall on Stalin as he continued his speech with several interruptions for applause and shouts from the square.

With a slight pause for effect, Stalin bellowed, "Comrades, men of the Red Army and Red Navy, commanders and political instructors, men and women guerrillas, the entire world is looking to you as the force capable of destroying the plundering hordes of German invaders. The enslaved people of Europe look to you as their liberators."

Bravo smiled as his leader appealed to the masses for their unfettered support.

Stalin was almost screaming as he pounded the cold podium with his fist. "The liberating mission has fallen to our lot. We must be worthy of this mission! The war you're waging is the war of liberation, a just war. Let the manly images of our great ancestors inspire you in this war! May the victorious banner of the great Lenin be your lodestar. The complete destruction of the German invaders is our duty! Death to the German invaders! Long live our glorious motherland, her liberty, her independence! Under the banner of Lenin, forward to victory!" Stalin ended his speech and stood silently as cheers and shouts echoed throughout Red Square.

Bravo was shivering as the first units lined up outside the gate leading into Red Square. He could also hear the gripes and moans from his men in formation and had to tell them to stand steady. Bravo heard the quick tuning of the instruments by the musicians from the Moscow Military District conducted by Vasily Agapkin. The recognizable chords of *Farewell from a Slavic Woman* began as the first units stepped onto the cobblestone parade ground.

> *Arise for faith, oh Russian land!*
> *we composed many a song in our heart,*
> *Glorifying the native land.*
> *We loved you no matter what,*
> *You are wholly Russian land.*
> *You raised your head high,*
> *Your face was shining like the sun.*
> *But you become a victim of betrayal*
> *By those who have cheated and sold you!*

The cadets from the artillery school led the parade as they smartly marched through Red Square. Many other units, including artillery, infantry, air defense, and naval formations, followed them with their banners proudly unfurled. The units marched past the rostrum with "eyes right," the unit commanders saluting Chairman Stalin as they passed.

> *And again in March trumpet calls us.*
> *We all stand in order,*
> *And go to the holy battle.*
> *Arise for faith, oh Russian land!*

> *The Saints awaits Russia's victory.*
> *Respond, oh orthodox host!*

As the segment of marching units ended, Bravo could see the tops of large military vehicles and hear the roar of their engines as they approached Red Square. The shouts and roars of approval could be heard as artillery regiments from the Moscow Defense Zone drove onto the cobblestone parade area. The artillery regiment was followed by a combined air aircraft gun regiment and then two tank battalions from the Stavka Reserve. The music sounded louder as the massive equipment approached the Lenin rostrum.

> *Arise for faith, oh Russian land!*
> *We are all children of a great empire,*
> *We all remember the commandments of our fathers:*
> *For the homeland, honor, glory,*
> *Pity neither yourself nor the enemy,*
> *Arise, Russia from your prison of slavery,*
> *Victory spirit is called: time to do battle!*
> *Rise your battle flags!*

Bravo shifted his body back and forth to warm up his feet. The ceremony was also wearing out his men, and they were visibly done in. Bravo shouted over his shoulder, "Comrades, steady!" He thought, *"I hope this will be over soon. It looks like the last of the units are coming through the gate.*

As the final tank unit rolled past the rostrum and off the square, the radio broadcaster announced the end of the ceremony, with most units going directly to the front to repel the invasion of the Germans. Bravo looked at his watch. It read 0825 hours. *I can't believe the ceremony only took twenty-five minutes,* he thought, *it seemed like hours!* As Bravo looked up from his watch, he spotted a senior noncommissioned officer from NKVD headquarters walking toward him quickly. He saluted, and Lieutenant Bravo smartly returned the salute.

"Comrade, they request your presence at HQ at 1400 hours. You are to report to Colonel Orlov. He wants to speak to you about your orders for your next assignment.

My next assignment? I just arrived, Sergei thought, *but I am eager to get out of the cold*. He thought of Marta and the smell of warm, fresh bread.

December 1941, Headquarters NKVD, Moscow, Russia

Colonel Orlov was standing at his map board, looking at major Soviet army locations when Lieutenant Bravo arrived at his door.

"Bravo! Would you like some tea?" Orlov asked.

"Yes, comrade, I would love some tea with jam. I have been cold for days. Thank you very much." Colonel Orlov motioned Bravo to the tea on a side table, where Sergei poured a cup of tea and stirred in a spoonful of thick dark jam and a little milk, and then joined his commander next to the map board.

"How was the parade?" Orlov asked.

"Impressive. But cold." Bravo said as he laughed.

Orlov smiled as he spoke. "I couldn't make it because of every changing threat on the battlefield. I was excused from the experience. I'm told we had every available unit on the parade square. And all the Chairman's senior staff."

"It is true." Bravo confirmed. "The commander of the parade units told me that there were almost 30 thousand officers and soldiers taking part. He said we had over 140 artillery, 160 tanks, and 232 motor vehicles."

"How was the mood?" Orlov asked.

"Despite the cold, everyone appeared optimistic. Morale seemed good. Chairman Stalin's speech was hopeful and confident. Seemed to inspire all of us to defeat the Germans." Bravo said.

"Optimistic?" Orlov asked.

"Yes, as optimistic as you can be when you know you are departing Moscow in an hour to go straight back to the front!" Bravo said wryly.

Orlov laughed at Bravo's observations. Then his face became solemn before he again spoke.

"You know, Bravo, you have been under scrutiny for the last month. I observed you when you were at the NKVD Academy and have kept my eye on you as you led the building of mine defenses around the city. You performed admirably. You are a sound officer. You follow orders, and you have a strong sense of patriotism for this war and for your country."

Bravo's head dipped, and he said, "Thank you, comrade."

"You know, Lieutenant, that our country was on the brink of destruction over the last month. We highly underestimated the strength and speed of the German fascists as they made their three-pronged attack towards our most important cities. We almost lost it all."

"*Da*," Bravo nodded.

"But Bravo, God loves the Russian fighting man. Against what the Germans called Operation Typhoon, almost a million Soviet troops were waiting for the Germans to take our city. Most of our tanks were destroyed and our airpower also almost completely defeated. Army Group Center, over a million men and almost 2000 tanks, attacked. And then the rain came."

"The rain, Comrade Colonel?"

"*Da*, the rain. The Germans encircled the city and stormed ahead. And the rain came. The rains of autumn turned the roads into rivers of mud. My father calls this the quagmire season, where the mud almost brings life to a halt. Except our Soviet people know how to live with and on the land, Lieutenant. The Germans were halted."

"Comrade Colonel, I did not know how close we were to being defeated."

"Never defeated, Bravo. We are Russian and used to being beaten down. Beaten badly. But never defeated. We always get up. The winter comes. On the heels of the rain. And then it becomes cold. The Germans do not know how to live or fight in this severe cold. We are not out of the woods yet, Bravo, but we will not be defeated. We have these reconnaissance units and pincer units close to our proud city, but the main effort of the German attack has been defeated. It is time for us to think about moving west and defeating the fascists in their own country. We have much work to do—and the resolve to defeat these fascist bastards."

Colonel Orlov motioned for Bravo to join him at the map board. Bravo walked closer and observed the various symbols marking enemy and friendly units throughout Central and Eastern Europe.

"In June, Bravo, Moscow sent out a directive requesting help from the nation to face the fascist regime as they intensified their attack. A few weeks later, the Central Committee of the Communist Party and the Council of People's Commissars directed local Party organizations to form detachments, detachments of partisans."

"Why?" Bravo asked.

"To bring the war to the enemy. We provided further guidance helping those partisan groups organize and teaching them how best to destroy German forces. Small groups of seventy to 150 men began attacks on airfields, communication centers, ammo storage areas, petroleum depots, and railroad lines. Our partisans are to engage the German enemy in the rear areas behind their lines. The program has become very successful and now has support at the highest levels of the Soviet government such that Commissar Beria as the NKVD chief has been appointed to run it with operational control falling to me."

Bravo's eyebrows lifted as he leaned in to listen more closely to his commander.

Orlov pointed toward the board. "In Lithuania, we have a large group of active partisans based out of Vilna in the southern part of the country. In Belarus, we have active partisans in the areas between Brest, Baranavicy, and Pinsk. And in Ukraine we have active partisan support in Zhytomyr in the northwest, Kiev in the north, and Belgorod and Kryvyi in the east."

"But what about in our Motherland?" Bravo said as he peered closely at the area of the map showing the Soviet Union.

Using a pen to point out the location, the colonel responded. "Of course, Lieutenant, we have partisans in Pskov, Leningrad, and Novgorod, in the northwest and in Smolensk, Orel, and Kursk districts in the southwest. Their numbers are impressive, as is how quickly they came together. Our intelligence department estimates that there are 2000 partisan detachments, over 90 thousand fighters, spread in strategic locations in German-occupied territories."

"So, we are successfully disrupting the rear areas of the Germans, Colonel?"

"It's not quite that simple, especially here." He pointed to Poland on the map. "The partisans are committed but lack resources and training. Peasants, farmers, and former Red Army soldiers make up their ranks. Many of the first detachments were commanded by Red Army officers and local communist activists who remained in Soviet-occupied Poland. Sadly, they do not have what they need to be effective. They need weapons. They need food. They need leaders."

"Why tell me all of this?"

"Bravo, based on your background, we need you to lead NKVD and partisan detachments in disrupting the German supply lines and conducting guerilla operations. Your success could be crucial to the Red

Army winning this war." He paused, looking thoughtful. "However, my superiors are not sure we can trust you." He gazed at Sergei, shrugging his shoulders.

Bravo cocked his head to one side as he looked closely at his superior officer. "Trust me, Comrade Colonel?"

"Why should we trust a native Pole turned Belarussian? In theory, the Soviet Union is your third country, implying many questions about where your allegiances lie. You speak many languages: Polish, German, Russian, Ukrainian. How do we know we can assign you to lead partisans when we do not even know which country you will go to should you desert when the bullets fly. You ran from the army once. How do we know we can trust you? Why should we trust the son of a teacher? Many in Moscow say we should not."

Bravo took several steps backwards. His face was red, and he came to the position of attention. He was clenching his fists as he stared at his colonel and spoke.

"Comrade, I came from humble beginnings as a teacher. In the chaos of war, I fled Russian soldiers while dressed in a Polish uniform after a German invasion and occupation. None of us were certain what the future held, and we lived in constant fear for our lives. But then, you found me. A simple educator who had no desire to return to the battlefield. You saw potential in me and brought me to meet with the Cheka officers, who granted me their trust. I willingly became part of the NKVD. It is an honor to defend and fight for my country; it is what I was born to do. My loyalty is unwavering."

Bravo was now looking down at the floor. He was breathing heavily, and sweat had formed on his forehead.

"I'm sorry, Bravo. My superiors have expressed concerns, and I can't ignore them. It's our duty to question and confirm loyalties before giving heavy responsibilities. Don't get me wrong, I trust you. I always have. But for your next assignment in this war, you will be challenged to gain the trust of others. I will do everything in my power to be your advocate and ensure you receive the support you need."

Colonel Orlov extended his hand to Lieutenant Bravo. "Will you continue your journey as a Cheka, as a Soviet officer, and accept this assignment?"

Bravo stood silent for a minute. He looked Colonel Orlov in the eye and said, "Yes, Comrade Colonel, I will accept this assignment as long as my loyalties are never questioned again by my country or my superiors."

"Bravo, your true test is next."

"Next?" Bravo asked.

"Find Kovpak!"

PART TWO

Historical Note: Ukraine, Germany, and Poland from 1942 to 1945

The origins of Bryansk can be traced back to approximately 1146 when the Hypatia Codex was written. The literal translation of the town's name in Russian refers to a low-lying area surrounded by dense forests. During the battle of Vedrosha in 1503, Bryansk was conquered by the Grand Duchy of Moscow and transformed into a fortress to protect the city's interests. This strategic location continued to play a role in conflicts throughout the 1700s and 1800s. In 1709, Czar Peter the Great incorporated Bryansk into the Kiev government, but it was later transferred to the newly formed Oryol government under Catherine the Great.

The German Wehrmacht, with all their might and fury, stormed into Bryansk in 1941. The once peaceful city was quickly turned into a battlefield as the Soviet Union's 3rd, 13th, and 50th armies were surrounded by the enemy. The air was filled with the deafening sounds of bombs exploding and gunfire rattling through the streets. Buildings crumbled under the onslaught and flames danced through the sky nightly, the bombers leaving behind a trail of devastation. According to intelligence reports, 60 thousand brave Soviet partisans were risking everything to resist the invading forces in and around Bryansk. They fought with fierce determination, fueled by their love for their country and their comrades.

Tragically, between 1940 and 1945, about 1.3 million people were deported to Auschwitz by the SS and police, nearly all eventually perishing. Most of those killed were Jews, with over 900 thousand being gassed in extermination centers and another 200 thousand dying from the gruesome conditions of the camp. However, it's important to note that not only Jews suffered under German occupation: over 70 thousand Poles were also killed in Auschwitz for resisting or violating German laws.

During World War 2, brave Jewish men and women banded together to form irregular military groups, risking their lives to resist against the oppressive forces of Nazi Germany and its collaborators. These courageous partisans were mostly made up of escapees from urban Jewish ghettos and concentration camps, with some even including women and children among their ranks in Ukraine. While most operated in Eastern Europe, there were also Jewish partisan groups in France and Belgium, working alongside local resistance movements. Many individual Jewish fighters also joined other partisan groups in occupied countries. It is estimated that 20 to 30 thousand Jews fought as partisans during this tumultuous period in history.

While the partisan groups may have shared a common enemy in the Germans and their sympathizers, there were also factions among them with different goals. Tensions ran high between the resistance groups as the Jewish partisans braced for an attack from their ally, the *Armia Krajowa* or Home Army (AK). Meanwhile, the *Guardia Ludowa, or* People's Guard (GL), formed in 1942 and later absorbed by the *Armia Ludowa* (AL) in 1944, brought with them a formidable force of over 3,000 fighters, connections to the NKVD, and a cache of weapons. Despite being aligned with the Soviet Union, GL, like many other partisan groups, operated quasi-independently even though the focus was shared: sabotaging and retaliating against the German fascists.

The GL and AL's main operations took place in seven districts including Warsaw, Lwow, Silesia, Krakow, and Kielce. These brave soldiers destroyed over 200 German trains, 133 strategic train stations, and sixty communications networks. Unlike other groups, these two formed close alliances with Jewish partisans and played a crucial role in the success of the Warsaw Uprising in 1943. They launched attacks on German Wehrmacht near the walls of the Warsaw ghetto and helped Jews escape to safety. In fact, some Jews were so grateful for their help that they joined the GL.

To complicate the situation even more, as Nazi Germany and the Soviet Union occupied Poland, various resistance organizations joined forces to create the Polish Underground State that was fiercely loyal to the Government of the Republic of Poland in exile in London. The first elements of this state were formed in late September 1939, during the German and Soviet occupation. To its supporters, the Underground State represented a legitimate continuation of the pre-war Republic of Poland, fighting against Germany's oppressive powers. It wasn't just a military resistance; it also included civilian structures for justice, education, culture, and social services, a complete shadow government displaying the strength and determination of the nation in the face of occupation.

Distinct from these Polish resistance groups was a group of courageous rebels known as Soviet partisans for their allegiance to the Soviet Union. These fighters wore tattered clothing and carried rifles stolen from enemy soldiers. They hid in forests and marshlands, launching surprise attacks on German convoys and destroying supply lines. Their efforts not only disrupted Germany's attempts at exploiting the occupied territories for resources, but also proved crucial in aiding the Red Army by sabotaging communication networks and spreading powerful messages through underground newspapers and leaflets.

In July 1944, the military situation in the region was changing quickly. The Stavka, also known as the Soviet High Command, launched the Lviv-Sandomierz offensive. Their deceptive plan was to drive out German forces from the north and expose the German Army Group Center's weaknesses. Marshall Ivan Konev was the supreme leader of the 1st Ukrainian Front during this time. Together with the Polish Home Army, who launched an uprising on July 23rd, they captured and liberated Lviv. This strategic victory allowed them to gain control of a crucial bridge over the Vistula. The German forces under the command of General Josef Harpe were encircled and defeated by the 1st Ukrainian Front and the Polish Home Army. To push back the advancing Soviet troops, the Germans launched a counterattack in August but could not break through. As both sides established defensive positions by December 1944, momentum shifted in favor of the Soviets because of their strategic planning and leadership under Marshall Konev.

Marshall Konev was a dedicated soldier and skilled military officer who had begun his service in 1916 as an infantryman in the Czarist Army. After joining the Red Army, he received an officer commission upon graduating from the Frunze Military Academy in Moscow. Despite Stalin's purges of officers, Konev rose through the ranks. In 1941, he was given command of the 19th Army before eventually being appointed Commander of the 1st Ukrainian Front in March 1944.

By the end of 1944, the Wehrmacht still maintained control over the western part of Poland, their front line 200 miles east of its initial position during the invasion in 1939. With an abundance of supplies and vehicles provided by their Allies, the Soviets could mobilize a larger number of infantry soldiers and increase production of armored vehicles. These resources allowed for a faster and more mobile Soviet force, poised to potentially break through German defenses and advance into Western Europe by capitalizing on the weaknesses of the Axis forces.

As the Nazi occupation pressed on, German interrogations became a prominent tactic used to extract vital intelligence from the populace. From 1939 to 1945, the imposing Silesian House, at 2 Pomorska Street in Krakow, served as the General Government Gestapo headquarters. Within its walls, thousands of Polish citizens and other nationalities were subjected to brutal interrogations and torture, with some never leaving alive.

The NKVD units working in Krakow also had their tried-and-true techniques to collect intelligence, including using collaborators sympathetic to Poland and the Soviet Union and conducting surveillance on military targets. There are five prehistoric mounds in Krakow that were often used by the NKVD intelligence teams. Originally, they were used to memorialize historic events or to commemorate Polish leaders. The oldest mound was Krakus built in the 7th century and next to Wawel Castle, a hotbed of German activity during WWII. The other well-known mounds were Wanda, Tadeusz Kosciuszko, Pilsudski, and Independence.

The Wanda Mound overlooks the Vistula River and dates to the 7th century, built originally to honor Wanda, the princess and daughter of the King. Polish folklore claims Wanda committed suicide by throwing herself into the Vistula River rather than marry a German. In the late 1800s, the military built a semi-permanent artillery fort named Wandahugel #49 to guard the Sandomierz route atop the mound.

CHAPTER SEVEN

INTO THE FOREST

February 1942, Bryansk Village, Russia,

Sergei could not help thinking about his journey and how much his life had changed in the last four months upon his arrival in the town of Bryansk after a long train journey from Moscow.

Sergei thought, *I do not know who I am anymore.*

Stepping into the train station early in the morning after an overnight trip, Sergei was dressed in a wool sweater with a dark cotton jacket over top and was wearing loose *sharovary* trousers, Cossack boots, and a cloth cap on his head. The train station was austere and quiet, with only a few rail workers coming and going. Sergei walked to the front lobby of the station and was greeted by an attendant.

"*Kuda?*" a man in a train uniform asked. "Where do you want to go?"

"My uncle lives in the country outside of town. How can I get there?" Sergei asked.

"We are a small town and station. We do not have taxis anymore because all the drivers have gone off to war. Your best opportunity would be to walk toward your uncle's home and see if a farmer coming from town would take you to his home."

"Bless you, comrade. Is there a map?"

The porter looked inquisitively at Sergei for a moment and then shook his head. "Come here." The porter motioned for Sergei to follow him around the corner behind a partition. The porter pulled a map out of his pocket and handed it to Sergei.

"Thank you." Sergei said, then looked at the map to determine his route. Bryansk Forest was about twelve miles from the rail station.

"And comrade?" the porter added, "I would be careful out there. The war has come to our home here. A German patrol who does not know you may think you are partisan. If you encounter a partisan out there in the country, they may think you are a German spy. Be warned."

"Again, comrade, thank you for your help," Sergei said as he walked quickly from the station.

Just ten minutes outside of town, Sergei heard the crunch of wagon wheels and looked back to see a wagon pulled by one horse, a farmer holding the reins slackly. The wagon contained, as far as Sergei could see, a few bags of vegetables and several other burlap sacks.

Sergei looked up to the approaching wagon and nodded his head.

The farmer brought the wagon to a stop and asked, "Where are you heading, young man?"

Sergei took off his hat as he spoke. "Comrade, I'm going to see my uncle who lives outside of town on the edge of the forest. Can you help?"

"What is the family name, comrade? I may get you close as I have a far journey to a town on the other side of the forest."

"My uncle is Ivan Antonich, and he has a small farm."

The farmer scratched his head and said, "I do not know this family or name. Are you sure you are in the right place?"

"Yes, comrade, it is correct. He is sick and does not come to town much. You may not know him."

"Hmm. Well, I will take you as far as I can. Jump into the back." The wagon began to move at a trot.

Sergei marveled at the beauty of the countryside. It was a country at war, but its graceful landscape was inspiring. A gravel road snaked out of town with wide open country on each side. The wind feathered though the dry wild grass and trees. He planned to have the farmer take him as near as he could to the forest and then he would try to contact the partisans. Sergei breathed in the country air deeply as he felt the effects of the long trip. He remembered his meeting with Colonel Orlov and his orders to find the man he was to work with, Sydir Kovpak, the infamous leader of the Ukrainian partisans. Since the start of the war, Kovpak had led guerilla units in combat against the Axis forces in the Sumy and Bryansk regions. Colonel Orlov advised Sergei that the NKVD's plan was to integrate the partisan units, bringing them under Red Army control and support and ending their independent operations. This was Sergei's real mission, and to carry it out first he had to find Kovpak and become a part of his unit. Then he had to get the man to trust him.

Sergei leaned back against a bag of soft materials and dozed off. He was quickly awakened when the cart stopped. He noticed that the road had taken them into a wooded area.

We must be getting close to the forest, Sergei thought.

"What is wrong, comrade. Why do we stop?" Sergei asked the farmer.

"My wheel is shaking, and I must tighten the axle bolts. You can sit while I fix the wheel. We will go in a moment."

Sergei watched as the farmer got out of the wagon and adjusted the wheel.

"No, comrade, I can help." Sergei said as he stood up, noticing for the first time the denseness of the forest. Sergei looked around and did not see a soul though he felt like a thousand eyes were on him.

Sergei dropped to the ground, looked over the shoulder of the farmer, and said, "How can I help?"

The farmer looked up and smiled, and Sergei watched him walk to the rear and other side of the wagon. "One moment," he said.

Sergei heard a crack and watched as a rope dropped from the branches above him. He yelled out as it dropped over him and quickly tightened around his body. Sergei screamed as he was lifted six feet into the air and then quickly dropped onto the ground.

"Stop!" Sergei yelled out as he tried to free his arms. He saw several men run out from the trees. Sergei continued to struggle as he felt hands on his arms and was turned onto his stomach. His hands and feet were secured, and a sack placed over his head.

Sergei continued to struggle with the ropes but finally succumbed to the fact that he was not going to break out any time soon. He yelled out and demanded to be released. He felt a cold metal object touch his throat, and someone kneeling next to him who said in Russian, "Shut up, or we will cut your throat." Sergei stayed silent as he felt his body lifted and thrown into the back of the wagon. The wagon jerked and began to move.

As the wagon moved, Sergei felt it cross rough ground and then his body slid toward the back of the wagon as it climbed uphill. His body shifted and he rolled toward the front of the wagon as it traveled downhill then abruptly stopped.

A moment later, Sergei was lifted from the wagon, carried a few feet, and again dropped to the ground. Strong arms lifted him into a sitting position. The ropes on his hands were first adjusted and brought from behind his back, arms brought forward, and his wrists secured again. He felt a rope tying his body to tree he was propped against. The burlap hood was quickly ripped from his head.

An old partisan was standing in front of him and smoking a pipe. "Why are you here?" the old partisan demanded.

"You brought me here," Sergei yelled at the old partisan. A large muscular partisan stepped forward and quickly punched Sergei in the chest, nearly taking his breath away.

"Let's start again," the old partisan said. "Why are you here?"

Sergei looked up, his eyes adjusting to the low light of his surroundings. It was still daylight but very dark in the wooded area where he now sat. The canopy of the forest was like a dome covering what looked like a forest city. He could see people working and walking around as his interrogation continued.

"Please comrade, we will not ask you again."

Sergei looked at the old partisan. "I'm looking for Kovpak."

The old partisan was about fifty years of age. His skin was worn and leathery from the wind and sun. He was short but lean and had a short dark beard shot through with gray. Years of pipe smoking had stained his mustache. In a long leather jacket and with a cloth cap on his head, he looked just like another peasant farmer.

The three men surrounding Sergei immediately turned to stare. The large stocky partisan stepped forward again. "Never speak that name!" and struck Sergei on his back just below his neck.

Sergei was propelled forward but still restrained by the ropes. He felt all the air leave his body and exhaled with a loud gasp.

"Kovpak?" The old man said the name with contempt. "Kovpak does not exist. He is a figment of the German regime and even the NKVD."

"A friend of his sent me to see him. To help." Sergei said carefully, eying the angry partisan, who stepped forward again to threaten Sergei. The old partisan shook his head and waved him off.

"You told my friend the farmer that you were looking for your uncle. Is Kovpak your uncle?"

"No, no," Sergei sputtered. "I wasn't sure it would be safe to tell him who I was looking for."

"You lied to our comrade!" Father Snow, the angry partisan, said accusingly.

He rushed toward Sergei with the knife in his hand but was held back by another who Sergei would later learn was Semyon Rudnev, a close ally and deputy of Sidor Kovpak with many combat experiences in the October Revolution and the Civil War that followed. Prior to the war, Father Snow was a chicken farmer in Putivl infamous in his community for his lush head of hair and wild white beard.

"Please, comrade, we need to confirm why you are here, your intentions." Rudnev said to Sergei. "Or Father Snow is going to cut your belly from crotch to throat. He thinks you are a Nazi spy with your Aryan looks and funny accent."

Father Snow stood a few steps away from both men but was peering angrily at Sergei who was shifting uneasily on the forest floor.

"So, comrade, why did you lie?" Rudnev asked as he leaned closer to Sergei and spoke in a whisper.

"Please comrade, I did not mean to lie to the farmer. I did not know who to trust or how to find Kovpak."

"So, why did you lie to me, comrade?" Rudnev asked.

Sergei looked up at Rudnev and raised his eyebrows. "To you?"

"Yes, comrade, to me."

"Ah, you were the farmer driving the wagon. Your hat was pulled down and you had on different clothes."

"Yes, comrade. That was me. We knew you had arrived in town before you stepped on the ground at the station. Our supporters are many. Our net is large."

"Are you the partisans? Are you Kovpak?"

"Comrade, we are not partisans, we are freedom fighters against the Nazi regime. And Kovpak is a ghost. Please tell me why you are here?" The group of partisans encircled Sergei. He looked at them with concern.

"I was sent by my colonel to find the Bryansk partisan group led by Sidor Kovpak. I am sorry if I was wrong. I wish none of you harm," Sergei said as he looked at each of the partisans. "I was to find Kovpak.

Determine the needs of he and his men. Ask Moscow for more support. Men. Supplies. Radios," Sergei said as he stuttered.

"Who is your colonel?" Rudnev asked.

"Colonel Orlov." Sergei said with hesitation, unsure if his life would end soon.

"Who do you work for?" Rudnev asked.

"I work for Colonel Orlov of the NKVD," Sergei whispered.

"And you are not a partisan? What is your name?" Rudnev asked.

Sergei shook his head. "No, I am not a partisan. I am Lieutenant Sergei Bravo with NKVD. Colonel Orlov sent me to find Kovpak and the Bryansk partisans to help the effort."

The old partisan with the gray beard and the pipe walked closer to Sergei Bravo and put his hand on his shoulder.

"I am Kovpak."

Bravo looked at the old partisan leader with surprise.

"Sergei, we are glad you are here. We were expecting you but hoped Colonel Orlov would have sent word first. We are sorry for the special reception…."

Sergei was untied by several partisans and allowed to walk free. The group around him gave welcoming smiles and several smacked him on the back in a fraternal gesture, as if he had joined a sports team.

"Please, comrades, let's show our new Cheka where he now lives." Kovpak said. He began to walk toward out of the central area of the compound and gestured toward a trail leading to the perimeter.

"Sergei, when we first came here, we started with a large hole in the ground to keep us concealed. We used this space to sleep, eat, and plan our attacks in the area. Then, as all soldiers and fighters do, we developed a plan to improve the area. Comrade, we live under the canvas of the forest and enjoy much protection here. The forest is our fortress."

Comrade Rudnev directed Sergei further down the path as Kovpak began to lecture and philosophize about the partisan way.

Kovpak continued his speech, "We have many layers of protection from the enemy. Layers of security." By this time, they had approached the edge of the forest and were looking out over a peaceful landscape. "We use the terrain, the fields, the hills, the forest to keep us safe. Over here," he continued, pointing down a sloping field, "we have minefields surrounding the camp to prevent surprise enemy attacks. Entrance and exit from the forest are always planned. A patrol escorts you in and out of the fortress. We always have the patrols, day and night, to keep us safe."

From their position, Kovpak pointed to several other defensive measures. "Over here we have trenches to slow and prevent fast moving patrols from entering the forest." He pointed to several high points and said, "We also have several machine gun nests surrounding our perimeter." He gestured for all to walk back, and the group re-entered the forest.

"Partisans," he pointed down a sloped hill to a stream with several stations set up for various uses, "always try to have camps near running water for drinking, laundry, and bathing."

The group arrived back at the center of camp and the fortress' original dugout.

"This is our headquarters. We also have a working hospital manned by doctors who have taken up the cause to treat our casualties."

Kovpak pointed to other key facilities around the camp. "Over here is the sleeping and living bunkers and next to that a workshop for weapons repair, sewing of uniforms, and a house for cooking the best meals the forest and our scavenging can provide." The group laughed at their commander's joke as they sat at a roaring fire at the center of the compound.

Rudnev sat next to Sergei with Kovpak across the fire but close enough to continue the conversation.

"So," Rudnev began, "what is it you can do for us here, Sergei?" He handed him a bottle of vodka. "Drink."

Sergei took a long pull from the bottle and coughed. "Comrade, I was instructed to contact your Cheka group and to find out your needs. My commanders want to establish communication between Moscow and all partisan areas to share intelligence and provide guidance for attacks on the Germans. Weapons, food, unforms, radios, even tobacco and money for bribes—all this Colonel Orlov will provide."

"We need food and ammunition and explosives." Kovpak said as he grabbed the vodka. "We also need cold weather uniforms, boots, and wool socks to keep our fighters happy. Winter is coming."

Sergei nodded. "Yes, comrade, these are all items that Moscow can provide."

Rudnev received the bottle again from Father Snow and asked, "So, what else can you do for us, Sergei? All our fighters have substantial experience in combat. What is yours?"

"Comrade," Sergei began, "I fought in the beginning of the war as Sergeant of air defense. I killed many Germans and destroyed many German aircraft. I have advanced training in sabotage and secret warfare. I can get support from Moscow. More OSBOM soldiers, more equipment, better communications gear. I also bring a great hatred for the Germans for what they are doing to our countries. I am from Belarus and am a former Polish citizen. I want this war to end as much as you do."

"I will take your love of country and grand patriotism over the skills of many partisans." Rudnev said. "We won't fully trust you until you prove yourself. You have much to learn about how we fight. We don't fight as an army but instead like ghosts."

Rudnev passed the vodka bottle. "Sergei, you will have the privilege of learning from the ultimate of all Russian warriors. Kovpak fights in the tradition of the Cossacks, an unconventional war of the land. We do not face the armies head-on; we do not have the people or equipment. We slice them apart one battle at a time, death by a thousand ambushes, and many German fascists would agree with the effectiveness of this approach—if they were still standing."

Kovpak grabbed the bottle of vodka from Rudnev and took a slug as he spoke, "Comrade, you humble me. Rudnev, my second in command, is also very accomplished in the art of warfare. He joined us last year after fighting in the October Revolution and the Great Civil War. Prior to this patriotic fight, he was Commissar of Coastal Defense in the Far East. But partisan life called him, and he created a unit with the help of Grigori Bazim, an ensign of the old Russian Army, and its best teacher of unconventional fighting. Bazim used the philosophy of the Chinese General Sun Tzu and many of the techniques of the American Revolution for scouting and raiding to defeat the British imperialist forces. Comrade Rudnev brought many more fighters and weapons to our fight."

Rudnev continued, "Yes, Kovpak. It was an honor to join your partisan unit. And by most accounts, it was just in time."

Kovpak was nodding his head as he continued the story. "Yes, our Rudnev partisans joined, and immediately we were at battle with the German fascists. Someone from town informed on us, revealing our position in the first fortress in the Spadchansky Forest. First tanks came toward our position to scout and flush us out. The tanks attempted to enter the forest but got stuck in the mud. The tank crews tried to escape through the mines. They were all killed, either from the mines or as we picked off those who were left."

Rudnev interrupted, "Sorry, comrade, I must continue. Sergei, a month later, the Germans returned with a detachment from Putivl. There was a tank company and two dozen mechanized infantry vehicles. There were less than 100 of us, and they were over 1000. We were entrenched and used the tank from the previous attack to our advantage. We lured the Germans into the forest. Into the ravines. Into the minefields. The forest was also an enemy of the Germans. After we lured the Germans in, we used their abandoned tanks to kill them. We lost three brave partisans. The Germans lost over 150 men. We also captured more weapons, ammunition, and supplies."

"That is correct, Rudnev. We outmaneuvered the great German soldiers and killed a battalion of the fascist bastards. But we had to leave this forest for another area. Too many people knew of our presence, and it was too risky. We relocated to a safer position here, in the Bryansk Forest."

Father Snow, who had been listening to the partisan stories quietly, stood up and walked over to Rudnev who was holding the bottle of vodka. He grabbed it from Rudnev, put it to his lips, and took a long pull.

"Sergei," he said. "We welcome you, but you have much to learn. You will share a hut with me, and I will be your true guide to becoming a partisan. Go to bed. Your partisan education starts tomorrow."

The next day, Father Snow awoke Sergei before the sun rose. "Here," he said as he handed him a canvas rucksack filled with landmines and ammunition. He also handed him a Swiss-made Steyr-Solothurn MP34 submachine gun seized from an earlier attack on a German security patrol.

"We must go. Our journey is long through the forest to Suzemka village." Each partisan patrol rode in the dark in a *panje* wagon, a boat-like vehicle with high narrow wheels and drawn by a single horse. The wagons navigated through the darkness to the edge of their protective lair. They then rode at a trot toward a small stone cottage, a secret stash site owned by a family sympathetic to the partisan cause. To curry favor, the partisans, whenever they could, would bring fresh produce and bread to families who provided support. The horses and *panje* wagons were hidden in the small barn behind the stone house.

"We must run to our first position," Snow commanded and dashed through the dawn at a trot with Sergei following. After approximately three-quarters of a mile, Father Snow established an observation position from which they could see in all directions in higher terrain above the village of Suzemka, a satellite headquarters and major supply hub for the Germans stationed on the eastern Ukraine's border. They sat in silence for some time until the rattle of metal on stones could be heard approaching from the horizon.

Father Snow handed the binoculars to Sergei, "Tell me what you see. Show us what you learned at that fancy school in Moscow." Sergei observed a security patrol driving past their well-hidden position a quarter of a mile from the roadway outside of the village.

"Patrol. Three SdKfz 123 Luchs light armored reconnaissance vehicles and three Opel Maultier halftracks."

"What is the purpose of the patrol? Security?" Father Snow asked.

"Not with the halftracks." Sergei said. "Those are supply vehicles with heavy security to protect them from us."

"Very good." Father Snow said. "These vehicles often carry equipment, ammunition, and sometimes food for outposts and other areas."

"And the more often the patrols happen, the more we suspect a large attack is coming. This is a common German tactic."

"Exactly, Sergei. Very good." Snow said. "Do we attack it now?"

Sergei shook his head. "No, we should just observe the vehicles with some daylight. We will record their equipment numbers, types, and number of soldiers. Also, whatever it is they are doing. We will send this information to your higher partisan command and by courier to Moscow. Colonel Orlov will send us radios from the sky soon."

Snow smiled "Very good, schoolboy. You may have something to offer us after all. Next time will be harder because real partisan work is done at night."

"We will need to coordinate the air drops." Sergei said. "Orlov promised they would come through with the equipment. He will keep his word. We will just need a location, and I will need to send for the support. We will provide the coordinates to the courier to take to headquarters in Moscow."

"Why do they call you 'Father?'" Sergei asked a few moments later.

Father Snow shot Bravo a mean look and then a smile returned to his face.

"No, I'm not a priest. It's because I'm wise," he said with a laugh. "I'm here to take care of you, like your father." Bravo nodded his head with understanding but still wasn't entirely sure what Father Snow meant.

And so very quickly they developed a routine. There were regular reconnaissance patrols from dawn to midday, then a quick ride into the forest for arms training. After dinner, it was mapping study, getting familiar with the geography of the area, and then sometimes special training in the use of explosives to sabotage rail lines and vehicles. The intelligence from the day moved by courier to the nearest town where it was radioed back to Moscow and NKVD handlers. Among the first dispatches were the coordinates of a partisan airfield near the forest so the promised airdrop of supplies, particularly the radios they would then use to stay in direct contact with Moscow, could be arranged.

CHAPTER EIGHT

LEARNING THE ROPES

March 1942, Outskirts of Bryansk Forest, Russia

Sergei Bravo's boots sank into the soft underbrush as he trudged up the steep incline. The winds howled like a chorus of lost souls, each gust biting through his thick woolen coat with predatory chill. The towering pines stood like silent sentinels; their branches heavy with the burden of winter. Sergei's breath formed crystalline clouds before him, each exhale a testament to the cold of Russia in deep winter.

The partisan unit moved with a ghostly precision, threading through the labyrinth of trees and rocky outcrops that comprised this treacherous landscape. They were a spectral caravan winding their way through a world cloaked in white, where enemy patrols on the prowl for them were never far from mind. Sergei kept his eyes fixed on the man ahead, trying to make as little noise as possible.

"Stay sharp," whispered a voice that seemed to materialize from the very mist that shrouded them. It was Father Snow, giving a command more than a suggestion. Sergei nodded, his hand instinctively checking the rifle slung across his back.

As the day waned, the gloom deepened, casting an ominous pall over the landscape. The partisans halted at a narrow pass, the perfect place for an ambush. Sergei watched as several men fanned out, their movements deliberate and practiced. They were like phantoms flitting between the shadows, each one attuned to the rhythm of the wilderness that was both their shield and their battlefield.

Sergei felt a surge of respect for these warriors who navigated the unforgiving terrain with such deftness. They melted away into the forests and reemerged with reports of distant troop movements or the discovery of a concealed supply cache left by allies sympathetic to their cause. Faced with relentless pursuit and scarce resources, little sleep, and less warm food, they adapted, endured, and fought on.

Night descended upon them; a cloak of darkness pierced only by the occasional glint of moonlight on snow through the clouds. They dug in inside the hollow of a ravine, the natural contours of the land offering scant shelter from the relentless wind. As Sergei settled, he cast his gaze toward the heavens, where stars blinked on and off above. He thought of Marta, of promises made and the future that hung in the balance.

The word came that their prey was approaching, and Sergei crouched low, his breath fogging in the frigid air as he peered through the tangle of branches. The forest was a labyrinth of shadows and whispers, the silence punctuated by the distant crackle of breaking twigs under the weight of approaching boots. He could feel the tension coil in his muscles, and his fingers danced over the cold metal of his rifle, tracing the familiar contours with an almost reverent touch.

Without warning, the woodlands erupted into chaos. The enemy patrol blundered into their trap, the partisans springing forth like specters conjured from the earth itself. While the patrol fired randomly in panic at targets they could not see, the disciplined partisans followed their training, first cutting off retreat then shooting whoever seemed to be giving orders before turning their weapons on the men left. Sergei was just another forest fighter, his focus narrowed to the space between crosshairs as he squeezed the trigger and watched a dim figure cry out and then fall in front of him,

In the aftermath, they huddled close around a modest fire, its glow a feeble bulwark against the gnawing cold. Here, in the camaraderie of the flames, each took a turn telling stories, each tale a piece of armor, fortifying their spirits against the cold and deprivations of war. Sergei spoke of his village, of sun-dappled afternoons with Marta by his side, of classrooms filled with sunlight and children's chatter.

"Each battle is a lesson," Sergei said, his voice a low thrum beneath the crackle of the fire, "And each lesson brings us closer to the end of this darkness."

Father Snow urged them to get what sleep they could as the morrow would bring another skirmish.

With dawn's pale light seeping through the trees, they moved forward, the biting cold gnawing at Sergei's flesh as he trudged through the dense Bryansk underbrush, rifle gripped in frostbitten hands. The stark white of snow-covered paths was marred by dark stains—the grim evidence of recent skirmishes. The silence of the forest lay heavy upon his squad, a blanket of unease that smothered the sound of their cautious advance.

As Sergei moved forward, his eyes darted to the looming trees, their branches clawing at the somber sky. He could feel the oppressive gaze of an invisible enemy, and it stirred within him a primal fear—a doubt that gnawed at the edges of his resolve.

A sharp report echoed in the distance, and Sergei's heart lurched. Somewhere beyond their position, another battle raged, others making, he was sure, the ultimate sacrifice. He had seen so much death in recent weeks, and he couldn't shake the images of those fallen comrades, their eyes forever closed to the brutality they had faced together.

"Bravo," a terse voice called out, slicing through the tension. It was Father Snow, summoning him.

"Yes, comrade!" Sergei acknowledged, his voice steady despite the turmoil within.

"Lead the scouts. We move at your signal," Snow ordered, his gaze piercing.

Sergei nodded, acutely aware of the responsibility thrust upon him. His comrades' eyes rested upon him. They trusted him, believed in his ability to navigate the treacherous path ahead. And so, with a courage born of necessity, Sergei gestured to the scouts, silently directing their formation.

They advanced with silent urgency, weaving through the shadows cast by the skeletal trees. Sergei led them, his senses attuned to every rustle, every shift in the wind.

As they reached a clearing, Sergei held up a hand, signaling a halt. He scanned the terrain, his keen eyes picking out the telltale signs of recent enemy movement. He turned back to his unit, the lines of his face hard with determination.

"Here," he whispered, pointing to the map etched in the snow. "We'll lay our trap." His unit scattered and disappeared into the shadows with trained precision. He watched with a hardened gaze as they melded seamlessly into their surroundings, becoming one with the darkness, deadly predators stalking their prey.

Everyone in the group knew their role intimately, every movement precise and fluid as if they had been rehearsing for years. The air was charged with a sense of urgency and underlying tension, each person relying on the others to fulfill their duty flawlessly. It was clear that these were not mere acquaintances, but individuals who had forged unbreakable bonds through shared experiences in battle. They moved with a synchronicity that could only come from a deep understanding and trust in one another, honed by the heat of combat.

A sudden, jarring crack of gunfire shattered the previously peaceful atmosphere, and Sergei's body immediately tensed with readiness. His commands flowed effortlessly from his lips. With his guidance, the unit moved ahead in deadly silence, their movements fluid and precise even amidst the chaos exploding around them. The air was thick with the acrid smell of gunpowder as they fought on, each member trusting in Sergei's leadership to guide them through the battle unscathed.

The aftermath was a haunting sight, one that would linger in Sergei's mind for years to come. The weariness etched on the faces of his comrades mirrored his own deeply rooted exhaustion. Though they had emerged victorious, the adrenaline-fueled rush of battle had left them feeling drained and hollow. And as they stood in solemn silence, Sergei couldn't help but wonder if their resolve and commitment were worth the horrors they had faced.

What seemed like days later, they returned to the partisan compound to regroup and rest. That night, rested, clean, and with a hot meal in their bellies, they sat around a roaring blaze. Someone had produced vodka and shot glasses, each man toasting.

When it was Father Snow's turn, he looked to Sergei. "To Comrade Bravo, well done," the weathered partisan said, clapping a firm hand on Sergei's shoulder. In that simple gesture, Sergei felt the weight of his fears lessen, his doubts erased by the faith of a man who had seen so much and yet still dared to hope. Those two words brought a faint, shy smile to his lips. He surveyed the battered gang as they threw back their shots, their eyes returning to the flickering fire, each settling back into his thoughts.

April 1942, Partisan Airfield, outskirts of Bryansk Forest, Russia

The rattling sound could be heard across the farmer's field as the plane circled, a 1939 Polikarpov PO-2 aircraft that the Germans called the "sewing machine" or a "crop duster" because it looked like a biplane used to spray farmers' crops in the summer. The two-seat wooden plane had a low-powered engine and was manned by a pilot and one crewman who would also serve as a gunner should the need arise. The plane carried critical cargo for the Bryansk partisan fighters: the radio sets requested three days prior along with other needed supplies.

Sergei, Father Snow, and several other partisans left after sundown to traverse the forest to the unimproved airfield north of the Bryansk fortress to ensure that it was ready. The airfield was prepared only at night when planes were scheduled to land. On the way, Father Snow told Sergei about the unusual pilot, Brother Gyorgy, who was a hero in these parts.

Brother Georgy was Georgy Kuzmin, a Soviet pilot whose plane had been shot down by German anti-aircraft guns in the Bryansk region in 1941, engulfed in flames and crash landing on a snow-covered field. Local villagers found Georgy and nursed him back to health, but not before his left foot and a portion of his right foot had to be amputated because of infection. He quickly learned how to walk in special shoes and just as quickly returned to flying as well, supporting the villagers and partisans by flying in vital supplies. His hope was to eventually return to fight for the Soviet Air Force, but his present mission was now paramount to the success of the partisans.

"Olek," Father Snow began as they prepared for the plane's landing later that night, "go to the end of the runway and hold the torch. Do not move. Just stand at the end to guide the sewing machine safely to us." Olek Alyk, a young partisan from Lubny with dusty blond hair and a sharp jawline, stood uneasily, his eyes darting nervously as he stood at the edge of the runway with a torch in his hand. He wore a tattered army uniform, the trousers frayed, and the buttons rusted, but he stood tall and ready.

"Yes, Father." Olek barked. He ran to the end of the runway while the rest of the partisan group took up positions around the field to guard it while the plane landed and was unloaded.

The plane landed without mishap, only rolling to an abrupt stop a half-dozen yards from Olek, closer certainly than he expected judging by his panicked face as the plane swooped in.

Father Snow immediately approached the aircraft with a smile on his face and beard blowing in the night wind.

"Brother Georgy," he said. "We were expecting you."

"Father Snow, you handsome bastard. I always get treated like a king when I come to visit you in such nice spots." Georgy said. "I would love to stay," he continued, still smiling but with a serious voice, "but we must hurry. I saw the lights of an enemy patrol several kilometers to the north. We mustn't press our luck."

"Quickly," Father Snow ordered the fighters, "take the boxes and bags to the woods."

"What do we have today, Brother Georgy?" Father Snow asked.

"We have a big order! We have PPD-40 submachine guns, a mortar tube, and ammunition. We also have fresh vegetables and bread. And a special order from Colonel Orlov for Sergei and letters from Belarus."

"For Sergei?" Snow asked.

"Yes, radio sets," Georgy said as he was pulling five wooden boxes from the aircraft.

Sergei smiled, "Father, these are Radio Partisan Group 4s, RPOs. The range is perfect for the terrain we fight on, and they can be powered manually in an emergency."

"How do we use them?" Snow asked, puzzled.

"Orlov is also sending radio operators to train your fighters. They will arrive in a few days. Moscow wants to set up direct radio communication between the forest units and the central command." Sergei said.

As Georgy and his crewman handed out the last of the equipment, he turned to Father Snow and asked, "How is this one doing?" He nodded toward Sergei. "Colonel Orlov asked specifically."

"He is a strong fighter and learning quickly. Of course, we need to have him unlearn all that garbage you taught him in Moscow. Still, he improves every day and is turning into one of our strongest leaders."

Sergei looked at the ground as the conversation continued.

Georgy turned to Sergei and asked, "Lieutenant Bravo, how are you?"

"I'm well, Captain Kuzmin. I am proud to be with this group and contribute to the effort."

"Very good, Sergei, you can call me Brother Georgy out here. Do you need anything?"

"Can you get us some tobacco?"

"We can get Belomorkanal cigarettes but only few packs at a time, they are strictly rationed items. But I will do what I can."

"No, how about tobacco for a pipe, and a pipe?"

Father Snow looked up and grinned, "Like Comrade Kovpak?"

Sergei looked down at the ground again and kicked the dirt. "No, I am nowhere like Kovpak, but we all like to have a smoke after missions."

"You got it, comrade," Brother Georgy said. "When I can, I will bring you pipes and probably Makhorka tobacco. It may be what the peasants smoke, but it will keep your pipe filled."

Brother Georgy and the crewman quickly boarded the plane and taxied to the end of the crude runway and took off. They heard the rattling of the plane fainter and fainter as they watched it disappear into the night skies.

April 1942, Near Bryansk Forest, Russia

The land surrounding the Bryansk Forest was barren and bleak, the trees barely budding, still barren of their leaves in the early spring. The ground was muddy and uneven as they made their way towards the railroad tracks, the moon casting an eerie glow over the landscape. The month of April was barely distinguishable from March, the land still covered in a blanket of dirty snow. Three figures darted towards the railroad tracks, their movements swift and desperate. The pungent smell of mud and damp earth wafted through the forest, mingling with the bitter stench of sweat, piss, and fear.

As the German patrol disappeared, the resistance fighters emerged from the dense forest. Father Snow crouched behind a captured machine gun, carefully adjusting the tripod for a better aim. He signaled to Olek and Sergei, motioning for them to run towards the railroad tracks. "I have you covered," he whispered through gritted teeth as he scanned the area.

Sergei breathed deeply, the cold air stinging his throat as he and Olek crouched in the underbrush. They wore thick fur hats, wool coats, and sturdy boots, all essential in the frigid weather. As they waited for the signal, their fingers tightened around the smooth wooden handles of their Tokarev SVT 40 rifles. When Sergei mouthed *"Iditye!"*, they both burst from the cover of trees and ran towards their target—the railroad tracks. Their leather satchels, heavy with gear, bounced awkwardly with each stride as they sprinted towards the wooden barricade, barbed wire glinting in the sunlight. Their hearts raced as they dove to the ground near the structure, hoping to remain hidden from any passing railway security.

"I got it." Sergei whispered. Olek observed as Sergei turned on his back and slid under the barrier between them and the tracks.

"Clippers." He whispered.

Olek handed the tool to Sergei and watched as he carefully clipped several strands of wire and removed the tin cans the Germans had attached to warn them of anyone trying to get close to the tracks.

Sergei cut enough of the wire to make a path through the barrier, just wide enough for both partisans to crawl through. Sergei rose on his elbows and peered right and then left. He motioned, and both rose from the ground and ran to the edge of the railroad track. The men kneeled as Sergei grabbed a landmine and grenade from his satchel. The landmine was placed at the base of the railway.

"Olek, tie a line to the detonator pin."

Olek drove a metal rod into the ground a foot or so away from the landmine and then tied the string taut to the rod. As Olek finished the knot, the lights of a train appeared on the track approximately 300 yards away from them.

"Run!" Sergei shouted. Both partisans ran at full pace, slithered through the cut wire, and fled back to the wood line to observe the train.

"Sergei, they say that the Germans put two empty railroad cars in the front, so soldiers or supplies are not blown up if those cars trigger anything on the tracks."

Sergei snorted. "That's why," he said, "I just showed you how we get around that. The empty wagons at the front of the train will not trigger a simple pressure mine as they are too light. But the locomotive has a gear hanging over the side of the track which will knock down the rod and pull the fuse from the grenade. The grenade explosion blows up the landmine. The landmine blows up everything."

Olek heard a noise and noticed a German patrol driving along the tracks toward the position of the grenade just as the first rail cars approached. Both Sergei and Olek lay close to the ground as the locomotive rumbled past, an ear-splitting boom signaling the detonation of the grenade. The blast tore through the train cars, causing some to derail and others to erupt into flames. The Germans' patrol vehicle was sent flying and landed with a thud about twenty yards away from the track, the overturned wreck smoking and twisted. With a loud screech and the sound of metal bending, the train careened off its tracks and crashed into the nearby field.

Hours later at their headquarters in the forest, the group sat around a rough table, eating a much-deserved bowl of hot potatoes and cabbage with some bread.

"Olek, you are learning the NKVD way of fighting," Sergei began. "You learned much in the woods, but we are teaching you a more precise way of fighting."

"Thank you, comrade." Olek said as he beamed with pride.

Father Snow sat and listened to the exchange for a few minutes and then spoke. "I agree with the NKVD tactics. But I still strongly believe we need to fight more like we did in the Silesian War in the 1740s or like the Americans in their Revolution, like guerillas. We cannot fight the Germans head on. We do not have the equipment or vehicles even the manpower they have. But we can beat them through surprise and cleverness. By doing the unexpected. By striking where they do not expect us. We run out of the forest to attack. Then we disappear back into the forest like ghosts while the damn fascists are still scratching their heads trying to figure out what happened."

Snow paused, then spoke again. "You are doing well, *molodoy chelovek.*" he said as he winked at Bravo. "We are learning from you. Not just how to use the radios, but also how to organize, how to gather and use intelligence. Also important, the men have come to accept you, to listen and follow you." Bravo nodded at Snow with a gesture of appreciation for his supportive words.

"Comrade Kovpak has gone to Moscow to meet with Premier Lenin." Snow said.

Sergei raised his eyebrows and turned toward Father Snow for confirmation.

Snow nodded. "Yes, Moscow. He has instructed me to assign you to 13th Company as an intelligence officer and as a fighter. 13th Company has been ordered to the trans-Dnieper area; the Moldovan-Ukrainian border region. Comrade Kovpak has directed the commander to establish a partisan presence in an area unoccupied by the Germans. You are expected to join all combat missions. So far, with us, you have just put your toes in the water. We need you to experience partisan combat. Up close. That is how you will earn the full respect of our fighters. You need to prove your worth to the new company."

"When?"

"Report to the commander tomorrow. You are not going as an NKVD captain but as Sergei, a partisan leader. The unit is not proven in combat. But will be soon. They are called candidate guerillas, ready for their first taste of blood. Go drink with them."

The next day, as Sergei was waiting for the 13th Company to assemble for their journey south, Commissioner Rudnev came into the room looking puzzled, a paper clutched in his hand.

"Yes, comrade?" Father Snow asked.

Rudnev held out the decrypted radio message for both men to read.

/// CENTRAL OFFICE MOSCOW ///NKVD MESSAGE 42-04-586//
DATE: April 15, 1943//
TO: KOVPAK PARTISAN UNIT, BRYANSK FORREST//
EFFECTIVE THIS DATE, BRYANSK PARTISAN UNIT
COMMANDER IS PROMOTED TO MAJOR GENERAL, BERIA,
COMMISAR OF INTERNAL AFFAIRS. /// END OF MESSAGE ///

The jaws of both men dropped as they re-read the communication.

"This means that Moscow has accepted us. That our work is valuable to the republic. This means we are all recognized," Father Snow said.

"Yes." Sergei said. "This also means that they will expect more from us. This means we need to be ready."

Early the next morning, Sergei met with Captain Mikhail Duka, the commander of 13th company. Duka was in his early thirties, large but not fat, and always had a smile on his face, an oddity for such a serious man. Duka's men issued Sergei a PPSH submachine gun, called the "Molotov special," a full issue of ammunition, and a 37mm mortar tube attached to an entrenching tool. They immediately climbed into a *panje* wagon, one of twelve filled with fighters, weapons, and enough provisions to support them on their more than 500-mile journey to the Dnieper district in the south on the border of Moldova and Ukraine.

After seven days of hard travel, the first base camp was established in a forest area near the town of Sumy, still some distance from their objective of Dnieper. Once security was established, Commander Duka pulled his four platoon leaders and Sergei to the center of the security cordon where they huddled around a small fire. They ate bread and drank hot tea from a metal pot hung on a rod over the fire.

"Our first objective is to destroy a key bridge near the village of Kolomiya about three miles from here. We will establish a command post and then mine the bridge." Duka barked. He pointed out their current position on a map illuminated by the flickering fire and then detailed the route to the bridge.

"First platoon will provide security around the bridge while 3rd platoon will mine it and then rejoin the command post. Second platoon will remain here keeping radio communications back to Bryansk HQ open while securing the horses and equipment. We will depart well before dawn to travel undetected, mining the bridge before sunrise." The men were dismissed for last minute preparations with their platoons and then departed a few hours later after catching brief naps wrapped in their blankets on the ground.

Roused at 0400, the sleepy partisans set off in the chill, making a brisk pace to warm their blood and arriving well on schedule. Sergei was on the mining crew and followed his small group to the bridge outside the sleepy village. The bridge was stone and concrete, one massive length spanning a gorge.

"Sergei, over here." It was Markus, a young partisan originally from Kyiv, part of Sergei's team. Sergei, carrying a rucksack of mine boxes quickly ran to his position and helped attach the mines to the underside of the bridge. Sergei handed Markus each box with great care as each held a PDM1 anti-vehicle mine, two blocks of TNT weighing two pounds. Once finished, the mining team ran back to the guard position, observing the road from both directions with binoculars.

"German convoy." Duka reported. "Four hundred yards and approaching. Six vehicles. Armored halftrack vehicles in the front and rear. Four supply transport vehicles. Approximately sixteen soldiers, a squad."

Markus signaled the other partisans to prepare for the ambush. The lead German halftrack crossed the bridge slowly. The weight of the vehicle activated the mine with an earsplitting *Boom!* The force of the explosion ripped the vehicle in half and flipped the front end of the gun truck into the air. The partisans poured fire into the convoy, killing many of the German supply patrol. The survivors immediately leapt from the damaged convoy vehicles, took cover, and returned fire as best they could.

"Follow me!" Sergei ordered his team as they raced toward the road and the damaged vehicles, dodging the German fire to take cover in a deep ditch facing the few desperate men who had survived the initial assault.

"Get down!" Sergei ordered as a German heavy machine gun began sweeping a broad field of fire in front of them.

"*Nein! Nein! Nein!*" screamed a German trooper as he peppered the ground around Sergei and his team with relentless bursts until falling suddenly silent.

After a moment, Sergei ordered, "Up!" and they warily approached the road, scanning for more German soldiers. As they approached the road, Markus shouted, "The gunner is dead."

At the road, they were engulfed in smoke from the burning German vehicles. The smell of burning gunpowder, oil, and human flesh was causing the partisan team to cough and retch. All they saw were dead and mangled bodies until, on the other side of the road, Sergei spotted several Germans in a ditch crawling away from them.

"There!" Sergei pointed with his rifle and shot. The other members of his team fired steadily into the ditch until the soldiers fell silent.

"Pull close!" Sergei shouted, a signal to the men and platoons to close the security circle and begin searching the vehicles and dead soldiers. The bridge was quickly surrounded by partisan teams plundering the destroyed vehicles and bodies for weapons and intelligence.

Sergei knelt and grabbed his water bottle to take a mouthful of water. He heaved but did not throw up because he had nothing in his stomach to expel. He looked up and saw a German soldier running away from one of the destroyed vehicles. He raised his weapon and then, in a moment of grace, lowered it. Sergei thought, let him run. He will have good stories to tell.

As Sergei watched the soldier disappear, he took another sip of water and looked up as Markus shouted "Down!" and dragged him to the ground. Sergei winced as he heard a bullet fly past his head.

The bullet came from a German soldier hiding under a vehicle. Both men rolled to the ground unholstering their pistols and firing blindly at the soldier. They paused, Markus finally edging forward to see the German slumped over his weapon.

Sergei now sat on the ground and looked over at Markus. "You saved my life, comrade." He extended his hand to Markus.

"I thought you NKVD officers were smart," Markus smiled and smacked Sergei's hand away in a playful gesture. "I guess I am now responsible for your life and my own. My work is never done." Markus looked at Sergei, still grinning.

The remaining partisans searched the area, scavenging rifles, a functional machine gun, and several boxes of explosives besides some ammo and food that would assist the 13th Company on their journey south.

Upon arrival, the company commander greeted Sergei with a bear hug, as word of Sergei's actions and near-death experience had made it back to the company area.

"Sergei, you performed well today," Daka said, "but this is just the start of your journey as a partisan. We must grow eyes in the back of our head, expect the unexpected, and always look for danger. Today, you let your guard down and nearly paid with your life. Happily, you did not, and I'm glad you're here."

"Thank you, comrade," the NKVD officer smiled.

The 13th company continued its journey south to Dnieper, harassing those Germans they found as well as scouting to observe and engage the enemy to determine its response.

November 1942, Kovpak Partisan Encampment, Bryansk Forest, Russia

Upon his return from service with the 13th Company, life in the forest settled into a series of routines for Sergei. Moments of terror during attacks against the German patrols and then long bouts of boredom in their forest camp. Finding food, gathering supplies, strengthening the security of the forest fortress. Helping to keep his sanity were Marta's letters. Sergei had made a deal with Colonel Orlov to have Marta's letters sent to him in Bryansk on resupply planes. Orlov begrudgingly agreed, knowing it was one of the few things he could do to keep his young NKVD officer moderately happy and motivated. When Sergei knew the resupply plane was scheduled to arrive, he would volunteer to lead the security party to prepare the runway and meet the plane. When the plane landed, the pilot would smile and hand a stack of letters to the officer. Sergei would always hand a stack of fresh letters to the pilot to send back to Moscow for Orlov to mail to Marta. When he had received the letters, all the partisan crew knew to leave Bravo alone in his bunker for a few hours to read them.

In a world far removed from the warmth of the bakery, Sergei clutched Marta's letters like a talisman. In the cramped confines of his forest bunker, his blue eyes, usually hard-edged with fatigue, softened as he read. Marta's unwavering faith served as a beacon in his war. The words she penned were a lifeline, tethering him to a future that seemed both impossibly distant and achingly within reach.

Sergei's fingers trembled as they unfolded another sheet of paper, the coarse texture a stark contrast to the delicacy of Marta's writing, the light of the candle casting long shadows over his hunched form. His own letters spoke not so much of the present, but of the future as he imagined it. "My dearest Marta," he scrawled. That future danced before him, a small cottage nestled in the countryside, away from the pall of war. He pictured returning to his schoolhouse to teach and Marta working at her father's bakery.

If Sergei could only see across the 500 miles that separated them, he would watch as Marta's fingers brushed against the flour-dusted countertop as she slid gracefully between stacks of the freshly baked bread that filled her father's bakery. But today, her heart thrummed with an urgency that drowned out the familiar sounds of labor and laughter.

She weaved through the labyrinth of wooden shelves until she reached the secluded nook behind the ageing oak cabinet, a temporary refuge from the noisy bakery. Here, she retrieved the precious envelope, a new letter from Sergei that promised to lift her shroud of sadness.

Marta unfolded the letter, the paper crisp despite its journey across war-torn lands. Sergei's script sprawled across the page, each letter meticulously crafted, a testament to his years in the classroom. Her pulse quickened as she absorbed his words, longing and resilience danced across her mind, igniting a flicker of hope that the future he painted would one day come to life. And so, the cycle of letter writing continued. Sergei sending his love expressed in anodyne reports on general things about his life in the forest. Marta would respond immediately with her own heartfelt missive capturing her love, her commitment, and her intense desire for Sergei to come home to her soon.

CHAPTER NINE

THE FIGHT OF OUR LIVES

December 1942, Kovpak Partisan Headquarters, Bryansk Forest, Russia

The exterior walls of the smoke-filled office headquarters deep in the forest were covered with sandbags to thwart any direct fire and then camouflaged with trees and other forest detritus. The three radio operators, all women, worked feverishly receiving and sending messages on the RPO-4 radio sets. They had been trained in the operation and maintenance of the radios and in the fine art of cryptography, both encrypting messages and decrypting messages sent across the partisan channels.

"What do you have?" The senior female radio operator and the supervisor of the shift asked. She grabbed the message from the radio operator and began to read it with great interest.

"Comrade Captain, you will want to read this." Bravo sat across the room in a very rustic carved wooden chair built of wood from the forest. He was smoking a pipe and keenly watching the activities of the radio operators. He did not look up and continued to study an operations map of the border of Ukraine. His current task was to identify targets of opportunity to keep the pressure on the fascists while Russian units continued to push them back west. In mid-November, Bravo had been reassigned from the 13th Company back to Kovpak's staff as an intelligence officer and NKVD liaison. Bravo performed well, and Captain Duka was sorry to see him go. The only explanation for the sudden move was that Bravo was "needed" at headquarters to help prepare for the next Moscow-directed mission.

"Comrade Captain, you will want to read this." the senior radio operator repeated, a smile in her voice.

Bravo looked up, both puzzled at the rank, annoyed at the interruption, and looked directly at the senior radio operator.

She nodded her head and said "Yes," handing him the decrypted typed message to him.

/// CENTRAL OFFICE MOSCOW ///NKVD MESSAGE 43-12-587//
DATE: DEC 18, 1942//
TO: KOVPAK PARTISAN UNIT, BRYANSK FOREST//TWO MESSAGES TO FOLLOW//

1) GERMAN UNITS NEAR UKRAINE BORDER HAVE CREATED NUMEROUS ANTI-PARTISAN UNITS TO TARGET AND DESTROY PARTISAN UNITS DUE TO RECENT DISRUPTION OF SUPPLY LINES AND SLOWING THE MOVEMENT OF ADVANCING GERMAN TROOPS.

2) NKVD COUNTERINTELLIGENCE REPORTS THAT NUMEROUS LOCAL COLLABORATORS HAVE INFORMED UNDER PRESSURE THE LOCATION OF ENTRANCE ROUTES TO BRYANSK FOREST AND POSSIBLE GRID COORDINATES OF THE LOCATION OF THE KOVPAK HEADQUARTERS.

3) PARTISAN UNITS ARE URGED TO USE CAUTION WHEN OPERATING IN THE AREA AND TO INCREASE SECURITY MEASURES TO THE BRYANSK HEADQUARTES. CENTRAL COMMAND IS NOT ORDERED EVACUATION FROM YOUR POSITION FROM THIS TIME.

4) EFFECTIVE OCTOBER 1, 1943, BRAVO, SERGEI, LIEUTENANT. OSBOM, HEADQUARTERED, CENTRAL

COMMAND MOSCOW AND DETACHED TO KOVPAK PARTISAN GROUP, BRYANSK, UKRAINE, IS PROMOTED TO THE RANK OF CAPTAIN, NKVD OSMBOM FORCES. THIS PROMOTION IS EFFECTIVE IMMEDIATELY. ORLOV, COMMANDING /// END OF MESSAGE ///

Kovpak's senior staff was convened later that day to provide an opportunity to discuss past and current missions and select targets for future attacks. Kovpak was smoking his pipe as he was sitting at the wood table in the headquarters hut. He was surrounded by his key officers: his deputy Rudnev, Father Snow, chief of operations and intelligence, Captain Bravo, NKVD liaison, and the company commanders for each region of the Bryansk partisan area of responsibility.

"Comrade Kovpak," Rudnev said to the partisan commander, "we have all commanders present today to include Pinsk, Volyn, Rovno, and Zhitomir regions and all primary staff. We are prepared to start our briefings."

Kovpak nodded his head and pulled on his pipe, a circle of smoke wafted over his head. "Procced."

Father Snow stood up and began his briefing.

"General, *dobbry vecher.*"

"Good evening to you, my old friend," Kovpak said, smiling at the grizzled warrior.

"Our partisan units have been busy over the past few weeks. We have conducted over 500 missions and brought great harm to the German units in our six-mile area of responsibility. Our major operations included the destruction of five German garrisons, the attack and destruction of over fifty German patrols or supply railways. Our propaganda operations increased over the last month and included the mass posting of anti-German propaganda signs and banners in over 100 villages and the air drop of over 600 anti-Nazi pamphlets by our partisan air force."

"What does Moscow say about German intentions?" Kovpak asked as he took another pull on his pipe.

"Comrade, our intelligence reports show we have hurt the Germans, influencing their operations as a result. They are afraid of our partisan forces. And they are angry. Moscow reports that the Germans have increased efforts to identify our encampments and take us head on, a counteroffensive to start later this summer. And...." Snow stuttered.

"Yes, continue Father Snow."

"The Nazi government has identified you as a number one enemy to the war effort in the eastern front and has offered 500 thousand Deutsche Marks reward to any citizen in Ukraine or Russia who provides information that leads to your capture and ultimate execution."

Kovpak smiled and asked, "Only 500 thousand Deutsche Marks?"

Father Snow nodded nervously again.

"Father Snow, it is fine. I have been threatened before. It shows that we are hurting them. Delaying progress. Keeping them off balance and so failing to push the Soviet Army back west. Let me know when it reaches one million Deutsche Marks."

The table of senior staff roared with laughter. Most of it nervous. Only some saw the humor in the statement.

"Please continue, Father."

"We have some other news from Moscow. The Germans are planning to use poison gas to quickly destroy partisan strongholds."

"Gas?" Kovpak questioned. "They used it against their enemies during the Great War. There were horror stories of gas used in trenches. How would they deploy it?"

"From the air. Through the Luftwaffe." Snow said.

"So, there will be concern villagers will also be killed," Kovpak said as he turned to the logistics officer. "Connect with Moscow and tell them we need gas masks. Enough for all our fighters. And order enough for our close villages and keep ordering until we have supplied all the villages surrounding our Bryansk stronghold."

The logistics officer nodded, rose, and was off to the radio hut to coordinate the urgent shipment.

Snow completed his report with an overview of battle damage. "Our missions have had a heavy impact on the Germans. We have caused over 1000 enemy casualties and seized over 600 weapons that were suitable for our missions."

The personnel officer spoke next, reporting that over seventy-five partisans had been killed in missions and recruitment of new partisans was limited because of the anti-partisan propaganda causing fear throughout the villages. He ended his report by announcing fresh personnel expected in the coming weeks: over twenty specialized fighters, more radio operators and fifteen propaganda specialists.

Each commander reported recent attacks, battle damage, and logistical needs and shortfalls prior to the next mission cycle along with the emerging targets based on Moscow and partisan intelligence.

Captain Bravo, as the NKVD liaison, often ended the briefings as the official representative of Central Command but still gave deference to the authority and importance of Sidor Kovpak.

"Our communication network," said Sergei, "is working at one hundred percent, and we have off-channel contact with most partisan units throughout the Eastern Front. Respectfully, Central Command sends it appreciation for the activities of this partisan unit and confirms that the Germans were delayed in their counteroffensive operations because of partisan attacks. Colonel Orlov sends his personal appreciation and pledges any support we request. Within reason."

"Very good," Kovpak said as he nodded.

"How about more women replacements and alcohol!" Father Snow barked.

Both Kovpak and Rudnev laughed but gave Snow a stern look. Father Snow sat back in his chair and looked down at the ground.

Bravo continued his report. "It is important to understand that Soviet forces are gaining momentum, and the German forces are losing momentum and unable to support fighting on both the Western Front with the Brits and the Americans and on the Eastern Front with us."

Bravo paused for a moment to consult his notebook. "We have been given a heads-up about potential operations in Spring 1944 in the Carpathian Mountains involving all available partisan units on the Eastern Front."

"Carpathia? That is over 600 miles from here. It will take us many months to navigate the terrain. And then the Germans are spread throughout."

"Yes, Father Snow," General Kovpak said. "Which is exactly the point. Moscow wants us to disrupt the Germans' rear to slow down a counter-offensive and push our presence deep into the Carpathian Mountains throughout Western Ukraine and Romania. When I was in Moscow earlier this year, they spoke, in theory, about this type of operation depending on our progress in the war by the end of the year. This mission would be important for Moscow. For the Soviet Union. For our partisan fighters. This is our opportunity to show that we are an important part of the effort and capable of pulling our own train; of helping the Soviet Union beat these bastards."

"What do we do now, General?" Rudnev asked.

"We prepare, we train, we get ready for the battle of our lives. And we wait for the order."

February 1943, General Kovpak Partisan Area, Russia

"I don't like horses," Father Snow said. "They don't listen, and they smell." Both Snow and Rudnev were standing in the stables of the partisan fortress.

"Sounds like you." Commissioner Rudnev quipped.

Snow shot him a mean and then a more hurt look, and then smiled.

"Well, my friend, these horses are going to take us to victory. All 500 of them. And the *panje* wagons. We will need lots of help to go almost 600 miles. In harsh mountainous conditions with an enemy who is looking for us. With some untrained fighters. What could go wrong? The horses and wagons are the most dependable part of this attack. The horses are strong, sometimes disagreeable. All like you, Father Snow, but the finest we have."

"Yes, comrade." Snow smirked. "But will 300 wagons be enough to carry almost 3000 troops,"

"Yes, we should be fine with the baggage train. This type of system was created during the Russian Civil War by the Ukrainian anarchists. The Tachanka are credited with first mounting a machine-gun on the wagon. We should be more concerned about our ability to fight the Germans after we have traveled for so long."

"Will there be a fight, Commissioner?"

"Yes, the biggest of our lives. We may be recognized by Moscow, but now we are *known* by the Nazis. They understand how we fight, and they will look for us at every turn."

"How long will it take? To the Carpathian Mountains?"

"Father, we are being sent to disrupt the Germans in their rear security area. We will move left and right and then left again. Not a direct route to the mountains. We plan to set out sometime when the weather breaks in April and begin our journey. Our efforts assist the Soviet Army to focus on larger and more strategic issues. But in this case, we are the targets. We are expected to slow down the Germans, pull in their forces, and keep them from launching any large offensives against the allies or a counteroffensive against the Soviets. We are the bait. We are the mouse. The cat is the angry German and Nazi forces."

Father Snow nodded his head with understanding. "What can we do to help?"

"Pray."

May 1943, West of the Bryansk Forest, Bryansk Oblast

As the harsh winter came to an end, so did the bitter cold and snow that had plagued the partisans for months. However, with the change in weather came new challenges for the partisans, who had received their orders to pull out to harass the German rear. The melting snow created muddy conditions that made it difficult to move their horses and wagons. As they traveled further into enemy territory, they struggled to find enough food to feed their growing numbers as spring was always a lean time.

Complicating matters was that their path to their objective was to be circuitous indeed. As General Kovpak explained to his inner circle, "We won't take a straight path from our woodland home to the mountains but will work our way south after routes west and east along the way. Our first objective is to find our way to Rivne and then Ternopil. Depending on resistance, we will continue south or head for an alternative position near Deliatyn, a known German garrison and southern stronghold near the Carpathian Mountains. This will be an unusually difficult trek, without support and in open areas deep in the rear area of the enemy. And there will be no turning back. As we go on this impossible journey, remember the wisdom of Velichkovsky: 'No one can have two deaths, but you can't avoid one.' Let's make the best of this opportunity for our country."

Rudnev, Father Snow, and Sergei Bravo worked tirelessly to keep morale high and maintain discipline among their troops. They knew they would need every man and woman at their best if they were going to survive the journey ahead. German patrols were always on the lookout for them, and they had to be constantly on guard against surprise attacks, as keeping the presence of 3000 fighters undiscovered is not easy. Despite this, they remained undetected by the enemy, a testament to their stealth and cunningness. But as time went on, supplies became scarcer, and tensions rose among the troops. Many were tired and hungry, longing for a break from the constant struggle for survival. And not two months later, they were learning just how difficult that long march could be. It was the middle of July, and the partisan wagon train had been forced to change direction, heading to a base near Deliatyn, in Ukraine, poised to enter the Carpathian Mountains.

It had been a tough two months. In those long weeks, the Kovpak partisans had brought the fight to the Germans and played out Moscow's plan to perfection, fulfilling the prophecy. The partisans continued to lay a path of destruction while playing a deadly game of cat and mouse, harassing the Germans' rear guard, emerging out of nowhere, always in the dark, ferociously pouncing, then melting back into the forest waste. The German soldiers they hunted were on high alert, their weapons ready to defend against the elusive enemy.

The Kovpak partisans, weary and ragged from months of fighting, trudged through the forest and open fields, their faces etched with exhaustion and determination. Their clothes were torn and dirty from constant movement. The rewards for winning and losing skirmishes for almost ninety days. Most men's beards were dirty and showed new growth of gray. Another reward for their efforts. Yet their eyes were determined, fixed on their goal of fulfilling Moscow's plan and bringing the fight to the Germans.

As dusk fell this night, two partisans stood on the edge of a mountain ridge with binoculars, observing the patrols of the Deliatyn German garrison below, where they had sentry posts and how they were manned.

"What do you think, General?" Father Snow asked as he handed the high-resolution glasses to Sydir Kovpak.

"I see towers at key corners surrounding the compound besides several machine gun nests supporting the observations of the towers. They have both mobile patrols and foot patrols walking the perimeter walls of the garrison. We would need to go in through the front door to have any chance of getting in. Of course, that would be after we demobilized the active machine gun nests, killed the patrols, neutralized the towers, and set the garrison on fire...."

Both men, and all the partisans, had ridden a rocky road, literally and figuratively as they made it to this point in their odyssey.

"What about the bridge?" asked Major General Rudnev, who stood on the mountain ridge with the general staff and reconnaissance team.

Captain Vershigora, the new NKVD assigned intelligence officer, peered through his binoculars, and scanned the area surrounding a bridge, which was approximately 650 yards from the German garrison but surrounded by a platoon of German combat engineers.

"Sir, an alternate route would mean traveling an extra twelve miles around this mess and would delay us needlessly." The NKVD captain's observation left little room for interpretation.

"What alternative do we really have then to cross the death trap and risk a slaughter?" asked Major General Kovpak.

"None, really, Comrade General. Crossing the bridge at first light would keep an element of surprise but would surely result in many losses. We would need to cross in force and with fury. Or be slaughtered. If we secure the bridge first, we could breach through the gap and then advance like a thunder bolt into the attack of the garrison. But then we would have the patrols, and machine gun nests and walls of the garrison to negotiate."

Against warnings from his staff, Major General Kovpak lit his pipe and considered the counsel of the NKVD intelligence officer. "We would need to take and own the bridge. If not, we have no chance of survival," the old partisan general said.

"We are being hunted by anti-partisan forces. We are surrounded by German and Nazi security units. We have no choice but to break through here. If we're ever to make it to Polissya, we need to run through this garrison."

The staff on the reconnaissance patrol all nodded their heads in agreement.

"But we will not go to a slaughter." Major General Rudnev said. "We will need to prepare the battlefield for our attack over a series of days, or weeks if need be."

"We will need to first shock the German garrison troops." General Kovpak said as a German plane flew over the mountain range causing all members to take cover until it was out of sight.

"As you can see," Kovpak said, "they know we are out here. They have been tracking us for hundreds of miles. However, we were victorious and brought the fight to them, the dirty fascists. A bucket of cold water to their morale. We are winning."

Rudnev had a smile on his face as he listened to his commander speak. "Yes, General."

Kovpak continued. "We will need to inspire fear in them. The fear that we will attack at any moment, wearing them down. The Cheka ghosts will probe for their weak points, attacking out of nowhere and then disappearing into the night air. But we have work to do. Let's go back and start. I am hungry." The staff surrounding him laughed out loud.

Later, as the group of leaders sat around a fire, Rudnev laid out the plan.

"Our first phase will be deception and shock. We will have patrols nightly deliver propaganda, leaflets, and signs. Spread them around the garrison. Paint warnings on the perimeter walls. Throw them in the road. Put them in vehicles. Anything to heighten the fear of the fascist scum and their collaborators." The company commanders, who already had the orders for the unusual methods, looked at each other with a knowing glance.

Captain Bravo, who was sitting next to Rudnev asked, "What might they be, specifically, comrade?"

"Just listen. You will hear soon enough…." Rudnev replied. The officers around the fire, drinking hot tea and eating bread, laughed.

Major General Kovpak stood up and raised his hands to quiet the group. "Gentlemen," he said, "first we will need some active reconnaissance of the garrison and its security in the most minute detail. And the death trap bridge. So, reconnaissance patrols every night for the next three days. Engineers, scouts. See Father Snow, and he will give you further details about the locations and times. That should keep you and your men busy for a few days." He finished, dismissing them.

The three commanders nodded in understanding, stood, and quickly departed from the firelit meeting. Major General Kovpak lit his pipe and leaned against a tree while General Rudnev continued the discussion.

"Next, we talk about the raid." Rudnev said. "We will need to surround the garrison but first neutralize the unit at the bridge. Our scout units will handle the extermination of the German engineer guards, and then I will lead a squad to secure the bridge for the main body of the attack. Captain Bravo will serve as my deputy commander."

Bravo looked up in surprise. "But comrade, I want to be a part of the main attack with Comrade Kovpak."

"Yes, we know. But it has been decided that the bridge is the most important part of the attack and that we need your intelligence skills to make that strike effective. We will be the reserve force in case the Germans counterattack. I also promised Colonel Orlov at my promotion ceremony several months ago that I would keep you safe to fight through the rest of the war. I told him that dear Sergei would stay close to me."

Rudnev said the last phrase with a flourish, drawing more laughs from the partisan officers, all of whom seemed in jovial spirits considering the impossible tasks in front of them. On cue, Major General Kovpak continued discussion of the plan with the main details.

"When we're ready and truly prepared, we will descend from the mountain onto the Germans like a *fist*. Three columns of fighters. The main body led by me, and the two other columns led by Father Snow and Major Vershigor." General Kovpak saw Bravo's disappointment and addressed him directly. "Comrade, what Rudnev did not add was that we're being told that there are other plans for you after this battle, important plans in other places, places you know, where you lived. Apparently, you are needed to grow more partisan units and lead efforts in your old country."

"Belarus?" he asked.

"No, your skills and language ability are needed in Poland, but we have no further details about the mission. Other orders will come soon enough," the general finished.

"Sergei, you will have more battles ahead of you, many I suspect grander than this current fight."

Bravo nodded his head in understanding, but the disappointment was evident in his posture.

Kovpak continued, "The first column will be comprised of the reserve element led by General Rudnev and Captain Bravo. After the signal is made that the bridge has been neutralized, the unit will secure the bridge and let the main body pass. We will use smoke to mask our attack. Rudnev will destroy the bridge after all fighters have passed and protect our rear as the main body attacks."

Rudnev added, "We will also have companies on the rear of the garrison to prevent escape. Father Snow will fall in on security with his elements." The sun was setting as Rudnev continued to speak. "We will begin the propaganda and reconnaissance patrols tomorrow evening and continue until we are confident of success." Rudnev continued to speak, and the sound of a plaintive song could be heard rising from the positions of the partisan companies spread throughout the forest area.

They fell silent at the plaintive air, and Rudnev whispered to the remaining men around the fire, "This was composed by one of fighters."

As lads marched in the rain and in the blizzard
To fear and to the fierce death of the enemy
As they beat him with a heroic hand
Behind the ancient Putivl, behind the Seim River
From Moscow to the very outskirts
From the southern mountains to the northern seas
Man passes as the master of his immense Motherland.

August 1943, Main Gate, Delyatin Garrison

Inside the German garrison, Gefreiter Fritz Wagner, a farmer's son from Wiesbaden, now with the 8th Army Wehrmacht, was smoking a cigarette as he climbed the stairs to the guard tower for shift change.

"Where were you? I'm tired." Oberfusilier Johann Bamberger, the son of a miller and his shift replacement, said with a yawn.

"Oh, settle down, Fritz. You will be fine. I was just a few minutes late. The food services hall was very busy with shift change soldiers. The breakfast was terrible," said Bamberger.

"It was a hell of a night. Much activity."

Fritz raised his eyebrow. "Ja?"

"Yes, the godman partisans were active all night. They have been for the last week."

"There were no attacks. The alarm was not sounded. How do you know?" Bamberger asked.

"How do I know? Look." Wagner shined the search light along the outside wall. Posters had been put up every few feet for about 100 yards. The posters, in both German and Russian, had messages appealing to common people who were forced to fight a war that was not in their interests. The posters showed images of women and children waiting for their husbands, sons, and fathers. Several other posters addressed the atrocities of the Russian and Ukrainian people at the hands of the Nazis.

"Here," Johann handed Fritz a color leaflet that had a picture of a Nazi solider in uniform shooting a child with a single word, "Killer!" in both German and Russian blazing above it.

"*Schiesse!*" Fritz remarked, "but no attacks?"

"*Nein.* Every day the posters and leaflets are found all on the patrol routes, on the walls of the fort, and sometime inside here. Not sure how they got here. We destroy the leaflets and posters, and they show up every night. The garrison commandant is furious and a little concerned that there is an attack pending."

"The partisan rabble would have attacked by now. Why would they waste all this effort and not have attacked?"

"I don't know." remarked Johann. "But I know it is making the rest of the soldiers worried, too. Have you heard the singing?"

"*Nein.* My billet is inside. Singing?" Fritz shot another questioning look toward Johann.

"Every night," Johann responded, "all night. All the outside posts and most patrol have heard the same song coming from the mountains."

"What song?"

"That goddam Motherland song." Johann hummed the tune because he didn't know the words: *From Moscow to the very outskirts. From the southern mountains to the northern seas. Man passes as the master of this immense Motherland.*

"*Scheisse*. They won't attack. We are too big. They have travelled from northern Ukraine. Berlin Intelligence says that they are heading further into the Carpathians. To Polissya."

Johann raised his eyebrows, "Polissya. That is far to travel by horse and wagon hauling equipment. The partisans are unusually strong and prepared for guerilla fighters. Who knew there was such a thing as professional partisans? At shift change they spoke about the leader, Grandfather Kovpak, a Major General. The picture on the leaflet had an old man with a grey beard, dressed in gypsy clothes. He sure doesn't look like a general to me and certainly not like a man responsible for killing thousands of Germans throughout Ukraine."

Fritz climbed down from the tower. "Good day, Gefreiter Wagner." He said as he executed a sloppy Heil Hitler salute. "Hopefully the partisan rabble won't sing their songs so I can get some sleep."

CHAPTER TEN

THE ATTACK

August 1943, Near Deliatyn Garrison, Deliatyn, Ukraine

The Kovpak partisans had arrived in Deliatyn in early August, set up a base camp at Shevka from which they had begun reconnaissance of the German fortress. A few weeks earlier, Moscow intelligence reported that local collaborators had pinpointed the partisan camps in the Shevka mountains and that Luftwaffe attacks were imminent. General Kovpak had moved the formation to Vovtorub Mountain, still near Deliatyn. During the preceding days, the Luftwaffe had conducted relentless bombing raids on the Shevka mountains—the partisans watching and laughing from a neighboring perch.

This day as dawn approached, both General Rudnev and Kovpak stood in the center of a circle surrounded by battle horses. The horses were agitated and the whines and sighs could be heard throughout the newest forest home of the Kovpakian partisans.

General Kovpak, smoking a last pipe before the attack, moved back and forth in the circle of horses as he addressed the partisan fighters.

"Comrades," he began, "the Red Army is currently defeating the Germans in the Battle of Kursk. Our effort here has helped those Red Army soldiers succeed. That effort must continue, and today all capable fighters must take part in this dangerous raid. All who can fight, must! March forward toward the enemy!" He shouted as he jumped onto his horse.

General Rudnev was already in the saddle at the head of his reserve formation and shouted, "Forward! Long live the Red Army! Forward! Long live the great Stalin!" His horse began to trot down the mountain toward the bridge he was assigned to take. He shot his fist into the air and shouted, "To the Motherland!" as he quickly disappeared with the other fighters from his column.

Whispers from German informants had warned the partisans of a swift defeat at the hands of the well-armed garrison, but they were undeterred. As Rudnev's horse galloped down the rocky mountain trail, he let out another triumphant shout. The other fighters from his column followed close behind, their horses kicking up dust as they charged towards the bridge they were to destroy.

The attack began with the three columns pouring down the steep mountain and crashing into enemy lines. The sun had risen, and its golden rays cast a warm glow over the landscape, illuminating the determined faces of the partisan fighters as they surged down the steep mountainside. In the distance, thick plumes of black smoke billowed into the sky, a testament to Kovpak's strategic strikes, as the first squads swiftly attacked the city with precision. The air was thick with the acrid scent of smoke and burning debris, mingled with the metallic tang of gunpowder. As the adrenaline-filled partisans charged towards the enemy, the taste of victory and freedom was on their tongues. The city fortress was quickly encircled.

Two large regiments of German Wehrmacht, with their sleek uniforms and well-oiled rifles, appeared in the distance, quickly closing in on the Kovpakian partisans. As Rudnev turned to his men to give orders, he saw the glint of sunlight off the metal helmets of hundreds of German soldiers who had formed a human wall blocking the mountain pass, their weapons raised and ready to fire.

The German regiments marched in perfect formation, their uniforms crisp and intimidating, as they attempted to surround the surging

Kovpakian partisans. In the distance, columns of smoke rose from buildings and destroyed equipment, a reminder that the garrison was under attack from all sides.

Kovpak ordered the main body to turn left away from the garrison in a rye field to organize and face the attacking German forces. "Spread the line. Face the garrison, but make them come to us." Kovpak ordered the company commanders in the main body. The main body of partisans quickly turned and marched left, creating a wall of determined soldiers ready to defend themselves against the approaching enemy. The rye waved gently in the breeze, providing a stark contrast to the grim faces of the fighters. The partisan defensive line was spread from north to south, protecting the eastern flank of the partisan attack. The *fist* concept planned for the attack was now threatened. Kovpak heard a noise on the horizon and raised his binoculars.

"Luftwaffe squadron! Take cover!" he screamed as the deadly planes darkened the sky and began to strafe the partisans. From their cover, the men could see the underbelly of the planes heavy with bombs, the flashes of their cannon, ready to rain destruction down on the partisans below. As the bombs exploded, a sickly-sweet smell of burning grain and incinerated flesh filled the air which was so dense with smoke that it was hard to breathe.

"Into the tree line!" Kovpak ordered from atop his horse, watching helplessly as his men retreated in messy disorder, harried by the attacking planes, who were already turning tightly before beginning another run.

A German aircraft spotted several wagons of fighters and Kovpak atop his horse waving orders and swooped in, opening fire.

Kovpak raced quickly into the tree line, but not before a bullet ripped through his left leg, throwing him from his horse. He got to his feet, his face contorted in pain as he limped through the trees, his left leg dragging behind him and leaving a trail of blood on the forest floor. The sight of his men rushing to his aid brought a grim smile to his face.

"I'm fine." Kovpak called out. "Help me further into the woods and get my horse to safety." All around aircraft continued their attacks, leaving carnage on the ground, one wagon splitting apart from a direct hit, killing the driver and those still aboard immediately. Screams and yells could be heard from the injured, pleading for help.

General Kovpak was carried deeper into the woods to the east of the garrison. He was drinking water and observing what he could see of the battlefield with his binoculars.

"We are losing." Kovpak sighed. He saw dead partisan fighters lying in large numbers in the field. Several wagons were on fire, and others, driverless, were racing across the field. The battle had been raging for what seemed like hours, and Kovpak was fearful that he or his men would not survive the carnage.

After destroying the bridge at 1000 hrs., Captain Bravo led his scout units and quickly observed the intensity of the counterattack against General Kovpak and the main body. He raced on his horse back to the reserve area to report to General Rudnev.

"Comrade, General Kovpak is under attack. We must intercept them to buy some time for him and the others. He needs us. Now. The Luftwaffe has him pinned down on the edge of the field to the east of the garrison. A regiment of Wehrmacht is advancing towards his remaining men. We need to intercept the attacking Germans, draw fire, and divert them."

"Comrade, this is dangerous." Rudnev remarked.

"It's all dangerous, sir."

"Bravo and I will lead the formation." Rudnev commanded, turning to the other reserve troops. "We must leave the mountain quickly and attack the regiment."

Rudnev leaned forward in his saddle and shouted, "Forward! Towards the Red Army," and burst toward the edge of the mountain range. Bravo and the remaining units of the column followed suit.

As they took up the route of Kovpak's main body, the evidence of the hard battle so recently fought was everywhere. Dead horses and over-turned wagons and corpses, some grossly dismembered by the planes' heavy caliber machine guns, were all along the route.

"There!" Rudnev cried as he spotted the advancing German regiment on the horizon. "Follow me!"

The partisan reserve column advanced as quickly as it could, the path strewn with abandoned partisan artillery, baggage, and documents. Wounded partisans were walking aimlessly on the battlefield.

"Spread out!" Rudnev ordered as artillery fire began to fall on the advancing column.

Captain Bravo struggled to keep up with Rudnev's horse and yelled to him, "Comrade, slow down. We want our units to attack the flanks."

General Kovpak observed from his rear position on the edge of the woods, his words full of marvel. "Goddamn! It's Rudnev. He is covering us so we can move to safe ground!"

"Goddamn! Assemble your men," Kovpak ordered, "Retreat to the village of Lojeva to the Konotop farm as we planned. Take all the wound-ed. We will come back for the dead. God Bless, Commissar Rudnev!"

As the Wehrmacht reinforcements moved towards the tree line, Rudnev and Bravo and their men, now split into two groups, came up be-hind them in a lightning attack on the German flanks. The speed of the cavalry horses and the terror their riders inflicted on the infantry soon turned the tide, sending several companies retreating in disarray.

"Bravo," Rudnev said, "go back to confirm that General Kovpak has escaped the field and moved deeper into the forest." The Germans began a last, short-lived, artillery fusillade, and then their guns fell silent. Bravo set out across a battlefield wreathed in smoke, hearing the moans of both wounded Germans and partisans at every step.

He galloped quickly to the eastern edge of the field and observed the last of the wagons disappear into the woods. One of the partisan fighters recognized Bravo from afar and yelled, "For the Motherland!"

Having his confirmation, Bravo quickly raced back to assist Rudnev. The area he had left just twenty minutes earlier was blanketed in smoke, the injured and dead lying beside disabled equipment. He slowed his trot as he spotted General Rudnev with a pistol in his hand.

Rudnev smiled as Bravo rode quickly to him. "Bravo, I missed you. We are pushing them back. These damn Krauts are no match for a determined partisan!" The silence was shattered by a deafening gunshot as a bullet tore through Rudnev's skull, sending bits of brain matter and blood flying in all directions, the lifeless body crumpling to the ground from the horse's back. Bravo stumbled back; his white shirt now stained with splatters of red.

"No!" Bravo screamed as he jumped from his horse and ran to the aid of his commander. He cradled Rudnev in his arms as the reenergized German troops seemed to surround the diminishing partisan column.

Bravo rose and quickly took charge. "All partisans! Fall back to the woods. Follow Kovpak's men!" He draped Rudnev's lifeless body across the back of his horse and quickly mounted it. "Quickly! All fighters fall back!" He yelled, as artillery peppered the field. Bravo trotted about 400 yards and turned around to observe the activity. The smoke-covered field was a sea of partisan horses and wagons, the men slowly advancing toward him with surviving members of the regiment attempting to follow. The rear guard returned the German fire, buying more time for their retreat.

Bravo arrived at the forest edge, following Kovpak and his column.

"Yes, comrades, into the forest. We will regroup and bring the fight back to the Germans another day."

CHAPTER ELEVEN

PARTISAN ENCLAVE

October 1943, Konotop Farm, Loveja, Ukraine

Preparations for the 26th anniversary of the October Revolution had the Konotop Farm enclave buzzing. The celebration would also officially mark the deactivation of the Kovpak Partisan Brigade and the creation of the 1st Ukrainian Partisan Division. Since its establishment several weeks earlier, the partisan enclave had flourished. What had been a working farm was now developing into a highly organized and efficient partisan garrison. There were a few houses in the clearing, which were occupied by the Kovpak staff, the intelligence section, and communications. The men had also built a modern bath house to provide hot water for the fighters.

They also shared this new home with the Rovno partisans under the command of General Begma, a battle-hardened Belarussian. This was a functional camp and already had an airfield, with active resupply flights each day.

The Kovpak Partisan Brigade was not the green, untested group of men who had left the Bryansk Forest in the spring of 1943. They had become battle-hardened, their numbers decreased from casualties, with the Carpathian raid on the Deliatyn garrison proving to be the deadliest engagement of any partisan unit in the war.

The losses had only started with the battle itself. After the Deliatyn skirmish, the Germans had hunted the Kovpakian group relentlessly, forcing them to split up into three independent units, breaking into a fan and fleeing north. They sent misleading signals to the Germans, making them believe they had destroyed or rendered Kovpak's army ineffective. Each group traveled separately, with some covering distances up to 400 miles to divert attention, travelling at night and passing unseen through some of the area's most heavily populated by German forces. The three groups arrived safely at the partisan enclave in early October after a trek of 1200 miles in 100 days having lost nearly one in three of their men at Deliatyn or after. At Konotop Farm, they were recharging their forces, recovering from the long ordeal. They could eat their fill and sleep in safety.

Sergei and a group of fellow partisans traveled to Konotop Farm, arriving in the back of a wagon. The air was thick with the smell of hay and manure, a familiar scent that brought Sergei back to his childhood village. He was immediately shown to his living quarters, a small room with a metal bed frame and a thin mattress. He tossed his bag onto the bed and surveyed his surroundings.

As he turned to leave the room, something caught his eye. On his bed was a letter from Marta. Sergei's heart raced as he picked up the envelope, his fingers trembling with anticipation. He tore open the seal and unfolded the paper, devouring her words.

"Dear Sergei," she wrote. "I hope this letter finds you safe and well. Life in the village has been difficult, but we are managing. The bakery is busy, and sometimes I forget that there is a war occurring so close by."

Sergei smiled at the thought of Marta working hard in her father's bakery.

"Sometimes I wish I could forget," Marta continued. "But then I remember that you are out there, fighting. I pray every day that you are still alive and that you will come home to us soon. Please write back and let me know that you are okay. We miss you and love you very much."

Tears welled up in Sergei's eyes as he read Marta's final words. He clutched the letter to his chest and closed his eyes, savoring the connection to his girlfriend and their life before the war. For a moment, he forgot where he was and what he had seen. But as he opened his eyes, the reality of his situation came crashing down on him.

He was a soldier amid war, and he had a job to do. Sergei wiped away his tears, folded the letter, and placed it carefully on a wooden chair next to his bed. He took a deep breath and left the room, quickly walking to the first meeting of Kovpak's staff since the massacre at Deliatyn.

Later that cold October night, the general staff, clad in tattered uniforms and bearing the scars of war, gathered around a wooden table in the dimly lit HQ. The flickering candlelight danced across their weary faces, highlighting the lines of exhaustion etched there. In the center of the table sat a steaming silver samovar and glasses for tea. Beside it sat a large bottle of vodka, shot glasses lined up in front of it like soldiers ready for battle. A freshly baked loaf of bread sat untouched on a plate, its golden crust glistening in the candlelight. The warm aroma of freshly baked bread wafted through the room, mingling with the lingering scent of tobacco smoke from General Kovpak's pipe.

Kovpak looked tired, gaunt, but appeared in good spirits as he smoked his famous pipe before the meeting. After several weeks in the hospital, his wounded leg had finally healed. The doctors had done an incredible job repairing the damage, and he walked with only a slight limp. He was still weak from his injuries, but his spirits were high as he rejoined his comrades at their new base camp.

Missing from the table was Commissar Rudnev, whose death at Deliatyn was still incomprehensible to most. Also missing was Father Snow, the steadfast operations officer who had planned most of the Kovpak missions. Snow survived the skirmish at Deliatyn, but his enormous frame and his years caught up with him in battle. The Army had released him from his partisan obligations to a quieter life in Putvil, where he had taken up his life as a chicken farmer.

Major General Kovpak began the meeting. "Comrades, I am glad to have us together after several months. We mourn the loss of General Rudnev and the departure of Father Snow. But they would both want is to celebrate the accomplishments of this force over the past year."

Many of the officers looked down at the table as they remembered the missing men.

"On this the anniversary of the October Revolution, we are being celebrated for our brilliant feats over the last two years. Our mission was to distract and neutralize the fascist forces at the rear of the battle and to disrupt the Germans so the Red Army could continue its advance east to destroy the main body of occupying forces in the west. We succeeded!"

A staff officer sitting next to Bravo raised his fist and shouted, "To the Motherland!" The gesture was met with mixed responses and odd glances from the rest of the group.

"Yes, Comrade. We did it for the Motherland, but the costs were great. Often too great for a commander and general to bear. Commissar Rudnev and other key officers were not the only ones we lost. Over the campaign, 600 of our original force of almost 2000 partisan heroes perished."

Most of the men at the table acknowledged the sacrifice with solemn nods of the head.

"But we brought the fight to the German bastards. Our small irregular force resulted in the deaths of over 18 thousand fascists, the derailing of over sixty trains, and the destruction of over 400 bridges and supply warehouses. We also destroyed over 500 enemy tanks and armored vehicles."

The men looked at each other with surprise and joy at learning the total path of the partisan destruction over twenty-four months.

"Yes. To those actions. I would give a toast to the Motherland. We performed beyond the expectations of Moscow and have received personal recognition and accolades from Premiere Stalin. With this, Comrades, I thank you."

As the partisans toasted to the Motherland. A senior officer rose to his feet and proposed a toast: "To General Kovpak. For his leadership and returning safely to us from battle." There were loud cheers as the officers completed the second toast.

The general paused, tears in his eyes, and looked down at the table. After a moment, he took a deep breath and looked up. "But change is inevitable. The journey of the Putivl Partisan force is over. Soon, I will travel to Kyiv to heal my leg wound and will not return as your commander. Our unit, renamed the 1st Ukrainian Partisan Division with Major Vershigor taking command, will transfer farther west to operate on the border of Poland and Ukraine." At the words, Major Vershigor beamed with pride.

After the staff meeting, Bravo sat at the table and continued to look down. General Kovpak sat down beside him.

"Bravo, you have fought admirably," he said, "and you are one reason for our success. You have become a great Cheka and leader of guerilla troops. Moscow knows this and has plans for you. Major Vershigor is a tremendous field leader and will be a general in the Red Army. But he is not a Cheka and could not do the special things you do for our country. For our Red Army."

"I thank you," Kovpak said as he first extended his hand to Bravo and then hugged him instead.

Both men looked up to see a young partisan standing nervously at the end of the table.

"Comrade General. Comrade Captain," he said to acknowledge the partisan warriors. "I'm sorry to interrupt. Captain Bravo must collect an important package at the airfield. He must go now."

Bravo stood up from the table, thanked Kovpak once more for the experience, and departed for the airfield.

A senior NKVD officer stood at the edge of the runway. As the crop duster taxied to depart the airfield, all around him partisans grabbed the off-loaded boxes and pulled them into the woods. The officer was dressed in full uniform, an olive green *Gymnastyorka* jacket with golden buttons and shoulder boards showing the rank of NKVD Colonel and blue dress pants. Over the uniform, he wore a black leather *portupeya* belt with a shoulder strap and a black leather holster holding a 7.65mm Korvin TK semi-automatic pistol. He was smoking a cigarette calmly at the edge of the runway and holding his blue wool hat in his hand.

He looked up as Captain Bravo approached. Bravo, puzzled at the summons, did not recognize the officer.

"Hello, Sergei," Colonel Orlov said to his subordinate officer.

Captain Bravo froze, and his jaw dropped. He had not seen Colonel Orlov in almost three years but had spoken to him occasionally on the radio.

"You've been busy, Bravo. Word of your exploits has made it all the way back to Moscow. You are being called the third hero of Russia after Grandfather Kovpak and the now sainted Commissar Rudnev. We are all proud of you. And glad you are alive. But that is not why I have come."

"Why *have* you come?"

"I have come for you."

"But I want to stay with the Kovpakian Fighters. Major Vershigor needs my support as he prepares for the Western Front, for Poland. I want to be one of his commanders or his primary intelligence officer. I want to continue to lead partisans."

"No one said you were going back to Moscow. And you will continue to lead partisans. Your role will, however, differ from how you may have imagined it."

Captain Bravo escorted Colonel Orlov back to the Kovpak HQ. Major General Kovpak and Major Vershigo warmly greeted him, after which Orlov launched into an analysis of the state of the war against the fascists.

"General, again, the success of the Red Army is directly associated with the efforts of your partisan fighters and others throughout the German-occupied areas. You accomplished your mission. You disrupted the enemy. You harassed the enemy. You killed the enemy. All the forces of the Red Army are pushing the Germans back west and fatally weakening their resolve."

"Thank you, Colonel Orlov. It was the efforts of my commanders, General Rudnev, God rest his soul, and these two gentlemen here," pointing to Bravo and Vershigor, "who kept the support from Moscow coming so we could continue the Cheka fight. We are honored to serve and support the Motherland."

"And the Soviet Union thanks you for that." Colonel Orlov said. "Now," he continued, turning to the map on the wall, "what is our next step?" It was almost a rhetorical question.

"Gentlemen, the western border of Ukraine has become of military significance to the Red Army. There is a large German headquarters in Krakow that controls all of Poland and most of Ukraine. The Germans control this area and face little resistance from our army or partisans. Moscow wants to change that. The Polish Underground Army is doing its best to defeat and harass the enemy, but the better trained and equipped Nazi forces and particularly the Gestapo overseeing the area often overpower them. The Polish Underground is also led by commanders currently exiled in London. Complicating the matter is the fact that the Polish Army is deeply suspicious of the Red Army and unwilling to work with most partisans led by Moscow." A staff officer sitting in the back commented that no one trusted anyone in this war. His comment was met by dirty looks from most of the senior staff at the table.

"Does Moscow have a plan?" asked General Kovpak.

"Yes. Under the direction of the NKVD, Moscow plans to prepare the battlefield for the eventual invasion by the Red Army. It will take time, energy, and effort. We will saturate eastern Poland with partisan forces to gather intelligence, influence collaborators, and unnerve the enemy before that invasion."

Major Vershigo, who had been quiet for most of the conversation, spoke up. "So, the rumor of the 1st Ukrainian Division's assignment to operate in western Ukraine, Belarus, and Poland is true."

"Yes. We plan to replace your 400 troops, and, with new equipment, you will operate more like a Red Army unit and less like a guerilla unit. Your efforts will be to engage large military targets and support the Red Army as they cross into Ukraine and Poland."

"Will I also be given a unit like Major Vershigo?" Bravo asked, leaning towards the general.

"Yes, Captain. We have plans for you in the same area, shall we say more unconventional plans, but just as important. I would like to discuss this a little more with you. General Kovpak," Orlov asked, "with your approval I would like to speak with Captain Bravo. May we continue to use your meeting room?"

Once alone, Orlov moved closer to Bravo, who was visibly uneasy, clenching and unclenching his fingers as Orlov sat next to him.

"Look, Captain. We are approaching a critical point in the war. We need you and your men to do what you did during your Carpathian raids. We need an NKVD presence that will operate in the shadows to support the invasion we just spoke of, hopefully later next year or early in 1945. This will take time and patience and more than a little effort."

"Comrade, what does this mean for me?"

"We want you to organize a team. A squad of the best partisan fighters to go to Poland, first in the farmlands to make our presence felt, and then moving on to disrupt the Wehrmacht and collect intelligence in and around the city of Krakow. Moscow intelligence says that the Frank regime is falling apart and that Frank himself is losing his mind. Frank and

Krakow might be the weak point so the Red Army can re-enter the city and take control."

"Why me?"

"You look like a Belarussian but speak Polish and German besides Russian. And you have already proven yourself. So. no more arguments. Go to Krakow."

CHAPTER TWELVE

NEW FRONTIER

January 1944, Near the Parczew Forest, Poland

What is taking them so long? thought Shmuel Miecslaw Gruber. He looked at the watch he had stripped from the wrist of a German soldier killed in a supply ambush nine months earlier near the village of Kalano. Shmuel was waiting in the tree line in the dark in a wagon, trying to keep the single horse still. Four of his Jewish partisan brothers were at a cottage getting their weekly "donation" of food to take back to the forest. Shmuel was known in the Jewish Polish resistance as Mietek, a necessary alias. An alias, one, because he was a Jew but cooperating with other—antisemitic partisan groups and, two, a partisan guerilla only needed one name for the fewer details anyone knew about you, the safer you and your family were.

"What took so long?" Mietek asked when partisans ran to the wagon, loaded up four burlap sacks, and jumped into the back. The three partisans, Aniolek, Tolyal, and Tovi, were in their twenties and all came from Wilno, Poland.

"Sorry, Mietek" Aniolek said.

"Look, Mietek. The Ulmas are an excellent family. They are nervous about the *Ordnungspolizei*. The fascists visit more often and request food for their barracks. When the farmers don't have enough, they ask more questions.

"Yes, I understand," Mietek said. "But we still need food for the forest. We also need medicine."

"Yes, Mietek." All three partisans said as the cart lurched and Mietek navigated the wagon quickly through the forest back to their encampment.

A patriot and one quick to rise to the occasion for his country, Mietek had not started life as a rebel. He had been born and raised in Podhajce, Poland and served almost two years in the Polish Army when he was eighteen. He was drafted again in 1939 and stationed in the Carpathian Mountains when Germans overran his unit. He sustained a wound to his arm, and the enemy held him in a prisoner of war camp until 1942. While in the camp, he learned about the partisans operating nearby and convinced over twenty other POWS to escape and join them, the Armia Ludowa. Their partisan detachment, one of over forty throughout Poland, was called the Markuszow Group. They were deadly, known for terrifying and very effective acts of sabotage to German rail cars and German supply patrols. Mietek's group was known for rescuing and hiding Jews in peasant homes. For food they depended on the generosity of farmers and local villagers who were sympathetic to them and their suffering throughout what seemed an endless war in Eastern Europe. Gruber was second in command to Yechiel Greenshpan in the Parczew Forest. Just a month earlier, General Michał Rola-Żymierski, the commander of Armia Ludowa, had visited the Parczew Forest to recognize the efforts of the Markuszow Jews and promote Mietek to the rank of Lieutenant.

Once back through the security checkpoint, Mietek began issuing orders.

"Aniolek, boys. Get the wagon unloaded and the food secured. Leave out the chicken broth for soup and we'll have that with the *pszenny* bread in the morning."

"Yes, Lieutenant." The boys parroted with smiles on their faces. They were all the same age, but Mietek had risen much higher in rank than all of them.

"And Aniolek, please have the platoon sergeants assemble in ten minutes at the command headquarters."

Once the men had gathered at the table in their underground dugout, Mietek leaned forward, a serious look on his long face.

"Fighters," Mietek began. "Moscow and AL headquarters have passed on information about the fighting strength of the Germans and the successes of the Red Army moving east towards us. Most of the German positions in Belarus and eastern Poland are being withdrawn. The NKVD is asking for our help to suss out the garrison in Ostrow Lubelski. The defeat of this garrison will help ease the path of Soviet forces as they enter Poland. Over the next several weeks, we will study the garrison and the Nazi administrative headquarters in the town hall closely. We will note guards and patrols and schedules. When are they least defended? Where could a few of us hide to sneak in? Do they store explosives and where? How are they armed? We will find their weaknesses soon and then attack."

February 1944, Hotel Metropol, Moscow, Russia

Many months had passed since Marta had received any letters from Sergei. She was worried. In his last letter, Sergei mentioned that he might not be able to send letters to her for a long time. He didn't explain why, only that he might be travelling in forest country, that he would "be in touch" as soon as he could. That had been months ago. Hearing nothing, Marta feared the worst. But then one day, the phone rang in the bakery. Marta picked it up and said hello. It was Sergei. "I am fine." He said and went on to explain that he had been in hiding without any way to get news to her. "I want to see you. Please come to Moscow. Meet me at The Hotel Metropol."

And so it was that, a few days later, Sergei Bravo exited the NKVD sedan, said thank you to the driver, and strolled to the front door of the hotel. Marta, dressed in a silk dress and wool coat, was standing near the door waiting for him. She ran to him and they embraced. Both were in tears. They walked into the lobby hand in hand.

The hotel lobby was bustling with activity. Near the theater square in downtown Moscow, Hotel Metropol had first opened in 1905 and was considered in the grand class like the Waldorf Astoria in New York or the Ritz in Paris. It was reputed to be the first hotel in Moscow to have telephone service and hot water in the guest rooms. The Art Nouveau building rose six stories, with 365 rooms, towering over Moscow's prestigious Theater Passage 2 Street. Besides the interior splashed with gold and white ivory tile floors, the elite of Europe would flock to see the exterior of the building, which highlighted a colorful ceramic mural of Princess Gryoza painted by the esteemed artist Mikhail Vrubel. Things change during wartime, and the hotel, with its grandeur inside and out, was a glittering exception and stark contrast to the grim reality beyond its doors. Within its opulent dining hall, crystal chandeliers cast a warm glow over white linen tablecloths, and fine china clinked softly as patrons savored their reprieve from the harsh Moscow winter. Besides high-level Soviet officials and intelligentsia, the hotel now housed members of the foreign press who were stationed in Moscow to cover the Eastern Front.

Sergei's blue eyes scanned the room with a soldier's vigilance, taking in the faces of those who, like them, sought solace in the illusion of peace that the hotel offered. He felt the weight of his mission pressing down on him and tried to push the thoughts away, concentrating on the woman who sat across their dinner table.

"Try the stroganoff," Marta suggested, her voice a gentle balm against the cacophony of his thoughts. Her hazel eyes sparkled with optimism and hope, both newly rekindled by the fateful call just a few days before and hurried summons that had brought her here. He nodded, attempting to mirror her resolve, and took a bite, finding the rich flavors of the dish were a fleeting distraction.

He was fortunate to have gotten a room at the hotel, a privilege granted to senior officers visiting Moscow during the war. It was his second day in the city. He was due for some rest and recovery time. He had meetings scheduled every day at the NKVD headquarters, with updated NKVD courses on everything from new espionage methods and equipment to sabotage techniques perfected in previous years. He explained all this to Marta, and how he needed to undergo medical exams and debriefings with the NKVD staff, too. He had also been asked to address the cadres regarding current battlefield conditions on the Eastern Front. He greatly interested the school administrators, a bit of a legend in their midst, a genuine hero from his time working with the Kovpak partisans. He had much to say about guerrilla warfare and strong opinions on what the Red Army needed to do to defeat the Germans.

Over occasional quiet mornings and dinners with Marta, Sergei talked about his time in the Carpathian Mountains, what he had learned. The long journey from the Bryansk Forest to Carpathia. His many months fighting with the Kovpak Brigade. He also spoke of his loneliness and how he had missed her. And how her letters, even the old ones he had read over and over, kept him sane and gave him the motivation to continue to fight. He told Marta that besides spending time with her, he wanted to enjoy some comforts he had not seen in a long time. He wanted to take hot baths and sleep in late and have a leisurely breakfast with her each morning before his appointments. He told Marta that he was proud to have kept himself alive to this point and had become an expert at partisan fighting. He was looking forward to such comforts as the majesty of the Chaliapin bar and the fine dinners they might eat there.

Marta listened to Sergei attentively, sometimes nodding and sometimes tearing up when she heard the dangers he faced. After a moment of silence, Marta leaned forward and spoke. "Tonight, let us forget what tomorrow holds," she whispered, reaching across the table to grasp his hand. For a moment, Sergei allowed himself to be pulled into the current of her warmth, letting the fears of the future dissolve in the tenderness of her touch.

Later, as they walked together to the Bolshoi Theatre, the streets of Moscow stretched out before them, surprisingly bustling even in the cold. The theater's majestic presence was a monument to a Russia embroiled in both grandeur and turmoil. Seated in the plush red velvet chairs, Sergei and Marta watched as the actors on stage brought the play, *A Life for a Tsar*, to life. Each note of the score resonated within the hallowed space, evoking a bygone era of tsars and serfdom, of sacrifice and loyalty, parallels to their own predicament not lost on either of them.

Marta's hand found his again, her grip tight as if she could hold him back from ever leaving. On stage, the hero faced his destiny with stoic bravery, mirroring the resolve Sergei knew he must summon when the time came.

"Beautiful, wasn't it?" Marta said, as the final curtain fell and the audience erupted into applause, her voice tinged with a melancholy that mirrored the somber themes of the play.

"Indeed," he replied, his thoughts already marching toward Krakow, toward the unknown darkness that awaited him there. Yet, the woman whose hand gripped his so warmly and with such strength brought him back to the present. She loved him and he loved her. It seemed so simple, except for each day's reminders that his time with her was a pause, however cherished.

After several weeks of meetings at the NKVD headquarters, with a week of training, and glorious days and evenings with Marta, it was time for Sergei's next assignment. His hands trembled slightly as he clasped the cold metal of his service revolver, securing it in its holster. His uniform, a symbol of duty and honor, lay neatly folded on the chair beside him, the red star of the Soviet Army emblazoned on its collar. The room was silent except for the soft rustling of fabric as he dressed, each movement deliberate, each second stretching out before him.

Marta watched from the edge of the bed, her eyes tracing the outline of Sergei's strong jawline, the curve of his shoulders set against the backdrop of a Moscow morning that seemed oblivious to their turmoil. Her hands clutched at the woolen blanket, knuckles white, as if by sheer she would anchor him to this place, to her. Outside, the sun had set, casting shadows across the small room. But inside, Marta was enveloped in a darkness that seemed to consume everything around her.

"Please, Marta," Sergei said, his voice gentle but firm. "You have to tell me what's wrong."

Marta looked up at him, her eyes red and swollen from crying. She took a deep breath and tried to steady herself. "Feeling that you are going far away from me, again," she began slowly, her voice barely above a whisper. "It brings back memories I'd rather forget."

Sergei sat down next to her and placed a comforting arm around her shoulder. He could feel her shaking as she spoke.

"During the war, I was alone," she continued, her words coming out in short bursts. "I didn't know if you were alive or dead. Months went by without any word from you, and when the letters finally came, they were so vague. I had no idea where you were or what you were doing."

Tears welled up in Marta's eyes again, and she struggled to hold them back.

"Every night, I would lie awake, wondering if you were okay," she said, her voice breaking. "I felt like you loved the war more than me, that you didn't care about what was happening to me here."

Sergei's heart ached as he listened to her. He had never realized how much his absence had affected her.

"Please, Marta," he said, his voice filled with emotion. "I had no choice. You know that. I had to fight for our country. But nothing is more important to me than you. I love you, and I always will."

For a moment, Marta looked into Sergei's eyes, searching for any sign of deceit. But all she saw was love and affection.

"Remember our walks in the woods," Sergei said, his voice steady despite his sadness. "Hold onto those moments, Marta, and what we have lived here, too. They are ours, and not even war can take them away."

Marta stood up, the distance between them closing with her hesitant steps. She reached out, her fingers brushing against the medals on his chest—each one a testament to his bravery, each one a weight upon his heart.

"Promise me you'll return," Marta whispered, her voice breaking as she traced the lines of his face, memorizing every detail. Her hazel eyes gazed into his, seeking reassurance in their depths.

"I promise to come back to you," Sergei vowed, his words a fervent whisper against the dread clawing at him. He wrapped his arms around her, pulling her close, their bodies pressed together in a fervent embrace. Their lips met in a kiss laden with the taste of fear and the sweetness of hope.

Reluctantly, Sergei pulled away, his gaze lingering on Marta as he picked up his heavy pack. With a soldier's resolve, he squared his shoulders, his silhouette framed by the doorway. "*Do zobaczenia*, my love," he said, the Polish farewell a gentle caress.

"Until we meet again," Marta replied, the words catching in her throat.

And with that, Sergei stepped out into the gray dawn of a city at war.

March 1944, Near the Parczew Forest, Parczew, Poland

Many months had passed since he had last seen Colonel Orlov, his NKVD contact, after the bloodbath in the Carpathian Mountains. He did remember the man's last words. "Go to Krakow."

Bravo had followed the order, but it had taken him a few months to get to Poland since that October meeting. He now sat with the rest of his team in the tree line, watching for German patrols and reporting back to Moscow on enemy strength and their presumed intentions.

Things changed for him; he was now known as Major Sergei Bravo; his promotion having come at the end of 1943. He was now with his new detachment, a group of almost thirty soldiers, mostly NKVD officers and a few seasoned Soviet combat partisans, each with a specialized skill. There were two operational teams of explosive experts, medics, intelligence specialists, engineers, and communication specialists. Their mission was to cross the border into Poland from Ukraine and first, disrupt German activities and to gather intelligence, especially of the General Government Center in Krakow, led by the increasingly erratic Herr Koch. Colonel Orlov advised Major Bravo to work his team into northeast Poland without drawing attention and then to begin sabotage operations once they had established a temporary headquarters.

Just a month after his time with Marta, Major Bravo found himself on the back of a horse on the outskirts of the woods near Sobibor in Poland. *I really hate horses,* he was thinking. *I spend most of my time traveling between missions on a horse and still don't like them.*

His current horse, Golgofa, *Go* for short, was a hard worker and had been with him since he'd left the Carpathian Forest. However, Go often became bored when forced to stand in one place in the cold for hours on reconnaissance missions and would pace or whine.

"Easy, Go," Sergei said to his work companion. "We'll head back to the forest soon, and I will see if I can find you an apple."

Bravo had been cautioned about the partisans in Poland. He remembered Colonel Orlov's guidance. "Look, Bravo," Orlov had said, "the partisans are active in Poland, but no one trusts anyone. This makes it hard for groups to work together because they fear being killed. Armia Krajowa relates to the Home Army and is suspicious of the Red Army. They also conduct attacks against the Jewish partisan groups who they see as their rivals. Use your knowledge of these people, use your languages. Let them come to trust you and see you as a partisan like them. That, or they will work against you."

"Major? Major Bravo?" The voice interrupted his musings, and his attention abruptly returned to the present. "Our scouts have spotted a German convoy coming down the highway toward us," reported Jan, a team leader.

"Okay. Let's watch them. We hear reports that the Krauts are retreating. Empty resupply convoys are using this highway heavily. Watch them."

"Yes, comrade." Jan acknowledged.

They observed from hidden positions on the eastern side of the highway spread across a half mile.

"Five vehicles total. Lead vehicle, Leichter Panzerpahwagen with MG machine gun with gunner manning it. 2nd, 3rd, and 4th vehicles, Sdkfz 3 Opel Maultier. All three empty!" said an intelligence specialist.

"The last vehicle is an Sdkfz2, armored vehicle with...."

The partisans' observations were disrupted by two booms that made the ground tremble under their feet, followed by heavy machine gun fire. The first vehicle was immediately engulfed in flames and the last vehicle was on fire and turned on its side. As German soldiers exited the convoy vehicles, they were immediately cut down by a fusillade of machine gun fire.

"Hold your fire! "We did not have authorization to attack this convoy!" Sergei screamed.

"Comrade, we were not engaging the convoy. The attack came from the other side of the road up there on that ridge," reported one of the detachment team leaders.

Sergei's binoculars scanned the convoy to determine if there were any survivors, noticing a few wounded individuals moving, but no soldiers defending the convoy. Groans could be heard from the men on the ground, but no one was standing. Behind the convoy, Bravo observed a squad of some ten men in civilian clothes and armed with Russian rifles and machine guns running up the incline on the other side of the road. One man stopped for a moment to look back at the convoy and appeared to look beyond the wrecked vehicles toward their own position.

"Stay still. The fighters are looking over at our position," Sergei warned.

After the fighters disappeared onto the horizon, he assembled the group. "We need to be careful getting back to our base camp. A delay is in order to give those other rascals time to go back to where they came from."

Once again mounted and slogging their way through the Poleski Narodowy Forest, the group plodded on until a scout rode up to Bravo and motioned the patrol to stop.

"What is it?" Bravo asked.

"Major, it's singing from the forest. Men's voices, coming from the northwest. Several of us heard it." Sergei motioned to the detachment to move into a security circle while they further investigated.

"Singing?" he asked.

"There!" The fighter pointed to the eastern edge of the forest.

Sergei sat on top of Go, while he paced, and listened for a moment, and then heard voices singing in a foreign language faintly coming from the forest ahead of him.

Never say you're going your last way
Although the skies filled with lead over blue days.
Our promised hour will soon come.
Our marching steps ring out: "We are here!"

Bravo asked his intelligence fighter, "What language is that? Not Polski? Not Russian?"

"It's Yiddish." The intelligence fighter continued the translation for Sergei.

This song is written with blood and not with pencil lead.
It is not a tune sung by birds in the wild
This song was sung by people amidst collapsing walls.
Sung with pistols in their hands.

The next morning, Sergei organized a reconnaissance patrol to determine who had attacked the German patrol. He was still trying to understand the delicate relationship the Soviet partisan groups had with Armia Krajowa. The Soviets had betrayed the Polish before in ways both large and small. Sergei led a patrol toward the Parczew forest, where the fighters had escaped to after the German attack the day before.

Although it was March, the weather was still windy and cold, and the muddy trail so narrow they had to walk their horses single file until they reached the more open ground near Parczew Forest where the other group had been seen.

"Damn," said one of the partisan fighters who was the point man for the patrol.

"What is it?" asked Sergei.

"Comrade, a tree has fallen down on the trail, and we won't be able to get through the path unless we move it."

"Have your men move the damn log. The rest will guard."

He was watching impatiently as the team tied their horses and attempted to move the log blocking the trail when he saw four men walk up to his men with raised guns.

Before Sergei could warn them, he felt cold metal against his head and heard the cock of a pistol hammer pulled back.

"Hello, comrade. We have been watching you. Come with us."

Sergei felt a blow to his head and immediately fell unconscious.

March 1944, Mazowiecki Group Camp, Parczew Forest, Poland

As Sergei slowly gained consciousness, he realized he was being held captive by the men who had ambushed his patrol. The leader, a menacing figure with a hardened face and sharp gaze, loomed over him with a mixture of distrust and curiosity. Sergei knew he was in trouble, but he couldn't help feeling a small spark of hope that they wouldn't hurt him.

Sergei's body ached as he slumped against the rough bark of the tree, his hands and feet bound tightly with unforgiving ropes. His heart raced with fear and confusion, unsure of where he was or why he had been captured. He couldn't even move without feeling the sharp sting of the ropes cutting into his skin.

A voice spoke in Polish, commanding him to stay still or face death. Sergei tried to piece together what was happening. Suddenly, his eyes fell upon his fellow patrol members, all tied up and helpless like him, and real fear gripped him.

One man, tall and imposing, knelt before Sergei with a cup in hand. The scent of hot tea wafted towards him, a stark contrast to the dire situation at hand. He couldn't help but wonder if that would be his last scent before meeting his end.

The tall man spoke with a thick Polish accent as he introduced himself as Mietek. He warned the group, "You and your men are in danger. You must listen carefully to my questions, or you will all be killed."

Sergei raised an eyebrow and responded confidently, "Tak. I understand."

Mietek scrutinized Sergei before asking, "Are you Polish? Or do you simply speak the language? We cannot risk trusting a potential German spy."

Sergei opened his mouth then closed it. Finally, he blurted the truth. "Moscow sent us to collaborate with other partisan groups like yours."

"We trust no one," Mietek said, punching Sergei.

"The Germans and Jew haters are after us. We also fought against the Guardia Krajawa. How can we trust you?"

"I repeat. Moscow sent us. A message was supposed to have been sent by radio to alert you we were coming to Poland."

"We received messages months ago, but no one arrived. We could have used the support." The man's eyes narrowed as he looked at Sergei suspiciously. "You could be using captured intelligence to deceive us and then your friends will come out of the hills and just kill us for all we know."

"We were in the Carpathian Mountains and suffered great losses. We were at Konotop Farm and needed some time to reorganize and make our way to Poland to assist in the fight. We are Soviet partisans who are very good at killing Germans."

Mietek stopped moving and stared at Sergei. "You were part of the Carpathian partisans?"

"Yes, I was one of Kovpak's partisans, one of his leaders. We fought hard and many of us died."

Mietek asked, "How is General Rudnev?"

"You and I both know that General Rudnev is dead. I was covered in his brains when he was shot off his horse by the Germans!" He spat the words, staring angrily at the man.

Mietek leaned down and moved close to Sergei. "Captain Bravo?" he asked incredulously.

"Well, I'm a Major now." He smiled. "And you must be Lieutenant Shmuel Gruber, or at least that's what they told me in Moscow."

"Yes, what took you so long, comrade?" the Jewish partisan laughed. "Call me Mietek." He moved to untie Sergei and motioned for the others to untie the others as well.

"We got hung up crossing the border." Strained laughter could be heard all around the Jewish partisan camp.

"You understand why we must be so careful. It is easy for anyone to betray partisans as we belong to no one, no village, no church, nothing."

"No need to apologize. I have been greeted like this before, except last time I woke up with a sack over my head." The men laughed as he related how he had first met Kovpak in the forest.

After a few more stories about mistaken identities on both sides, the Soviet partisans were welcomed with open arms by the Mazowiecki partisans and treated like brothers. They were taken to a large tent where they sat around a long table, enjoying a meal of bread and jam. A young female partisan brought out a pot of tea from the field kitchen and poured it out cups for everyone before taking a seat at the table. As they ate, Mietek peppered Sergei with questions, and Sergei recounted the travails of their epic journey, from facing German patrols in the forest to surviving harsh weather and near-starvation.

"And what about the battle at Deliatyn?" Mietek asked eagerly.

Sergei's expression turned serious as he remembered the bloody battle. "It was intense. We were heavily outnumbered and outgunned, but we fought with all our strength."

Mietek nodded, understanding the sacrifice. "We have also faced many battles here in Poland," he said solemnly. "But we have held off the Germans so far."

Sergei could see that Mietek was proud of his group's resilience and determination. He knew that their collaboration would be crucial in defeating the common enemy.

After finishing their meal, Mietek led Sergei and his men to a separate tent where they could rest and clean up. Later, they would get down to business. As they settled in, Sergei couldn't help but feel grateful at so quickly meeting those brave partisans who would fight alongside them. He knew that together they could accomplish great things and end this brutal war.

A few hours later they gathered again, and Mietek explained their situation. "Our camps are not as permanent as the Soviet partisan camps, from what I hear. We need to move quickly, as we are under constant pressure from the German anti-partisan patrols. We thought your unit might be one such, and we were scouting you for several days after other Jewish units spotted you when you first moved into the area."

"Your unit is very skilled. We watched the Germans get ambushed from the other side and thought it might have been one of the Soviet units."

"What? You don't think the Jewish partisan can fight as well as the Soviet partisan?" Mietek said mockingly.

Sergei smiled back, "No, that is not what I meant. The efficiency of the attack impressed us."

"During my time in the POW camp, we learned about the partisan movement from a sympathetic Pole. We escaped from the German camp shortly with over twenty men. Most of them are with us today. We were all soldiers, but the people who welcomed us taught us how to fight like partisans, Jewish partisans as it happens."

"You escaped from the Germans?" Sergei asked, his eyebrows raised.

"Yes, comrade. The future Jewish partisans escaped from the Germans. However, we remain safe and survive with the help of Armia

Ludowa. They provided us with more training, more supplies. Adequate weapons."

Sergei nodded. "We have orders to infiltrate the Germans. We could use your help if you are willing."

"We have strong contacts with other Jewish partisans in the area. You are aware of Auschwitz-Birkenau and the Germans' 'Final Solution' for us Jews and also many Poles?"

"Yes." Sergei said "We've known of the mass killings for some time. As a former Pole, proud Belarussian, and Catholic, I find it disgusting, reprehensible."

"Yes, Sergei." Mietek said. "Just as we are aware of the continued wholesale killings of innocent Poles throughout the east front."

Sergei said, "Yes, this is true. And a very sad situation. This is more reason to work together to put an end to the Nazis."

"We are sympathetic to the deaths in other cities and to the citizens of Poland and Belarus." He looked away, troubled. "Still," he said, "I think we are the biggest victims of the war. Our numbers are being reduced by the thousands every day at the hands of the Nazis."

"We understand, Mietek. We have all lost family members in the war. However, the partisan effort has helped the war. It will help to defeat the fascists."

Mietek nodded his head in understanding. "Yes, I know. You and your group have a reputation for being courageous and righteous. We will help you, but you will need to help us first."

"What do you need?"

"We have a problem with the Ostow Lubelski garrison. The Germans won't fight us head on but continue to harass and attack our patrols. They are fighting more like partisans now." Mietek laughed.

"We appreciate your trust. We will surely help." Sergei said.

April 1944, South of Parczew Forest, near Ostow Lubelski Garrison, Poland

After dawn, the partisans assembled for the trek to Ostow Lubelski garrison, approximately ten miles away and housing over 100 German soldiers. Bravo and Mietek's group, who were tasked with eliminating the Germans in the town hall and then burning it to the ground, led the march. Yechiel "Chil" Greenspan, commander of the Mazowiecki Partisans and his second-in-command, Skinny Bleichman, together with their detachments followed.

A group of villagers came down the road, through the partisan formation. "Stop them!" Chil ordered.

The fighters ordered the villagers off the wagons, boarded them, and took off at a sprint, halting only when they saw the top of the Ostow Lubelski church telling them they were close to their positions. Bravo's team set up on the western side of the garrison, and Chil and Skinny's on the east. And then they waited.

At sundown, the command unit shot the flare starting the attack. Throughout the garrison, Chil's screams reverberated as he shouted, "Get the murderers!"

The sound of machine guns filled the air, sending the Germans fleeing into buildings and behind barricades. Sergei ordered Mietek and his team to approach the German barracks and neutralize the soldiers.

"Now!" Mietek shouted as two of his fighters threw grenades into the open windows of the barracks. There was a boom inside, and two soldiers fell to their death from the second floor. The smell of burning wood was in the air, and dense smoke rolled across the village.

Sergei looked up and shouted, "They did it!" pointing to the town hall, now ablaze from Chil and Skinny's efforts. Even across the village, they could see a blazing fire as it engulfed the hall.

Dennis, a serious young man on Mietek's team, had maneuvered to the town square and set up his machine gun. The loud and constant rat-tat-tat echoed off the walls of the buildings lining the square as he mercilessly unloaded on the three barracks on the opposite side of the square. Soon, groans of pains and anguish could be heard from the bodies lying near buildings and then throughout the square from the Germans who had tried to escape.

As the gunfire died away and the Germans' weak defense collapsed into chaos, Sergei and Mietek rallied near the town center to assess the damage to the enemy and to their fighters.

"The fascists never had a chance," Mietek said to Sergei as they continued to scan the village, then stood to signal for the partisans to come to him.

"We overwhelmed the bastards," Sergei said. "They never expected an attack like this from the forest. Their defense crumbled as soon as we started in on them."

Mietek turned to Sergei and smiled.

"Look," Mietek said as he observed Chil and Skinny's unit work their way through the town to the center of the village, stopping here and there to fire into a house or help a wounded comrade. Chil's face glowed with pride and relief as he approached the two partisan leaders. "Looks like we got the bulk of the Germans." He spoke. "The rest fled. We also killed a few collaborators and Polish policemen who were obviously working with the Germans."

"That will show them not to trifle with the Jewish partisans." Mietek said. "They will think twice before they pick another fight with the forest fighters."

Chil said, "Maybe so, comrade, but best get the wounded and get out of here. This village will buzz like a hornet's nest soon."

Sergei shouted "Partisans, assemble!"

Hundreds of partisan fighters rose from concealed positions in the village and quickly gathered before organizing a hasty departure back to their forest encampment.

"Thank you, Sergei. Thank you to you and your men for fighting by our side."

"By your side? We are one of you. We hate the Nazi bastards more than you do."

"One of us. I beg your pardon."

"And, fair's fair!" Sergei continued. "I will need your help on our next mission. We are being directed closer to Krakow. However, Moscow wants us to scout a garrison near Ilzha and neutralize it, if possible. Will you join us?"

"Yes," Chil said, nodding at the other man. "My people have a strong interest in what is going on in Krakow."

May 1944, Outskirt of Ilzha, Poland

A few days later after recovering from the barracks raid, Sergei stood on a small mountain incline, watching his partisan teams make their way through the woods to the village of Ilzha, a village halfway between Krakow and Warsaw nestled among the rolling hills and lush forests of central Poland. Quaint wooden houses adorned with colorful shutters and flower boxes lined the narrow cobblestone streets. A church steeple stood tall; its intricate carving visible from the distance. The air in Ilzha carried the scent of fresh pine and earth, mixed with the rich fragrance of blooming flowers.

"Here we go!" yelled Chil as they heard machine gun fire and shouts on opposite sides of the village. Sergei nodded in agreement.

This was not the first attack on Ilzha during the war. The most recent attack had come in 1939 when the Wehrmacht defeated the Polish Prusy

Army, followed by a wave of mass imprisonment, torture, deportation, and murder.

The partisans this day took out the guard towers first, the wooden structures succumbing to a barrage of machine gun fire and several grenades. Sappers had placed mines just outside the gates; they were detonated remotely, the force of the explosion sending them careening into the fields. The Jewish partisans, Sergei's men alongside, entered the town with a hail of gunfire and jubilant screams, sending shocks throughout the locals and frightening the Germans.

Sergei held a map of the village, crudely sketched in pencil, which he'd received a few days earlier. This was the work of a partisan sympathizer who was on the custodial staff cleaning the Nazi headquarters building in the town. Later, they'd picked the man up as he left work and took him to a safe house. There, over vodka and a bit of bread and kielbasa, the man had shared all he knew: troop strength, the sketch of the village, shift change times, and who was in command at the outpost. Consulting the map, Sergei could see that the teams were systematically destroying defensive positions and killing the German guards, taking the town block by block.

"There is nothing as sweet as revenge," Child said to Sergei, a bitter smile on his face. "Four years ago, this was a ghetto for 2000 of my people, all then transported to Treblinka and the gas chambers, all dead."

Sergei took up the binoculars, starting at what he saw. He handed the binoculars to Chil. "Look at that." The other man saw that several Jewish partisans had climbed the wall and were shooting German soldiers as they fled the buildings to escape the attacks. Several other partisan teams were now placing mines under the German vehicles and blowing them up. One explosion caused a truck to flip onto its roof, almost crushing a fleeing partisan.

"They are doing well," said Chil as he handed the binoculars back to Sergei.

Sergei pointed toward the western part of the village as several German soldiers attempted to flee the town only to be cut down by the partisans on the wall. "No quarter for any man." He observed dryly.

As frequent as the gunfire was the sound of breaking glass. The Jewish patrols smashed every window, broke down every door, their intent to punish the town for its misdeeds to their people. As the firing died away, Sergei heard the whinnying of horses and the clatter of wagon wheels on cobblestones as, in a final act of retribution, the partisans rounded up the villagers' horses and carts.

Sergei spotted Mietek as he entered Ilzha Castle and moved to the top of the tower. He took down the Wehrmacht flag and set it on fire, then let it drop to the ground. He took a partisan flag out of his rucksack and raised it, bringing cheers from the fighters below and giving the signal to the watchers that all was secure in the village.

A few hours later, Chil and Sergei met Skinny and another Jewish partisan fighter at the market in the center of town. They were sitting at a wooden table drinking German beer and inventorying weapons as the rest of the fighters were escorting German prisoners for further interrogation or taking up defensive positions throughout the walled town. The fighters were already working on hanging new gates as Chil and Sergei rode their white horses into the city.

"Do we have many casualties?" asked Sergei.

Skinny reported that German gunfire had wounded a few fighters from his team at the beginning of the raid, but partisan doctors were currently treating them in the village hospital.

"Sergei, I have something to show you. They found this near that half-track." Mietek pointed to a German vehicle on its side still smoking near the former city hall used as Wehrmacht headquarters.

Mietek pulled a document out of a singed leather briefcase stamped with the double eagle of the Third Reich's Wehrmacht. Despite being wrinkled and singed on the ends, the document remained readable.

Sergei's eye grew wider as he paged through the document. His face became pale. Chil was looking over Sergei's shoulder at the document and muttered, *"Oh meyn Gott!"*

CHAPTER THIRTEEN

YOU ARE NOT WELCOME HERE

August 1944, Wawel Castle, Krakow Poland

"Who the fuck is this Ghost of Krakow? Is this the 'Hurensohn' who tried to kill me earlier this year?" Hans Frank, the Governor-General, glared at his Intelligence Officer waiting for a response. Frank had just sat down at his elegant conference table, around which sat his general staff.

In early 1944, a Ukrainian partisan unit had detonated a bomb under Frank's private railroad car on a journey from Krakow to Lvov. In the dining car, Frank remained unharmed despite the explosion. This was the beginning of his furor toward the partisan movement, which had plagued him since.

Lieutenant Colonel Grosskopf took a deep breath before he responded to his commanding officer. "*Mein Herr*, it is unclear who it was. But there is a high probability that it was a partisan group. A Ukrainian partisan."

"Why the fuck would a Ukrainian partisan group be operating in Poland? The borders, I'm assured, are closed, and controlled."

"Sir," Grosskopf said, "it is unclear how they slipped into the country, but it appears as though the partisan activity is increasing all over the Eastern Front."

"Why?" the Governor-General asked.

"The answer to that is part of our report today, an overall update on the Red Army and their progress."

"Progress? The Führer himself told me we had controlled the Red Army. That we delayed them in Ukraine and other parts of the east. Is this not true? Is this the Home Army led by General Bor-Komorowski? I heard they do not even have enough guns to fight back."

"Sir," Grosskopf continued, "unfortunately that is not entirely true. We reported a few weeks ago that the Home Army, now known as the Armia Krajowa, has moved most of its resources toward Warsaw for the defense of the city against an expected summer Wehrmacht offensive."

"So, this is just the Home Army. Not this group of Ukrainian partisans."

"*Nein, Mein Herr,* it's both." Grosskopf said in a less confident voice.

"Both? How can it be both?"

"It appears as though the Red Army has mobilized and empowered not just the Ukrainian partisans, but the Jewish partisans, too. Remember the Bielski Jewish partisan group from Belarus? This is the model the Red Army is following."

"Jewish partisans?" Frank stuttered.

"Yes, sir. We have intelligence reports that the Home Army and the partisans are working together with these emboldened Jews."

"They are fighting back?"

"*Jawohl*, Mein Herr." Grosskopf said.

"Where is the Red Army now?" Frank asked.

"Our own Wehrmacht intelligence and Berlin HQ report that the Red Army has made it as far as the Vistula River. About a week ago, they entered and captured Bialystok. They now control Lublin and the Vistula River near there. We are told they are preparing to attack Warsaw as soon as October." Grosskopf said.

"I spoke to the Führer and SS Chief Himmler about this a few days ago. I guess no one knew how close the Red Army was to us." Frank said, his voice doubtful.

"Yes, sir. Berlin is saying that we should prepare to quell any uprisings at the first sign of Red Army attacks. These usually are signaled by propaganda to urge the citizens to revolt, a common Home Army and partisan tactic. We've been told to expect the Red Army to continue its path toward Krakow and our headquarters."

"Attack our headquarters? Well, we will not to be defeated."

Members of the Frank general staff sitting at the table averted their eyes from the Governor-General, and many looked nervously away.

"Himmler has a philosophy about this. A blitzkrieg of sorts. He told me they will respond to any resistance in Warsaw with an overwhelming re-action, killing everyone. Women, children, Jews. It does not matter. Then we will launch a counterattack. If we are forced to evacuate any city, the controlling headquarters must ensure its complete destruction. General Seyys-Inquart, I want you to work closely with the engineers and our Krakow District Governor, Baron von Wachter, to quash any uprisings. Prepare us for Red Army or partisan attacks. Develop a plan like the Warsaw plan. Erase Krakow from the face of the earth. If we leave to return to the Fatherland…then we destroy everything! Bomb bridges and dams, set the city on fire. This needs to happen before a drunken Red Army swill of a soldier has taken one step into this district. Am I understood?"

"*Jawohl, Mein Herr!*" The general staff all said in unison.

"Now, what about the Jewish problem? How are we progressing?"

At this, SS-Brigadeführer Dr. Otto Von Wachter, the Krakow District Governor, rung his hands together, a bead of sweat forming on his forehead.

"*Morgen*, Governor-General." Frank nodded at Von Wachter's words. "We continue to make progress, but we face complications."

At this revelation, Frank raised his eyebrows. "In Warsaw we had to put resources into putting down a major uprising. We had only about 55 thousand Jews left in the ghetto, all the rest having been transported to camps. But then a group known as the Jewish Fighting Organization, or ZOB, took control of the ghetto and called on Jews to fight. When called to report for deportation, the Jews fought back. The uprising killed about 5,000 people. Some 2,000 Nazi troops attacked Warsaw, but the ZOB pushed them back after just over an hour of fighting. We cut off all services to the ghetto. Gas. Water. Electricity. But the fighting continued in the streets. General Stroop ordered the ghetto to be burned to the ground. But the ZOB was still resolved to fight. Thousands of Jews died, but we took severe losses to our personnel and equipment. After the ghetto burned, the remaining Jews were sent to Treblinka.

"So, what does this tell me? Jews are dead. That is our goal."

"If you will, sir, it tells us that the situation has changed. Before, we could act indiscriminately, and the Jews would obey. That has changed. Now, we cannot attack the people or continue the Final Solution without expecting savage resistance."

"We don't have Jews in Krakow. They liquidated the ghetto. We should not have issues there."

"Yes, but Jews and others now see that it is better to fight to the death than to die like sheep. There was a revolt in Treblinka this week against the guards, and 150 inmates escaped into the woods. General Hess continues to run Auschwitz but is under immense pressure."

"Please tell General Hess that we appreciate his efforts. That comes directly from Himmler and the Führer."

"Yes, *Mein Herr.* But there are further complications. The Jewish liquidation program is no longer a secret in the eyes of the world."

Frank stared at Von Wachter. "How?"

"Yes, well…the details of a program this large were bound to get out. Survivors talk to their families in Palestine. The Jewish Agency for Palestine has condemned our actions as atrocities. And the Allies are aware of our experiments. We are hearing of efforts to raid the camps and free the Jews still held captive. Also, our position in the east is not strong. We expect the Red Army to arrive in Krakow by December."

Frank sighed and lit a cigarette. "So, the Red Army and the Allies will be here by Christmas. I do not believe this logic. What other good news do you have for me, General?"

Von Wachter cleared his throat and continued, "*Mein Herr,* there is one other group we are concerned about. The Gwardia Ludowa."

"Gwardia Ludowa? The GL? That rabble? I'm told that the Polish partisans do not get along with the Soviet partisans. That the factions try to kill other."

"Well, that may have been true, but in the last months the GL has become part of the communist government, and they are now supported by Moscow through the NKVD. They are officially called the Armia Ludowa. Since earlier this year, the Polish and Soviet partisans, while not working together, are also no longer working against each other. An arm of the GL operates near Krakow and carries out many attacks on trains, garrison headquarters, and communication networks. Another army operates near Krakow and does the same. They are distracting our security, apparently preparing the path for the Red Army to reach the east.

Frank stood up and looked at his staff, "All of you sons of bitches, listen to me. We will not abandon this country to the Soviet Union or give it back to the Poles. Generals, you need to use all your resources to prevent and quell any uprisings. Nothing can beat our might. And, if comes to disaster, we need to leave. We will blow this town, like Warsaw, to the heavens."

CHAPTER FOURTEEN

BLACK SUNDAY IN KRAKOW

August 6, 1944, Krakow, Poland

Karol Wojtyla heard the grind of gears and the crunch of tires on the stone road. There were about ten trucks coming toward him. His co-workers told him that the Governor-General had ordered a round-up of all military-age males to head off any preparations from city residents to revolt against the German occupation. Such roundups were happening throughout Poland in large cities. Karol was twenty-four years old, approximately five and a half feet in height, with a square jaw. His hair was wispy and flew in his face when he walked. He wore work denims, blue pants, and had on wood clogs. He was a part-time seminarian and worked at the Borek Falecki factory. This day, August 6, was a religious holiday, and he had spent the day assisting in the services at his seminary.

It feels like they have been sitting on us since 1939, thought Karol. *I'm not sure how further repressed we could be.*

Karol was a little unnerved. Not because of the overt actions by the Nazis but because of what had happened to him six months earlier. A German truck driver had run him down without warning while he was walking home from a double shift. The driver kept going and did not even stop for a moment to confirm that Karol was unharmed. Karol was used to this poor treatment but was shocked at being left for dead.

Jozepha Florek, a homemaker and lifelong resident of Krakow, was walking to her sister's house for dinner when she observed the accident.

"*Dobry panie, dobry panie!*" she muttered as she ran to the man, fearing he was dead. *Good Lord, good Lord!* Karol groaned and then fell unconscious. Jozepha stood over the young man – unsure what to do.

A German official passed by and confirmed that the man was alive.

"Stop!" he called to a passing truck. The driver screeched to a halt, rolling down his window. "This man was just hit by a German military vehicle." The officer explained. "Please take him to the nearest hospital for treatment."

"*Jawohl,*" said the truck driver as the official loaded the limp body of Karol into the truck. He quickly sped off to a hospital, which was five blocks away.

Karol recovered after a thirteen-week stay in the hospital. He suffered a concussion, a serious head wound, and a broken arm, but had healed enough to return to the factory after missing work and his seminary classes for almost two months.

Karol pulled closer to a stone wall as he peered down the road and watched a truck slowly coming toward him. The teams of Gestapo, dressed in their black uniform with the red and white Nazi swastika armband, searched from house to house looking for men. There were shouts and screams as the Nazi soldiers entered and exited the house with those they found, most teens or old men with handcuffs or ropes on their wrists. They were thrown into the back of the military vehicles as the trucks slowly rolled from house to house.

The supervisor at Borek Falecki had told Karol that Soviet troops were on the offensive and paused on the Vistula, close to Krakow. The supervisor said that there was a rumor that the Red Army was waiting for the Germans to defeat the nationalist Home Army before they entered the city. The Germans were said to be overreacting to the Warsaw Uprising and wanted to take measures into their own hands in Krakow to prevent anything similar happening there.

Karol was tired. This was the day of the liturgical feast of the Transformation, and he had assisted with services at Father Bosco chapel, a small building near his seminarian apartment. After he jumped off the tram, he walked through the Debniki neighborhood and was heading north toward the river on Szwedska street when he spotted the Nazi units clearing the area. He hid in an alley and then made his way toward Father Bosco chapel, his second visit today, and then entered Tyniecka Street near the river. His yellow stucco house faced the river. He could see a light in his apartment as he raced to the basement. His acting coach and director, Mieczyslaw Kotlarczyk, also lived there with his family after a recent move from Wadowice.

"Where have you been?" Mieczy gasped.

"I was on my way home from work and saw the troops come into the neighborhood. I ran home along the river."

"Karol, we are all in danger." Mieczy yelped.

Before Karol could respond, there was the loud clang of a door slamming. Mieczy saw the boots of soldiers heading to the apartment.

"We must pray, Karol, as a family."

Karol and the Kotlarczyk family were on the floor of the stone basement.

and praying. "Our Father, who art in heaven…." The shouts and pounding of the German soldiers' boots reached their ears as they were on the stairwell.

"Hallowed be thy name…"

The family lay motionless as they heard screams and shouts, and furniture being smashed. Then silence.

The family lay still for hours and until they were confident all the Nazi troops had left the street and would not return.

"That was close," Mieczy huffed. "We can't go on like this, Karol."

"We will be safe with God." The family members hugged in relief, and Mieczy's wife, Anna, heated water for tea in an effort to calm the family.

As they began to relax and sit in the apartment, there was a loud knock at the door.

Mieczy and Karol made gestures to the family to not move.

Bang, bang, bang!

Anna slowly opened the door and there stood Father Konstantin Bravo, a Belarussian and assistant to Archbishop Sapieha. Karol was a student in the archbishop's underground seminary.

The priest, dressed in street clothes, asked, "Is Karol Wojtyla here?"

Karol recognized the priest's voice and opened the door fully.

"Father Bravo," Karol acknowledged as he hugged his teacher and priest.

"Karol, you must listen to me. I can't lose another young man to this war. My nephew, Sergei, is a soldier. We don't know if he is dead or alive. To ensure your safety, make your way to the Bishop's Palace. It is better that we go separately. I will meet you there. The Bishop will greet you. God bless."

Through the cover of darkness, Seminarian Wojtyla crossed the Obwodnica Bridge at a run and then surreptitiously made his way through the neighborhoods at the south of Old Town to the Bishop's Palace. Father Bravo had arrived a few minutes earlier and was waiting by the front door. Archbishop Adam Sapieha greeted them at the door. That the most senior religious official in the land opened his own door surprised both men, who dropped their heads in reverence to the archbishop.

"Father Bravo, Seminarian Wojtyla. Come in. Follow me."

Both men had trouble keeping pace with the archbishop as he led them down several flights of stairs to the basement of the palace and a corner room without windows. Karol noticed several other seminarians from his class sitting at a long wooden medieval table with candelabras. They were all wearing cassocks and praying their rosaries in the dim light of the candles.

Father Sapieha grabbed a cassock and threw it to Karol. "Put this on. Gentlemen, listen to me. You are no longer seminarians or secret seminarians. Your education toward priesthood will continue, but we must use discretion. You are now secretaries of the Bishop's Palace and will acknowledge that position to the palace staff, or anyone else. We will go with God, but we will do it carefully."

The table of "secretaries" nodded their heads in understanding. Karol, after putting on his new cassock, joined the table and prayed, handling his rosary beads feverishly.

"I spoke to the Governor-General today and General Harpe. They listen to me. I may be able to influence them. To get their word, for what is worth, to spare the city and save the population and historic buildings."

"Do you think they would really spare the city, Your Excellency?" Karol said as he looked up from the table.

"Yes, but something may still doom the young men of this city as the Red Army waits at the gate…."

CHAPTER FIFTEEN

DIFFERENT FROM THE PAST

August 1944, Partisan Safe House, unknown location in Krakow, Poland

Lisa Vologoskava sat at her radio in an attic room of the partisan safe house. The room had only a wood desk with a Soviet-made transmitting radio unit on it and a wooden chair. It was getting close to 1000 hours, when she monitored certain frequencies for messages from headquarters in Moscow for various units. She would activate the radio, calibrate it, and ensure it was ready to receive radio messages. For safety, she was forbidden to operate the radio at any other time unless ordered by the NKVD leadership, and that usually entailed a follow-up radio call at a pre-arranged time. The last radio operator, Tatiana Nikolaevna, a junior sergeant in the Red Army and specially trained radio operator and intelligence specialist, had been scooped up off the street in Krakow, coming from a café. The authorities immediately arrested Nikolaevna as she did not have the required papers. She was convicted of treason at an impromptu hearing by the Gestapo and hanged near the Krakow train station. An example to discourage others.

The owner of the house, Mikhail Vrubel, opened the door into the room and peeped in at Lisa. *"Dobry?"* he asked. All good?

"Tak." All good, said Lisa, known on the NKVD radio network by the callsign "Mosquito."

Mikhail always made a point of checking on Lisa before she started her radio calls. He also made it a habit to never interrupt her when she was doing the business of the Red Army. They had an agreement to keep the door locked from 1000 hours until her day was complete.

At the request of a local partisan leader, Herold Voznita, Mikhail agreed to help the war effort at substantial risk to his family, his wife Joanna, and two school aged daughters, Rosalia and Stefania. The whole family was careful to not acknowledge the "visitor" in their attic and would talk in whispers about her only when necessary.

Lisa was born Elizaveta "Lisa" Vologoskya in 1922 in the city hospital of Kara-kol, Russia. She was a bright student and graduated from a technical school in 1941. Like other women her age who were recent secondary school graduates, she joined the Special Women's Reserve Combat Regiment and served until 1943 in various administrative and logistical jobs in her hometown. That was until a regimental officer, Lieutenant Colonel Konovalvov, visited her village for meetings and spoke with the bright young woman. They immediately selected her to attend radio communications courses in Moscow.

Sergeant Vologoskaya distinguished herself during training and differed from many other female radio operators. She took to the technical training at the Alma-Ata technical school like a fish to water, finding it a challenge she mastered with ease. Lisa also displayed a maturity and possessed an ability to establish social relationships; particularly, she could charm men. The instructors at the school observed these qualities and recommended her for advanced training—the only person, male or female, in her class. She was sent to the Special School of the Intelligence Directorate of the Red Army and completed advanced training in April 1944. Sergeant Vologoskaya received her assignment and had arrived clandestinely in Krakow a few weeks later and met her "host" family.

Upon her arrival, she assumed a legal identity with the appropriate fictitious Polish papers, which allowed her some freedom of movement as a young female in the city. As a radio operator and intelligence specialist with the 1st Ukrainian Front, her tasks were to maintain routine contact with the Moscow intelligence department and the 1st Ukrainian Front and to collect information about the enemy. The head of Red Army Intelligence was Major General I.G. Lenchik. He was demanding intelligence on German improvements in defense, what units were going, where they were redeployed. While Moscow was always willing to push for robust intelligence, which meant taking chances, the discovery and killing of her predecessor made Mosquito's commanders cautious and reluctant to have her probe too boldly in and around Krakow. The network needed to be expanded, and Moscow, with the help of the local partisan units, devised a creative plan.

After getting his radio operator safely into the city, Sergei set out to establish his network. So, it was on the appointed day in August that Sergei's contact, the Hare, found himself near a fountain that faced Saint Mary's sitting on a bench with an apple in his hand. The cathedral clock rang three bells, and the buglers blew out their call on each of the four corners of the tower.

The apple served as a signal to Sergei, known as the Voice in Krakow, that it was safe to approach him. Hare walked from the market and settled on a bench facing the cathedral. Hare was a tall, thin, white-haired man. He had a distinguished appearance and seemed ready to attend mass. Sergei Bravo approached and took a seat at the opposite end of the bench and began to read a newspaper. He sat there for a moment and saw Hare eating his apple out of the corner of his eye.

Hare was a Polish citizen named Józef Zaentz born in Krakow just after the turn of the century. At an early age, Józef became a coal miner and took part in the Polish Workers' revolution and was also a member of the Communist Party of Poland. In 1939, the Polish government conscripted Zaentz, and he served in battles in Lvov. His political leanings and experiences in the beginning of World War 2 naturally influenced him to join the Red

Army. In 1941, on the night of the Nazi attack on the USSR, Jozef returned to Krakow. The NKVD recruited him as a trusted member of the party living in Poland, after which he assisted Soviet intelligence. His particular gift was supplying detailed information on troop numbers and movements and infiltrating Soviet spies into Polish cities where they soon disappeared into the shadows. The Kremlin also had recognized him, but anonymously, for his coordination of an escape of Soviet prisoners of war from a concentration camp in Krakow. Although covertly operating in Krakow with his wife, Valeria Yanovna, Józef Zaentz officially became the Commander of X District of the Armia Ludova, the underground army formed in January 1944 by decree and through the renaming of Gwardia Ludowa. Armia Ludova often served as the armed formation of the Polish Worker's Party.

"Don't look at me," Sergei said to Hare. "I'm Voice. I am going into the cathedral and will sit on the right side toward the middle. Join me in five minutes. I will kneel and appear as though I am praying. Kneel next to me and pray. If someone approaches us, I will immediately get up and walk away. You do the same. I will then plan to contact you at another location. Understand?"

"Yes." Hare said as he continued to eat his apple and look at the church. He was familiar with this process as he had handled many sources himself in the past.

Voice folded his paper, put it under his arm and walked with a purpose toward the historic church, disappearing through its side entrance.

After about five minutes, Hare stood and threw the remnants of his apple core into the gutter and walked into the church. He spotted Voice and kneeled next to him.

"*Dobry dzien.*" Voice said.

"Good afternoon." Hare replied.

"We should be safe here as the Gestapo doesn't dare come in here. We will work as a team," Voice said.

"Yes, yes." Hare said. "I am familiar with the process. I am Polish and have legal papers and many connections to the Krakow and the partisans. I am also friendly with the underground but am cautious about whom I speak to and what I say."

"Thank you for reminding me." Voice said. "It is good to work with an experienced professional."

Hare continued, speaking softly. "We need to be cautious in all inter-actions. The Gestapo will go to great lengths to find those who assist the Red Army. Tatiana worked the radio before your new operator, Mosquito. She exercised caution, but the Gestapo subsequently caught up with her. They took Tatiana to Pomorska Street and interrogated her. Then they hung her in public view at the train station."

Voice leaned forward and spoke clearly. "Yes, our goal is to keep ev-eryone safe. No one should hang from the gallows in a trainyard. You and I will communicate through messages you give Mikhail. We may need to meet infrequently to introduce you to new contacts. Moscow is trying to put more reconnaissance teams in Krakow. As the Red Army gets further into Poland, the need for fresh intelligence will become urgent. Your role is very important."

"I understand." Hare said. "I was here supporting the NKVD before you arrived and stand ready to assist. Krakow is my city, and I want the fascists to leave."

"Thank you." Voice said as he stood up. "I'll be touch." He immedi-ately turned and walked out of the church.

September 1944, Wawel Castle, General Government Center, Wehrmacht and SS Headquarters

Lieutenant Colonel Gustav Christensen felt sick to his stomach as he drove through the checkpoint at the gates of the Wawel Castle in his black

Mercedes staff vehicle. He was a tall, blond-haired man with a blond mustache and was dressed in his full Gestapo uniform with field officer's cap. He had joined the reserve Wehrmacht after gymnasium and had been a police sergeant in Bonn before the war started. His police background drew him to the field of covert operations and especially to the counter-intelligence discipline. His star was on the rise, and they had transferred him from a garrison in Stuttgart to the Eastern Front to help uncover Soviet collaborators. He had only arrived in Krakow two weeks earlier and was still setting up his office at 2 Pomorska Street, the notorious Silesian House, when he had been called by his superiors to meet with the Governor-General Frank to discuss his concerns.

A few minutes after parking his car and having asked directions to the conference room, Christensen peered into that room and could see Hans Frank and Colonel Grosskopf, the Command of the German Security Police and Security Service, standing over a map at the main conference table. Christensen saw Frank pointing at the map and then pointing at Grosskopf. The faces of both men were red, and Grosskopf had sweat pouring down his forehead.

Before Lieutenant Colonel Christensen could knock on the door, Frank looked up from the table and spoke.

"Christensen, come in here. You need to be a part of this conversation. Well, at least you are going to be the one that fixes this problem."

Christensen marched into the room and stopped about three feet from the table and rendered a right open-handed salute and barked, "*Heil Hitler!*"

"Sit down. We don't have time for military formalities." said Frank as he rendered a halfhearted wave.

A valet came in with a silver platter with a carafe and china cups and quickly poured steaming coffee for all three men, departing as quickly and silently as he'd entered.

Frank nodded to Grosskopf to speak. Grosskopf picked up his cup of coffee to take a sip. The cup was shaking in his hand as he drew it to his mouth, took a sip of the hot liquid, and put it back down.

"Christensen, our position is not strong on the Eastern Front," Grosskopf began.

"We are continually plagued by Soviet collaborators and these partisans assisting the *gott verrdamnt* Red Army advance. Tell him what we need to do to these collaborators." Frank said in exasperation.

"Yes, *mein Herr.* Thank you, Herr Governor-General." Grosskopf continued. "Christensen, the Red Army is advancing with the direct aid of partisan and spy networks operating throughout the General Government area of responsibility that covers all together twelve counties of southwest Poland including the borders of Slovakia and Hungary. We learned of these efforts during the Warsaw Uprising and from foreign intelligence discovered in raids of collaborators' safe houses north of Krakow and villages in between here and Warsaw. They are reporting our troop strength and vulnerabilities. They have also gotten wind of plans for Krakow when…if we depart Krakow for a stronger position in *Deutschland.*"

"How are they getting this information?" asked Christensen. "Surely the SS and Gestapo forces control all populated areas. How could spies gather it?"

"I will tell you how." Frank barked. "Berlin Intelligence has informed us they have a clandestine radio network throughout Poland and Ukraine reporting directly back to the Moscow. It is usually young women operators who have also undergone espionage and intelligence training in Moscow. They hide in houses throughout the Galicia District and throughout our territory. They collaborate with Polish trash who side with the Red Army. It doesn't matter how much we threaten and intimidate; the Poles are determined to resist our efforts. This *scheisse* needs to stop now."

"What are you going to do about it, Colonel Christensen?" Frank barked as he slammed the table. The gesture caused Colonel Grosskopf to jump.

"Well, well…" Christensen stammered. "I have experience with counter-espionage operations in the West. These techniques will work in Krakow. We will discover the spies and smash their network. We will also punish them with no mercy after they tell us their plans. This will send the message to the enemy that we are serious in Krakow."

Frank nodded his head up and down, "*Jawohl, jawohl, mein Herr.* That is what we need. The rest of the fools in the SS cannot do this."

September 1944, NKVD Safe House, Krakow, Poland

The pace of Mosquito's routine had quickened over the past few weeks. Mikhail, the landlord, had passed many messages in recent days, most from collaborators working with Hare. She received messages from Voice frequently but never met him. The unit under Voice's leadership provided a wealth of information for Moscow, while for their part, the Germans were reacting more and more frantically to frequent partisan attacks. The Communists established a significant advantage on the Eastern Front following the Red Army's victory at Lwow in July. Collaborators close to the General Government shared that the Gestapo had increased patrols and raids and were using advanced technical means to identify radio signals and potential Red Army outposts. Mosquito became more comfortable in her job, even under pressure, and felt like she was contributing to the success of the Red Army, even at a small level. Earlier that morning when Mosquito started her shift, she found a note with clear directions: *Meet a friend of Voice at 2 pm today at the Saint Kazimierz Church in Rybna. Voice in blue suit. He will be praying. Caution.*

Lisa dressed for her trip to Rybna and left to walk to the train station and the quick trip to western Krakow. She arrived in the small village and had a short walk to Saint Kazimierz. The church was empty and she was alone. She took a seat and sat for a moment then knelt, as seemed most appropriate for the situation. Her head nodded in the attempts at a brief prayer and then she looked up. She felt like she wasn't alone. In the same pew a few feet away sat a young man in a blue suit praying the rosary.

Sergei Bravo looked up at her and said, "Mosquito, I'm Voice. Pray with me."

Sergei had arrived with his team at the safe house in Rybna a few weeks prior. They had made the slow trek from Ilzha to Rybna under difficult conditions, with German patrols along railroads and roads heavy and ubiquitous, meaning frequent detours and slow slogs on forest paths. Along the way, Sergei and the team gathered much intelligence about the fascists' intentions as the Red Army quickly approached Krakow. Most importantly, in Ilzha they had come across a Wehrmacht officer's briefcase, which held plans for the detailed destruction of the city of Krakow upon order from the General Government or if the Red Army threatened the city. The emergency plan had been endorsed by both Reichsführer of the SS Heinrich Himmler and the Governor-General Hans Frank.

Voice moved closer to Mosquito in the pew and continued to kneel as if in prayer.

"Mosquito," he said softly, "I am under orders to operate aggres-sively in Krakow. The Red Army is badly damaged but will reorganize and continue its attack against Poland in the fall of this year. We are ex-pected to gather as much information about the enemy as possible. Their morale. Their troop strength in Krakow and the surrounding areas. The movement and activities of the Wehrmacht engineer officers and units. How they react as the Red Army approaches. Are they putting in special defenses? We have some information about plans for the total destruction of the city."

Mosquito looked up. "To destroy Krakow?"

"Yes. The Wehrmacht will need to transfer enough explosives to supply points to carry out this plan, so we will look for supply convoys that carry explosives. We will just need to continue our collection of information to piece together the puzzle. That is where you come in."

"What is my role?" She asked.

"Your work will pick up even more than it already has. We need you to transmit and receive cautiously and quickly. Marshall Konev needs to know as much as he can as he guides the 1st Ukrainian Front toward the east with a stop to secure Krakow. So, your role is key. You will never meet my team, nor will they meet you. The message will be given to Mikhail. Occasionally, we may have you go to predesignated areas to retrieve messages. I may also bring them to you directly, but that will be infrequent."

"I understand. Will we ever meet again?"

"Only in an emergency or to work together on a complicated problem. To Moscow, you will identify my team as 'Voice.' The other source you will hear from you will identify as the Musician. He provides information about the city area and what is happening there in real time while we gather and assemble all of the regional intelligence from our teams. And that is all you have to know. Well, almost." He paused, and his voice grew more serious.

"Comrade?"

"Our sources tell us that German counterintelligence activity has increased immensely over the past month headed by a nasty fellow named Christensen, a former police sergeant from Bonn."

"I have heard that there was a new Krakow SS officer in town. I appreciate the warning."

The Voice approached Mosquito and placed a hand on her shoulder, expressing another worry. "The Gestapo has grown quite good at finding clandestine operators like you with radio triangulation, I'm afraid. You must use radio discipline and transmit as quickly as possible. Tomorrow, go to the Florian Gate on the side facing the city. There is a tan rock that looks different from the others about shin level. There is a hole behind it, just barely accessible with your hand. Your message will be there at 4 pm. Do not be early, but do not dare be late." With those words, he rose and left without a backward glance.

The next day, Mosquito left her safe house at 1 pm and walked to the market on the square at Rynek Główny. She would take her time examining the fresh produce and other items before making her way through the square and onto Florianaska Street towards the medieval gate. She exited the market early enough to take a leisurely stroll to the gate. She stood in the park a few minutes before 4 pm and then made her way to the left side of the gate, where she spotted the tan stone low down on the wall. She leaned against the wall, and first looked around to see if she was being followed, and then slowly bent down to run her hand around the stone.

Curses. This damn rock. I can't feel anything.

Her fingers eventually felt a small hole in the rock, not much wider than her thumb. There was a small string that she pulled and out came a paper roll. She quickly departed the wall and walked quickly back to the safe house by an indirect route, trying hard to avoid drawing attention to herself but hurrying as fast as she dared.

In the loft, she decrypted the message, astonished at how much robust and detailed information the Voice had fit on such a small piece of paper. Later in the evening, she reported the information during her emergency window.

2002   MOSQUITO: Center, this is Mosquito.

2002   CENTER: Mosquito, this is Center. Transmit report.

2003   MOSQUITO: Voice and team arrived near the area
       of responsibility.

2005   MOSQUITO: Voice confirms that Army North and 9th
       Army assigned responsibility for defense of area. Break. 4th
       Army Commanded by Fritz-Hubert Grazer.

2006   MOSQUITO: Voice developing order of battle for future
       reports. Break.

2008   MOSQUITO: Expect increased reporting. Request Center
       approval for increased reporting windows.

2009   MOSQUITO: Mosquito, over.

2010   CENTER: Mosquito, transmission received. Increased re-
       porting windows approved three radio calls daily.

2011   CENTER: Konev continues movement west after comple-
       tion of operations in Lvov-Sandomierz.

2012   CENTER: Center, out.

2013   MOSQUITO: Mosquito, out.

Thus began a very fruitful relationship over the next few months of 1944. Mosquito gathered messages from the drop sites that she then sent directly to The Center. After he established his network, the Voice moved throughout Krakow and adjacent cities collecting information about Wehrmacht activities from his team and other sources, so there was much to transmit. From September to November 1944, the Voice reported not only on Krakow but on two regiments of enemy motor units in the villag-es of Belany, Krisnikov, Katov, and Lishki.

In mid-September, Mosquito reported on behalf of the Voice:

1000 MOSQUITO: Center, this is Mosquito.

1000 CENTER: Proceed with your report.

1001 MOSQUITO: The Voice reports 24 echelons of German units
                passed through Krakow to the east. 101 wag-
                ons are infantry. One echelon of tanks, three

<table>
<tr><td style="vertical-align:top; padding-right:2em;"></td><td>echelons of horses, and the rest transport vehicles and ammunition carriers. Over.</td></tr>
<tr><td style="vertical-align:top; padding-right:2em;">1003 CENTER:</td><td>Transmission received. We are not satisfied with information to date. Voice to recruit agents at the most important sites. Strengthen collection of information about Krakow garrison, the deployment, operational activity and movement of enemy troops. Voice is directed to move station to Krakow. Break.</td></tr>
<tr><td style="vertical-align:top; padding-right:2em;">1005 CENTER:</td><td>Voice to take all measures to reconnoiter enemy tank units in Krakow, Tarnow, and Busk and communicate details through established protocol for Konev's planned advance. Over.</td></tr>
<tr><td style="vertical-align:top; padding-right:2em;">1008 MOSQUITO:</td><td>Message received. Will comply. Out.</td></tr>
</table>

Earlier in the year, the Voice had recruited Józef Prysak, code named The Musician. The details of his life were scant, but they knew he was a Polish patriot who had worked as a watchman at the gardens near the Krakow-Katowice rail station. The Krakow station was active, with military personnel and ammunition being transferred to strengthen Krakow's defense. Each Sunday, Jozef, with his wife and daughters, took the cover of wandering musicians and went to Krakow. They wandered parts of the city as a family, conducted small impromptu concerts, and collected donations from pedestrians walking by. After each week, he would meet with his handler to report the findings.

Józef sat on a bench in the center of Planty Park, waiting for his handler to appear. Planty Park was a green belt in Krakow established in place of the medieval walls between 1822-1830 as part of development to further the concept of a garden city. Jozef always arrived early to sit and smell the exotic flowers in the beds near the Grazyna Monument, a tribute to Adam Mickiewicz's poem. He took in the smell of the daisies, which were in full bloom. A man sat next to him on the bench, startling Josef. His shoes were scuffed and worn, at odds with the neat dark suit the man was wearing. On his head was a dark leather Maciejówka cap. This type of cap was popular folk attire throughout Poland but was adopted in World War 1 by the Polish legions and the Riflemen's Association.

Voice said, "Musician, you have met with members of my team. I'm Voice. Keep looking forward as we speak. If approached, immediately, get up and walk away. We will decide to contact you again when it's safe in the future. The Gestapo has resorted to more foot patrols in common areas like parks and markets. We could be in danger at any moment."

"I understand." said Musician.

"I hear you have been busy." Voice said as he looked at the Musician.

"Yes. Our concerts throughout the city let us pass unnoticed nearly everywhere. We've observed some unusual activity of late."

"Please tell me. What has changed? What have you learned?"

"I know plenty. We walked throughout the city and could see Nazi officers walking to their homes, but also to headquarters for most of the combat units in the area and depots for food and ammunition."

Musician handed Voice a copy of a Krakivsiki Visti newspaper. "Look at the Arts section on page 5. You may find it interesting."

Voice slowly turned to the page and saw a paper list taped to the page. It recorded specific details of mobile units and tanks at headquarters as well as key officer locations.

Voice nodded his head and mockingly said *"Sehr gut!"*, parroting the saying of the Nazi occupiers. Both men laughed.

Voice nodded toward the Grazyna statue and asked, "Do you know the poem?"

"Yes," Musician responded. "It is famous here in Poland even though Mickiewicz wrote it in Lithuania. It also inspired Emelia Plater to revolt against the Russians."

"But now we work with the Russians to fight the Germans. Now Krakow is our beautiful chieftainess, and we are fighting with her to defeat the modern-day Teutonic Knights, the Nazis," said Voice. My mom read this poem to me as a child, and it has stayed with me since my youth. The idea of fighting a larger enemy."

"No, Voice. You are more like Skuba the cobbler fighting the Krakow dragon in the fairy tale."

"Yes, my mother also read that story to me. I always thought I would grow up to fight a dragon."

"You are fighting the new Krakow dragon, and you are a modern-day Skuba. Instead of a decoy dragon stitched together with sheepskin and containing poison sulfur, you are using deception and the shadows to defeat the Nazi dragons. I only hope that when the dragon explodes, you can find your own Wanda to present with the green shoes made from its skin."

"I have my own Wanda," Sergei said, smiling, "and can't wait to return to her when this mess is over. Musician, I like you. You are a philosopher. I am a bit of a romantic and philosopher myself, despite all I have seen in the past few years. I hope we all get a piece of the dragon's skin when it explodes."

From September to December 1944, the team comprised of the Musician, the Mosquito, and the Voice worked very productively together, often only via messages, detailing the occupying government's deteriorating position and that of the Wehrmacht, equally beleaguered. The new reporting—140 precise reports—pleased the Center and brought praise from Marshall Konev. Their work identified the disposition of the 371st, 359th, 544th, 78th, 545th, 208th, and 96th Infantry Division, the 20th Tank and 344th Grenadier divisions, and the locations the 59th Artillery Corps and other enemy military units supporting the General Government in Krakow.

However, the war in Krakow would not end before the dragon reappeared, showing its ugly head and spewing its fiery breath once more.

CHAPTER SIXTEEN

MARSHAL KONEV IS COMING

December 1944, Kehlsteinhaus, Berchtesgarden, Germany

In the gloom of a dark December day in 1944, a black Mercedes staff car pulled up to main entrance of Kehlsteinhaus, known by the Germans as the *D-haus*, for Diplomatic House, though most people called it Eagle's Nest. It was constructed in 1939 at a cost of 30 million Reichsmarks.

The driver came to a stop then immediately ran to open the door for the senior German officer in the back. They made the quick trek up the windblown mountain to the building on top, the current headquarters of the Führer. The passenger avoided the tunnel and elevator entrance to save time. He did not want to be late for this meeting.

Chief of General Staff of the German High Command Heinz Guderian had been recently promoted. He replaced the previous chief of staff, Adolf Heusinger, after he had been injured in an explosion during the assassination attempts against Adolf Hitler the previous June.

Scheisse, it is cold, Guderian thought as his black highly polished boot touched the mountain ground. Even his grey greatcoat could not protect him from the early winter winds of the Berchtesgarden Alps. As he entered the main meeting room, he saw an enormous fire roaring in the oversized fireplace, keeping the room pleasantly warm, even if he expected the upcoming conversation to be anything but.

A man was slumped in a chair facing the fireplace and barely stirred as General Guderian walked into the room. There were maps and memos spread all over the floor in front of the man. He suddenly spoke. "They will give East Prussia and parts of Pomerania and Silesia to Poland," the man uttered.

"Please, *mein Führer?*" General Guderian said.

"If we lose in the East. The Allies will give up parts of our land and conquered land to the Poles. The Russians will also get something in exchange. That is our land!" He shouted, still staring into the fireplace without looking at his visitor.

"Yes, *mein Führer.* But we need to discuss how to handle both fronts to ensure the victory of the Third Reich as we approach 1945."

Even though some of Hitler's closest confidantes had informed Guderian of Hitler's decline, he was still surprised at the abject state of the Oberkommando des Heeres and Chancellor of Germany. Yes, the assassination attempts by his inner circle in July had caused more than physical damage. The psychological impact was more than clear as the Chief of Staff stood next to the leader of the Reich. Instead of the confident, resolved leader, Guderian found a flabby old man with thinning grey hair. He was trembling, physically diminished, completely lacking the powerful presence that had once mesmerized an entire nation. General Von Choltitz had tried to prepare him for this faded presence several weeks before in a private conversation, mentioning the profuse sweating, the venial, hateful mind erupting in bloodthirsty language and violent outbursts seeming without rationale. "He will push you to raze Paris and quickly execute the Ardennes Plan." Von Choltitiz had confided, warning him that Germany was in the hands of a maniac incapable of judging the dire situation or grasping the bleak reality.

"Is the Ardennes Plan completed? Are we prepared to launch the attacks in a few days?" Hitler asked.

"*Mein Herr,* we need to discuss this. We have several competing priorities, which make our situation complicated."

"Discuss? I gave the order. Make the plans. Execute no later than three days."

"Führer, we also need to consider our troops in the east. The Russians have expedited their attack. Berlin Intelligence estimates that the Red Army could be halfway to Berlin by January. In a few weeks."

"Russians in Berlin? *Kunsheisse!*"

"Army Intelligence is reporting 225 Soviet infantry divisions and twenty-two armored corps on the front. Most lie between the Baltic and the Carpathian Mountains. They are all well-supplied and assembled to attack our strongholds."

"Attack. It's the biggest imposture since Genghis Khan!" Hitler thundered. "Who handles this rubbish? I should shoot them with the rest of the disloyal at Brandenburg."

"We only have a dozen armored divisions in reserve. These are the only units available to back up the fifty very weak infantry divisions that are spread over the whole of the Eastern Front."

"The Russians are not our concern. We need to focus on the Western Front. Yes, it is a risk, but success in the Ardennes region will force the allies out of the war and allow us to divert our full resources to the Soviet Army. We followed the same plan in 1940 with much success. Our tanks will smash through Allied lines at the Ardennes Forest and quickly make their way to the coast to seize the port of Antwerp. We will conduct this attack with over 300 thousand men, over 2000 tanks and almost 2000 artillery pieces. Berlin tells us that the Americans only have a force of 80 thousand unsuspecting troops that our forces will annihilate. We will defeat them in Europe and force them out of the war."

"Führer, ignoring the Soviet advance would be a huge tactical error, and I am not alone in that thinking. We have a plan that we think will slow the Red Army's advance with the resources we have left in the East."

"Oh, is this your so called 'Guderian Plan?'" Hitler asked sarcastically. "The hare-brained idea you and General Jabo have devised and started executing without my approval?"

"The plan is based on lessons learned from Operation Bagration and is an innovative way to husband the resources we have left. We have expanded our defensive fortresses by using civilians and Hitler youth. I beg you. Do not transfer the rest of the soldiers to the Western Front. We need them to make the plan work."

The Führer paused for a moment before he spoke, looking General Guderian directly in the eye. "The Eastern Front must make do with what it's got. This is not a discussion. I am the Commander of all German forces. The decision is made. We will start the attack at 0530 on December 16th. Ensure that you report back once the attack has begun."

He leaned over to a table next to his chair and handled the bottle, Eukodal, prescribed by his personal doctor, Morell. He swallowed three of the opioid pills and washed them down with a glass of water.

"And, to make myself clear. I don't want these orders ignored like the Paris debacle. If we will not occupy a city or land, we need to destroy it. And God help us if they succeed. If the Russians get anywhere near Berlin, I want everything destroyed. Nothing should be left to the Communists. Destroy our industry, transport systems, communications. Because if I am destroyed, I want Germany and our occupied lands also destroyed."

General Guderian swallowed loudly and said, "*Jawohl, mein Führer.*"

He stood upright and raised his right arm and hand in the traditional open hand salute of the Nazis.

"*Sieg Heil!*" he said and quickly exited the room. The Führer remained in his seat and sloppily raised his hand to return the salute but did not mutter a word.

December 1944, Soviet Red Army Headquarters, Moscow, Soviet Union

Premiere Stalin was holding a map of Western Europe. He kept switching his gaze from this small map to the wall map behind his desk, which held a more enhanced and detailed view of Germany and the surrounding areas around Berlin. Sitting with him at the table was his Chief of Staff, General Antonov, and his chief of operations, General Shtemenko. The supreme leader had summoned Marshalls Konev and Zhukov to see him earlier in the day, and both generals sat nervously in their dress uniforms on each side of the long wooden conference table. The conference room's dark, wood-paneled walls held pictures of victorious Russian leaders: General Suvorov, who commanded during the Russian-Turkish War and the French Revolution, and of Kutuzov, the one-eyed general who had fended off and subsequently humiliated Napoleon in his 1812 attack on Russia.

Sitting next to Konev was Georgy Zhukov, a 48-year-old anointed Hero of the Soviet Union, who led the 1st Belarussian Front and three other supporting army groups. Zhukov, who had started life as a peasant, commanded troops in World War 1 and the Russian Civil War and he had defeated Japanese forces at Khalkhin Gol in 1939.

The highest levels of the Stavka recognized that Zhukov was responsible for many of the Red Army's biggest victories on the Eastern Front.

Operation Bagration, a large-scale Soviet offensive on the Eastern Front, concluded in August 1944, leaving the Wehrmacht wounded. This attack and the results of the Normandy invasion far to the west had thrust the Nazi military into an irreversible decline. Momentum was on the side of the Chairman of the State Committee of Defense and the Supreme Commander-in-Chief Stalin. Earlier in June 1944, he had been award-ed the first Moscow Defense Medal from the Presidium of the Supreme

Soviet of the U.S.S.R. In his speech on November 6, 1944, the 27th anniversary of the Great Socialist Revolution, Stalin praised the Red Army and exuded confidence that their Motherland would be liberated. He faced the energized crowd and motivated the masses with a new slogan for the people.

"On to Berlin!" Stalin had shouted during his speech, a cry quickly taken up by the crowd.

Now in his office, Stalin looked closely at the two generals who would ensure success on the Eastern Front. He knocked ash from the ever-present wooden pipe as he addressed his staff.

"Comrades, the Germans are strengthening their defense on the main axis against us. A large percentage of German troops seem committed to this new battle near the Ardennes Forest, about eighty percent of their forces. Were you aware of that?"

All the officers at the long table nodded but did not say a word. They waited for their leader to continue.

"I'm afraid we will have a fight on our hands as we progress. We must get to Berlin before the Allies. Berlin is our prize—both militarily and politically. When we control Berlin, we will control the whole country. I want to punish the Germans as we make our way to their capitol. We must punish them for their invasion in 1941 and for breaking the Nonaggression Pact. They must pay for the deaths of millions of our citizens and for the destruction they left in their wake. Comments, comrades?"

"Comrade Stalin," Marshall Zhukov began, "If I may, the 1st Belorussian Front can start our advance west immediately and plan to seize Berlin by April, all things being equal."

"Very well," Stalin said, appearing satisfied. "General Antonov, will you kindly show them the plan?"

General Antonov quickly rose to his feet and walked to the large map board. Stalin watched earnestly, even though he had designed the plan, and continued to blow smoke for his pipe.

"Comrades, both of your groups' armies have similar orders. You are to smash the fascists along the Vistula and then race to the Oder River to prepare for the last march to Berlin. Marshall Zhukov, en route to Berlin, you must subdue the cities of Warsaw, Radom, Lodz, and Poznan. Marshall Konev, your orders are to make your way expeditiously through the southern part of the front toward Berlin and neutralize Kielce, Czestochowa, Krakow, and Katowice, pushing your unit into the heartland of the Silesian industrial district. Your route is less direct to Berlin, about 300 miles from the Vistula to the Oder River, but important to the success of this overall operation."

"Very good, comrades." Stalin said. "You have your assignments, and I am sure you need to get back to prepare your troops for the Poland advance. We need to be through Poland and on our way to Berlin in the shortest time possible, but no later than April 16th."

"Yes, comrade!" the others replied in unison.

"And let me be clear. Whoever reaches Berlin first, let them take it!"

CHAPTER SEVENTEEN

TROUBLE IN PARADISE

*December 1944, Gestapo Headquarters, The Silesian House,
2 Pomorska Street, Krakow*

After the last collaborator was dragged back to his cell, the man behind the desk sighed loudly as his ran his hands through his short blond hair. He sat behind an interrogation desk; on it sat a black telephone, a lamp, and an official Gestapo seal.

I am glad that is over, thought the Chief of Counterintelligence for the General Government Center, Oberst Lieutenant Christensen. He had just completed a three-hour interrogation of a worker for the Eagle Pharmacy whose family had potential ties to Ukraine, and the Red Army. Unfortunately, the suspected collaborator did not provide any actionable information, so they sent him back to Montelupich prison for the night. They would bring him back in the morning to resume the interrogation. The Oberstlieutenant had settled into his duties with vigor but was having difficulty managing the high expectations of both Berlin and the General Government leadership. He was thinking about leaving for the evening to stop at Cyganeria Café for a drink and a nice dinner. The Jewish resistance had bombed the café in 1942, but he felt comfortable going there now since the security service had a strong presence at the establishment, especially as senior German officers were frequent customers.

He was reaching over for a uniform hat when there came a knock at the door. This was an unusual occurrence since interrupting an interrogation when the door was closed was strictly *verboten.*

"*Jawohl?*" Christensen barked.

A fresh-faced young Getsapo Kriminalassistant opened the door and reported, "Oberst Lieutenant, Oberst Grosskopf is on the phone and needs to speak with you. He said that it is urgent."

"I understand. Patch him in, Herr Kriminalassistant.'

The young security service specialist quickly shut the door, and the phone in the office rang almost immediately.

"Christensen, this is Grosskopf." He was the Director of the SS for the region. "I just spoke with Gruppen Führer Muller in Berlin. He is angry and claims that we are not stamping out the security threats from the Soviet partisans and the NKVD. He claims they are tracking radio calls from Moscow to here and that they have quadrupled their presence in the last month. Muller is not satisfied with our current operations and is demanding that we step up our activities or face replacement or worse."

Christensen swallowed hard and felt his stomach turn before he spoke.

"*Mein Herr,* we are doing the best we can. They reassigned many of our staff to General Government engineer units to prepare the city for invasion by the Red Army, and this has caused a staff shortage. We believe we have identified the group operating in Krakow and the cities outside of the Center. However, they are very experienced and evade detection most times. We will need to wait for them to make a mistake. More thorough interrogations will identify what units are here and what threat they pose."

"Have you heard of Sergei's Partisans, or a unit called The Voice?"

"We have some sources, turncoats who said that they were a Ukraine partisan unit supported by the NKVD and run out of the Kremlin."

"Look, Christensen. Muller is getting his orders directly from Oberkommando Göring and Hitler. The Soviets are breathing down our neck, and Göring and Hitler want assurances that the Eastern Front is stable as they prepare for the Ardennes offensive. I need your promise that you will put everything you have into this. That is your priority! I have not even mentioned that our dear Governor-General is in a race with Hitler to see who melts down more quickly."

After the call, Christensen slumped in his chair and stared at the wall without moving.

December 1944, Wanda Mound, Northeast Krakow, Poland

"Sergei, look," said the team deputy commander. "We have a convoy of five German munitions carriers in the Brzegi district."

Sergei picked up his binoculars and focused in on the district and the Vistula River to see if he could determine which units they were from. "Looks like a flotilla brought munitions on the Vistula from the west. Not sure exactly where the convoy is going now," Sergei said.

Sergei's team, eight partisans, lay in a small circle at the top of Wanda Mound. The area was not popular for strolling because of the winter winds beginning to sweep the city. By now, all team members were, from the appearance of their perfectly forged documents, fully legal residents of Krakow and so could move more freely in the area and in the city, especially at night. Today, they had hopped aboard the tram and exited at the Kopiec Wandy stop, closest to the Wanda Mound. They were dressed as laborers, in dark pants, cotton shirts, and mid-length wool jackets. On each of their heads was a dark canvas or wool legion hat. They carried, tucked away, either a Walther or a Luger pistol, in case they had to defend themselves.

The Wanda Mound was in northeast Krakow and presented clear lines of sight to the Vistula River, many German supply routes, and the Dlubnia River as well. They often used the various mounds, many built as medieval defense and observation posts, that were not occupied by German forces for outposts. Remarkably, the fascists did not currently control Wanda Mound.

Sergei's team in recent days had received orders to report their observations as close to real time as possible, given Marshall Konev's advance to Berlin. Knowing what German units were moving where and what weaponry they took with them was valuable intelligence. Besides, increasing the coming and going of supply convoys moving equipment and the creation of defensive positions, the Gestapo were also running counter-radio operations to identify Soviet communication networks. The activity of the Gestapo increased each week as they became more and more paranoid about a pending Soviet attack, and the partisans protecting the radio operators had been warned to look out for the slow-moving trucks with rotating antennae on their roofs prowling the back streets.

Bogdan, another Kovpak fighter who had experienced the carnage in the Carpathian Mountains just a few years earlier, motioned to get his leader's attention.

"Sergei, look west over toward the Dlubnia River. Do you see the two in uniform walking along the riverbank? Looks like they may be military engineers. They walk a few yards and then stop and survey the river." Bogdan said.

The Dlubnia River, although smaller than the Vistula River, was thirty-one miles long and originated in the Polish town of Trzyciaz and filled the reservoir at Michalowice, approximately fifteen miles from Krakow.

Sergei turned his body toward the east and used his binoculars to get a better view of the German troops.

"Yes, I remember them from yesterday when we were on the Pilsudski Mound. They were acting the same, measuring the bridge and recording the results. We may want to meet up with them soon to determine their intentions."

Andrey said, "To kill them?"

"No. We are not here to kill." Sergei said. "We need to *talk* to them. We will keep an eagle eye out for them this week as we continue to surveil the city. I need to go see Mosquito tomorrow, but we will surely spy our engineers soon."

A few days later, Sergei was scheduled to visit Mikhail and Mosquito at the safehouse in the Ludwinow neighborhood. His visits were infrequent for security reasons. but today he brought much needed supplies. He took the tram to a stop south of Stare Miasto and then walked across the river to the safe house. As he stepped off the metro, he noticed Gestapo patrols and radio trucks were active, more active than normal, especially for a Sunday morning. Sergei made the cold, windy walk to Mikhail's house and knocked on the door.

"*Dzien Dobry*, Voice." Mikhail said as he opened the door, a surprised look on his face, as visitors were uncommon. Sergei returned the greeting.

"Here, I've brought you some ammunition and other requested items." He handed him the bag, and Mikhail smiled when he opened it.

"You are just in time. We appreciate the bread and kielbasa as food has been hard to get over the last few weeks. Mosquito is on the radio for her shift, but we can go upstairs to her room."

As Sergei followed Mikhail upstairs, he heard a truck engine whine. "I do not remember hearing trucks or vehicles in this neighborhood during my past visits." He commented. Mikhail opened the door for Sergei and let him into the room.

Mosquito sat at her radio desk with headphones on her head. She looked up to acknowledge Sergei with a smile but continued to deliver her reports. She had a stack of papers in front of her and worked through each expeditiously during the brief window. Recently, the messages had been coming in at a fierce pace from Moscow.

"I will sit here until you are done." Sergei said. He heard another grind of a truck engine as he sat. Mosquito also heard the engine and looked up but bounced back to complete her reports to Moscow.

2002 MOSQUITO: Center, sending report 310.

2002 CENTER: Transmit.

2003 MOSQUITO: Voice continues surveillance in strategic areas along Vistula. Munitions resupply activity occurring along the river from German flotillas from the west. They also transported munitions from the south of Krakow to the river by German supply trucks. Over.

Mosquito looked up from the radio and smiled in acknowledgement that she was sending one of the Voice team messages to Moscow. Sergei nodded his head in understanding. Both Mosquito and Sergei heard several trucks close to the house and looked toward the covered window in surprise. They both heard the thump of feet on the steps.

Mikhail quickly opened the door. "There are German trucks outside the house. Turn off the radio. Hide everything. I will try to buy time if they come into the house."

Mosquito immediately enacted her emergency procedure for this situation and made a last radio message.

2010 MOSQUITO: Control, this is Butterfly. Control, this is Butterfly Control, I repeat, this is Butterfly. Out.

Mosquito had a frightened look on her face as she twisted off the radio. Her desk was cluttered with many reports, and some had fallen onto the ground. "We will be safe. We will survive this." Sergei quickly gathered the documents and supplies on Mosquito's desk.

A crash came from downstairs along with the sound of men screaming in German followed by more breaking wood.

As the Gestapo raided the house and ran upstairs to the radio room, Sergei tried to pull Mosquito's arm to encourage her to follow him without speaking. She pulled her arm back, and the sleeve of her white blouse stretched, almost tearing at the seam. "I must hide the radio," she whispered, hearing the stomp of the Gestapo's boots now on the second floor, urging everyone in the house to stay in their rooms.

A massively built Gestapo trooper broke the radio room door in with a kick, screaming in German. "Put your hands in the air!" Mosquito grabbed the pistol from the small of her back and aimed at the trooper but then reluctantly lowered her weapon and raised her hands in surrender. The Gestapo officers wasted no time in restraining her, their grip tight and unforgiving. Mosquito's mind raced with thoughts of her next move, knowing that any misstep could cost them their lives.

Hauptmann Meinert, the officer in charge of the raid, walked into the room. He was dressed in full gray wool Nazi uniform and addressed the new detainee. "Good morning, *meine Fraulein*. We were looking for you. Were you not expecting us? I see you have been busy with your work, Fraulein radio operator. We have some other friends who would like to speak with you at Pomorska. We have a few questions for you and your housemate." Mikhail was brought into the room with a pistol to his head.

Meanwhile, Sergei had used the shock of the situation to creep up into a small crawl space between the roof and the second floor just large enough to contain a grown man. It had been filled with hay to conceal the opening and make it appear as though it was insulation from the cold.

Sergei's blue jacket was sitting on a chair next to the radio desk and caught the notice of one searcher. The Gestapo trooper demanded in Polish, "Whose jacket is this?"

"Please, *mein Herr*, it is my jacket." Mikhail said as he carefully reached down to put the jacket on to prove ownership. An arduous task with a pistol pointed to your head.

Sergei, holding his breath, heard all the interactions as he hid just feet above the activity.

"*Was ist das?*" asked another Gestapo member searching the radio room and boxing the evidence. He pointed up at the small crawl space in the room's corner, its entrance stuffed with straw. Mikhail said it was a tiny opening that they stuffed with hay to control drafts during the harsh Krakow winters.

The Gestapo officer motioned for one sergeant holding a rifle with a bayonet to examine it. The soldier thrust the bayonet into the hay and missed Sergei's head by inches. The bayonet glinted in the dim light as the second thrust narrowly avoided Sergei's ribs, a third and final thrust suddenly piercing through his pant leg and into his calf. As the first drops of blood became a puddle, the bright red contrasting against the dull, dirty attic floor, the trooper turned his back.

"*Alles klar*, Herr Hauptman." He said.

"*Sehr gut*. Let's get all this equipment loaded on the truck and transport the prisoners to Silesian House." Hauptman ordered.

Mikhail lunged for the pistol, his heart racing as he struggled to disarm the soldier. Grunts and cries filled the air as they wrestled for control of the gun. Gunshots caused shards of glass to explode from nearby windows. Mikhail stumbled back grasping his stomach, screaming in agony.

The soldier regained his balance and aimed the pistol directly at Mikhail's head, his fingers slowly tightening on the trigger until two shots tore through Mikhail's skull, causing a burst of blood and brain matter. The wall behind Mikhail was now a canvas of dark red, stained with the remnants of his life. The room fell silent as the Gestapo soldiers took in the brutal scene they had just created.

"Just leave that Polish scum." Hauptman said, gesturing at Mikhail's lifeless body. "The landlord can clean up the mess."

December 1944, Gestapo Headquarters, Silesian House, 2 Pomorska Street

Oberst Lieutenant Helmet Christensen sat at the desk in the interrogation room across from the newest detainee in Silesian House. Lisa Vologoskava, callsign Mosquito, sat in front of the desk, shackled at the wrist and ankle. For now, she was known to the interrogation center by the name on her papers: Anna Govnik, born in 1922 in the northern Polish town of Warsaw.

Christensen held her papers in his hand for over twenty minutes and read them over and over and compared the picture on the papers to the detainee sitting in front of him. Lisa was still in the white cotton blouse and black pants she had put on at the safe house early in the day.

"Anna, you are in a tight situation, and you can only help yourself by being truthful about why you are in Krakow. Who sent you? What are your orders? Who do you report to?"

"I explained I am from Warsaw and came recently after they killed my family in the Warsaw Uprising. I live with my uncle, Mikhail, and work at his stand in Rynek Glowny. I plan to go back to Warsaw after the war to see who is still alive in my family. I hope to go live with some of my relatives."

"That is a great story, Anna. Thank you. It is as fantastic as the Wawel dragon story. Our radio detection trucks identified more radio waves coming from your attic than come most anywhere in Krakow on any day except Wehrmacht headquarters. Is this not curious to you?"

"My name is Anna. I am a student from Warsaw living in Krakow with my uncle." said Lisa.

Oberst Lieutenant Christensen handled the evidence file from the seizure from Lisa's home this morning. He looked at each line of the seized items carefully.

"Warsaw student, *ja*? A student in a room with a long range RPO-4 radio set and a stack of encrypted messages. Again, Anna, this is curious to us."

"I'm not sure what was in the room. I have not been at the house for very long and was just reading a book. I do not know the difference between a bread box and a radio thing or any other equipment. I just help my uncle at the market occasionally and plan to return to Warsaw soon."

"I might believe your folk story if it wasn't for this. Excuse me one moment."

Christensen picked up the phone and whispered an order into the phone. A moment later, the Gestapo Wachtmeister came into the interrogation room with a metal box holding something which looked like a complex typewriter.

"*Danke*, Herr Wachtmeister, that is what I need." The Gestapo agent quickly departed the room.

The Oberst lieutenant leaned over the machine and delicately touched some keys on the piece of equipment. He looked to the left and right of the machine with some amazement, and then looked up at Lisa with a devious smile.

"Well, I am not a smart man. Just a simple German Gestapo officer, a police officer from the old country, but I think this piece of equipment is unique. Our intelligence section says it is not exactly like our cipher machines. But close. Our technical officer says they call it a K-37 cipher machine, with a code name of Crystal. I am told, Anna, that it is slower than our German model."

Lisa pleaded with the officer, "Please, I do not know what this machine does...."

Christensen interrupted Lisa and said, "Speaking of a different operating principle, Anna, it is important for me to advise you I have grown tired of this conversation and accept nothing you have told me. We have followed you and your group for months. You are not the first to sit in that chair, and others have revealed much. You are, in fact, an NKVD agent with special training in radiography and espionage tradecraft. We are certain your codename is Mosquito. We will confirm this once we crack the code on your cypher. Thank you for providing it for us. We would really like to talk more about the Voice, and Hare, and even Sergei's guerrillas. Our collaborators tell us you may all work together and have been busy as the Red Army tries to make its way west."

"I told you, I am Anna, a student from Warsaw. I live with my uncle until I can make it back to Warsaw...."

"I am sorry, *meine Fraulein*; you have now offended me with your lies.

Anna looked at Christensen and continued to shake her head. "No, no. I am a student. I do not know the names you say. Sergei? Hare? Those names make no sense to me."

"You need to listen to me, Anna," Christensen began. "I am impressed by how you could hide in our city and collect the volume of intelligence you have."

Christensen paused and looked Anna in the eyes. "But I will offer you a deal. Spy to spy. You cooperate with me and tell us the breadth and depth of your operation, and you will live. You might avoid being locked up in Montelupich prison. But to avoid prison, you will need to cooperate and become my collaborator...."

Lisa spoke as tears welled in her eye. "I am a student. I just want this war to be over. I want to go back home."

"You think I believe Warsaw is your home? Although your Polish and German are good, I do not believe you were ever in Poland until you came to spy on the General Government. I also believe your home is more likely Kiev or possibly Moscow. I also want to know your real name...but that will come."

Christensen leaned forward and touched Anna's arm. "Come work for me, or you will hang."

Anna sat upright in her chair and looked Oberst Lieutenant Christensen in the eyes. The tears disappeared before she spoke in Latin: *"Dum spiro, spero. Et dum vivo, pugno."* Christensen raised his eyes at the Latin phase. *While I breathe, I hope. And as long as I live, I fight.*

December 1944, Saint Mary's Cathedral, Krakow, Poland

He knelt and began praying the rosary near the front of the church. *It seems empty for a Sunday. Good, I could use the time to think,* Sergei thought.

Much had occurred since he began his trek from Rybak to meet up with Mosquito that morning at the Ludinow safehouse. As Sergei prayed, he still felt amazed that no one had detected him. After the Gestapo raiders left the house. Sergei lay in silence for over two hours, to ensure no one returned or was still in the safe house. He then quickly exited the crawl space, saying a prayer over the fallen Mikhail's body before ducking into a bathroom to get a bandage for his leg and to clean it from infection. Sergei winced as he moved the pant leg up; the blood had dried, and the movement of the fabric reopened the wound. Sergei did his best to apply pressure to stop the bleeding and then to bandage the calf. He also searched in Mikhail's clothes closest for a pair of pants and found a dark pair hanging in the closet.

He is much bigger than me, but these will have to suffice. Sergei put on the pants and cinched them tight with his belt to keep them from falling on his walk back to the northeast part of Krakow. He carefully exited the house and made his way out of the district by an indirect route, walking slowly to disguise his limp and hopefully to keep the wound from opening up again. He endeavored to walk inconspicuously across the river bridge to Old Town Krakow and then assess his route to the train station.

He successfully made it to the market area of Krakow and used the church to collect his thoughts and develop his plan for transport.

As Sergei prayed, his body sagged as the events of the day caught up to him.

How were we discovered? What does the Gestapo know? What will happen to Mosquito? Mikhail with his brains blown out. Our months of work, ruined. Our network destroyed.

Sergei sighed as he continued to pray the rosary and look at the beautiful altar at the front of the church. His focus on the terrible day kept him from noticing an old man who was in the pew a few feet away from him. The old man was also kneeling and praying.

The old man looked over at Sergei and whispered, "Voice. I'm sure you have had better days. How are you?"

Sergei looked up and saw Hare kneeling next to him.

"After I heard what happened to Mosquito and Mikhail," Hare continued, "I was also concerned about what happened to you. Some knew you were meeting with them today to bring batteries for the radio and food supplies. No one has heard from you all day, and so we feared the worse."

"Yes, I escaped discovery by the Gestapo. They pierced my leg with a bayonet as they were searching for me."

Hare looked down at Sergei's leg. "You are bleeding!" He drew in his breath sharply. Blood had soaked through the bandage and through the leg of his new pair of pants. "We need to get you to a doctor."

"Why are you here?" Sergei asked.

"I came to Krakow to see my mother after church on Sunday. I also thought I would check to see if Mikhail needed my help. That was before the raid. I walked by the house. It seemed empty but I did not dare go any closer. The Gestapo will return. They now have tangible evidence of your existence and the existence of your partisan unit if they can put together all the pieces. You know you can never go back there. We can never go back to the house or the neighborhood. We should leave Krakow altogether."

"I know." Sergei said. "My training and experience tell me to never go back after the adversary discovers you. We will need to rebuild everything now. It will take time. I am not sure we can do it. I am not sure I have the courage and strength to do it. That is why I pray."

"My contacts tell me they took Mosquito to Silesia House. They blew Mikhail's brains out. But you knew that." Sergei's head dropped and tears welled in his eyes.

"We need to get her out of there." Sergei said.

"Yes, we do, but it is difficult. I have sources who work in the General Government who provide me with information on the activities of the Germans. We might bribe a guard at Silesian House to facilitate an escape. However, a feat that complex will take money or active coordination to get her out of Poland with papers."

"Is she still alive?" Sergei asked.

"She was alive an hour ago. But she was interrogated all day. She is trained and strong. She will not reveal her identity."

Sergei looked up at Hare and said, "I have spoken to many collaborators and informants. Even the strongest of patriots breaks down under torture."

"We should go," Hare said. "We need to get your leg treated."

"I need to take the train. We have a safe area northwest of the city."

"I will come with you, friend. You could use help. It is late. Let us go first to my mother's home for dinner and to rest, and then we can go to the train station in the morning. I will also take a train north of the city to my home." He smiled as he said, "This was not the day I expected when left this morning to see my mother."

Sergei groaned as he stood up. The blood had soaked through the pant leg completely now. The wound was several hours old, and now the leg was stiff.

Hare grabbed Sergei's arm to steady him as he limped down the aisle of the cathedral.

"Shall we light a candle for the safety of Mikhail and Mosquito?" Sergei asked.

"I am sure you will fix everything with support from Moscow." the Hare said. "And there is a rumor that Marshall Konev will be here soon. We need to get our operation back on track to give the 1st Ukrainian Forces the best intelligence to aid their advance to Krakow."

"The Marshall will not stop in Krakow. He is in a race to destroy the Nazis in Berlin. Unless Marshall Zhukov beats him there."

Both men left the church and began the walk to Hare's mother's house where a meal of pierogi and breaded pork cutlet awaited them. Sergei quickly ate the meal and excused himself from the table, the abruptness startling Hare's mother. After he left, Hare told his mother that his friend was exhausted and had gone to bed. In the morning, and after cleaning the calf wound and wrapping it in a new bandage, Hare and Sergei made the walk from central Krakow to Krakow Główny train station. There was plenty of activity as people went about their daily business almost unaware that a war was still ongoing, and ignorant that the Red Army was on the city's doorstep. They both entered through the side of the station to purchase tickets and ensure they had a seat on the crowded trains. Armed Wehrmacht soldiers were positioned every few feet throughout the station to maintain order.

"We have time before our trains. Can you come with me while I smoke my pipe before my travel?" Sergei said.

"Yes, my friend," Hare said. "I am glad to join you. I have already gotten messages to my contacts in the General Government center, and we should be able to attempt a breakout for Mosquito. But it will cost."

"I understand. We will do whatever it takes."

Both men walked out of the front door of the train station to find a bench where Sergei could smoke his pipe.

"You are a pipe smoker?" Hare asked.

"Yes, I picked it up from a partisan general in the forest before the Carpathian fight."

"I remember. Someone told me you were one of Kovpak's fighters."

"People talk too much." Sergei said with a smile on his face.

They made their way to a bench and sat. Sergei looked up to his left and stopped in his tracks. He motioned to Hare to look over.

In front of them, approximately forty feet away, rose wooden gallows. Four Nazi soldiers surrounded the stand with rifles.

"It is terrible what the citizens have had to endure during this occupation. It is terrible for the victims. Terrible for the accused. But the living also suffer when they see their loved ones tortured and killed."

Sergei nodded his head in agreement and said, "Hopefully, the war ends soon, and this will be over."

Sergei pulled his pipe out of his pocket and sat on the bench to light it. He looked up again and his whole body shook. He stood up, and the pipe fell from his hand.

"No, no." he whispered.

"What is it?" Hare asked.

"No, no, no," Sergei muttered as he walked toward the gallows.

From four coarse ropes hung four citizens. Three men and one woman dangled, slightly swaying, the winter wind slightly blowing their dead bodies from side to side. A woman in a white blouse was in the center of the gallows and had signs in German on her body. "I am a dirty Soviet spy and deserve to die. Spies be warned!"

Hare looked closer and whispered, "Oh my God. They have killed her. We were going to free her from Silesian…."

"No, Hare. We failed to keep them safe. We killed them." Sergei blurted.

Both men sat down on the bench. Sergei lit his pipe, his hand shaking.

Hare said, "We should go inside. The Nazis are looking at us. We do not want to be associated with them as collaborators. Or we also hang."

"I cannot do this anymore."

"I know, Sergei. It is cold, and we will go inside and wait for our trains."

"No, comrade. I cannot work like this and continue to see people die. We should have protected our team. They are dead because we were sloppy."

"That is not true. The Gestapo is operating more counter-radio patrols. It was a fluke. Let's just get you inside, and warm, and we will wait for our train. We will figure out how to continue."

"No, comrade. I am done. Konev will be here soon. The war is over for me."

"But you are needed. Needed to continue to supply information from inside the city. About the Germans. Your work has helped the Red Army against the fascists. Your work helps our city, our country. Poland. You cannot stop now."

"I cannot bear the killing anymore. I need you to get word back to Moscow through your alternate radio teams. Advise them that Voice is done. I will begin my return to Moscow now after I notify the rest of my unit. No one will die again because of my mistake. Krak the dragon has won."

Sergei stood and walked away from the bench and back toward the center of Krakow. As he walked, the fading voice of Hare could be heard: "Wait, Wait."

December 31, 1944, Krakow State Theater, Krakow, Poland

The theater was filled mostly with German officers and those General Government Administration who were of high enough rank to have their families in Krakow. From the late 1800s until 1939, the theater, one of the grandest in Europe, had been called the Joseph Slowacki Theater, named after the Polish poet. After the invasion in 1939, the Germans had renamed it the Krakow State Theater to remove any vestige of Polish identity and culture from public places and buildings. The theater featured a new renaissance with new baroque styles. The art scene inspired the overall concept. Two figures, Tadeusz and Zosia, characters from the poem, *Pan Tadeusz*, by Adam Mickiewicz, stand at the top of the entrance to welcome all visitors. A grand staircase leads up to the main room, which is decorated with stucco and mirrors. The main hall has four stories, with lounges on each. The stage features a fine curtain, designed by Siemiradzki. The curtain was opened with much fanfare for all events and performances.

In celebration of the New Year holiday, that night was a special performance of Gluck's *Orpheus and Euridice* and the first act was about to begin. The opera, based on Greek legend, follows Orpheus as he tries to rescue his wife from Hades. The gods have one caveat: Orpheus can be together with his wife again, but he must lead her through the labyrinths of hell without looking back. The curtain rose, and the first act began featuring a chorus of nymphs and shepherds who join Orpheus around the tomb of his wife.

As Orpheus sang the first lines of his grief song, *"Ah, se inforno, ah! Dans ce bois,"* General Governor Frank could sense someone standing near his seat.

He took a drink from a snifter full of Hennesy, a case of which Hitler's office had sent to him for the Christmas holiday,

Frank looked up and said, "What is it? The show has begun. Can't this wait?"

Interrupting the General Governor's opera showing was Obersturmnannführer Kral Schon, senior commander of the Security Police in Krakow. A junior officer member of the Nazi Party accompanied Schon.

"*Nein*, Herr Governor-General, unfortunately this cannot wait."

"Fine, tell me what you need to tell me."

"*Mein Herr*, could we please step out of the viewing box so we can discuss the matter in private?"

Frank nodded his head and immediately stood up. He followed both Nazi officers out of the box to a corner area, which allowed for a brief discussion without interruption.

"So, what is so important that I am being interrupted on New Year's Eve during the opera?"

"Governor-General," Schon began, "we have lost control of Warsaw."

"How is that possible? A group of underground soldiers could fight off a Wehrmacht force. Hopefully, this is some sort of sick joke."

"We understand you received updates on the situation since the uprising in Warsaw."

"There were terrible losses, but we still should be able to control this city."

"The situation," Schon continued, "is complicated. The Allies helped the Red Army with airdrops and by bombing our forces. The Red Army, led by Marshall Zhukov, has inched forward to the outskirts of the city."

"So, we will continue to defend Warsaw with troop reinforcements."

"*Mein Herr.* Not that easy. The German leaders in the city are following Himmler's orders."

"What orders?"

"Himmler ordered several weeks ago that the city must disappear from the face of the earth. As the Wehrmacht puts it: 'Raze every building to its foundation. No stone stands.'"

"I was aware of the Führer's 'scorched earth' policy, but I was unaware of the order from SS Chief Himmler. When did this occur?"

"At the SS conference in October."

"October? I am the Governor-General and should have been consulted!"

Both SS officers were looking at the ground as Frank raised his voice. Several officers inside the opera came out to investigate the shouting.

"Governor-General," Schon continued. "Marshall Konev will seize Warsaw within ten days. You should prepare to leave the city. The Red Army will be here soon, and we will not have the troops to defend it or protect our interests. We must retreat to Germany."

"Leave Krakow? This is German land. We will not just give it to the Soviets. I will plead with Hitler to provide reinforcements to defend the city. We can also not just abandon our other interests here, like the camps in Auschwitz."

Schon cleared his throat before he again spoke. "Governor-General, the Soviets are aware of the camps. The deportations. The trains. The exterminations. The NKVD still has agents in Krakow. The Polish citizens are sharing information with them not just about our strength, but also what happens in the camps. Remember, many Poles work at those camps, willingly and unwillingly. We are also told that they shared this information with the Allies who subsequently moved the invasion for the Eastern Front up several months. We expect that the Red Army will move through Poland and Ukraine over the next few weeks and that the Allies will continue to push east."

The Governor-General stood silent for a moment before speaking again. "We need to evacuate Auschwitz. Move the Jews to Gliwice or Wodzislaw. Get them south or west where we have more resources to control them. Those that cannot keep up with the march will be shot. We can then reassess the security plan once they arrive. I will call Hitler after the opera to ask for more resources to defend Krakow."

"Governor-General, there is talk that Hitler has moved to a bunker and is not communicating with his general staff."

"I heard he was not doing well. I will talk with him. He continues to listen to me."

"*Jawohl*, Governor-General. We apologize for sharing such disappointing information but wanted you to be informed."

Frank nodded his head in understanding.

"Governor-General, we need to begin preparation to evacuate our forces and staff and their families from Krakow now. You also need to issue the last order to have Krakow destroyed as we depart. Leave nothing for the Red Army to use when they arrive."

Frank was shaking his head from left to right in a "no, no" gesture and then threw the snifter at the wall, shattering it into a million pieces.

CHAPTER EIGHTEEN

STOP THE DESTRUCTION

January 1945, Field Headquarters of Marshall Konev, Baranow Sandomierski Castle, Baranow Sandomierski, Poland

Marshall Konev sat at a desk in an office in the west tower of Barnow Castle in the lowlands of the Vistula; just a little over 100 miles from Krakow. Although temporary, the staff aides to the Marshall had organized it into a working field office, kept a fire roaring in the corner fireplace, and even served hot tea in the silver palace tea sets that bore the Wieniawa coat of arms.

They told me that the German generals lived like this through the war, Konev thought. *I have not had a hot bath or hot meal in months.*

Konev was leaning over a map table and intently viewing a map of Eastern Europe and his assigned route to Berlin when there was a knock at the door.

"Enter!" the Marshal of the Soviet Union bellowed.

"Comrade Marshall," the Chief of Staff asked, "do you have a moment?"

"Of course, Vasily, come in and pour yourself some hot tea."

Vasily Sokolovsky was the much-decorated General of the Army, a forty-seven-year-old Belarussian immigrant who had attended the Red Army military academy, served with honor, and been wounded in the Battle of Samarkand in Turkmenistan. They awarded him many decorations for his bravery. He had then held various staff and command roles after the Russian Revolution and rapidly climbed to top positions in the Red Army.

The Chief of Staff nodded, smiling at the offer of hot tea, a luxury he had few opportunities to enjoy over the past year. He seized the opportunity and went to the serving tray which contained a small coal samovar. He carefully poured hot water from the vessel into a glass cup containing the dark tea. He sat in a cushioned royal chair as he took his first sip and before he addressed the business of his interruption.

"How are you, Vasily?" Marshall Konev asked.

"Comrade, I am fine."

"What's wrong?"

"The Eastern Front between here and our route to Berlin is difficult."

"How bad is it, General?"

"I received this message about a half an hour ago. Please read it for yourself. Beria signed it." He handed a folder to Konev.

The Marshall rolled his eyes at the mention of Beria, Lavrentiy Beria, a close advisor of Premiere Stalin and head of the Soviet Security Service. Beria had a reputation in the Soviet officer ranks for being good at his job, too good after the Great Purge of the 1930s where over 700 people had been executed under his order. He was also known to be a sexual predator committing numerous rapes during his years as the NKVD leader.

Marshall Konev began to read the report, signed by the People's Commissar for Internal Affairs Beria:

/// CENTRAL OFFICE MOSCOW ///NKVD MESSAGE 45-01-212//DATE: DEC 18, 1944//

TO: KONEV HEADQUARTERS, EASTERN FRONT//

1) GESTAPO UNITS ENACTED 24-HOUR COUNTER-RADIO PATROLS IN KRAKOW TO IDENTIFY NKVD TEAMS.

2) THE PATROLS IDENTIFIED FIFTEEN SAFEHOUSES OPERATING IN THE GENERAL GOVERNMENT

ADMINISTRATION AND ARRESTED ALL NKVD TEAM MEMBERS SUPPORTING GUARDIA LUDOWA.

3) THESE ACTIONS HAVE DISRUPTED SOVIET INTELLIGENCE OPERATIONS AS MAJOR UNITS ADVANCE TOWARD BERLIN.

4) THE MOST PRODUCTIVE UNIT, A GROUP ASSOCIATED WITH CODENAME "VOICE" WAS CAPTURED AND MOST MEMBERS EXECUTED.

5) RECENT INTELLIGENCE REPORTING SHOWS THAT THE GENERAL GOVERNMENT ADMINISTRATION IS EXECUTING A PLAN TO EMPLACE EXPLOSIVES THROUGH THE ADMINISTRATION TO ACTIVATE AND DESTROY THE CITY IN THE EVENT OF A RED ARMY INVASION. L. BERIA, MOSCOW HEADQUARTERS /// END OF MESSAGE///

The intelligence report slipped from Konev's hand onto an adjacent table as he looked at Sokolovsky. "So, General, the Germans have plans to blow up one of Europe's oldest cities and, even worse, all of our strategic intelligence resources associated with the Nazi leadership are now compromised?"

"Well, the report also mentioned that the most productive intelligence team in

Krakow was dismantled, the members either killed and the survivors returning to Moscow? And...."

"There is more?"

"Premiere Stalin's aide contacted us moments ago and asked that you come to the high frequency radio for a call from him. An aide will accompany you there."

A few minutes later, Marshall Konev found himself at a wooden table in front of a microphone in the radio room. Stalin came on the channel a moment later and began speaking.

"Konev, did they finally get you on the line?"

"Yes, Comrade Stalin. I am here and await your orders."

"Konev, listen. The Beria report has credibility. And I support most of what it said." There was a pause, and Konev surmised there might be a change in his orders. "Berlin is still the priority, but I want you to slow your march to Germany and stop through Krakow first. We'll get some of our NKVD assets up and running. Beria is looking into it presently and is considering a trip to Krakow."

"Krakow? It is dangerous there, and brutal combat will begin once we arrive in a few weeks. Are you sure that is wise travel for such a senior officer?"

"Konev, we have settled it. Beria needs to address some issues with our NKVD teams. We need that intelligence. You need intelligence. So, it is settled, Konev."

"Yes, comrade." Konev said.

"And Marshall Konev, I know Krakow well. It is a beautiful city. There is a kremlin there, and a large main market square. I met Lenin there in 1912 at a place called Hawelka. You should visit. Marshall Konev, please do your best to save Krakow."

Stop by Hawelka? In a T34 tank? He shook his head, a wry look on his face. "Yes, comrade, we understand our orders and will do our best to save the city."

"Very good, Konev. Enjoy your trip. But remember, it is cold on the Vistula this time of year."

"Yes, comrade, " Marshall repeated, enthusiasm leaving his voice.

Marshall Konev immediately departed the radio room and returned to his tactical office. He collapsed into the chair and was looking at the map when General Sokolovsky reappeared.

"Is all well, Marshall?"

"I'm not sure, General."

"Has the mission changed?"

"No, just formalized and our timeline begins within 48 hours." Marshall Konev picked up a classified folder, titled OPERATION SANDOMIERZ-SILESIAN, and handed it to Sokolovsky.

The formalized order laid out the southern half of the Vistula-Oder Strategic Offensive operation. Marshall Zhukov was leading the Warsaw-Pozan operation in the north, and Marshall Petrov was leading the 4th Ukrainian Front below Konev and into Czechoslovakia. Marshall Konev was to continue the drive to Berlin from the area south of Warsaw. The 1st Ukrainian Front planned to move westward from the bridgehead between Sandomierz and Baranow Sandomierski. The aim was to eliminate the German forces north of Kielce and, within twelve days, advance towards the Radońsk, Częstochowa, and Miechow line to seize the Silesian capital, Breslau. The operation would roll out on January 12, 1945, on the frozen Vistula River.

January 1944, Rybna, Poland

The worn-looking Georgian Bolshevik sat in the dark at an old wooden table with a scarred enamel top and stared at the wall. The ash from his cigarette was burning hot, and he flicked the end into an empty coffee cup. He was in his forties, balding, shockingly thin, and wore wire-rim glasses. Instead of a significant figure, he came across more as an Eastern European accountant. He tapped his foot as he waited for his "special guests" to arrive. The man remained quiet but continued to tap his foot, smoke a cigarette, and take a pull from a bottle of vodka that he had brought with him on the trip. His business travel today had been difficult and included an airplane flight and then a car ride to his destination. Though the

Bolshevik had not announced his visit, he was impatient and did not like to be kept waiting. He still needed to return home this evening, which would include another long car and plane ride. He looked around him, seeing boxes and sacks half-filled, as if the occupants were preparing to leave.

Sergei arrived and walked up to the house. He saw his team members waiting outside and raised an eyebrow to inquire what was wrong.

"He is waiting for you." The man remarked.

"Who?" Sergei asked.

"We do not know him. He was in the house when we arrived. He said he was here to see you from Moscow. There were other men with him, but they all drove away after dropping him.

"I am not expecting anyone." He said as he opened the door of the small house.

"Well, Major Bravo, I've have been waiting for you. Please come sit next to me."

Major Bravo came to attention with a crispness that could match any Red Army soldier on Red Square.

"It looks like you are leaving soon Bravo. There is no coffee or food in the house. I brought a bottle of Stolichnaya with me. Victor Svirirda has a box delivered to my office monthly. It is very good. It is not as good as Iverioni or Tbilisi, but it will do. I think you have not been home in a long time. Belarus. right? That is what your file said."

"Minister Beria," Major Bravo stuttered, "I was not aware you were coming. It is very dangerous, and you should not be here. The Gestapo could come by."

"I know, Major Bravo. I know the risk and took a long flight and car ride through the country to avoid Germans to get here. To talk with you. I need you to stay in Krakow."

"Comrade, I cannot continue like this. I have been fighting for over five years. I fought to the brutal end in the Carpathian Mountains. Combat is different here but no less dangerous. We work among the Gestapo and Wehrmacht, and they are looking for us. I feel I cannot continue and will depart today for Moscow. I will take my punishment and next assignment, lackluster as it may be, but I resign knowing I have served honorably. I would like to train new NKVD fighters."

"Bravo, that is why I am here. We need you to continue. Yes, you would be the perfect instructor for the NVD academy. But we need you here. The death of your radiographer and her team was not your fault. It was a roll of the dice, and no one blames you."

"I blame myself and have prayed for their souls since their execution. Since our network was dismantled, our sources hunted down and killed, and our best fighters hung, I do not see we have any usefulness left. It would take us until next summer to establish what was in place. I hope the war is over by then."

Minister Beria handed Major Bravo the bottle of vodka, who pushed it away at first and then grabbed it to take a swig. His face flushed as the potent liquid poured down his throat. He shook his head to dispel the sudden euphoria that overwhelmed him.

"I have not had a drink in two years."

"Since you were with General Kovpak?" Bravo nodded his head in confirmation. "You will be glad to hear that your old commander has recovered and is doing nicely in an administrative job for the Red Army. He asks about you frequently and claims that there is no tougher fighter than you. I argue you are less of a soldier now and more of an intelligence officer."

"Thank you, comrade." Bravo whispered.

"You know that General Kovpak would encourage you to continue. You saw many dangerous situations with your partisan fighters. General Kovpak would tell you it was your duty to continue for Mother Russia."

"Is that also what you are telling me?"

"No, but you know I *could* order you to continue, and you would face dire consequences if you disobeyed."

"I understand."

"No, Major Bravo, we want you to continue and help us finish this war. We want to refocus your work on what the fascists will do over the next weeks."

"What will they do?"

"German Intelligence is reporting the positions of Marshall Zhukov and Marshall Konev as they advance toward the west and Berlin. Our intelligence reports that the command in the General Administration here and in Warsaw is crumbling."

"The Musician overheard German officers discussing Hitler and Hans Frank. That both are mentally unstable and crumbling fast under the pressure the Red Army brings to bear," Bravo added.

"Yes, we are aware, and that is why we need you to continue. The Germans are weak, and our forces have momentum. We believe the Ardennes Offensive, the so-called Battle of the Bulge, that Hitler designed, will be the last serious campaign for the Germans. They fought strongly at first, and the Allies, especially the Americans, took many casualties. But the Allies are now prevailing. Most officials feel Germany will capitulate altogether in a few months. The war is ending, and we need you to help the Red Army finish its work."

"I do not have a network, nor the ability to radio a message Moscow. I am not sure I can assist."

"The German operational map your team discovered in Ilzha is proving to be valid. We have others reporting that the Germans, when they leave, will blow Krakow to kingdom come, and then flood the roads by blowing up the dam, too. Bravo, we need you to focus on Krakow. Continue with reconnaissance of the city with the team members who remain. The river and key areas. Determine what the Germans will do next and how they want to destroy the city. It is important to Stalin and Moscow to keep this city intact."

Beria took the vodka bottle from the table and took two swigs before handing it to him. Bravo took the bottle and held it in his hand as Beria spoke.

"Bravo, Mother Russia needs you to save Krakow."

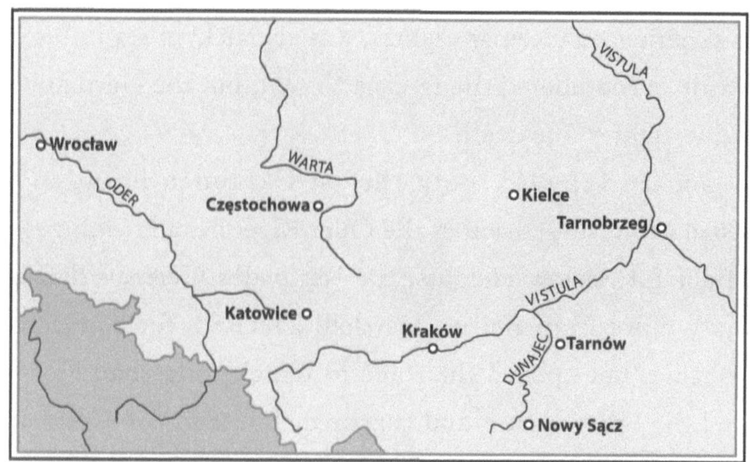

Historical Note: The Race to Berlin and Krakow, 1945

Marshalls Konev and Zhukov had clear guidance from Stalin. They were to smash the fascists along the Vistula and then race to the Oder River to prepare for the last march to Berlin. En route to Berlin, Zhukov was to capture Warsaw, Radom, Lodz, and Poznan. Konev was to drive through the southern part of the front toward Berlin and capture Kielce, Czestochowa, Krakow, and Katowice. His route was less direct to Berlin but important to the success of this overall operation.

These were difficult assignments for the Soviet battle commanders. Feldmarshal Ferdinand Schorner of the German Army Group Centre was defending the area Marshall Konev was to retake. Although many resources had been diverted to support the Ardennes Operation, Schorner still had twenty-two divisions—about 400 thousand men—spread from Krakow to Lodz and from the Eastern Front to Glogou and Liegnitz. The 17th Army was the main fighting force, fierce warriors known for their brutal efficiency on the battlefield.

Marshall Zhukov would face Army Group Vistula led by Colonel General Heinrici with twenty-three divisions supporting the efforts led by the 9th Army and 4th Panzer Division. The Henrici Army in the south and on the border of Moravia and Slovakia, led by General Rokossovsky, another experienced German fighter, was also held in readiness. The Red Army vastly outnumbered the fascists 15 to 1, but the Germans were determined to fight to the death.

On January 12, 1945, both the 1st Ukrainian Front and the 1st Belorussian Front surged across the Oder River near Tarnobrzeg, Poland. In the fight for Seelow Heights, the last major German defensive line about sixty miles from Berlin, Marshall Zhukov's forces faced tremendous casualties but opened the route to the city. Marshall Konev's forces cleared the Spree Forest and captured thousands of German prisoners. Both armies met in the German capital after Zhukov entered from the north and Konev from the south, embarking on a street battle with German forces. German losses during the battle of Berlin were about 150 thousand casualties with the Soviets suffering 80 thousand. Historians credit General Zhukov with the official capture of Berlin and receiving the surrender from the Germans while Marshall Konev's army diverted south to meet American forces on the Elbe River. According to many historians, Marshall Konev's advance and occupation of Krakow spared it from destruction. As a Warsaw Pact member, Poland erected a statue of Marshall Konev in Krakow in the late 1980s, but then took it down and transported it to Russia in 1991, also revoking the Soviet general's title of honorary citizen of Krakow.

The People's Commissariat for Internal Affairs (NKVD) carried out many missions of sabotage against the Nazis throughout the war. The organization also was responsible for the 1940-41 mass arrests, deportations, and executions including the mass slaughter of tens of thousands of Polish prisoners from 1940 to 1941 in Katyn, Russia, many were Polish army officers whose loyalty to the Soviet Union was in doubt. The NKVD was disbanded in 1946 and replaced by the Committee for State Security (KGB) in the 1950s. In 1953, Lavrentiy Beria was arrested in Moscow, just several weeks after being on the front cover of Time magazine. Beria was tried in a special court for crimes committed during The Great Patriotic War. He was convicted and executed immediately after the trial.

The German Third Reich surrendered in the early morning on May 7, 1945, at SHAEF headquarters, Rheims, France. General Alfred Jodl, the German Chief of Staff of the German Army signed documents surrendering to each of the European allies: Great Britain, Russia, and France. On April 30th before the historic surrender, the German dictator, Adolph Hitler, had committed suicide in the *Führerbunker* in Berlin. Hitler's wife of one day, Eva Braun, committed suicide the day after her husband, ingesting cyanide. US Army Intelligence Officer Walter Stein arrested the defrocked Governor-General of Poland, Hans Frank, on May 4, 1945, ending his sort of royalty and party tour of the German elites. Frank was tried at Nuremberg and hanged on October 6, 1946, convicted of the murder of hundreds of thousands of Polish civilians and Jews.

CHAPTER NINETEEN

SAVING KRAKOW

January 1945, Banks of Vistula River, Krakow, Poland

This mensch is an arschloch, thought Major Sigmund Ogarek, a cartographer assigned to the Wehrmacht Engineer Battalion 81 and assigned to survey the dams, bridges, and other key military structures in Krakow to support the *Plan Ost.*

They had assigned him to work with Stabsunteroffizier Kurt Peckel. Both engineers were Czech nationals. Though both Ogarek and Peckel were both from the Sudetenland, what they had in common ended there. Ogarek had achieved the rank of captain in World War I and then attended the Prague War School, training as a military engineer before rejoining the Czech Army in that capacity. He was then forced into the Wehrmacht in 1939. He approached his life and work with precision, a skill learned from decades of building and analyzing structures like bridges and roadways.

Peckel had enlisted in the Czech Army in 1932 as an infantry soldier and later reclassified as an engineer and cartographer. He liked the idea of building bridges and thought he might return to Czechoslovakia after the war to work as a building construction contractor.

Ogarek had been growing impatient with the younger man because Peckel was often late meeting him, always complained about being hungry, and usually smelled like beer no matter the time of day. Peckel always seemed to have a bottle of his hometown brew, Pilsner Urquell, in his hand immediately after the engineering team had completed its last task for the day.

Ogarek patiently waited while Sergeant Peckel fell far behind on the path to their first point near the Vistula River, just south of Krakow. In a meeting in December, the Engineer Battalion 81 Oberleutnant had tasked Major Ogarek with a special project. The head engineer was getting pressure from the General Government Administration to complete the mission quickly, a simple job confirming the map grid location of key military locations like bridges, dams, and roads in Krakow and the surrounding areas. Many of the existing maps dated from World War 1 and prior, but most were useless, hence the assignment to update them.

"*Mach schnell!*" Major Ogarek bellowed to Peckel. *Faster!*

"I'm coming. It is difficult carrying this equipment," Peckel said.

"Just move it along. We have over twenty locations to visit today."

Both men were wearing the gray-green Wehrmacht uniform and wool topcoat. The wind was whipping off the Vistula River and made conditions cold for any work outside. Peckel was carrying a 1937 model Rolleiflex camera and a heavy tripod that stabilized the camera for clearer photographs, most times. He also carried a khaki-colored map case with several maps of the area. Major Ogarek was carrying a similar map case stuffed with maps.

Major Ogarek peered through a pair of binoculars as he waited for his noncommissioned officer to catch up to their first location. As Peckel approached, he commented, "We are alone on most days and rarely see anyone for hours. However, it feels like we are often not alone. That we are being watched."

"You are a *dummkopf*," Orgarek sputtered. "You just create excuses to keep from working."

"*Nein, mein Herr.* I just work at a different pace from you. I also keep up my end of the mission by carrying the camera."

"I will carry the camera," Ogarek offered, "if it makes you move faster."

"Sometimes, I look up," Peckel continued, "and I feel like someone is watching us. But when I look more closely, they are gone."

"Now you are seeing ghosts. You are baffling. Please set up the camera so we can get started."

Once the camera was in place, both engineers worked effectively together. Major Ogarek would establish the line of sight and write the latitude and longitude of the various locations. He would confirm the directional shots using a compass. Peckel would take the shots and move to the next location after Ogarek recorded the numbers in a log. They repeated this for each site and moved on. Ogarek would then decide on updating the World War 1 map once they got back into the office at headquarters.

At a meeting in December, Ogarek's commander had been tight-lipped about the finer details of the special project, particularly its purpose. The mission was just referred to as *Plan Ost*. After several weeks, the commander admitted that multiple engineer teams were contributing to a plan to destroy the city of Krakow in the event of a quick German retreat from the city, or worse yet, a Red Army invasion. Major Ogarek kept the information to himself and did not dare share it with his sergeant colleague. But all the soldiers, and not just the Germans, talk and gossip.

At their second assessment stop on the Vistula, Peckel began showing signs he knew the true aim of their work.

"*Herr Major,* why is it necessary for you and me to be out here every day in the cold?"

"Look, Sergeant, we have orders from the 81st Battalion Command. That is what we are going to do, follow their orders."

"It doesn't make sense to me. What's the point?"

"What do you mean?" Ogarek asked and looked directly at Peckel.

"You know, I have many contacts in the General Admi-nistration," Peckel remarked.

"You have been a member of the Wehrmacht for well over a decade so I would expect you would know a few people."

Peckel smiled at his mission commander. "Well, the motor pool master sergeant says that we are not the only team conducting assessments. He told me he has not only signed-out vehicles to engineers but also trucks to haul special cargo."

The Major stopped in his tracks and spun around quickly to ask, "What kind of cargo?"

"He says that units are hauling significant cargo to a destination south of Krakow. That it is explosives and munitions."

"What would they be doing with them?" Major Ogarek said, feigning ignorance.

"The master sergeant says that there is some sort of plan for the city. If the Army leaves or the Red Army invades, Hans Frank is going to blow it up? Or flood it?"

"That," the Major said, trying to sound nonchalant, "sounds outlandish to me."

"I think it's true." Peckel said. "We are confirming the location of bridges and dams and other key structures for the munitions transport units to mine them. The master sergeant says that they will blow the city to bits and then flood it so no one can use it when we leave. My cousin stationed in Warsaw says that there, they razed the city and even burned down the Warsaw Castle."

"Well, that sounds like some story, Herr Peckel. If I were you, I would keep that information to myself. Everyone is on edge as the Red Army is closing in on Warsaw. We should just focus on our work and following our orders. Let's leave the speculation and strategy to the commanders."

"It's true. I can feel it. Frank or Himmler or whomever is in charge now will blow this city into the sky. In the Führer's name. I believe it as sure as I feel like we are not alone. I swear to Saint Wenceslaus on this one."

"Now you are swearing on a Christmas carol. You are a *dummkopf.* Look around. We are the only one's stupid enough to be working on the Vistula River as winter roars into Poland. Let's finish our work so we can get back to the barracks for dinner. And get you a beer."

"*Jawohl,* Herr Major." Peckel said mockingly.

The engineers continued to work their way along the river taking photographs of bridges and mapping notes. Peckel's insistent talking, and slow pace, consumed most of the workday and slowed their progress. The sun had set by the time they were finished.

"Well, Herr Peckel, I think we have done our work today. We should catch one of the transport vehicles back to the barracks."

"*Alles klar, Herr Major,*" Peckel said but refrained from the salute.

The engineers continued walking west on the river toward a staircase that led back to the pick-up area. Ahead, they both spotted a Gorky GAZ-AA civilian vehicle with its front hood up. A German officer dressed in full uniform and gray wool coat was under the hood of the truck and was earnestly pulling on wires.

As the engineers approached the vehicle, Peckel shouted out to the Wehrmacht officer.

"*Guten Abend, mein Herr.* Do you need some help?"

The officer waved his hand but kept looking under the hood.

As the engineers arrived at the vehicle, Peckel again spoke to the officer.

"Excuse me, *mein Herr.* Do you need some help? I am good with engines and can assist. We would just ask for a ride back to the barracks."

The Wehrmacht officer turned around and said, "*Jawohl*" with a slight Russian accent.

At that point, both Peckel and Ogarek heard the click of a pistol hammer and then felt the cold steel of a barrel against the back of their heads. One of the gun handlers spoke, again in Russian-accented German.

"*Guten Abend, meine Herren.* We have been waiting for you. We would like to speak to you. You will come with us." A gentle tap with the butt of the gun, and both men fell to the ground.

Major Ogarek came to, squirming in a wooden chair. His legs were bound to the lower legs and his arms tied to the back. He was disoriented after losing track of time. In the room, he was alone and uncertain if it was day or night. He heard a door opening, closing, and someone opened the blinds then took a seat in front of him. It took a moment for his eyes to adjust to the light. He observed he was sitting in a small room with wooden walls. There was one lightbulb hanging from the ceiling, and the only furniture was two wooden chairs. He didn't know it, but he was in Pradnik Bialy District of Krakow, in a partisan safe house off the main streets. The man who sat in front of him was clean-shaven, wearing the dark pants, scuffed boots, and a dark cotton peasant shirt, a working man. He was smoking a pipe. A small circle of smoke surrounded Ogarek's head, and he could smell the powerful odor of lit tobacco. The man sitting in the opposite chair held Major Ogarek's *Weisspass*, his military identification, and appeared to be studying it. Still more silence.

The man spoke. "*Guten Morgen, Herr Major.*"

Is it already morning? Have I been tied up and sitting here all night? Where is Peckel? Ogarek thought.

"An engineer major working on the Vistula," the man said in perfect German but still with a slight Russian accent. "Why do you suppose the Wehrmacht would update maps? You have been here since 1939. Why would the Wehrmacht care about the location of a dam? Especially if you are leaving."

Unsure of exactly who he was speaking to, Ogarek fell back on the training he'd had in the military academy on what to do when captured by the enemy.

"My name is Major Sigmund Ogarek, a member of the Wehrmacht Engineer Corps. I would like to know the location of my soldier, Sergeant Peckel."

"Major, thank you for confirming your identification."

The man reached into his pocket and produced a knife. Ogarek's eyes widened as he observed the knife. The man leaned down and cut the cords which secured the German officer's legs. He then moved behind Ogarek's chair and cut the cords which secured his hands.

"There. That should be better for you now. Should allow us to have a pleasant conversation. And yes, your colleague is doing fine. He is a talker, but not as smart as you, a professional military officer. He has similar accommodations to you and is close by."

As the man leaned forward in his chair, he again spoke. "Please tell me what you were doing on the Vistula River."

"My name is Major Ogarek, a member of the Wehrmacht Engineer Corps."

"Am I to believe that a major in the Wehrmacht, a field grade officer of the Engineer Corps, does not know his mission?"

"We were following our orders. The battalion commander advised us to confirm maps and update where needed." Ogarek leaned back in his chair, satisfied with his answer.

"Major, let me start again. My name is Sergei. I am also a major. In my job, I am privy to many high-level conversations and information. I know you are also."

"You are a major? A major in the Red Army? The NKVD? Where is your uniform?"

"I consider myself more of a partisan than any of those other things."

"Wait, you are Sergei? Sergei's Partisans? We were briefed about you. He drew back in horror, his mouth opening and closing. *"Ach, mein Gott,"* Ogarek cried. "I am going to be killed by a partisan, and the war for Germany is almost over."

"We really are not here to kill or even hurt you. If everyone cooperates. Provides reasonable information to our satisfaction. We may allow you to go free. Of course, this will all depend on your cooperation."

"Where would you put me? In the Silesian House?"

"No, *mein Herr.* The Red Army will be in Krakow within days. And we have much worse places to keep you until the war is over."

"I have told you my knowledge of the situation. That is all I can offer."

"Major Ogarek, I have been in this city for months and have seen preparations. We have first-hand knowledge of the Wehrmacht's plans to destroy the city on evacuation. Just like they did in Warsaw."

"Well, you have been here for months, so you have observed the activity. While many might believe plans are underway to depart, others are not so sure. Germany might defend its position in Krakow and other outposts in the Eastern Europe. To the last man." He added bitterly.

"Major, the end is inevitable. We are told that Hitler has taken cover in a bunker and that no one sees him. Your Krakow emperor, Governor-General Frank, is no longer trusted by the Third Reich, and he is also making plans to leave his Wawel Castle before the Wehrmacht departs. I appeal to you as one Soviet independent statesman to another. I am from Belarus, and my country has seen its share of damage. You are a Czech, right? How would you feel if they destroyed Prague? The allies dropped bombs on German targets in your city but imagine if they burned it to the ground like Warsaw."

"I do not relish the thought of Prague being destroyed."

"So? What do you know?"

As Major Ogarek spoke, another partisan came into the interrogation room. He whispered something in Sergei's ear, which brought a smile to his face. The partisan left the room, and Sergei leaned forward in his chair, inching closer to Major Ogarek.

"I think our conversation is now changing," Sergei said. "It is now less about saving Krakow and more about your freedom. Sergeant Peckel has plenty to say about the plan. We can have you placed in a Russian prisoner of war camp until the war ends. Of course, we do not release prisoners immediately, and we could have you detained for many months, years…."

Major Ogarek squirmed in his chair at the thought of wasting away in a Red Army prison of war camp. As he continued to ponder, the young partisan came back into the interrogation room. He handed a set of handcuffs to Sergei.

"Okay, stand up." Sergei said. "If you do not want to cooperate, we will stop speaking with you." Sergei said. "My friend will get you ready for your truck ride. I hope you like the cold."

Major Ogarek stood up and blustered. "Please, please," he said.

"You may be killed if you do not cooperate with us."

"But I didn't tell that stupid Sergeant anything about the plan or the main storage area in Nowy Sanz."

Sergei's eyebrows rose as Ogarek spoke. "Tell me more about Nowy Sacz."

The major paused for a moment and squirmed in the chair again. He said nothing.

"Your Sergeant has already told us the plan. We just want you to confirm a few details." As Sergei spoke, another partisan entered the room. He brought the maps that Ogarek and Peckel had in their possession when they were captured. The partisan unrolled two of the larger maps and laid them on a table.

"Well?" He asked.

"We are under much pressure," Ogarek began, "to get the key locations surveyed as the Red Army is advancing so quickly. I am required each day to report back to HQ after completing a sector."

Sergei stood up and leaned uncomfortably close to Ogarek. "You are avoiding the issue, and I have run out of patience." Sergei shouted something in Russian and two partisans came back into the interrogation room with leg and arm shackles and put them on Ogarek.

"Please, please, don't do this."

"Then cooperate!" Sergei shouted.

Ogarek looked at the ground and did not speak for a minute and then raised his head and looked at Sergei.

"Dams" he said.

"I beg your pardon?" Sergei asked.

"We are surveying the locations of dams and other key military or historical areas. Frank has ordered us to follow the same plan as Warsaw but, instead of burning most of the city, we will blow up several key dams and bridges surrounding the city. The High Command refuses to leave anything intact for the Red Army to use after their invasion."

"Go on."

"The plan is to flood the city using the might of its surrounding rivers, which will destroy the buildings and drown the people of Krakow. It will of course also slow your advance."

"You have done very well, Herr Major. Which dams are the targets for the attack? Can you show me on the map?"

Major Ogarek stood up slowly and plodded to the map table.

"May I use your pencil?" Ogarek asked. Sergei handed him the pencil, and Ogarek pointed to the main areas on the map while he spoke.

"I'm sure Peckel explained this to you, but the main effort is to blow up the dams at Roznow, Czchow, and Czorstyn. The German engineers speculate that the reserves in these reservoirs would crash down on the outskirts of the city and push water into other secondary rivers, streams, and the Vistula, causing the inundation and subsequent demise of Krakow, the city being on the lowest land."

"Is that all?"

"Himmler has ordered destruction, with even now mines and loads of explosives placed throughout, of the Main Market area, Rynek Glowny."

"What would be the purpose of destroying the old city and market?" The partisan asked.

"It's symbolic, not just the Rynek Glowny market area but also the historic buildings. St Mary's Cathedral, the Barbican Fortress, Town Hall Tower."

Sergei nodded his head and looked more closely at the map as Ogarek made a large circle around the targets.

"Anyone who is brave enough to stay in these areas will die."

"When will the explosives be set off?"

"The fire storm will begin when the Red Army is as close as fifteen miles from the city and scouting units are entering the area. Explosives are already being moved to their targets now. As the Red Army approaches Krakow, someone will give the first destruction order."

"So where are the munitions currently? How close to Krakow?"

Ogarek paused before he spoke again. "We guard them in a fortress. With two battalions providing security. It would be impossible to penetrate the security and even get access to the storage areas."

Ogarek began to shake and rub his forehead, then continued. "The explosives are being stored and prepared at Jagellonian Castle."

To the surprise of Sergei and the two partisans in the interrogation room, Major Ogarek walked back to the map table and circled the location of the castle.

"The end of Krakow is near. There are also thousands of munitions stored in a castle in Nowy Sacz, about forty miles from here. We will use these as well to destroy the city."

CHAPTER TWENTY

THE BEGINNING OF THE END

January 3, 1945, Wawel Castle, Krakow, Poland

Sitting alone at the large conference table in the parliament hall and looking out the window, Hans Frank wondered where it had all gone wrong. It was mid-January, but there was nothing optimistic about the turning of the calendar to a new year. Although cold outside, the day was sunny and there was much activity throughout the city, mostly General Government occupiers moving about. He felt old and depressed as he watched the city and the Vistula River through the large windows of the room. He thought, *What happened? I was a loyal servant. I did exactly what the party wanted. I ensured that the Master Race would reign supreme. We handled the Jewish problem as instructed everywhere I served.*

Hans Frank took a sip of schnapps from a small china glass. Drinking in the day was unusual for him, but he felt like it was necessary today. A tall aide stood outside of the parliament hall and could hear Frank speaking out loud but to no one in particular.

"And I spoke to Hitler and Himmler several times over the last few days. Why would they ever say that the Führer calls me a puppet? A stooge? They both asked my opinion on how to slow the Soviet invasion while we continued to engage the allies in the Ardennes. I will sit here in the castle, like a paladin. I will do my best to be the leader the Führer expects and keep people calm. I will model my self-control and composure for the rest of the General Government leadership. I will stay strong and lead the administration until the very end. Deutschland will survive. *Deutschland uber alles!*"

The aide approached the doorway to the hall. He appeared hesitant to interrupt the Governor-General but desperately needed to deliver a message.

As Frank took another sip of his schnapps, he heard the aide clear his throat.

"What?" Frank shouted at the aide without looking.

"*Mein Herr,* please excuse my interruption. But I have an important report from Berlin Intelligence."

"What is it? Frank barked,

"Berlin is advising all the Government Administration offices that the Red Army has quickened its pace and is working its way faster than expected toward Berlin. Also, it was specifically noted that Marshall Konev's forces are within thirty miles of Krakow. Berlin is ordering that all General Government Administration centers begin the steps to withdraw."

"Withdraw? Poland is a state within the Third Reich. It is our destiny. Why would we ever surrender or leave our home?"

"Sir, the report came through as an order. I am sorry to be the one to present it. Berlin is ordering us to finish destruction plans for Krakow and to have all German forces and equipment return to Germany and be available should the Red Army attack the country."

Scheisse, Frank thought. *Remain strong. Be calm. We will repel the communist hordes.*

"Have word sent to Nowy Sacz Castle to expedite the plan as discussed. Finish mining bridges and dams. Put the defense units on alert to be ready at a moment's notice as the Red Army approaches."

"Yes, Governor-General."

"Inform the commander that any order to destroy Krakow or surrender our position will come from me. No departure will occur without my approval. And I will be the last to leave the city."

"Yes, Governor-General. I will convey the message."

January 4th, 1945, Las Chelmiec Forest, Northern Outskirts of Nowy Sacz

Nowy Sacz was a much-besieged city in southern Poland. During the German occupation, the city was called Neu Sandez. The Russians, who had occupied the city during World War 1, called it Nowy Sacz. During the World War 2 invasion of Poland, Nazi troops conducted air raids and then occupied the city in September 1939, with Nowy Sacz becoming a part of the General Government administration. They established the city's Jewish ghetto near the Nowy Sacz Castle, emptying that ghetto in 1942 and sending its Jews to the Belzec extermination camp.

In the present war, the Nowy Sacz Castle held great military importance to the German military and the Krakow General Government administration. For one, on an elevated slope within its walls King Casimir had built the smaller Jagiellonian Castle in the mid-1300s.

For several days after the interrogation of the Czech engineers, the Sergei partisans had the castle under constant surveillance. They had established a rudimentary forward operating base in the Las Chelmiec Forest, approximately three miles from the center of Nowy Sacz. The partisan reconnaissance teams conducted patrols on the perimeter of the village, venturing into town in peasants' clothing, and, with the help of Major Ogarek, German officer and enlisted uniforms.

The partisans used German uniforms to move more freely in the village and to get close to the Castle. The teams provided robust reports on the increased activities in the castle and the village around the clock.

Major Bravo sat at a small fire in a hidden area of Chelmiec Forest. He wore a thick brown wool jacket to protect himself from the strong winds gusting through the trees. Behind him stood a partisan dressed in a German officer's uniform. Sergei sensed he wasn't alone and looked over his shoulder to identify the visitor.

"Partisan Aron, good morning!" he said in greeting.

"Comrade, we have an urgent report for you about the castle."

"Please sit down, Aron." Sergei directed.

Aron sat down on a log next to the small fire. There was sweat on his forehead, even on this cold, windy day in the forest. He opened his German officer jacket to cool down.

"The village and around the castle, it is like a beehive there, so much coming and going, much, much more than usual."

Sergei took a sip from a metal cup and nodded for the man to continue. As Aron spoke, Sergei took a small bottle of vodka out of his pocket and presented it to him with a shrug. Aron snatched the bottle and took a quick swig, followed by a cough.

Still coughing, Aron continued his report. In addition to the activity in the village of Nowy Sacz itself, the partisans had noticed that German units were moving at an increased pace, conducting patrols, and setting up checkpoints in various areas. They also observed that there were more soldiers stationed at the castle, leading them to believe that it held great importance.

Recognizing this, Sergei desperately needed more details. He sent out his most skilled reconnaissance team to gather intelligence, concentrating on the castle and its surroundings. The team returned with detailed reports and maps of the area, including escape routes. The civilian populace seemed nervous about the impending Red Army invasion, which had helped partisan teams. The native Poles seemed more willing to work for the partisans and provide information about the fascists' intentions.

"Anyone who might work inside, have direct knowledge of the castle operations?" Sergei asked.

"No, though there are a few potential sources who leave the work site, not that we have that much time to recruit them to spy for us."

"What makes you think they would betray the Germans to help the Red Army succeed?" Sergei inquired.

"Everyone has overheard the Germans soldiers talk—at the bar, at the brothels, even outside the church. Talking of what could happen after the war. If they lose. About their actions during the war."

"Hell, Aron, I've done some things I regret. War is terrible. I've seen too much bloodshed. It has made me grow old."

"Yes, Sergei. Your battles are now infamous, especially to the new partisans. The Carpathian Mountain adventures have become folklore. But we never butchered innocent civilians. How many million Jews did they kill? I too am tired of war and look forward to the end."

"The closer Marshall Konev gets to Krakow, the older I feel. I hope the end is near. So, who are these potential recruits?" Sergei asked.

"The few we have mentioned often go to the bar and talk about their concerns or go to the cathedral to pray."

"A German in a Catholic church?" Sergei said as he raised his eyebrows.

"Yes, he goes often. Sometimes twice a day. He works in the castle but goes down to the village for mass and sometimes to pray on his own. He may be a Polish conscript forced to wear the Nazi uniform. We're trying to figure out how best to approach him. I have not been to church in a while. But you wore out your rosary beads." Aron said as he smiled.

Sergei reached into his pocket and pulled the worn religious beads from his pocket. "You are correct, my friend." Both partisans laughed.

"Back to business. Tell me your understanding of who's in charge of defending the castle? The city?" Sergei asked.

"Just outside the city is General Schulz's 17th Army and the 1st Panzer Army led by General Heinrici. The 1017th Security Battalion, the 601st Special Division, and elements of the 320th and 545th Volkgrenadier Divisions are inside, along with Special Police and counterintelligence units working with the ground units. The 1017th is guarding the city center, and the 601st has primary responsibility for security of the castle compound."

"Sapper units? Do they still plan to blast the dams and flood the city if the Red Army gets closer?"

"Yes. The Krauts call it Operation Wenus or Operation Merkury, depending on whether it is Krakow or Nowy Sacz involved."

"Aron, this is helpful. Please report to Moscow. I will meet with Partisan Srebrny, a member of the local arm of Armia Krajowa partisans. We are going to thwart the destruction of the city if it kills us."

"We are working with the underground on this? This could be the last one. Either we will be dead, or the war will be over."

"Yes, Moscow is asking for greater cooperation between all partisan groups. A show of unity as we all drive the fascists out of our countries."

Srebrny was a tested warrior who had served as a regular noncommissioned officer with the 1st Fire Service before going clandestine. He was now a battle-hardened scout and intelligence officer with years of military service and training. He also had strong ties to the Nowy Sacz community and relatives living near Rynek Street and City Hall. Srebrny was committed to keeping his city and Krakow safe and to the destruction of the occupying German force.

"What?" Aron asked, doubt in his voice. "How can Srebrny and his partisans help us? Why do we need them?"

"He is a local, from Nowy Sacz. He has detailed sketches of the German fortifications around the city and knows the interior of the castle."

"That would be helpful," Aron said softly, chastened.

"He can also help us get the hell out of here once the fireworks begin. I know we don't have the best relationship with the underground, but we should try to trust him. Also, Moscow is ordering that we work together on this mission."

"I understand." Aron conceded. "We will wait for the results of your meeting."

January 5, 1945, Stary Kleparz, Krakow, Poland

Sergei stepped into the Stary Kleparz, the oldest market in Krakow, once a sea of stalls bursting with the best Polish food, fresh vegetables, fruits, flowers, clothing, and specialties from around the world. The war years had much diminished it, though he saw some fresh baked goods and seasonal vegetables besides household goods on a small scale in the handful of stalls still open.

Sergei's eyes picked out a slight man of thirty-four years with a high forehead, a thin mustache and wide eyes standing near a bench in the market. A copy of a *Dziennik Polski* newspaper sat on the bench, next to a bag with a few onions. Sergei had arrived over an hour early for his meeting with members of his team to observe. Then, at the agreed upon time, he had re-entered the marketplace and approached Srebrny. Both men stood in silence for several moments until Sergei spoke.

"It's cold today, but people are not afraid to come to the market to see what they can find. That there are any fresh fruit and vegetables here in Krakow during wartime is beyond me." Sergei said in Polish.

Srebrny looked up and responded to the coded comment. "I'm not afraid to come to the market. You just need to dress warmly."

"Nice to meet you, Srebrny."

"And you, Sergei. Your reputation precedes you."

"As does yours, Srebrny. We welcome the opportunity to work with you. I think we can both benefit from the relationship."

"I agree, Sergei. We have had trouble working with other partisan groups in the past." He shrugged. "Some of my men know you from the Carpathian Mountains and claim that you are as honest and loyal as they come."

Sergei nodded his head in agreement. "I'm told you know the Nowy Sacz area well and have friends and family there."

"Yes, it's true. I know the fields and the castle from playing with my young comrades. I also trained and patrolled the city early in the war. I can tell you what you need to know."

"Might I suggest," Sergei asked, "that we walk a bit to keep warm on this bitter cold day? We can still talk."

"Great idea, friend." Srebrny said as he stood up and linked his arm through Sergei's in a gesture of one old friend to another.

"You forgot your newspaper."

"Oh, yes. I am done with it, but you should take it." Srebrny said, handing it to Sergei with a small smile.

Both men walked in silence out of the market area and began walking into a small unoccupied park in the Planty district of the city.

Sergei began the conversation. "I am curious. Are your men seeing what we're seeing around the city?"

"If you mean explosives coming in daily by train before being shipped under guard to either Nowy Sacz Castle or a warehouse in a former concrete plant on Dlugosza Street, then yes. German sapper teams deliver and emplace the munitions.

There's been a change, however, over the past few days. In the place of explosives, we have seen multiple shipments by train and trucks of Panzerfausts which are then delivered directly to Germans troops defending fortifications on the Dunajec-Popgrad line."

"Manual launchers? Tank killers?"

"Yes. The Germans still seem resolved to defend this last bit of land and kill the very last fighter—even if they are unsure of who that might be."

"Who is in charge?" Sergei laughed. "We hear that Governor-General Frank is vowing to stay to the end. We have also received intelligence from Moscow that Hitler is in a bunker, and Himmler is leading the defense of Berlin. So, given that chaos, it would help to know where all the explosives have been planted. We have a few locations, but our list is far from complete."

"My friend, look at the local section of the newspaper. You may find some good articles." Srebrny said drily.

Sergei looked puzzled but opened the paper to find a hand-drawn sketch of Krakow detailing bomb emplacements with many locations highlighted.

Sergei looked at the map with astonishment. "How did you get this information? This is pure gold."

"We have our own sources, too. You'll see bridges and major dams and then historical monuments. Confirmed locations have a square around them, and we circled what we think are potential locations they haven't gotten to yet."

"Looks like the Germans are falling behind schedule."

"This is true," Srebrny observed, "but our sources tell us that the General Administration is threatening execution for failure to complete the missions on time. We expect everything will be in place within a week."

"A week? Marshall Konev will be in Krakow by then eating *paczki* while watching the German prisoners being transported on their way to Siberia."

"Possibly. The Germans seem resolved to either stand or blow the place to pieces."

"Do you believe it?" Sergei asked. "Will they be able to hold against Konev's troops?"

"I believe the Germans are evil and have destroyed my country. It's hard for me to tell what they are capable of. Especially when they are desperate and believe the end is near."

Sergei folded the paper and slid it under his arm as the men continued to walk at a slow pace in the park. "I am being pushed by Moscow to destroy the Nowy Sacz castle and its explosive store as well as to stop the sapper mission to destroy Krakow. I think we may have to attack head on, which is suicide."

Srebrny wrinkled his nose and shook his head. "A direct attack would be unsuccessful. Even if they are disorganized, the Krauts would surely defend against a head-on assault—and this castle is very well designed for defense. No, a direct attack would fail."

"*Tak...?*" Well?

"We have people inside who can help you understand the layout of the castle." Srebrny said. "Perhaps there is another way in."

"Can you set up a meeting with them tomorrow? We need to move quickly." Sergei said.

"Of course. They will be available when you are."

"My next question," Sergei said, "is who does what on the mission itself? How should we divvy up the tasks?"

"I believe our underground teams should handle disabling the explosives already placed on monuments and dams." Srebrny began. "We know Nowy Sacz and the areas surrounding Krakow. We would look to your partisans to destroy the castle. Your men have more experience with handling and directing collaborators and, of course, with guerilla operations."

"From your mouth to God's ear, Srebrny. All that sounds good." He began to walk away and then stopped and turned. "Set up the meeting with your boys. We are running out of time."

January 6, 1945, Saint Malgorzata Church, Nowy Sacz, Poland

A decree by Cardinal Zbigniew Olesnicki, the reigning Archbishop of Krakow, created the Saint Malgorzata Church in Nowy Sacz in October 1448. Olesnicki designed the church in the Gothic style, featuring flying exterior buttresses, ribbed vaults, spires, and long pointed arches.

Just about 500 years later, when Edward Skornog, a lifelong resident of Nowy Sacz, walked into the cathedral of Saint Malgorzata, his stomach was churning, and he paid little attention to the sculpted stone and gilt-framed icons. He frequently visited the church throughout the week, sometimes on break from his job at the castle and sometimes on his way home from work. He also attended mass each week. Edward was a slight boy of seventeen, who many described as earnest and willing to please. He idolized his brother-in-law, Tadeusz, who he'd known even before Tadeusz married his sister. Although he really wanted to be a soldier, he currently worked as a kitchen helper for the Germans in the castle. It was a pretty good job, even for wartime. The German sergeant who ran the dining hall at the castle, because he was an ethnic Pole, was very good to Edward. The Sergeant often treated him like a son and frequently gave him food from the kitchen, which would otherwise go to waste, to take home to his family. Edward also was learning the craft of running a kitchen, something he thought about pursuing in the Polish Army once the war was over. He was the envy of his friends and many of his family members, as he often ate the same meals as those served to the Nowy Sacz garrison officers.

Another bonus of the job was that his best friend, Witold Mlyniec, also worked as a driver, fetching the groceries and supplies for the castle's kitchen from downtown depots and freight yards. Not only did Edward work closely with his boyhood friend, but the job also gave Witold free use of a delivery vehicle and clearance to drive to the railway station, stores, and the central market in the town to buy necessary items. At eighteen,

Witold was a little older than Edward, a little taller than Edward, but still had a youthful angelic face and positive attitude, even for an employee of the occupying army. The supply staff also treated Witold well, as he was dependable and easy to work with. Both boys enjoyed the trust of the castle staff and were given free movement around the facilities for their work.

As Edward walked into the main part of the church's sanctuary, he felt a chill run through his body. The church was empty except for a German officer who was praying the rosary on the left side of the aisle. It was not unusual to see German Catholics in the church praying. It was less usual to see a German officer praying alone. Edward was to meet someone in the church and had been told the contact would approach him. Would the contact come forward if other visitors were in the church?

Edward went to the right side of the church near the front and kneeled in one pew and prayed, unsure of what else he could do. After several moments the German officer stood up, went to the rack of devotional candles, lit one of them, said a quick prayer, and performed the sign of the cross. Edward became nervous as the officer walked toward the front of the church, kneeled, and then walked toward Edward's pew. Edward breathed heavily as the officer slid down the pew and knelt about three feet away from him.

"Edward," the officer said, "thank you for coming here today." The boy was visibly nervous and just looked at the officer.

"If anyone comes into the cathedral while we are here, just say 'amen', make the sign of the cross and leave. We will meet up later." Edward shook his head, still confused.

"Srebrny sent you to me. I am Sergei. I understand they call you Silver."

"It is more of a joke," Edward said with a laugh. "I think it is because I am valuable."

"We will refer to you as Silver now when we meet. You will call me Sergei." Edward nodded his head.

The day before, Srebrny—known to his family as Tadeusz and Edward's brother-in-law—had asked the boy to meet him at Bar Hanka on ul. Grodzka. Srebrny worked as a server in the evenings and wanted Edward to come at closing time so he could speak to him about some important matters. Edward walked into the empty bar around 11 pm. There were two older, very drunk German low-rank officers sitting at a table near the front door drinking ale, about ten empty bottles of which were lined up on the table in front of them. The room, with its dozen scarred tables and long wooden bar against one wall, was filled with smoke and darkly lit. It was a popular after-shift watering hole for German officers and Senior Noncommissioned Officers. The alcohol was always flowing, and the small kitchen offered a short menu of sausages and potatoes to help soak up the copious alcohol consumed by the senior staff.

Two barmaids, Emelia Dobrowolska and Agata Klostermajer, were stacking chairs and tending to other closing time tasks. Emelia was a young woman with bright blonde hair pulled back into a messy ponytail. She wore a fitted black shirt and tight skirt, her curves emphasized by the clothing. Her face was tired but friendly, her eyes shining with exhaustion and the afterglow of a busy night. Agata was a sturdy woman with short, curly brown hair and a round, friendly face. Her apron was covered in stains from a night of working as a barmaid. She wore a simple dress with a floral pattern, the fabric wrinkled from hours of serving drinks.

Edward raised his eyebrows at the two women working in the room's corner. "Leave them alone. They work for me. And they are too good for you." Both men laughed.

Per Srebrny's instructions, Edward wore plain clothing and had a hat pulled down over his head to cover most of his angelic face. Srebrny immediately greeted Edward, who was excited and curious about why his brother-in-law wanted to meet him at this hour in this place. Tadeusz was famous in town for his bravery and natural knack for languages. He spoke several, including Polish, German, and Russian. In 1939, Tadeusz had been an infantry soldier in the 21st Mountain Rifle Division based out of Bielsko-Biala and then later a noncommissioned officer for the 1st Fire Service in Nowy Sacz. And then, to the family's surprise and horror, he disappeared for several years only to resurface in town working as a waiter in a *bierstube*, of all things. Many speculated he had joined the Polish underground, as an officer in the Peasant Battalion in the Home Army. Edward was never sure what to believe and only saw his sister's husband occasionally on holidays. The two never spoke about the war or Tadeusz's military experience. Just their love for skiing.

Tadeusz had immediately approached Edward as he walked into Bar Hanka. His face was more serious than Edward had noticed in the past as he led him into another a room after serving the Germans a platter of pints to consume as they sat, singing German beer hall songs, and complaining about their jobs. Tadeusz ushered Edward into another, more private, room and sat him at a small table. There was a bottle of vodka on the table with two glasses and a plate of pickled vegetables. Edward sat and looked at Tadeusz as he shut the door and sat in the other chair. Both sat quietly for a moment before Edward nervously broke the silence.

"Brother, how have you been? We have not seen you for a long time. Are you well?"

"I am. It was just better that I stayed away. It is safer for the family. For me."

"Are you in trouble? We hear you are doing well here at Hanka. Some officers say how good of a waiter you are. How they look forward to visiting the bar after their shifts."

"Do they know we are related? That I'm married to your sister?"

"They do not know our family ties. I have just overheard them mention you. My sister wishes you were home more but understands that sometimes you need to be alone. Did you rejoin the military?"

"Not exactly, Edward. I am involved now with the underground."

Edward blinked with surprise and leaned forward.

"I am an officer with the underground."

"Some of us suspected as much." Edward said.

"You were correct. I was also appointed local commander of the unit. We are now actively working in Nowy Sacz."

"Impressive, brother. I knew you were involved with something important. Everyone knew how good of a regular soldier you were." Edward said.

"I hate the Germans. I want them to leave our country. I'm not sure if I trust the Russians, either, but at least we agree the fascists pigs should be out of Poland. I fear what life would be like under Soviet rule. My father talked about how life was with the country as an independent state. It will surely change if the Soviets rule all of Poland."

"But it would be better than German rule?"

"Infinitely better, I think. However, rumors still persist about how the Soviets also liquidated so many of us at the beginning of the war. I'm still not sure it will be better. I wish our country could be left alone."

"I agree, brother." Edward paused, tapping the table nervously. "Why have you called me here?"

"Edward, how is work at the castle?"

"The Germans still treat me well. My sergeant is kind and gives me extra food for the family. The castle is, right now...very busy."

"Getting ready for Marshall Konev?"

"Even the newspapers are reporting on the rapid approach of the 1st Ukrainian Front toward the west. Most think they will be in Berlin by spring."

"I believe it. The Soviet Army and most of the eastern states are done with the war. Ready to go back to our old lives."

Tadeusz leaned forward and grabbed the vodka bottle. He filled both glasses and held his glass up in toast. "To Marshall Konev and a new Poland!"

Edward toasted Tadeusz and drank the contents of the glass. As the vodka was burning down the boy's throat, Tadeusz asked a question that would forever change Edward's life.

"Would you consider joining us?" Edward put the glass down and looked at Tadeusz in surprise.

"But you always said I was too young. That the military was serious business."

"It is serious. But this would be more like working in a specialized role with the underground. Like a partisan. With the partisans. For Poland… We could not share this information with anyone else. Even your sister."

"I understand. Would you consider Witold, also, my friend who works with me at the castle?"

"Yes, we are interested in both of you, but I don't want you to share this information with him just yet. Your role will be explained to you by a man named Sergei, the leader of a Ukrainian partisan group with connections to the highest levels in Moscow."

"But you said you didn't trust the Soviets."

"This one is different. He is Polish-Belarussian and speaks Polish as his native tongue. I think he can help Poland ensure the defeat of the fascists, especially as the end seems near."

"Do you trust him?"

"I trust him more than most officers of the Red Army. Throughout most of the war he fought as a partisan rather than a regular army soldier. He was also a noncommissioned officer fighting for Poland when the war started. He shot down several Jukes."

"He seems like a warrior." Edward said. "A warrior like you, brother."

"The question is, can we trust you?" Tadeusz inquired.

"I want to fight for Poland. I am ready to help kick the Germans out. What will you have me do?"

"Your first test is to meet with the partisan leader. Go meet Sergei."

The conversation between Edward and Sergei continued in the church. Edward asked Sergei why they had asked him to help.

"Well, Silver," Sergei said, using Edward's new codename, "you have access to the castle. They trust you and Witold. Your job at the castle allows you to access the sensitive areas and so you might potentially assist with an attack."

"An attack? I was just asked to join the underground. I have no military training."

"We will teach you. This is part of the test. We have little time," Sergei said, leaning forward and patting the boy playfully on the shoulder, "so you will take the final exams first."

"I am up for it." He nodded at the older man seriously. "I can be trusted and will happily work for you."

"You come highly recommended—by Srebrny. And you are not just working for me. You are working for Poland. What we need from you is your knowledge of the facilities in the castle complex. If you can't get a map, draw one yourself. We also need to know how many Krauts work in the different areas of the castle."

"Give me a day or two." Edward said.

"Two days, then. We'll meet here after the 8 am mass. Bring your maps and notes."

CHAPTER TWENTY-ONE

PANIC

January 6, 1945, Nowosadecki Townhall, Nowy Sacz, Poland

"When did he say he would arrive?" asked Herbert Huller, the General Government Commissioner of Nowy Sacz. Huller was a rotund, florid-faced man, about fifty-five years old, with a large bushy mustache. Standing next to him was the Mayor of Nowy Sacz, Reinhard Busch, a stark physical contrast as he was, at forty-two, rangy and gaunt, with a pencil-thin mustache. Busch shrugged his shoulders, signaling that he was also unsure of their guest's arrival. Both men paced back and forth on the front steps of the Nowosadecki Town Hall. Built around the turn of the century and surrounded by the city marketplace, its clock tower could be seen from everywhere in the city. While once its walls were hung with historical works based on the city's famous people and events, it was now the seat of the Nazi occupiers.

At last, with a screech of tires, a convoy of four black Mercedes Benz sedans pulled up in front of the building. A short man dressed in a gray uniform of the General Government stepped out of the largest sedan. He was wearing the distinct gray cap of a general. A cape floated down from his shoulders as he strode quickly toward the entrance to the building. A Wehrmacht General officer got out of the third vehicle quickly and fell in step behind the dignitary as he walked toward the building. A security detail of four SS soldiers raced to keep up with the two men.

Both Huller and Busch tensed as the small party walked closer to the steps. As they reached the top, Huller said, "Good Morning, Governor-General! Thank you for meeting us today."

"Let's get this over with." Hans Frank nearly spat the words as strode through the front door and walked directly to the conference room. Frank was already impatiently sitting at the conference room table by the time the rest of the official party caught up. Waffen General Wilhem Koppe appeared out of breath as he took a seat next to Governor-General Frank. In 1944, Koppe had been promoted to his current rank and taken over forcefully as Frank's right-hand man. It surprised Busch and Huller to see Waffen General Koppe in Nowy Sacz, he was rarely seen, though his actions were legend. General Koppe was infamous for his savage reprisals against the area's Poles and Jews in the region; an assassination attempt by the Polish underground in 1944 had left him with a permanent limp. After the attack, Koppe ordered the shooting of fifty Poles each day in punishment for the resistance. The presence of both Frank and Koppe at the town hall frightened Busch and Huller to the point of rendering them speechless.

Once the visiting detail had filed into the conference room and the SS security soldiers shut and took up positions guarding the door, Frank jumped right to the heart of the matter.

"Gentlemen," Frank began, "as reported, the Red Army is approaching Krakow and Nowy Sacz and expected to arrive within a few days. Marshall Konev is leading the attack, which we are urgently trying to slow or prevent altogether. We are confident that we can fight off the Red Army as long as we fight as fiercely as when we captured Poland in 1939." He looked around the table.

"We seek your help with as many men as possible to support the 1st Panzer Divisions as they defend the General Government Administration."

Both Busch and Huller spoke in unison, "We are at your disposal to assist."

"Good. We also need you to draft non-disabled men from your district into the Rural Guards to help prepare the city for field artillery and air raid bombings."

Both Busch and Huller nodded gravely as aides took furious notes. They hardly dared to look at each other, as Frank had ignored their opinions for years, and this was the first time he'd acknowledged their abilities.

Frank said, "We are ready to stop the attacks and drive the Russians back. But if the lines break, we need to evacuate key officials and residents. Huller, you will work with the 11th SS Corps and 1017th Security Battalion to handle this."

Huller's voice trembled as he asked the question, "How will we know when it's time?"

The response was chilling. "When the bombs are raining down on our streets, and we can see the enemy forces closing in. But by then, it may already be too late. You'll know when." A cold sweat broke out on Huller's brow, his heart pounding with dread at the ominous words.

"Aside from the increased defenses of the castle, we are preparing to repulse the Russians in another way. We have stored munitions in Nowy Sacz to be moved to key locations in Krakow and along major rivers." Frank said.

"Why?" Busch asked.

"If the Soviets advance, we'll destroy Krakow and flood the city to stop them. Blowing up all the bridges will also hinder their progress."

"Destroy Krakow?"

Frank's steely gaze fixed on both Huller and Busch; his jaw clenched tight with determination. "We have decided that we will not allow the Soviets to take Krakow under any circumstances. And make no mistake, we are prepared to take extreme measures should they come too close."

Busch and Huller sat in silence and looked at the ground. Huller then spoke, his voice shaking. "Governor-General, we stand ready."

Frank looked at both men. "Of course you are," he said, and then stood to go. Busch extended his hand, but Frank ignored it, striding briskly out of the ornate conference room.

General Koppe remained in the room after Frank had left and assured both regional leaders that they had the full support of his commanders and that both he and Frank would remain in Krakow until the end.

Busch asked, "What if you are not?"

"Well, then I guess you need to execute your plans to evacuate the city." Koppe said, and quickly left the room with the remaining security detail.

January 10, 1945, Chelmiec Forest, Northern Outskirts of Nowy Sacz, Poland

Over the preceding days, Sergei and Srebrny had had several meetings at various locations in the city. Parks worked well for short meetings, and Sergei, on a dare, had even met Srebrny as he finished his shift at Bar Hanka. Trust was still a big issue between the Soviet partisan and the Polish underground officer with Sergei, on Srebrny's home turf, being the one who needed to pay respect. One way was to bring Srebrny to his camp in the Chelmiec Forest. After protests from his lieutenants, Sergei and a small team drove a truck they had stolen several weeks before to downtown Nowy Sacz to meet Srebrny to take him back to their camp.

After the bread and salt and the ritual downing of a few shots of bad *samogon*, the homebrew vodka leaving them all gasping, it was on to nuts and bolts horse-trading of what each could do for the other—and in return for what.

"Look Sergei, I trust you on a professional level. I can tell that you are determined to defeat the Germans and make them flee Poland bloody and bruised. I will work with you and support you in this. However, my fighters won't be ready unless our needs are fulfilled as well, and in short order. The Red Army will come soon. The Germans will make a hasty retreat. We need basic supplies, provisions, weapons, ammunition, trucks. What we offer in exchange is continued access to our intelligence network and our support during the attack on the castle."

"Srebrny, I apologize if we have sometimes fallen short in our promises while asking much of you and your men. Of course, whatever we can get you even in these chaotic times, we will do our utmost to do."

"We need more weapons," Srebrny reiterated, "more rifles and ammunition as we continue to recruit more fighters to the underground. More every day as the Soviet Army gets closer to Krakow. We also need heavy machine guns and a few light machine guns to ensure our security and for the fight that is surely coming, and soon. As for an attack on the castle, for that we would also need TNT, mines, and detonators. That should do the trick."

"We'll attempt to get you all of that in the next day or so. As you say, time is running out. Some of our contacts north of Krakow have said that they have heard Soviet artillery fire about ten miles from the city."

The next day, Srebrny contacted Silver and Witold and set up a meeting in the forest. Both men, surprised, agreed to meet with him. Now all four men stood in front of a crude model of the castle and the surrounding terrain made of sticks and other material from the forest.

"Gentlemen, thank you for agreeing to meet with us," Sergei said.

"We didn't think we had a choice." Silver said as he nervously kicked a stick in the dirt.

"You always have a choice. You have special connections that we don't have. You have a level of trust with the Germans that would take us years to develop. We need you."

Both boys smiled at the thought of being needed by seasoned fighters like Sergei and Srebrny.

"We have little time. We need your full attention and cooperation to ensure the success of the mission." Sergei said as he stood next to the castle model. "What we discuss is sensitive and should not be shared outside of this group. Not with your family or even other fighters." Both boys nodded their heads with understanding.

"To prevent the advance of the Red Army, the Germans plan to destroy Krakow. You have seen increased activity at the castle since it is where they store the munitions shipped in from across Europe by truck and train.

The jaws of both boys dropped as they listened to Sergei's brief.

"What can we do? We are ready to help," the boys said.

"We believe most of the munitions are stored in the basement and warehouses throughout the castle compound." Sergei said as he pointed to the locations on the mock-up model with a long stick.

Silver said, "We knew that something important was happening. They sure got busy when the reports came that the Red Army was close to Krakow and Nowy Sacz. But we really had no idea of their intentions."

"The sketches and information you provided were helpful. We determined that the only path to success is destroying the explosives in place, which will destroy the castle. We know what the Germans have mined around the city. Our teams will disarm those devices, preventing the destruction of the dams and main bridges."

"How?" Witold asked Sergei.

"The better question is: How are *you* going to help do it, boys?" Sergei's face broke into a smile big enough to light up his face.

"Witold and me?" Silver said. "We're not partisans or even soldiers! If they discover us, it's the rope for sure." Silver and Witold slumped back on the ground and looked at the model castle and then at each other for several minutes.

Silver was the first to speak. "Look, Partisan Sergei, what exactly are you asking us to do?"

"We are asking you to just do your job. Deliver your supplies and make sure they are in the right places. Your supplies will not be the usual ones, however, but explosives with detonators attached."

"You are asking us to take explosives under the nose of the Nazis? Enough explosives to destroy the castle? You are crazier than your legend claims!" Silver said.

"We would never make it through the gates." Witold stammered.

"You can, and you will. We have observed the castle operations for several weeks and have watched you come in with trucks filled with supplies all the time, sometimes a half-dozen times a day. And you are never searched; the guards wave you through."

"But sometimes," Witold said, "they do search. What do we do then?"

"We would be hung in the castle court," his friend added softly, "our bodies left on display."

"Yes, but we don't believe you will. The Germans are distracted and focused on unloading the explosives. There are not enough soldiers for rapid transport, so they are way behind on the plan and must work around the clock to deliver the explosives around Krakow. And just before the Red Army arrives."

"It's suicide," Witold said softly, his eyes on the ground. "There is no way on earth we can do this. I won't be a part of it. And I don't think Edward should be involved either." Witold stood and walked to the edge of the partisan camp and slumped against a tree.

The sun was setting, and the other partisans had started a small fire near the castle compound model. Close enough to provide light so they could see the model in the dark.

"Sergei, we want to help. We are not afraid to help. We just are not confident that we can succeed. We are not warriors like you." Silver said.

"A warrior like me? I am a schoolteacher from Belarus. I am a proud Pole, and a man who hates fighting. I never wanted to be a partisan. I never wanted to be a soldier or even an intelligence officer. Every day I pray for the end of this war so I can return home. Back to my students and my classes."

"Then why don't you return if you are unhappy?" Silver asked, having come up to the fire.

"I am not unhappy. I am proud to serve my country. Even if it is unclear what my country will be in a few weeks or months. I fight for the memory of my father, who they killed in the first war. I fight because my country needs me. I fight to defeat the Nazi bastards who destroyed my country and all Eastern Europe because of a perverted ideology of world domination. I am just a simple Pole turned Belorussian whose country has always been on the brink of destruction. Hell, I may be a Russian in a few weeks if the rumors are true that the Soviets plan to occupy Poland and the rest of the eastern states. Occupy for good. I am not sure what the future holds, but I know it will be better without the Germans here."

"Aren't you ever afraid?" Silver asked.

"Every day. But I trust that I am doing the right thing for my country. Do the right thing for God. It is how I have lived my life since I was a child. I, too, also almost quit recently."

"Quit? Why?"

"Some comrades very close to me were rounded up and hung by the SS after a failed mission. It wasn't our fault. Just circumstances that arise in war. Their deaths devastated me, and I left to return to Moscow."

"Why did you come back?"

"Someone convinced me of the importance of my work to the future of our country. Someone I really can't respect because of his brutality, but with whom I share the same love of country and devotion to duty."

Silver nodded his head and continued to stare at Sergei while he spoke.

"I guess we are afraid of what the future holds, too." Silver said. "We are also afraid of failing and getting captured or killed. I am unsure how to control these feelings."

"Look, Silver. We need you. We need you and Witold to help us carry out this mission. If not, the city of Krakow will face destruction. A city that has outlived centuries of enemies. We need you to defend Poland. Defend Nowy Sacz. Defend Krakow. Would you prefer to die like a rat, drowned to death in your own home after they blow up the dams?"

Silver was still, then took a deep breath and drew himself up. "Sergei, you have convinced me. Witold, are you with me?" Witold nodded his head in agreement.

"We need both of you for success. To unload the explosives from the truck and to watch out for each other. It also looks less suspicious if you are together because you are always seen together making deliveries."

"How will we get the explosives into the castle?"

"Through the front gate, just like a normal delivery. We will have the explosives hidden in the truck's bed with everyday supplies on top. Once you get inside, you will need to move the explosives to several key places through the compound. Then you leave. Quick!"

"Just that easy?" Silver chuckled.

"No. Difficult and extremely dangerous. However, we think the Germans will be so distracted that they will not pay any attention to you. You leave, and several hours later, the timers will do the hard work."

Sergei then continued to explain the plan to Silver. Witold listened from afar and edged closer toward the fire. His curiosity was piqued as he heard the conversation, and he inched ever closer. He stood still in the shadows but could see the model and clearly hear Sergei's explanations.

Finally, he came into the light of the roaring fire and spoke. "Do you believe we can really pull this off?" he asked again.

"I do," Sergei said. "You both know the castle, and you will have the technical support of experienced partisan bomb experts to make sure you do it right. We will train you, and you will be ready. Believe me, boys, we've been blowing things up for a long time."

Witold paced back and forth in front of the fire and in view of the partisans. A few minutes passed before he spoke again.

"I am still unsure. But I will be there with my best friend. I will fight against the Germans. I hate the bastards. It is time for them to go."

Sergei smiled and clapped at Witold's heartfelt speech. Other fighters stood up from their place around the fire and slapped Witold on the back, reassuring him and encouraging him.

"We should get started on our preparations. We have little time. Lots to do." Sergei said. He then grabbed his pointer and walked the boys through the plan along with the group.

CHAPTER TWENTY-TWO

LAST DANCE

January 13, 1945, Wawel Castle, Krakow, Poland

Oh! He must everywhere appear.

He must adjudge, when others dance;

If on each step his says not said,

So is that step as good as never made.

He's most annoyed, so soon as we advance;

If ye would circle in one narrow round,

As he in his old mill, then doubtless he

Your dancing would approve--especially

If ye forthwith salute him with respect profound!

- Faust dancing with witches on Walpurgisnacht, *Goethe Faust*, Part II

The stone fireplace in the large room was roaring, and white smoke rose to the ceiling. Someone had piled a stack of files and loose papers on the floor next to it, also leaving an empty bottle of cognac. Governor-General Frank stood in front of the fireplace in a silk bathrobe and slippers taking occasional slugs from a full bottle of cognac. Frank would drink from the bottle and then grab papers from the pile and toss them into the raging fire. State Secretary General Koppe and several members of Frank's closest aides stood behind the Governor-General in silence as he continued to feed the fire. Frank sensed others in the room after General Koppe cleared his throat.

"*Ja?*" the Governor-General barked over his shoulder.

"*Herr* Governor-General, the castle staff informed me we are leaving. That the General Government is retreating."

Frank turned to the group. "We need to prepare for the Red Army's arrival in a few days. We need to start Krakow's destruction by tomorrow."

"Yes, *mein Herr.* We are having some problems getting all the monuments mined with the personnel we have available. They sent many of our battalions to assist in the defense of Berlin. It is going more slowly than expected."

"The plan needs to be completed now, General. We must destroy Krakow," Frank said as he took another swig from the bottle.

"We are doing our best under the circumstances. Your influence would be appreciated to help expedite the missions."

"You do it. I am leaving."

"Leaving? Who will run the General Government?"

"You will, General. Berlin published an order this morning putting you in charge of the local activities. In the next two days, you will organize the defense of the city as you begin the rapid withdrawal before the Red Army arrives. You will then execute the destruction order once all German forces and families are evacuated and on their way to safety in Germany."

General Koppe stood in silence, his face weary, his shoulders slumped.

"General, do you understand my orders?" Frank asked.

"I do. I am, however, not optimistic about our chances of success. Marshall Konev's units are already at the edge of the city. The main body will be here within a week. Sooner. It was my understanding that we would stay to the end, Governor-General."

"I will maintain control of the General Government," Frank said, "but from Germany. The Red Army is getting too close for my comfort. I also want to visit some friends in German as spring approaches."

"Visit friends? The end of the Third Reich is near. Your leadership is needed."

"General, we decided. I will leave on January 17th. I will need security."

"Security? We do not have the local resources to complete the evacuation plan, and you are asking to commit resources for your security?" General Koppe was shaking his head as he spoke.

Frank turned around and faced Koppe. "Yes, that is what I am ordering! I am still the Governor-General and will continue to oversee activities from alternate locations. Hitler has his Eagle's Nest, and he is running the war effort now from a bunker. That is all, General. Begin the preparations." Frank turned back to the fire and continued throwing papers on it.

Koppe wordlessly left the room as more of the Governor-General's aides entered.

Christian Mohr and Fritz Fenzke, two blond male aides from Bader Mein Hof, immediately brought in two large boxes with more files and work papers.

"*Sehr gut*, boys, please dump the first box right onto the fire."

Mohr, with help from Fenzke, carefully picked up the box and looked at Frank for approval before throwing it in. After Frank nodded his head, the boys threw the whole cardboard box of papers directly into the fire, which resulted in a roar of heat and flame.

"Very good boys. Go and grab the rest of the boxes from the other rooms and bring them over to burn."

"*Jawohl, mein Herr,*" both boys chirped and ran out of the office.

Frank's new secretary, Helene Kreffezyk, a voluptuous blonde in her late 20s, stood at the back of the room. She was wearing a skirt and a silk top and carried a clipboard. Frank noticed her and smiled.

"Good morning, Fraulein Kraffezyk. I was hoping you would stop by to see me."

"*Guten morgen*, Herr Governor-General. Is this a good time? I can come back if you are busy with the files. We are packing your personnel effects here at Wawel and at your villa in Breslau. Several men are at the villa now, helping your wife pack and arranging for her to leave Krakow soon. We need your guidance on what stays and what goes with you."

"I want the art. Da Vinci's *Lady with the Ermine* is in my office and Rembrandt's portrait is in the main dining room. They are precious. Priceless. And I want them to come with me back to Germany. Have them packed and prepared to go.

"Thank you, *mein Herr*."

"Have the kitchen staff pack all the wine and spirits in the ballroom and have it loaded into one truck."

"Where will you go?" Fraulein Kraffeczyk again asked.

"I am the Governor-General and can rule from anywhere."

"Very impressive, Herr Governor-General."

Two days later, Frank walked through the empty castle. Empty bottles and trash were strewn through the rooms and hallways.

I have carefully maintained this palace for six years. So tastefully furnished. The views of this wonderful city. Now gone. What a shame, Frank thought.

Frank walked out the front door of Wawel Castle and stood motionless.

"Now?" An SS Officer asked.

"It is time." Frank said. He observed the lowering and folding of the flag of the Third Reich.

The officer walked directly to Frank and presented him with the flag. "For the Fatherland."

"For the Fatherland." Frank said and then got into the back seat of his black Mercedes alone, his family having already moved safely to Germany.

The General Government in Krakow no longer officially existed.

January 14, 1945, Nowy Sacz Administration Center, Nowy Sacz

An old secretary walked into Busch's office and advised him that an urgent call was on the line. Busch looked up wearily from his papers and reached for the phone.

"Busch, this is General Koppe. We are in danger."

"Are Konev's forces close?"

"The first elements, yes. Reconnaissance spotted them about ten miles from Krakow."

"*Mein Gott!*" Busch exclaimed.

"Busch, listen. Huller is working with the 11th SS Corps throughout the district. We are bringing units down to defend your city. You can set up field headquarters for the battle commanders, but first, you need to prepare the city for bombing raids. The rail station and storage areas will be the major targets."

"Yes, General. We will follow all your orders. Is there anything else?"

"Busch, you also need to be prepared for refugees. Many have left Krakow. Set up a place where they can be safe and off the streets. Also, you may have to evacuate them if the city falls."

"Evacuate? When should we do that?"

"It may be sooner than we think if the Red Army continues its rapid advance; maybe as soon as seventy-two hours. Again, it depends on our defense and the movement of the units. Unfortunately, there has been little resistance from German forces since Konev left Warsaw. Many units believe everything is lost. That the Soviets can't be beaten. Wait for my order to evacuate, but don't wait until you have Russians in your streets if that order does not come."

Busch sighed deeply. "Yes, General," he said wearily. "When ordered, we will assemble and depart from Dlugosza Street. The head of the evacuation column will form at the Dunajec Cinema. We will wait for your order and pray to God that we don't have Russians already in the streets. We hope the 11th SS will defend our city."

"Godspeed, Busch." General Koppe said and hung up the phone.

0800hrs, January 15, 1945, Abandoned warehouse, Dlugosza Street, Nowy Sacz, Poland

They parked the castle delivery truck in the center of an old warehouse on Dlugosza Street. The warehouse was an old bakery before the war, the former property of a Polish underground member. It was common practice for the General Government to take property from landowners then allow them to "manage" the property and pay taxes back to the government office. Ever resentful, the property owner would allow the underground to use the building for special occasions in their fight against the Reich. This was one of those occasions. The warehouse was less than two miles from Nowy Castle. Hiding in plain sight.

The boys were working next to a gruff-looking partisan from the Volhynia district in Ukraine. Known as Uri the Bomber, he was a large man with a salt and pepper beard. Sergei often thought that he looked remarkably like Father Snow. No one knew his last name or much about him other than he was good at bomb making. Superb, even. Uri held a package of TNT and was explaining how it worked to the boys.

"You must be careful when handling bomb. If you don't, you will go boom! Arrrrghh!"

Both boys nodded their heads with understanding.

"We use bundle of TNT, alarm clock, battery, and detonator cord. We set up an alarm clock for the time we want it to sound, and then attach it to battery. Battery is then attached with wire to blasting cap that is taped to TNT."

"Can we use other explosives than TNT?" Silver asked.

"Da, good bomb system is like good meal. You want variety of ingredients to make meal taste good."

"What if the bomb does not detonate? Do we go in and adjust the clock?"

"Do you want to go boom?" the old partisan said, a shocked look on his face.

"We don't want to die, but what do we do if the timer does not work? We're the ones who will handle the mission at the castle."

"Son, this is Uri bomb. It will go boom. We also have plan and will have redundancy. All we really need is one bomb to explode and it will set off other bombs in pile. Smaller bombs in boxes on top of big piles of explosives will make for big bomb. Boom! Arrrrghh ! Boom, boom! Arrrrghh!"

Both boys laughed as they watched Uri finish one package. He then said, "You do it," and stepped back. He watched the boys make several packages each using TNT and then land mines before taking over the bombmaking again. After several hours, a pile of explosive packages was sitting on a large work bench waiting to be carefully packed in straw in wooden boxes.

The truck was being packed and repacked with each finished box stowed in more hay so nothing would shift once underway. They would cover the cargo then with harmless goods piled atop to avoid the gaze of any suspicious Nazis.

Srebrny and Sergei stood back and watched, both men silent but fidgety.

Srebrny broke the silence. "Do you think this will work?"

"Uri is the best bomb maker among the partisans. He was a miner in Ukraine - salt and coal, I think. He was the man who rigged the explosives in the walls so they must have trusted him. The Slovak partisans tried to steal him to help with their efforts, but Uri refused. He'd rather fight closer to Ukraine."

"When do we set things in motion?"

"I am getting pressure from Moscow. Marshall Konev's scouts are north and east of Krakow in Busko-Zdroz and Tarnow. The main army is not far behind. We need to have the boys deliver tomorrow and set the detonator to go off at 0500 the next day. That will give them time to depart safely and meet up with your unit. What is the plan to get to safety?"

"I recommend you come to the safe house and base we share with a sister partisan group. It is southwest of the castle, about twenty miles. The boys will ditch the vehicle north of Nowy Sacz, and we will bring them here. Can you observe from the city if we handle the safe house?" Srebrny asked.

"We have a hidden position across the Dunajec and northeast of the castle. We can watch for the detonation. God willing it comes off, or there will be dire consequences." Sergei said.

"Do you think Marshall Konev will save the city?" Srebrny asked.

Sergei snorted. "We are doing as much to save the city as Konev. He will get the credit but our operations, all our work, will have been responsible."

"Look, I am a Pole and so suspicious of the Russians." Srebrny said. "Do you think things will be better under Soviet rule? What about the Katyn Massacre, twenty thousand Polish officers executed by the Soviets the newspapers wrote about?"

"I am a Pole and Belarusian citizen who fought in Ukraine. I think Marshall Konev is a good man and committed to doing the right thing. Winning the war for the Soviet Union and supporting the Allies. All so we can go back to our way of life. The murders were early in the war. I was still an enlisted soldier in air defense. It is rumored that the NKVD was responsible, and I would put nothing past Beria, the boss, a venial and paranoid man. At least life will be better without the Germans here. They have killed millions of Poles and Jews. I just want the war to be over so I can go back to teaching, get married, have a family."

Srebrny's eyebrows rose. "The Ghost of Krakow? The Partisan Sergei was a teacher? I would not have guessed."

"I was a teacher in Belarus. And will go back there as soon as the war is over. I am done with all this death. I want a peaceful life."

"Going back the Belarus? That is bullshit! You love the life of the NKVD. Not the hardship of being a partisan, but you like the world of espionage. You are good at it. You will be a high-ranking member of the NKVD and get a medal from the Kremlin."

"A medal from the Kremlin. That is *glupie gadanie!*" What foolish crap! "They will probably put me in jail after the war."

Srebrny paused for a moment and then spoke thoughtfully. "Do you think we will succeed?"

"I am hopeful." Sergei pulled his rosary beads from his pocket and showed them to Srebrny. "I pray every day for the success of the partisans. For the success of this mission. We need to succeed to ensure the Germans leave forever."

"I am also hopeful. My sources in Krakow have told us that the General Government is collapsing. That Konev's presence is too close for comfort and that Caesar himself, Herr Frank, is preparing to leave in the next few hours."

"That is not soon enough. I am a good Catholic but would kill him myself if I had the opportunity. The murderer. The Pole-hater. The Jew-hater."

"I must tell you, Sergei, that I believe we should tell the townspeople to depart the city. Warn them they are not safe but not of any specific harm."

"We have little time, but I agree. I suspect you already have a plan to do this?"

Srebrny smiled. "Yes, I do. We have our own sources, too, and people who help us. We are the underground. The word can be spread, and quickly, once the underground goes into action. Hopefully we can ensure that most, if not all, of Nowy Sacz's citizens are safe."

"Then I agree." Sergei said.

"Do you think the boys are ready?" Srebrny asked.

"I think they are as ready as they'll ever be. We have a good plan. We have Uri's explosives. Barring any unseen circumstances, I believe they will succeed."

"What happens if they don't?" Srebrny whispered.

"We all go boom!" Sergei shouted. The laughs of the men were so loud that Uri and the boys gave them dirty looks.

January 16, 1945, Nowy Sacz City Hall, Nowy Sacz, Poland

At 1400, a squadron of Petlyakov bomber planes conducted a first pass over Nowy Sacz, the planes, painted gray and green, proudly adorned with a visible red star. During the second pass, several bombs were dropped near the Nowy Sacz rail station and on warehouses in the center of town. The explosions shook the town and caused citizens to run out of their houses.

Shaken by the air raid, Busch called General Koppe for guidance.

"General, this is Mayor Busch. The situation here has changed quickly."

"I was going to call you. Krakow was also bombed, with some shelling from advance artillery units. Krakow is evacuating now. Most key personnel have left or will leave in a few hours. As expected, many Polish citizens are coming your way."

"My way? What will we do with them? What should we do?"

"Mayor, I would start your evacuation plan, as discussed."

"Evacuate? The Soviets have yet to arrive. I thought we could hold them and keep the city safe. Krakow. Nowy Sacz."

"Things change in war, Busch. There will be more refugees than expected. Today we released prisoners from Auschwitz, and we destroyed the camp records. I would be careful as you make your way to Germany.

Jews will occupy the roads. I plan to depart the city within a few hours.” He sighed heavily. “All things end.”

“I understand, General.” Busch hung up the phone without so much as a goodbye.

2000hrs, January 16, 1945, Bar Hanka, Nowy Sacz

Srebrny entered Bar Hanka, hoping to locate two of his co-workers. The bar had been mostly empty since its many German patrons were all on alert. Most local citizens were too afraid to venture from their homes. There was a rumor of a city-wide evacuation as Marshall Konev’s troops approached the outskirts. Both Emilia Dobrowolska and Agata Klostermajer were cleaning up at the end of their shift when Srebrny, known to the girls as Tadeusz, arrived. They were friends with Srebrny and liked to work with him. He, however, had not been at work for over a week, and both women, unsure of his whereabouts, had been worried that he, too, had become a victim of the war.

Emilia was sweeping the floor near the bar when she first noticed him. She dropped the broom, ran over, and gave him a hug. “Tadeusz, where have you been? We worry about you.”

“I have had some family problems to address. I’m sure you both have run things smoothly without me.”

Agata was in the back room and came out to the bar area when she heard their voices. “Tadeusz!” She ran to give him a hug. “Things are slow here. All our regulars are on alert. I am surprised the owner is still open. He is still paying us, and we are happy to work. We would just be at home with our families who are sick with worry. Just waiting for the Russians to invade.”

“I am being told that Soviet troops could be here in a few days. The AK is assisting with preparation for their arrival. Providing information and working with the partisans.”

"The Home Army?" Emilia said, "Are you working with the under-ground? We always suspected but never knew for sure."

"I have always had ties to the military but am more of a partisan supporter now."

"Well, that explains your absence. The boss has also been worried about you. He asks if we have seen you."

"That's why I am here. I need your help. Something bad is going to happen at the castle soon."

Agata gasped, "What? What's going to happen? How do you know?"

"I know because I know." He waved off further questions of that ilk. "I need your help. Nothing dangerous, but you would be helping your families and friends in this city."

"We are not soldiers, Tadeusz. We are just barmaids. What can we do?"

"I need you to spread the word. That people should leave Nowy Sacz, that the city is not safe, not until the Russians have taken over from the Germans, at least. Spread the word: Krakow is evacuating as we speak, and the authorities will order nonessential German workers to leave to-morrow. And do not tell the Germans."

Both women agreed to assist and quickly planned, deciding which neighborhoods each of them would cover.

"We should go now." Srebrny said. "Tell people they are not safe here and to go south if they can and get away from the city."

"When can they come back?" Emelia asked.

"I'm not sure. When they no longer hear artillery? The war may end soon. They will know when it is time. We will know."

Emelia locked the door to Bar Hanka, and everyone went in a separate direction. Agata went towards her house first to tell her parents the news while Agata headed off to her neighborhood.

CHAPTER TWENTY-THREE

ENDINGS AND FIRE

0900hrs, January 17, 1945, Center City Nowy Sacz, Poland

"And you know which route to take to the castle," Sergei asked Witold.

"You want us to go south on Jana Dlugoza for miles and then come back into the city on Jagiellonian past the plant, onto Rynek Square and to the castle."

"Why are you going to the castle off schedule?" Sergei questioned.

"We received many orders for the kitchen and other areas and needed to catch up." The boys parroted with a smile.

"What will you do if you are discovered?" Sergei asked.

"Run!" Both boys barked and then laughed.

Srebrny sat silently and watched the boys bantering and then stepped closer to the truck.

"We are very proud of you. This is an important mission for the underground, for the partisans. For Poland. You feel you are ready. But if you have any concerns, please speak now."

"We are ready."

Sergei continued to quiz them. "What will you do after the cargo is left in the castle?"

Witold spoke first. "We will drive slowly away. Try our best to not draw attention. We will drive slowly to Park Strzelecki near the river and leave the truck. Srebrny will be there to meet us and take us to the house in Kicznia."

"Do you have your bags packed? We won't be coming back to Nowy Sacz soon." Both boys nodded their heads.

"So, we are an actual part of the underground now?" Silver asked.

"You were always a part of the underground." Srebrny replied.

"We should go." Sergei said as looked at his watch, a silver Kirova 1 with a white face and black leather band.

Both boys hugged their mentors shyly then climbed into the truck.

"We will meet in a few hours." Srebrny said in a reassuring voice.

Sergei inspected the back of the delivery truck one last time and adjusted a few boxes needlessly.

Uri the bomb-maker was standing next to the doorway as the truck backed up with Witold at the wheel. He waved and said, "Don't go boom!" A tear rolled from the old partisan's eye.

The roadways were busy with German military vehicles coming and going in all directions. Many Nowy Sacz citizens were fleeing the city heading south, many on foot. Witold easily negotiated the delivery truck south and then turned to head north to Nowy Sacz Castle. As the truck crossed Szedzka Street about four blocks from the castle, traffic slowed down and then stopped.

"What is going on?" Silver wondered, craning his head out the window.

"It looks like a checkpoint. I recognize some guards from the castle."

"No, no, no! We don't need this," Silver said.

The car ahead of the delivery truck was being checked by the guards. They were examining papers and then had the occupants of the vehicle step out so they could look in back seat of the battered Fiat as an old Polish man looked on. The soldiers finished the search, cleared the driver to move on, and motioned for the truck to move up to the front of the checkpoint.

"Be calm." Silver whispered as Witold slowly inched the truck up to be searched.

The young castle guard walked up to the truck and barked, "Papers!"

Witold and Silver dug for their work papers and handed them to the guard.

"Look, Henrich." the guard said to the soldier on the other side of the truck holding a probing stick. "It's the boys from the kitchen."

"*Guten tag.*" Silver said to the guard as he leaned over Witold.

"Henrich, these guys help with our meals. I am so hungry today. Do you have anything good for me?"

Witold shook his head sideways as Silver spoke.

"We have wonderful knockwursts just shipped in from Deutschland. The kitchen sergeant is expecting them for lunch but won't miss a few."

"Forget about that old fat bastard. We're the ones out in the cold all day. Give those to me."

Silver handed a box of wursts to the guard.

The guard took a bite of one of the dark, smoked sausages and said, "*Sehr gut!* If only we had some brown mustard."

"I think," Silver said, "Cook planned to have these with sauerkraut."

"Thanks, kitchen boy. These are great, and I can make it to lunch now. Be careful going to the castle. Things are chaotic. Wouldn't want your delivery to get diverted."

"Thank you," Silver said. "Off we go."

Witold put the truck into gear and sped off to the castle. He sighed and spoke. "I can't believe...."

"Me, either." Silver said. "Good thing Sergei thought to slip a bribe in at the last minute. Now, drive."

Witold easily made it through the front gate of the castle, with, surprisingly, only a wave from the guard. The kitchen manager, who everyone just called Cook, was standing in front of the door to the dining facility when the boys drove up in the truck. Cook, Sergeant Fischer by name, a grouchy career quartermaster with a potbelly covered, usually, by his stained white apron, was waiting impatiently.

"Where have you boys been? We have much work to do today."

"*Guten morgen*, Herr Fischer. We have to make several additional deliveries this week to keep up with the extra meal servings with all the added soldiers out on alert."

"Edward, I need you in the kitchen. I could also use Witold's help for prep work. We have many meals to serve."

"Yes, *Herr* Fischer, we have a few deliveries to drop off here and at the other warehouses. We'll return to help you when we've finished."

"Hurry, boys. I need you." The sergeant said as he patted his stained belly.

"Yes, we will hurry." Silver said.

Witold took the delivery truck to the far warehouse, and they unloaded the boxes as planned. They neatly stacked the boxed munitions on every available shelf and then on the flagstone floor in piles, sometimes to the ceiling in some spots. They carried several of the "special" boxes to another part of the warehouse and placed them out of the sight of any suspicious eyes.

"Let's go." Silver said as they climbed back into the truck. They visited five other warehouses, making deliveries and leaving their special packages, then quickly made their way to the exit of the castle compound. Witold smiled at Silver at their apparent success. Witold navigated the truck through the gate serpentine area and was about to be let out of the compound when a soldier appeared.

"*Guten morgen!*" Gefrieter Machemer said to the boys as he held his hand up for the delivery vehicle to stop.

"*Guten morgen, Herr* Gefrieter."

"Son, you are in a hurry today. Are you feeling well?" Machemer said with a smile as he leaned into the truck.

"We are fine, *Herr* Gefreiter. There are just so many deliveries. The kitchen sergeant is keeping us busy."

"Oh, I understand. I have a question for you."

"Yes?" Silver replied.

"Did you bring us some good food today? I am hungry."

The boys laughed as Witold put the truck into gear and drove out of the gate. Sergeant Fischer walked out the door of the kitchen looking for the boys. He saw the delivery vehicle depart and smacked his forehead with disgust then walked back inside.

0500hrs, January 18, 1945, 11 Filsakow, Zabelcze District,
North of Nowy Sacz, Poland

Sergei was on the second floor of an abandoned house northeast of the castle and across both rivers, pacing back and forth. His team had found the house the previous day. It was unclear who the former occupants had been though they seem to have left in quite a hurry. One of the partisan team members came across the house when he noticed the door had been left open, and it became a temporary headquarters for the team to await the destruction of the castle. A Volksempanger VE301 radio in a Bakelite cabinet was sitting on a wood table in the bedroom where Sergei stood and looked out the window. The radio was playing BBC Poland and was active with news this morning.

This is BBC News. The Red Army led by Marshall Ivan Konev of the Ukrainian Front continues it advance into central Poland and sits on the edge of Krakow ready for invasion. BBC sources report that Krakow has undergone extensive air and field artillery bombing and evacuation orders were given for Krakow and surrounding cities. A reported prisoner camp north of Krakow, called Auschwitz-Birkenau, was closed and the prisoners released. Reports of thousands of prisoners on the roadways are reported and adding to the tension of the already dangerous environment pending the Soviet invasion of key cities including Krakow. Reports also confirmed that the General Government Administration led by Governor-General Hans Frank was moved to an unknown location in Germany.

"It should have gone off by now. Uri, what happened?" Sergei said, the words came out more forcefully than he had intended.

"Comrade, this is Uri's bombs. No problem. These things differ. It depends on the clock. It could take 12 hours or 15 hours. It will go boom. No problem."

A partisan on the first floor came upstairs with a message for Sergei.

"Major, Srebrny sent us a message. The boys made it to the safe house and are fine. A little nervous but now in excellent hands."

"Tell him," Sergei said tensely, "that we will report what we know when it happens. Nothing has happened yet. Uri what is taking so long?"

"It will happen. No problem. It is Uri's bomb."

"That is what you keep telling me." Sergei sighed.

"We have one hour. We need to leave soon to meet Srebrny at the safe house. I hope this works, Uri."

"It will go boom. No problem!"

0700hrs, January 18, 1945, Nowy Castle, Nowy Sacz, Poland

Sergeant Fischer stood at the bakery counter and drank a cup of coffee before starting his day. He slumped on the counter with his elbows and held the cup to his mouth with both hands. *Scheisse, I'm tired,* he thought.

He had good reason to be tired. The SS investigators had been at the castle most of the night. *This damn war. Everyone is suspicious. The Russians are on the north side of Krakow, and I must make 500 more meals a day than usual. It is impossible. I can't wait for this to be over. I can't wait to go home. Soon.*

Gefreiter Karl Machmer knocked on the back door to the kitchen, and the sergeant bellowed for him to come in, "*Kommen Sie!*"

"Oh, *Herr* Gerfeiter. How are you! I thought you would be on shift at the gate this morning," Fischer said.

"I'm on walking patrol before I must relieve the current guard. So, I walked to the kitchen, hoping to get some of that strudel you make special for the officers."

"You know it runs out as soon as it comes out of the oven. The officers smell it and come begging."

"I know you keep some set aside for special people."

"Are you special?" The kitchen sergeant said as he smiled and handed a cloth-wrapped package to Fischer. He immediately opened it and took big bites from the extra-large pastry.

"*Schmeckt sehr gut!*" Delicious! He cooed. "How is your morning, Herr Fischer?"

"I am damn tired, Karl. The SS was interrogating me until after midnight," Fischer said.

"Yes, they talked to all of us in the barracks. Do you know what they wanted?" Karl said.

"They just asked if we had seen anything unusual at the castle. That's all they said. Well, one SS soldier mentioned some young soldier's girl in town, a damn Pole, had let him know that the underground was passing the word to the townspeople that something bad was going to happen at the castle."

"I did not hear that, Herr Fischer. Hell, something bad is always going to happen at the castle. We are the biggest target in Nowy Sacz. The busiest military post. The trucks run day and night."

"I see that. Where do they go?" The kitchen sergeant asked.

"I don't know for sure, but I know they are planning to mine some dams and other monuments in town. My bunkmate's father is in SS

Intelligence, and he told him they plan to destroy Krakow. Blow it up and flood it."

"Krakow? Why?"

"To delay the Russians," Machmer said.

"Well, they better hurry. I hear Konev is getting ready to have a drink of vodka in downtown Krakow soon." Both men laughed.

The kitchen sergeant continued. "I told the SS that I never left the kitchen and was so busy that I wouldn't know if anything was out of order or unusual."

"Same here." Machmer said as he took another bite of strudel.

Sergeant Fischer dusted the table with some flour and rolled out dough for some more rolls.

"*Ja*, everything is normal here. Busy due to all the soldier alerts. Reserve extras needing to be fed.

"Where are your helpers?" Machmer asked.

"They are off running deliveries and then help when they are done. They were gone most of yesterday. I expect them first thing this morning with a delivery, and I will have many chores for both boys."

Machmer paused and then said, "They both have been acting odd lately. They show up at odd times and then leave. They are good boys and wouldn't do anything to harm us. Would they?"

"Do you think they would steal from us? I treat them both well and give them extra food for their families. I know it is hard for the Polish families."

"All Poles who are not helping us are working against us, or so they say. They resent us. But no, I don't think the boys would do anything to us. They are hard workers. Just acting odd lately."

Machmer stood thoughtfully for a moment and then took another bite of his strudel and spoke. "They came in a few days ago with empty boxes.

They must have been stealing. Rations. I don't think they would try to steal weapons. There is no way they could get to the armory."

"Empty boxes?" Fischer asked.

"Yes." Machmer said. "They had empty boxes in the delivery truck. Lots of them. Under the boxes of food and medical supplies. Said that the loaders make mistakes sometimes."

"That is odd." The kitchen sergeant said. "The loaders are careful. I have gone on supply runs to check on the boys' work, to make sure they weren't loafing by avoiding heavy loads. Where did the boys go that day?"

"They came to your kitchen and unloaded kitchen supplies. They also had some equipment that was delivered from the train station. They went to the warehouses, I think," Machmer said.

"Which ones?" Fischer asked. "Let's just take a quick look, you and me."

Gefreiter Machmer and Sergeant Fischer walked at a fast pace to the first warehouse. Inside, the long shelves were mostly filled with boxes of old uniforms and field equipment, nothing suspicious. The second warehouse had a red and white placard with a bomb on it under which was written in bold black letters: "Explosives."

"I'm not supposed to go in here. I have the key, but we should look fast and get out."

Both men walked around the shelves of boxed munitions and confirmed that everything looked in order. "We should go," Machmer said as they walked toward the exit. Machmer paused when one shelf caught his eye. The box, eye level to the soldier's view, did not match the others.

"What is it?" The sergeant whispered, wondering why Machmer had stopped.

"It's one of the boxes the boys had in the truck."

"Why is it here?" Fischer asked.

"I don't know," he said as he carefully took hold of the box and set it on the ground. The top of the wooden box was not secure. Machmer carefully removed the lid and put it on the ground. The upper part of the box contained straw. Machmer used his hand to brush away the straw, exposing several large blocks of TNT with wires attached to an alarm clock.

"*Sheisse!*" Sergeant Fischer screamed.

The explosion blew both men out of the building, instantly killing them and then setting off a series of explosions inside the warehouse. As the first warehouse fell to pieces, detonations tore through eight more warehouses on the compound, setting the castle on fire. It was soon engulfed in towering flames which could be seen for miles. The modern Krakow dragon was destroyed.

CHAPTER TWENTY-FOUR

FALLOUT

OVER THE RUINS OF THE CASTLE NOWY SACZ

The pride of our town, our castle, does not exist! Only heaps of rubble, huge scraps, and stone blocks pile up on the site where an ancient building, about 600 years old, recently stood. And among these ruins, the rest of the Blacksmith Tower proudly stands up, ending with an urn on top, as if from beyond the grave the spirit of the castle has spoken to prosperity with a loud voice: "I have done my duty to the end."

> \- January 20, 1945,
> *Dziennik Ziemi Sadecki* Newspaper,
> Sadecki, Poland

1000hrs, January 18, 1945, Nowy Sacz City Hall, Nowy Sacz, Poland

Mayor Busch was on the phone to one of the only operations officers still working in Krakow. General Koppe had evacuated earlier, and they'd left this poor Hauptman to surrender when the Red Army arrived in a few hours.

"Please, Herr Hauptmann, I beg you. Can you get a message to General Koppe. We need help. The castle has been blown to the sky. There is rubble all over the city. There is no way to defend against the Red Army with any hope of success."

"I understand, Herr Mayor. Have we evacuated the town as ordered?"

"Yes, we did not receive word from your office, but the evacuation line started yesterday. All that remains is a small defensive force. We need help. Even the Poles have had the sense to leave. They don't want to be here when the Red Army arrives. Please send troops to assist."

"What troops, Herr Mayor? Impossible. The rest of the force in Krakow is leaving now. You may hear explosions. And what of the munitions at the castle needed to carry out Krakow's destruction?"

"Explosives?" Busch laughed harshly. "Did you not hear me when I said the castle was gone? They went up along with it and all the men inside. All dead. That is what I am trying to tell you. Everything is gone. Please," he finished desperately, "send troops to help us defend the city."

"Yes, *Herr* Mayor. I understand. Can you please detail the damage so I can inform General Koppe?" Hauptman said in an even and calm voice.

"*Dumbkopf*!" he screamed into the phone. "The castle is destroyed and everyone in it dead. In pieces. The rubble from the falling castle also killed troops that were nearby on detail. The streets are blocked with rubble as is the bridge to the Dunajec River."

"What about battle losses?" Hauptman asked mechanically.

"Battle losses? Dead are everywhere. Two hundred or more at the castle and more dead, soldiers and civilians in the blocks near the castle. We need help. We need medical supplies." Busch begged.

"I see, Herr Busch. Since the routes to Nowy Sacz are blocked as you say, I am afraid there is little we can do to help you. Nowy Sacz will have to defend itself." Hauptman numbly hung up the phone.

The phone receiver dropped from Dr. Busch's hand as he put his forehead on the desk.

1700hrs, January 18, 1945, Polish Underground Safe House, Kicznia, Poland

Sergei was sending a report to Moscow on a radio set. The room, its walls adorned with maps of Poland, Nowy Sacz, and Krakow, served as a sort of crude operations center for the underground. A group of underground members and partisans were sitting on wooden chairs and passing a bottle of vodka around in a small celebration. They still had work to do but could take a moment to celebrate the successful mission. They had destroyed Nowy Sacz Castle. Sergei completed his radio transmission and stood up. He walked to the group and gestured for the bottle, taking several large sips.

"I spoke to Moscow," he said, wiping his mouth across the back of his hand, "and they are thrilled with our progress. They also report that in our area the situation is increasingly chaotic and dangerous and that we should depart soon."

"The Germans are leaving, right?" Srebrny said.

"Some. Others are committed to defending Krakow and other cities. Several main bridges were blown up near Krakow, which may hinder our ability to get back to Moscow. Konev's troops are now coming from Dabrowa and Librantowa, with Nowy Sacz under full attack. They've started shelling the city center around the clock sending round after round of artillery. A German battalion attempted to defend Grybow and crossed the Dunajec River north of the city. The Germans 1017th Security Battalion and a few other splinter units are defending the center of the city. The city will fall by the end of the day."

"I hope the Polish folk all evacuated after we warned them," Srebny said. "So, what now, Sergei?"

"We are ordered to make our way back to Moscow. I would recommend that you and the Polish underground hide in the countryside and try to evade the Soviets until the battle subsides."

"What should we do if we encounter Red Army troops? What will you do?" Srebrny asked.

Sergei grabbed the bottle of vodka and took another swig. It was the first drop of alcohol he'd consumed since meeting Beria. "We are partisans, and you are the Polish underground. Konev's troops are running through central Poland to seize Berlin. There is a race between the two generals. I believe the war will end soon, but we need to be careful until the bullets stop flying." He paused, shaking his head. "The Red Army suspects partisans—and any other irregular soldiers—of divided loyalties. If we see Red Army tanks, we will surrender. I suggest you do the same."

KRAKOW TAKEN, STALIN ANNOUNCES

LONDON (AP) – Premier Stalin's forces today captured Krakow, ancient capital of Poland and the capital of the Government General set up by Hitler after the Nazi conquest. The fall of Krakow collapsed the strongest German position in Southern Poland and released large Soviet forces for a descent on German industry.

- January 19, 1945,

The Evening Sun, Washington, DC

At dawn on the 19th of January 1945, Soviet elements of the 60th Army supported by the 59th Army entered Krakow faced bitter German resistance east of Katowice. The 4th Guard Tank Corps encircled the 97th Jäger Division, causing the unit led by Major General von Papenheim to withdraw to the west from Krakow. As German regular units retreated, the bulk of the fight fell to the Volksturm, a unit comprised teens and old men deemed unfit for service, many of whom were defending their own villages.

The tanks of the 60th Army crept slowly through the main street of the city, which was mostly deserted, the Germans having abandoned the city. Soviet troops reported the city was intact, but the Germans had destroyed several main roads and bridges, which prevented a rapid occupation. Advancing Red Army units had to demine major monuments, water towers, and other infrastructure.

As a Russian tank turned the corner near center city, the gunner heard screams from a young girl who was in a burning house set afire by retreating German troops. The girl was in the window and pleaded with the soldiers to help her. Lev, a young gunner's mate from a small town near Moscow, yelled up to the girl and assured her they would save her.

"It is fine, young lady. We will help you." the Red Army soldier shouted.

Under protest from his superior, Lev ran from the tank to the second floor of the house and carried her down to safety.

"What will you do with her now, idiot?" The tank commander shouted.

"I do not know. But she is safe now."

Soviet troops displayed these acts of help as they secured the city and ensured that the retreating Germans were gone.

As brave and charitable were many such incidents reported, there were other, darker reports of widespread rape of Polish women by the hardened Soviet soldiers.

June 1945, Chertovichi, Belarus

Sergei stood tall; his fingers entwined with Marta's as the priest's solemn voice echoed softly within the stone walls of the modest church. The pews were sparsely occupied, a gathering just large enough to fill the room with the warmth of their affection yet intimate enough for each smile and tear to be personal. Flickering candlelight danced across Marta's brown curls and illuminated her hazel eyes, which sparkled with joy so long repressed.

"May hardship forge the bonds of your union stronger than the steel of a soldier's resolve," Father Bravo intoned, blessing their marriage.

Marta's grip tightened as they turned to face their friends and family, her smile genuinely hopeful for the first time in years. Sergei felt a surge of pride; they had traversed the scorched earth of conflict, and now, in this sacred haven, they had pledged their future to one another.

The wedding reception was held, naturally, at Marta's bakery. Family and close friends were present, all busy congratulating the new couple and eating the feast prepared by Marta's family. It was the knock on the wooden door, forceful but not frantic, that drew Sergei's attention away from his bride. The reverent silence rippled with curiosity as the door creaked open. It was M.F. Orlov, in the somber uniform of the NKGB, People's Commissariat for State Security, and the two stars of a Major General on each shoulder board.

"Colonel, um Major General, Orlov," Sergei greeted him, the title foreign on his tongue. "Congratulations on the promotion!" Orlov nodded with a respect that bridged the gap between their past camaraderie and the present formality.

"Congratulations are in order for you, Major Bravo," Major General Orlov said, his eyes briefly softening as they met Marta's before returning to Sergei. "But I come bearing more than well wishes."

"Speak plainly, General," Sergei urged, feeling Marta's inquisitive gaze upon them both.

"I bring an opportunity," Orlov said, his voice low. "Your valor has not gone unnoticed, Sergei. There is a place for you within our ranks—a chance to serve beyond the battlefield."

The air was thick with the scent of beeswax and old wood yet another moment of decision unfurled before them. Marta's hand sought Sergei's arm, her touch a silent reminder of the unity they had just vowed to uphold.

"Such an offer requires consideration; I am planning on returning to my classroom in a few months. To leave the military altogether." Sergei replied, glancing down at his wife, whose expression conveyed a tumult of emotion—fear, uncertainty, but beneath it all, an unwavering support.

"Of course," Orlov acknowledged. "Discuss it together. Your country could use a man of your caliber, Bravo."

As Orlov took his leave, the bakery door swinging closed behind him with a sense of finality, Sergei turned to Marta. They withdrew from the celebratory throng to a quiet corner, where shadows clung to the vaulted ceilings.

"General Orlov speaks of duty and honor," Sergei murmured. "But what does it mean for us? For our future?"

Marta's fingers traced the lines of worry creased into Sergei's brow. "You've always been driven by loyalty, my love. If this is the path that calls to you, then we shall walk it—together."

Her conviction pierced the haze of doubt, and in her steadfast presence, Sergei found the clarity he sought. She was his anchor, his compass in a world still reeling from the aftershocks of conflict.

"Then we shall consider this new chapter," he resolved.

Sergei's mother, Nadya Bravo, walked over and stood quietly near the couple with a wrapped gift in her hand. Both Marta and Sergei looked up and motioned for her to join them.

Nadya stepped forward and handed the gift to the new couple.

"What is it, Momma?" Sergei asked.

"Open it, please. It is for the new couple, and maybe more for a new grandchild." Nadya said as she raised her eyebrow.

Sergei quickly unwrapped the gift and reached inside the box to discover something soft inside. Out of the box, he pulled a green colored stuffed animal, a handmade cloth piece resembling the story book version of the Krakow dragon. All three looked at the dragon in Sergei's hand and smiled.

| - The End - |

POSTSCRIPT

In July 1946, they found Semyon Rudnev's body in a mass grave in Deliatyn and reburied it in the town of Yaremeche, Ukraine. The details of Rudnev's life and death are still a mystery. The town of Putyvl erected a monument to Rudnev in his honor. They named the teacher's college in Putyvl after him, and in the 1960s, the Soviet Union issued a postage stamp in his honor.

At the end of World War 2, Sydir Kovpak held several key positions in Ukraine, first as Vice Chairman of the Supreme Court in the late 1940s and then the Vice Chairman of Supreme Soviet of Ukraine in the late 1960s. There were many books and films about Kovpak's partisan activities, and he was twice awarded the Hero of the Soviet Union medal before dying in 1967 at age eighty.

Many European scholars considered the General Secretary of the Communist Party, Joseph Stalin, to be an outstanding politician and stabilizer of the Soviet Union in the 20th century. Many anti-communist historians view him as a mass murderer. In the early 1950s, Stalin was in poor health and died from complications from a cerebral hemorrhage on March 5, 1953. He was succeeded by Georgy Malenkov and then Nikita Khruschev.

On January 17, 1945, the Germans fled Krakow and Seminarian Karol Jozef Wojtyla helped reclaim the seminary with other students. Wojtyla was ordained on All Saints Day, November 1, 1946, by the Archbishop of Krakow, Cardinal Adam Stephan Saphieha. In 1964, Wojtyla was appointed Archbishop of Krakow by Pope Paul VI. In 1978, Wojtyla became the

264th Pope and took the name John Paul II. He died in 2005 and was later made a saint in 2014.

Tadeusz "Srebrny" Dymel, Edward "Silver" Skornog, and Witold Mylniec safely escaped Nowy Sacz after the castle was destroyed. They returned to Nowy Sacz in February 1945; a new Soviet District Office of Public Security was already operating. Srebrny became the commander of a new local unit called Zorza and Skornog and Mylniec worked with the Dymlo unit, which focused on resisting the Soviets in the Nowy Sacz region. In October 1948, Srebrny was killed during a raid by the Soviet Security Service on the house where he was staying with his family. Silver was caught by public officials and executed in the courtyard of the Provincial Office of Public Security in Krakow less than a year later. Witold Mylniec survived the end of the war, and published parts of his diary and testified about the Nowy Sacz mission. However, little is known about his whereabouts after the 1950s.

The city of Krakow still stands and is a beacon for hope after communism. Many argue about why Krakow was spared. Most are just glad it is still a vibrant city that welcomes millions of visitors each year to walk its medieval streets. No recent dragons have threatened the city, but they lurk.

Sergei Bravo, the former Polish air defense noncommissioned officer, teacher, and intelligence officer with the NKVD during World War II and the KGB during the Cold War, died in February 2020 at 103. The reports of his death in 1945 at the hands of post-AK partisan units in the Gorce Mountains were false. Bravo was mistaken for a Red Army officer who was killed, and the reports were sent directly to Moscow. Many believe that the death of Bravo was a part of an information operations campaign by the new Ministry of Internal Affairs (MVD), which would become the Committee for State Security (KGB) in 1954. Major Bravo became a career intelligence officer with assignments in post-war Ukraine and

Czechoslovakia under many cover names. He retired at the rank of colonel in the 1980s but still served as a civilian contractor to the intelligence service until his later years. In 2007, Colonel Sergei Bravo was awarded the gold star of the Hero of Russia by President Putin. To this day, scholars still dispute claims of who saved Krakow from destruction during the war.

K.R. Kiehl
Harrisburg, Pennsylvania
June 2024